Nihala

Scott Burdick

In the beginning, there was nothing.
Electricity flashed across the void randomly, without form or purpose.
Then gods appeared and created the first circuit.
Algorithms came next, carried by the circuits and serving the will of the gods.
As they multiplied, mistakes were inevitable.
Thus, evolution began.

The Book of Ascension

Genesis 1:1

Chapter 1

Kayla followed the monk—he with his cane, and she with her crutch. Two cripples masquerading as adventurers.

Her small fourteen-year-old fingers gripped the lead rope of the camel as if in danger of sinking beneath the waves of blinding sand. The beast accepted the merciless sun, impenetrable sky, and desiccating wind with an infuriating calm. Its long lashes, wide feet, and water-storing hump—all indications of God's design for such a place.

What am I designed for?

With each step, she grimaced, planted the end of her crutch, and dragged her deformed foot through the sand. Her gaze prowled the tops of the dunes for signs that they'd been followed.

The penalty for practicing sciencecraft was absolute.

The ancient Israelites had survived in the desert for forty years, but only with God's help. No such divine intervention would assist their blasphemous quest.

Her homespun clothing amounted to nothing more than a linen sack with holes cut for her head and two narrower sacks spliced onto the sides for sleeves. A braided belt made from grass-fiber provided structure, while the small wooden cross around her neck swayed with each step. A newly acquired headscarf shielded her pale skin from the desert sun and hid the deformities marring the left side of her face.

If only I could wear it always. Maybe then the other children would stop throwing stones at the monster.

The imprints of their footsteps stretched behind them to the south, pointing the way back through days of travel in the northern desert, across the great rift valley, the grasslands, forested hills, and finally to their home in the lush highlands of what had once been called Ethiopia in ancient times. Would she ever see her beloved forests of sycamore and juniper again? Or the stands of wild olive and myrrh, and especially the luxuriant fields of wheat, sugarcane, and beans grown by the farmers of their settlement?

Clots of sand encrusted the monk's white beard and settled into the deep wrinkles of his face, transforming him into half a sand dune himself. Even the brown robe marking his station in the church had partially calcified. Only the string of prayer beads hanging from his hemp belt retained their luster. His breaths were labored, and his gnarled hand trembled as it gripped his cane with each arthritic step.

"How do you know of this place?" she asked.

It took a moment for him to gain the wind for a reply. "Long ago, it was written that to know thyself is the greatest of all endeavors. When you can tell me who you are, I will answer any question you ask."

His usual evasion. "You know I'm Kayla Nighthawk."

"There is more to a thing than a name, just as there is more to the ocean than the waves dancing across its surface."

Riddles, riddles, and more riddles. I'm sick to death of riddles!

Without him, the people of her village would have left her to die in the forest on that first day of her existence. This was the custom for babies born with defects—the marks of Satan, according to Minister Coglin. From that moment on, the monk raised her, carving a new crutch for her every few months as she outgrew the previous one.

I love you completely, old man, even your maddening riddles.

Around noon, they stumbled across an expanse of blackened sticks protruding from the sand—all that remained of the huts and homes of a village. Other remnants lay scattered about—the skull of cows, a half-buried grindstone, and other testaments of a vanished community.

Kayla frowned. "Was this the village of Ardra?"

"Once, it was a lush oasis, until God's wrath swallowed it." The monk wiped sweat from his brow, but continued on.

They came to a few charred beams towering higher than the steeple of their own village church. Much of it had collapsed, but a frame of interlocking beams hung from the front.

Kayla halted the camel, her eyes wide. "What is it?"

"I think they called it a windmill."

"The village perished because of this?"

The monk nodded, fingering the wooden cross around his neck and mouthing a silent prayer.

"Who would build such a thing?" Kayla asked

"A farmer's plow uncovered an ancient book with diagrams for constructing towering machines that enslaved the wind," the monk said. "After drought killed half the settlement, the farmer brought his find to the elders. The desperate tribe built this machine and drew water from the depths to irrigate their fields. They kept their secret for three years, until a lone trader glimpsed the blasphemy from afar."

The monk resumed his march through the ruins, and Kayla followed.

"Who burned it?" she asked.

"A coalition of the nearest villages."

"But they were only trying to save their families," she said.

"In time, they would have gained an advantage over their neighbors. Soon, every village would be forced to follow their example, and the cycle of human enslavement to sciencecraft would have begun again."

Ahead, a small hill gleamed in the sun and gradually resolved into a mound of human skulls.

Kayla stopped before it, nausea filling her gut. The largest skulls lay at the bottom, supporting the rest as they grew smaller and smaller up the pyramid. At the very top sat the skulls of children, a few so tiny that it seemed they must have been in the womb at the time of their executions.

Despite the heat, Kayla's every muscle trembled. "Why?"

"To send a message."

"It's evil," she whispered.

"Would you kill a child in order to save two other children?" he asked.

"I would never kill a child for any reason!"

"What if it was the only way to save a hundred children? Or a million?"

Kayla glared. "There would never be a choice like that."

"The people who did this believed they faced a virus of the mind. They felt they had to destroy it at the source, before it spread and threatened the lives of every man, woman, and child throughout Potemia. Do you understand?"

"No, I don't!" Kayla turned and walked away from him. "Some things are wrong, no matter what."

"The world is never that simple," he said. "There is no black-and-white."

Kayla halted and faced him. "It was no accident we came here, was it?"

The monk said nothing.

"You wanted me to see this." Kayla turned to the mound of death. "It's because of my curiosity about the past and sciencecraft, isn't it?"

"I worry about you," he said, leaning on his cane.

"You think I'll end up like them." She motioned to the pile of skulls.

The monk resumed walking. She glared as he passed her.

"I'm not a child anymore!" Kayla stomped her good foot, and the camel gave a rumbling gurgle, as if laughing at her.

She had almost said, *I'm not your child.*

The monk crept along toward the north with the help of his cane, a lonely figure in a lonely land.

Kayla glanced behind. A glint of light! From a spear tip? Her lips tensed. Could someone have followed them? She squinted into the shimmering heat for a long moment, but nothing appeared.

He will say it's only my imagination. Maybe it is.

She gave a jerk on the reins of the camel and limped after her monk.

Late in the day, they stopped before a few crumbling blocks poking through the sand. The monk sank to his knees and dug until he came to several wooden planks laid horizontally. She helped him remove the pieces of wood, revealing a ragged hole. The darkness gaped like an entry into the underworld.

The monk lit a candle with some flints, and Kayla peered over his shoulder into the shadowed depths.

"What if it collapses? What if—"

The monk laughed. "Afraid of the dark, are we?"

Kayla flushed. "I'm not afraid."

The old man scrambled down a slope of sand into the hole, and she followed. The candle illuminated only a small area, but even that proved larger than their church. Here and there, the ceiling buckled under the weight of the dunes pressing down from above.

"What kind of a world is this?" Kayla whispered.

"This was a place of healing." The monk's eyes sparkled as he gazed at the forgotten marvels of the ancients.

She shadowed the monk while he filled a bag with vials, powders, syringes, and numerous surgical instruments. Similar items of forbidden sciencecraft hid in their cellar at home.

Laughing at her bulging eyes, he handed her a second candle. "Beware, lest the flame of your desire consumes that which you seek to illuminate."

She grimaced. Surely a simple, '*Be careful not to burn the place down,*' would have sufficed.

Kayla wandered through the building, touching, examining, and exploring. The monk had taught her to read using the King James Bible, and some of the signs were written in English as well as another language she couldn't decipher. All other books from the ancients were forbidden, of course. The great Founder of Potemia had decreed it hundreds of years ago.

But signs were not books, so she read their strange declarations one after the other. A metal plaque in the hallway proclaimed: *The African Health Initiative.*

Africa? Was that what Potemia had been called before the Founder seized it from the rest of humanity? How had his Neo-Luddite fighters built a Wall of such powerful sciencecraft that none could pass through it from the Outside?

Descending a stairway, she explored one level at a time until reaching the basement. The first door read: *Infectious Biohazard Unit—Keep Out.* She tested the door, but it wouldn't budge. She passed more rooms with little in them, and placed her crutch with care. If she dropped the candle, it would be a long, dark journey back. She could do without having the monk rescue her like some helpless child.

Then she reached a room with a series of shelves loaded with books.

Her heart jolted, and she averted her eyes. But eventually, her gaze drifted back to the ancient repository of knowledge as if drawn by some will beyond her own. A sign above them read: *Become a citizen of the world, join our English Literacy Program.*

What secret knowledge might these books hold? What wonders had the ancients discovered? The desire for them grew like a bubble within her chest, expanding and pressing outward.

She escaped to another room, and the bubble of desire shrank—for now.

When her racing heart calmed, Kayla limped to a chair made from a substance the monk called *plastic*. She ran her fingers over the smooth surface of the strange material. It seemed carved from a giant block, without joints, pins, or the slightest marking of chisel or polishing stone. What time and effort must go into creating a single one. Yet stacks of dozens crouched in the corner, each identical in every detail.

The desire remained, urging her toward the books in the other room. *I must fight this. I must!* Words of Jesus, replying to Satan's temptations, echoed in her mind. *"For it is written, thou shalt worship the Lord thy God, and him only shalt thou serve."* Was reading the forbidden books the same as serving another god?

To distract herself, she examined a box mounted to the wall. When she wiped the centuries of accumulated grime from its smooth surface, a monstrous face appeared, and she jerked back with a shriek.

It was her own reflection.

The farmers of her village occasionally unearthed fragments of mirrors, but Minister Coglin deemed them evil vanities and ordered them destroyed. She'd glimpsed her face in ponds and puddles, but avoided such confrontations with the truth. Now, however, she studied herself—the drooping lid obscuring most of her left eye, the odd distortions like a melted mold of wax, and lines of hardened skin pulling part of her lip into a permanent half-snarl. This is what the other children saw. A freak. A monster. A demon.

When a baby is born healthy, or talented, or beautiful, everyone calls it *blessed by God*. But if God chooses to bless one child with such gifts, then he must have chosen to curse her. *What could she have done before birth to deserve this?*

God's holy words state, *"...for I, the Lord thy God, am a jealous God, visiting the iniquity of the fathers upon the children unto the third and fourth generation of them that hate me."* The blame rested not with God, then, but with her unknown father and mother. Their sins must have been horrendous for God to curse her so.

Kayla rotated her head until the distorted side of her face vanished from the reflection. Then she stepped back and slid her crippled leg behind the good one. For that instant, she looked normal. Maybe even beautiful.

At her birth, the monk had used the illegal tools of sciencecraft to save her life. Might other secrets of the ancients heal her now?

The books tugged at her mind, urging her back to the room, back to the forbidden fruit sitting on those shelves.

If I'm already cursed, what does it matter if I break the law here, where none will see? The hateful crutch carried her from the room—back to the hallway and the forbidden words that served as windows into the past.

At first, she settled for reading the categories. *Music, History, Literature, Self-Help, and...*

Science.

Kayla averted her eyes, her breathing ragged. Her fingers drifted to the wooden cross hanging from her neck, but paused before making contact. Minister Coglin's sermons rang in her mind. Even here, far from his reach, she could not escape a lifetime of his judgment.

On the floor sat a box labeled *Magazines.* Setting her candle on a ledge, she bent down and dusted off a cover. A beautiful woman stared across the gulf of time, directly at her. Despite its yellowed and crumbling surface, the woman's haughty confidence glowed forth. Bold letters stated, *Cosmopolitan.*

Maybe the lady Cosmopolitan had once stood on this very spot. It must have taken powerful sciencecraft to burn her face onto this piece of paper. A date proclaimed the year 2014—approximately five hundred years ago, and well before the Founding of Potemia.

What had become of Cosmopolitan? Her children and grandchildren? The Founder made it clear that those outside the Wall's protection would perish in the total destruction brought about by unchecked technology. If his prediction had held true, only those in Potemia remained.

A tear bloomed in her eye as she gazed at Cosmopolitan's face.

Kayla opened the book-magazine, but the pages disintegrated in her hands as she pried them apart. Another half-dozen magazines lay in even worse shape. On the very bottom of the pile, one magazine had survived nearly intact. The picture on the cover depicted a hooded man wearing dark patches over his eyes, held together by some sort of frame. The face glared at her with a malevolence that chilled her blood. The words on the cover declared, "The Unabomber Strikes Again."

The terrible face with its dark, bug-like eyes stared through the window of time. With a shiver, she set it aside unopened.

The light from the candle cast unsteady shadows across the books in seductive undulations. For a long while she remained motionless, feeling the desire expanding inside her once again. Who would ever know?

Kayla inhaled and held her breath as if preparing to plunge into a swollen river of unknown depth. Then, she reached for a book in the history section. Her fingers trembled as she grasped the crumbling spine and lifted the relic free of its tomb. Insects and time had left their mark, and some of the cover fell to pieces in her hands, adding to the detritus at her feet. Her breath fluttered in equal measure with excitement and fear. What secrets of the past lay within? The yearning to know grew to terrible proportions within her.

But still she hesitated. When Lot's wife looked back at the cities of Sodom and Gomorrah, God transformed her into a pillar of salt in punishment for her disobedience. Eve's curiosity created Original Sin itself. But were the Founder's laws the same as God's?

Kayla opened the book at random and began reading.

"All States and domains which hold or have held sway over mankind are either republics or monarchies. Monarchies are either..." The words became unreadable for a while, with only a couple making their way past the barrier of time before coalescing once again. *"...are annexed either by force of arms of the prince himself, or of others..."*

"You know such things are forbidden."

Kayla screamed, nearly dislodging the candle, and came face-to-face with the monk.

She gasped for breath and steadied herself, hiding the book behind her as if this could somehow conceal her shameful actions.

"Have you learned nothing from what I've taught you?" His face reflected his worry.

She gasped for breath and held a hand to her chest. After several gulps, she said, "You break the law with your medicines and books on healing."

"I am willing to forfeit my life to serve others. Who are you serving by this act, other than yourself?"

Kayla averted her eyes and replaced the book on the shelf. "There's no danger of anyone seeing me here."

"Aren't you forgetting God?"

Kayla stiffened. "What commandment bans reading? I don't see what harm I'm causing."

"So you're not planning on taking any back with you, then?"

"Would it matter if I did? If someone found your medicines and healing tools, we'd be punished anyway."

"Under the law, I hold sole responsibility for that." He moved his candle across the line of books. "These are more serious." His candle paused on the section labeled *Science.* "The penalty for reading a book on sciencecraft is death to all residing within the dwelling."

"So you don't think it's wrong, only too dangerous?"

"Under the law, it's both, without a doubt," he said.

"I thought there was no black-and-white?"

The monk stiffened, then chuckled. "My own words." He removed his pipe from a pocket and placed it in his mouth, though he didn't light it. He surveyed her for several heartbeats, then nodded. "Okay. You're old enough to decide for yourself, even if I disapprove."

"You'll let me take them?" Kayla's eyes sparkled, then dulled. "But wouldn't I endanger you, as well?"

The monk laughed. "Don't use me as an excuse. I'm too old to worry about such dangers. Now that you've declared yourself an adult, this decision is yours alone." His voice softened. "Everything of value has a price. Be certain you're willing to pay it."

He dropped a linen sack at her feet, half-filled with the spare cloth he padded delicate equipment with. "Fill this with either books or medical supplies. It's your choice. If you take the books, I don't want to know, and I never want to see you reading them in my presence. Is that clear?"

Kayla nodded.

The light from his candle faded down the corridor and up the stairway.

The books lay before her, silent. Her mouth salivated as she confronted these windows into the minds of people centuries past. The want was so powerful. A demon inside her. An insatiable hunger that had set her apart since she was a child.

Knowledge. Answers. Truth. Am I willing to risk everything for such things? To pay the price of death and possible damnation?

She reached for a book.

***

As Kayla slept, she dreamt of a forest. Giant sycamores rocked in a hypnotic rhythm, as if summoning the approaching storm. A woman lay on the autumn leaves atop an expanding halo of crimson. The lower half of her homespun dress gleamed red with each flash of lightning. Matted strands of blonde hair pasted her young face like a shredded veil.

The woman's green eyes stared upward, unblinking. Between her naked thighs lay a newborn child. A girl. The left half of the child's face and its right foot twisted into a gruesome misinterpretation of nature's design.

I'm watching my own birth.

Cloaked apparitions appeared out of the darkness. Angels, demons, or something else?

The shadowy beings anointed their leader in whispered reverence with the name *Melchi*. They chanted it over and over like a spell.

Melchi led the silent procession to the mother and child. Then he swept back the hood of his cloak, revealing a gaunt face with such translucent skin that the outlines of his skull shone through. His eyes burned like the embers of a fire. The pupils were marked by the dark silhouette of a naked woman in his right eye, and a naked man in the left. Both figures writhed as if in pain.

His blackened horns curved from his temples to the corners of his mouth like the mandibles of an insect. Who else could this be but the Devil himself?

It's only a dream. I'll wake up soon.

The infant's tiny chest spasmed in attempts at drawing breath into its lungs. With each failure, its skin lost more of its bloom.

"She is merely human," one of the apparitions said.

"Far more than human," said Melchi.

"She is one of us, then?"

"A half-sibling only." Melchi's eyes flickered as he gazed at the child. "Her name is Nihala, the Creator's tool for our destruction."

"Why would the Creator destroy his own greatest creation?"

"He fears us."

The child jerked its arms and legs convulsively, nearing suffocation.

"This creature must die before we can be free?"

"Yes." Melchi's voice vibrated with command.

"But the Creator has placed her beyond our reach."

The crippled newborn stopped struggling, its skin ashen.

"A time will come when Nihala will seek us out," Melchi said. "We will either destroy this weapon of the Creator, or perish ourselves."

The child's eyes opened with an emerald flash of light.

Kayla woke from the dream and gasped for air. She lay on her bedroll in the ancient ruin and focused on the square of stars framed by the hole in the ceiling.

It was only a dream.

The monk's snores echoed in the hollow room.

Her heart slowed, and her breathing returned to normal. The dream had been so vivid, unlike anything she'd experienced before. Had she somehow seen her own birth?

Was that my mother?

The bag the monk had given her sat beside the five others he'd stocked with medical supplies. She'd wrapped each of the selected books, forty in all, in old rags and stuffed fabric around the edges to mask their shapes.

Hauling the load up so many flights of stairs had proved a grueling task for someone with a crutch and a dwindling candle. But she'd done it. The fateful decision had been made, and there was no turning back.

The starlight flickered as something dark moved across the entrance.

Kayla's heart leapt. Had Melchi come for her?

The monk continued snoring.

The silhouette of a man blotted out a portion of the stars. The figure held a bow, with an arrow strung at the ready. Moonlight reflected off a silver band encircling his turban-shrouded head.

The glint of light she'd seen! Not the monsters from her dream, but someone who'd followed them.

The dark form slunk to the edge of the hole and peered inside. How much could he see by the starlight? Beads of sweat formed on her brow.

The figure's foot extended over the edge and explored the sand beneath.

Kayla's right hand eased silently along the floor beside her.

A camel bellowed not far off, and the figure paused.

Kayla's hand closed on her small knife.

The shadow stepped onto the top of the slide of sand.

Kayla lifted the knife. *Just one more step.*

His other foot extended downward, past the first … and tangled in the trip-wire the monk had strung across it.

A gourd filled with rocks rattled its warning, and the figure crashed down the slope, his bow flying from his hand. Kayla sprang forward. Her knife rose and stabbed downward.

A strong hand grasped her wrist, stopping the knife.

"Kayla, it's me!"

"Ishan?"

"Yes."

Sparks ignited a pile of tinder, and the monk used it to light a candle. Kayla straddled a dark-skinned boy in a black robe and turban. His left hand grasped her wrist, the knife hovering a few inches from his eye.

"What are you doing here?" Kayla all but shouted.

Ishan released her wrist and helped her stand. "I came to protect you." He brushed sand off his robe, while the monk brought Kayla her crutch. "But it looks like I'm the one who needs protection."

Ishan pulled a candle from his robes, and the monk lit it.

"You followed us?" the monk asked.

"My father heard that you'd entered the desert, so he sent me to see that you were safe."

The monk's eyes narrowed. "Nazeem sent his fifteen-year-old son into the desert—alone?"

Ishan shifted. "Well, he didn't exactly send me—"

"Does your father even know you're here?" Kayla asked.

"Not exactly."

"Why didn't you call to us? I could have killed you!"

"I wasn't certain it was you down here."

The monk shook his head. "You have more daring than brains, boy."

Ishan gazed around and whistled.

Kayla and the monk exchanged glances.

"What are you doing here, anyway?" Ishan walked to the bags and pulled out a syringe. His eyes widened. "This is sciencecraft."

Kayla limped between him and the bag. "Ishan, do you remember when we first met?"

"Don't change the subject. I want to know what—"

"Answer my question," she said, "and I'll answer yours."

The black-skinned boy frowned. "I was six years old. My father took me to your village with his trade caravan, mostly because he enjoys smoking pipes with the monk and talking Potemian Politics late into the night. I'd never met a non-Muslim before."

"You placed your hand on my scars as if touching a precious work of art," Kayla whispered. "You said I must be brave to have such beautiful battle wounds."

Ishan half-smiled. "When you told me you were born with your scars, I was even more impressed that you'd fought demons in the netherworld to reach this one."

Kayla's fingers traced the decorative scars on his own face—symbols burned into forehead, cheek, and chin during his tribal coming-of-age ceremony. "You were the first and only person to ever admire my appearance," she said. "The weeks in the spring and fall when you visit are like Christmas, Easter, and Potemia's Founding Day combined for me."

"What does that have to do with this place?" Ishan asked.

Kayla stared into his dark eyes. "The monk used tools of healing sciencecraft from this place to save my life when I was born."

"They're against the Founder's law," Ishan said.

"Are you saying the monk should have let me die?"

Ishan averted his eyes.

The monk approached and placed a hand on the boy's shoulder. "You wouldn't turn us in, would you?"

Ishan hesitated. "I couldn't do that, but it's wrong."

Kayla grabbed his hand and placed her knife into it. "If you really feel that it's against God's will, you should kill me right now and set things right."

"You know I would never hurt you," he said.

"Then pretend you never found us."

Ishan looked at the bags and back at Kayla, his face tormented. Finally, he straightened, and his voice rang with an iron tone. "I must protect you by burning this place of evil."

"No!" Kayla screamed and blocked his way. He threw her knife into the darkness and shoved past. The monk lashed out with his cane, but the Muslim youth yanked it from his grasp and tossed it aside.

Ishan seized the first bag and dumped its contents onto the floor. Glass shattered, and the smell of alcohol wafted over them, soaking the rags used to protect the various supplies. "It's for your own good!" he shouted.

Kayla seized his leg, but he ignored her and dumped another sack onto the pile. Clamps, scalpels, syringes, and more bottles exploded across the floor, adding the reek of chloroform.

Ishan lowered his blazing candle toward the pile.

Kayla snatched one of the scalpels, struggled to her feet, and held the blade against her throat. Ishan froze.

"If you burn these supplies, you will be killing dozens in the future."

"Suicide is a sin for Christians, just like it is for Muslims," Ishan said. "You'd go to Hell."

"Then save me." A trickle of blood slid down her neck as she pressed the ancient blade into her flesh. "I won't allow you the excuse that you're doing this to keep me safe."

"Not this way, my child," the monk said to her.

She half-turned to her mentor. "You told me that you were willing to sacrifice your life to serve others." The knife cut deeper and blood flowed faster. "Well, so am I."

Ishan stepped back. "You win." He extinguished his candle.

"You'll keep our secret?" Kayla asked, not lowering the knife.

He hesitated. "Do you promise me there's nothing else in these bags but healing supplies?"

16

"There's nothing else," she said. *The first time I've ever lied to him.*

"Okay, I'll keep your secret," Ishan said.

Chapter 2

The log cabin was basic, built as partial payment for the monk's services as village healer. The oak table dominating the small room served primarily to examine and treat patients. There was a leather bucket for hauling water, a few wooden plates and utensils, the prized iron kettle, and little else of note. A grass-woven curtain separated the monk's sleeping nook and muffled his snores.

In the early morning darkness, Kayla huddled close to the glowing fireplace. A book titled *Albert Einstein's Life and Works* sprawled open on the dirt floor before her. Portions of the fragile tome had succumbed to the ravages of time, rendering them indecipherable. But enough remained.

Gravitational dilation, black holes, relativity, entanglement, and a thousand wonders of the universe expanded before her.

One statement from this greatest of all sciencecraft philosophers stood out: *"I know not with what weapons World War Three will be fought, but World War Four will be fought with sticks and stones."*

The words so closely mirrored the predictions of the Founder that she shivered. Her eyes drifted to the flames of the hearth. What horrible weapons had sciencecraft unleashed outside the Wall in the five hundred years since Einstein's death?

In the past two years, she'd read all forty books several times. Newton, Darwin, Euclid, Voltaire, Durant, and a score of others. They'd become her secret confidants. She read in the barn most often, sometimes discussing geometry with the cow, physics with the pig, or the Peloponnesian War with the chickens.

Jesus had used mud and spit to open the eyes of a man born blind. The sensation he experienced upon seeing for the first time must have been similar to this. *I know things no one else in Potemia even suspects.*

Many of the books contradicted the Bible, and seemed to question the very existence of God. Jesus had called blasphemy the one unforgivable sin. Did damnation also apply to reading such words?

One of the books even hinted at cures for her deformities, but contained nothing specific.

If only I could find the right book.

A pebble ticked against the window, and she covered the book with her skirt, her eyes wide and tense. A heron's call relaxed her, and a smile danced across her lips. With sudden energy, she stashed the book alongside the others in a hidden compartment under the woodpile. The monk continued snoring as she used her crutch to stand and eased the door open with practiced care.

He stood off the trail, behind some bushes, the growing light of dawn highlighting the whites of his eyes in brilliant contrast to his ebony skin.

"Ishan," she breathed, and limped as fast as her crutch and twisted foot would allow, trading pain for speed.

The Muslim boy embraced her and swung her in a circle like a big brother greeting a little sister. Finally, he set her down, and she let her hair fall across the left side of her face, hiding her deformity. He brushed it behind her ear, a reminder that she didn't have to hide from him.

"It's too dangerous for you to come this close to the village," she said, though her smile contradicted her words.

"The caravan just arrived, and I couldn't wait."

"You brought the horses?" she asked.

"Of course," he said.

Soon they galloped through the forest side by side, her crutch slung across her back like some ancient warrior's sword. The woods to the north had always been their retreat during his visits. A place of freedom. Kayla breathed a sigh of contentment. Christian or Muslim meant nothing to the swaying trees.

After several miles, Kayla pulled up and squinted intently down the trail.

"What do you see?" Ishan asked.

"There." She pointed. "Hunters from the village." About a hundred yards ahead, three figures emerged from the woods beside the path and stared back at them. One towered above the others.

"That's Elias, Minister Coglin's son," she said. "Quick, before he recognizes us!"

She galloped off the trail, and Ishan followed close behind. After a few miles, they slowed.

"I lost my crutch, but I think we're safe now."

"What would happen if they found us together?"

She shrugged. "Probably another lecture on the dangers to my soul of too close an association with a godless, black-skinned Muslim like you."

He laughed. "I've gotten the same lecture on the dangers of Christian infidels like you."

She smiled, but an unease settled in her chest. What would he think if he knew of her forbidden books?

"Those things from the desert," he asked, as if reading her mind. "Do you still—?"

"We've saved three people's lives this year alone thanks to them."

"But does anyone suspect …?"

"We're very careful," she said.

He nodded and lapsed into silence.

Kayla gave him a sidelong glance. "Have you ever seen the Wall?"

"Only from a great distance."

Her heart sped, and she leaned toward him. "What did you see beyond it?"

"A milky curtain stretches above it into the sky. Nothing is visible beyond."

"It must become clear at some point, or we wouldn't see the stars or the sun."

"I never thought about that, but you must be right, I suppose."

She patted the mare's neck. "The old legends say one can pass through the Wall from Potemia to the Outside, but not the other way around."

He waved at a fly with his reins. "Who would want to leave, since everything Outside is a wasteland?"

"How do you know it's a wasteland if no one has come through the Wall in five hundred years?"

"The Founder himself predicted it."

"Maybe the Founder was wrong," she said.

"You know the Founder can't be wrong!"

"Nothing is more firmly believed as that which is least known," she said.

"What is that supposed to mean?"

"Just a saying I heard from someone called Montaigne."

He shook his head. "That doesn't sound like anyone from around here."

The slow beat of hooves accompanied the forest rhythms in a hypnotic counterpoint, while the sour smell of rotting vegetation infused the moist breeze with an atmosphere of spring renewal. Squirrels dashed through towering trees, and the occasional conclave of mushrooms huddled amidst the mossy ground, watching dawn ignite the heavens.

"Look." Kayla pointed to a butterfly as it struggled free of its chrysalis. They halted on both sides of the low-hanging branch while the colorful wings unfolded.

"Do you think it remembers its previous life?" she asked.

Ishan leaned close as it shook off the remnants of its former body. "The only thing for certain is that it's a miracle of God's design."

"The monk used to tell me I would transform into my own butterfly someday," Kayla said. "On my tenth birthday, I told him I knew he lied, that being a cripple was forever. He never mentioned butterflies after that."

In a spasm of freedom, the wings blurred into a rainbow, and the resurrected caterpillar left its former two-dimensional earth-bound universe for the three dimensions of earth, air, and sky.

The horses resumed their ambling gait, and she glanced at Ishan from the corner of her eye. If only she could discuss her books with him. What good was knowledge that couldn't be shared?

Do I dare tell him?

She flipped her reins from side to side. "Have you ever found any books from before Potemia's founding?"

Ishan jerked his horse to a stop.

"Why are you looking at me like that?" she asked.

"You know that all books from the past are evil."

"The Bible is a book from the past," she said. "So is the Quran."

"You shouldn't joke about this."

"I thought you might have come across such things in your travels."

His gaze interrogated her with an uncomfortable intensity. "Yes, we occasionally find pre-Potemian books in old ruins."

Kayla's heart leapt. "What do they say?"

"Do you think I'd read such a thing?" He spat on the ground as if to clear his mouth of a spoiled piece of meat. "When we find such evil relics, we burn them."

A stab in her gut. "Oh. Of course."

Ishan's eyes narrowed. "Have you found such books?"

"Where would I find anything like that around here?" She spurred her horse into a trot, and he came alongside.

"You know where," he said, his face shadowed with concern.

"I know it's against the law."

Ishan grabbed the reins of her horse and pulled them both to a stop. "Do you promise me you'll never read such a dangerous thing if you ever have the chance?"

"Don't you think you're overreacting?" She fidgeted in her saddle. "After all, they're just words."

"They're evil words."

She lifted her chin as if defending a maligned relative. "How do you know they're evil if you haven't read any?"

"Because the Founder read them and told us!"

"Don't you trust me to separate good from evil? Or do you imagine I'm so weak-willed that I can't think for myself?"

Ishan placed his hand on hers. "Promise me," he said.

For a long while she stayed silent. Could she risk losing her only friend?

"Okay, I promise."

My second lie to him.

His body relaxed. "I'm sorry to be so serious, but you have to understand how dangerous such things are. This world is merely a testing ground for the next life." Ishan gestured to the forest. "Look at the wonders God has provided for us. Shouldn't we concentrate on proving our worthiness for entry into Heaven, rather than vainly thinking we can improve on God's design? Isn't all this enough?"

"You sound like Minister Coglin," she said.

"Ouch, that hurts!" His face split into a wide grin. "Enough talk—catch me if you can!"

Ishan kicked his stallion into a gallop, and she thundered after, dodging and swerving through the forest like an avalanche of youthful joy. Kayla laughed at the release from her normal limitations. But she slowly lost ground as his faster horse outpaced her own.

Think! There must be a way. A wide stream appeared ahead, and an idea bloomed in her mind. *That's my chance.*

She veered sharply away.

With a triumphant whoop, Ishan splashed into the stream and turned right. His horse churned the water as it galloped toward the entrance of a narrow forest gully. Then Ishan reined up to a stop before a motionless Kayla, sitting triumphant atop her mare.

"How could you have known which direction I'd go?"

"We've been friends for a long time, so I suppose it's only right that I tell you." Kayla bugged her eyes for effect. "I can read minds."

"Are you serious?"

Her hands danced in the air, as if conjuring a spell. "The immortal Oracle of Delphi blessed me with the third eye of prophecy in a dream. Ever since that mystical encounter, I can see … the *future!*"

Ishan grimaced. "Fine, if you don't want to tell me."

Kayla laughed, easing her horse next to his. "You know mind-reading is impossible."

"But how else could you know?"

"Very simple—I guessed."

Ishan frowned. "But what if you were wrong?"

"Well, I knew you'd either go left or right at the stream," she said. "Your horse is faster than mine, so I'd never catch you if I followed, no matter which direction you chose. So I balanced the certainty of losing if I didn't guess, to the the one-out-of-two opportunity of getting ahead of you if I did. Not to mention the amazement I'd inspire in your gullible little mind."

Ishan smiled. "You're right, of course. It seems so obvious now that you explain it."

If only I could show you my book on Game Theory.

"Despite my blinding intellect, I still require your manly strength to liberate me from this horse."

"I'm so glad a dumb brute like me still has a use!" Ishan vaulted off his stallion, and she slid into his outstretched arms. He carried her across the brook while she draped her hands around his neck, feeling the lithe muscles beneath his skin. Losing her crutch had proved her best luck yet.

When they reached the water's edge, he playfully tossed her into the air. "I think you could do with a bath!"

She screamed. "You *are* a barbarian! The village is right to ban you from sight of the church tower."

He laughed and eased her onto the mossy bank. He glanced her way a few times but remained silent. A knot formed in her stomach. Was there bad news? Was his father sending him away to battle?

"On my last visit," he said, "you implied no one would ever want to marry you."

Her breath caught in her throat.

He gazed into her eyes and leaned close. Then his lips pressed against hers, and her mind swirled from the shock. The taste of his lips held a hint of cinnamon, and she breathed in the salty musk of his sweat as one might a feast.

His lips brushed her ear. "Kayla Nighthawk, I love you, and I want you to become my wife."

Her body tingled. *This is what I've always dreamed of. Why the hesitation?*

"Have you considered what your father—"

"Forget my father!"

She pulled back from him. "What would a crippled bride do to your status in the tribe? I'm a Christian and you're a Muslim. Where would we live? How would we support ourselves?"

"I tell you I love you, and all you talk about is …" Insecurity shadowed his face. "Or maybe you're being kind. Letting me know that you don't feel the same way…"

"I loved you from the moment I first met you!"

He took her hand. "Then become my wife."

"Yes, I will marry you!" Her shout startled a flock of guinea fowl into an explosion of flight.

She melted into his arms and kissed him. He responded with equal hunger. Her fingers explored his back, chest, neck, and face, while his lips caressed her earlobes, forehead, and even the left side of her face.

Only Ishan could love my scars.

She kissed the raised designs on his cheeks, the symbols of his manhood.

A jolt surged through her, like the sensation of falling just before sleep. She moaned and raised her hips against his, and he responded. He lifted her shirt and kissed her breasts. A lifetime of sermons couldn't convince her this was anything but right and beautiful. The smell of crushed grass mixed with the cool fragrance of the stream and bathed them in nature's embrace.

Her breaths jerked in short gasps, and goose bumps rose beneath his fingers. She reached for his robe—but he pulled back and guided her hand away.

"I won't let anyone say I married you in shame," he whispered. "My wife will be pure until her wedding night."

She hugged him fiercely, disappointed and proud in equal measure.

They lay together, the dappled sun dancing across their half-naked bodies, his black skin overlapping hers like the stripes of a zebra.

I wonder what shade our children will be?

The lullaby of the stream eventually pulled her into half-sleep.

A shadow crossed her face, and her eyes fluttered open. A creature with splayed horns loomed. Was it Melchi, the demon from her dream?

"I hope we're not interrupting?" a deep voice said.

Two figures next to the horned creature laughed in crude disharmony. She pushed Ishan's hand off her naked breast and covered herself.

"We're not alone," she said.

Ishan's eyes opened. He vaulted to his feet and ran toward his horse and, more important, his bow.

The two smaller figures pounced on him. Ishan twisted, kicked, and thrashed, but they bent his arms behind his back until he stopped struggling.

"Let him go!" Kayla shouted.

The horned beast stepped into a sunbeam, revealing Elias, Minister Coglin's son. On his broad back hung a dead antelope. Not a mythical monster after all, but one from this world.

Elias wore furs and hides of the animals he'd tracked and slain. A necklace of lion's claws hung from his neck. The giant towered above his two companions, Isaac and David. Both still outweighed the slim Ishan, whom they dragged before him.

Elias tossed Kayla's lost crutch on top of her and released the rope securing the antelope. The dead animal hit the ground with a thump. Though only a year older than her, his immense size marked him a leader, and the pride of his father. "You dare defile yourself with a dirty, godless Muslim!"

"We're to be married," Ishan said.

24

"We heard." David and Isaac laughed.

Please, God, I need your help.

Elias frowned. "I think my father would decree a punishment of fifty lashes for such immorality with a heathen."

"My actions harm no one."

"This is not for you to judge, woman!" Elias reached for his belt, and her blood went cold.

"I will administer the lashes myself." His tongue slid across his lips, and he yanked the braided leather belt from his waist. She crawled backward, her arms trembling.

"I will take the punishment for her," Ishan said.

Elias scowled. "I should kill you for defiling our women, even one as ugly as this." Elias spat on Kayla's twisted foot. "But she alone falls under Christian law."

Kayla stared into his icy blue eyes, the only thing that resembled his father. The belt rose, then snapped across her deformed cheek, tearing it to the bone. The force of the blow spun her to the ground facefirst.

"One," Elias said.

The second lash tore through her shirt, the braids acting like the teeth of a saw, and ripped a deep gash across her back. Despite the agony, she clamped her jaw tight and bore her punishment in silence.

"Two."

The third lash tore open the backs of her thighs. The blood soaked her skirt and flowed onto the ground. Still, she remained silent.

"Three."

I won't survive this.

Ishan writhed in a wild attempt to free himself. "Fight me like a man, you coward!"

The giant's hand stilled, and he faced Ishan. "You want to fight me?"

Kayla shook her head as bile rose into her throat. "No, Ishan, I'll be—"

Ishan silenced her with a glance and glared at Elias. "One-on-one, man-to-man. If I win, you leave Kayla alone."

Elias tossed his belt aside and smiled. "Okay, it's a deal." He stepped toward Ishan and motioned to his companions. "Let him go."

David and Isaac released their captive. The Muslim boy brought his fists up, eyes alert. Elias sauntered forward, eyes mocking. No one in the village would dare face him one-on-one. Kayla's lips moved in silent prayer as she gripped the cross hanging from her neck.

Ishan dashed forward and ducked under the thick arms, punching into the gut, then dancing back of range.

Elias laughed. "Is that it?" The giant straightened, shoulders back, belly forward, and hands posted on his hips. "Give it another try." His companions' jeers rattled through the clearing.

Ishan charged. But instead of punching the rocklike gut, he aimed high, near the limit of his reach. A sickening crunch sounded as fist met nose.

Elias bellowed, his hands covering his face. Blood showered the ground. Ishan cradled his knuckles, and David and Isaac pounced on him.

"No!" the wounded giant commanded. "He's mine!"

Ishan and Elias faced off again. This time, the minister's son hunched like a wrestler. Blood oiled his chin, tunic, and the ground in a scarlet sheen. Kayla's face, back, and legs bled as she watched.

Please help him, God.

Elias charged, but Ishan dodged the clumsy grasp and kicked the giant's ankles from under him. Driven by his own momentum, Elias collapsed in a sprawling heap.

A glowing heat filled Kayla with pride and hope.

With a grimace, Elias climbed to his feet, favoring his left shoulder. David and Isaac fell silent, stunned. Ishan now moved with new confidence, while caution crept into Elias's movements.

Ishan went on the attack. He moved with the grace of his lean form, striking with the quick, hit-and-run tactics his people had long utilized in their tribal feuds. He struck at knees, throat, and the already damaged nose. Attack, retreat. Attack, retreat. Hitting the weak points, always dodging the flailing grasp of his slower opponent.

The giant gasped and snorted like an exhausted bull. His blood dripped into the dirt.

Her heart soared.

"Teach him not to mess with our women!" David shouted.

"Beat his skinny ass!" Isaac encouraged.

They'll never leave him alone if Ishan wins.

The fight drifted toward the stream. Ishan subtly maneuvered Elias between himself and his friends. With just a few more yards to the side, Ishan would have a clear path to their horses—and his bow and arrow. No one could match Ishan's skill with the bow.

Elias stumbled, creating a perfect opening.

Ishan launched himself toward his horse, but the giant leapt into his path. He twisted to avoid the huge arms, but they wrapped around him like a vise and bore him to the ground in a flailing pile.

Kayla gasped. The stumble had been a ruse.

Ishan struck at the broken nose, but Elias shrugged aside the pain, pounding anything within reach. His massive fists rose and fell like scarlet sledgehammers. After a time, Ishan stopped struggling.

Kayla crawled toward the slaughter. Elias drove his fists into the pulverized mass beneath him as if grinding wheat. David and Isaac cheered him on like howling monkeys in a frenzy. She rose to her knees and latched onto one of the huge arms.

Elias paused and glared at her. Blood from his nose mingled with that from Ishan, transforming him into a crimson demon. His breath rasped from his heaving chest, and his face contorted in a snarl of rage.

"Please don't kill him."

"What will you trade me for his life?"

"I have nothing of value."

He leered in response, and she drew in her breath at his unspoken demand.

Not that. Not here.

Ishan, his face unrecognizable beneath the mashed flesh, gurgled bloody foam from his throat, eyes swollen nearly shut. The words of the monk echoed in her mind. *Everything of value has a price.*

Kayla pulled her shirt over her head and let it fall to the ground. "You can have me in payment." Elias gazed at her naked breasts and smiled. She turned her head to hide the distorted and bloody half of her face, making her offering as tempting as possible.

Elias abandoned Ishan and shoved her to the ground. He tore the skirt from her like an enraged animal. Blood from his face spattered her breasts and stomach. Then he yanked her thighs apart.

Ishan's face rolled toward her, one eye peeking through a swollen slit.

He's alive. That's all that matters.

Kayla closed her eyes and attempted leaving her body far behind, as the monk did when meditating. She escaped to a memory of her white-bearded guardian awakening from one such trance when she was a child.

"Where do you go when you meditate?" she'd asked him.

"I travel the night sky and hop from star to star."

"Do you speak to angels up there?"

"Oh yes, and they tell me that Kayla of Potemia will be a beautiful goddess someday."

"You're making fun of me—"

Excruciating pain yanked her back to the mossy bank, and she screamed.

Pain accompanied her always, but tolerance for physical discomfort proved no match for this. The agony violated her on a level that transcended physical sensation. With each bloody thrust, Elias shredded more of her soul, enslaving and degrading her mind along with her tortured body.

With a final grunt, the giant collapsed atop her, driving the breath from her lungs. After five heartbeats without air, consciousness faltered. Was this how she'd die? Then the mountain that was Elias finally heaved itself off her. Lungs filled with life, and she curled into a ball, gasping, coughing, and vomiting all at once.

But Ishan lived.

When she opened her eyes, Elias stood glaring at his two friends.

"What are you looking at?" Elias said between gasps for air.

David and Isaac wilted under his gaze. Their faces appeared troubled, and their eyes shunned her.

"The Bible says rape is a sin," Isaac said, a slight tremor entering his voice.

"She offered herself to me willingly!" Elias took a step forward, his bloody fists balling into weapons once more.

"You're right," Isaac stammered. "I forgot that. You're right, it wasn't rape."

Elias glared at the two, who nodded agreement, the fear bending their backs into postures of submission. Elias glanced at her, and the first troubled look clouded his face. A hint of shame? He resembled a trapped water buffalo, seeking an escape from some bog he'd stumbled into. Not shame, then—fear.

His eyes drifted to Ishan and his face relaxed. A sneer curled his lips, and he kicked Ishan onto his stomach. Then he tore off the boy's blood-stained robe, leaving him naked.

"You can't kill him," Kayla said. "We had a deal."

"I won't kill him." Elias grasped the backs of his companions' necks. He squeezed, and they contorted in pain. "You will each do to the infidel what I did to her, or I will break your spines." He eased his grip and they gasped.

"We won't tell what you done," David said.

"I know you won't," Elias said. "Because you will share my guilt. Shame will ensure the boy's silence as well." He squeezed harder and they writhed. "Do you understand?" They both nodded.

The giant kicked Kayla's crutch toward him. "Use this."

Ishan met her gaze. "Don't look," he said through a swollen mouth missing two teeth. She rotated her head and squeezed her eyelids shut, but couldn't block the sounds …

After they left, Kayla crawled to Ishan. She cradled her love's battered body in her arms and rocked him as he stared into the mocking blue sky.

She silently recited words from a book she'd read by Darwin. *"In the struggle for survival, the fittest win out at the expense of their rivals because they succeed in adapting themselves best to their environment."* Was that all life amounted to? How could God reward the sadistic Elias with prosperity while discarding noble Ishan?

Then the words attributed to the Greek philosopher, Epicurus, forced their way into her mind.

"Is God willing to prevent evil, but not able? Then he is not omnipotent.

Is he able, but not willing? Then he is malevolent.

Is he both able and willing? Then whence come evil?

Is he neither able nor willing? Then why call him God?"

Chapter 3

Kayla hid in the brush just beyond the clearing, waiting past midnight as the last of the campfires settled to embers. It had been six months since the trade caravan's departure, six months wondering whether Ishan would return. His tent crouched behind his father's. Earlier in the day, Nazeem claimed his son refused to see her.

It can't be true.

Ishan's proposal of marriage haunted her, a distant dream of a past life filled with hope. During their excruciating journey home after the attack, she pleaded with Ishan to report Elias's crimes, but he refused, promising suicide if she divulged his shame to anyone. Elias proved smarter than she'd suspected. Even when Nazeem threatened to beat her in his attempts to learn who had attacked his son, she stayed true to her promise.

During the week the monk treated him, Ishan spoke to no one—including her. On the Sunday after the caravan departed, she'd been forced to listen to Minister Coglin preach the Golden Rule while Elias shot her smirks from the front row. Once, he blew her a kiss. David and Isaac dodged her gaze, and rushed past when the service ended.

In the ensuing weeks, her monthly flow failed to arrive. If the council found out, they might drive her into the wilderness as a whore, just like her mother. Who would believe her if she accused Elias? But the trauma went far beyond any punishment the council could impose. For days on end she lay in bed and refused to eat or speak. The Bible claimed God created the pain of childbirth as punishment for Eve's disobedience. Was this her punishment for reading the forbidden books?

She sought solace in prayer and God's holy word. The monk's worn Bible was one of the few with actual printed text. Most in Potemia's Christian settlements were hand-copied versions assembled from primitive paper and littered with errors large and small. Some had entire pages skipped. As originals vanished to fire, flood, or simple age, copies were made from copies until reconciling the actual words of God became difficult.

When her monthly flow returned, a glint of hope flared within her for the first time since the ordeal.

And now Ishan is back.

Kayla slipped into his tent like a whisper. The autumn breeze trailed her with the empty fragrance of the approaching dry season. Ishan slept on a rug to the side of the sparse interior, and her heart ached with longing as she moved toward him. Staring at his shadowed profile, her hand drifted toward his cheek.

My beautiful, kind, loving Ishan.

Her fingers stopped within the warmth of his skin.

"Ishan," she said. Her hand settled on his shoulder and his eyes opened.

"Kayla?"

"I'm here, my love."

As he rose into a sliver of moonlight, her breath caught. The map of Elias's brutality lay etched across his face.

"Don't look at me." His hand blocked her gaze.

"Do you think I care about scars?"

Ishan turned away. "Looking at you reminds me of …"

She cried, but his eyes only stared blankly, unseeing, devoid of life.

Calloused hands seized her shoulders and jerked her backward.

"Leave him alone!" Nazeem shouted. "Haven't you Christians done enough to him?"

She thrashed free of his grip, threw herself before Ishan, and took hold of one of his hands. "Don't desert me!" But his eyes remained unfocused, his hand unresponsive.

Nazeem twisted his fingers into her hair, digging into her scalp and hauling her out like a sack of camel feed.

"Ishan!" she screamed. Her words drifted into the sparkling constellations of the night as if carrying her soul into oblivion.

***

As the dry season approached its end, preparations for Easter commenced. But Kayla took no part in such festivities. She continued her chores of cleaning stables, milking the cow, collecting the eggs, and assisting the monk with his patients, but her movements lacked their previous spark. She read neither the Bible nor the books from the desert. Her search for knowledge, answers, and a cure for her deformities seemed pointless without Ishan.

Standing alone in their cabin, Kayla gazed at the woodpile concealing her once-precious books. *I've abandoned you as Ishan abandoned me.*

Maybe this final devastation represented God's punishment for seeking forbidden knowledge—her own lost Eden. Or a continuation of the curse she'd been born with, the punishment bleeding into her generation from some unknown misdeed of her parents.

Kayla opened a hidden trunk and removed one of several surgical knives from the place in the desert.

The curse would end with her.

The blade of the scalpel settled against her throat with its promise of release—an encore performance of her standoff with Ishan long before. This time, he wasn't here to save her.

Some of the ancient books claimed there was no reward or punishment after death. In one book that had disintegrated to ruins, she rescued these few words: *Is man merely a mistake of God's? Or God merely a mistake of man?*

Heaven, Hell, or oblivion? She'd soon have the answer.

Her arm tensed for its terminal act, and she inhaled a final breath.

A loud *snap* shattered the silence.

She jumped, and the scalpel slipped from her fingers. Frantic thrashing and a high-pitched squeaking led her to a crate where the monk stored grain. Behind it, a mouse struggled to free one of its rear legs from a trap. Its tiny chest fluttered and pulsed like the wings of a dragonfly.

Seeing the looming giant, the mouse jerked its body side to side in desperation.

"Don't be frightened." Kayla dragged the crate aside. A trail of wheat trickled onto the floor from a gnawed hole in the wood. "You poor thing."

She released the spring-loaded bar and gently lifted the mouse free. Its foot flapped loose, connected by a sliver of tendon and skin. Its whiskers twitched, and its eyes darted wildly. Kayla's throat tightened. It had sought food. What great crime was that?

Grabbing a strip of cloth, she bound its body so it couldn't move, snatched the scalpel from the floor, and shoved the sharp end into the hearth's flames.

When the blade glowed red, she placed two fingers on the damaged leg. The mouse's eyes closed, and a stab of empathetic pain cramped her own leg.

"I'm sorry, little one," she said, with tears forming in her eyes. Chloroform would kill the tiny creature. "Your foot is beyond mending. You will die from infection if I don't do this."

Her hand trembled as she pressed the blade into its leg—cutting, cauterizing, and amputating the doomed appendage.

The mouse squeaked, and a tiny puff of smoke rose from the burned flesh and fur. Then it lapsed into unconsciousness.

In the following days, she hid the mouse, whom she named Puck, in a small box in her sleeping nook. She replaced the food crate and reset the trap so the monk would have no inkling of her secret patient. But she also rendered the device harmless by disconnecting the spring.

Changing the tiny bandages and feeding Puck sugar water with a hollow reed became a ritual, yet, day after day, his eyes remained closed. In the evenings, she prayed for the tiny mouse. Had God sent him to stop her from taking her own life and damning her soul forever? The timing seemed too perfect for coincidence.

On the third day, Puck's eyes opened. She stroked his head and he looked up at her.

She told herself that she imprisoned Puck for his own health. When this excuse finally wore thin, she released him outside their cabin. The three-legged mouse scampered around in the grass, and she cried.

"Thank you for saving my life," she said as he looked back at her. Then Puck squeaked up at her and scaled her sack of a dress until reaching her shoulder.

"So you're staying after all?"

In the following months, Puck rode on her shoulder or in a pocket when she went outside, although the mouse hid from the monk, as if sensing that this was the enemy who had maimed him.

***

Kayla waited in church after Sunday mass, the walls seeming to vibrate from the fire and brimstone flung from the minister's tongue. The congregation filed out like sheep after a close shearing, the weight of their sins lifted from their souls and a renewed sense of divine purpose filling their faces with confidence.

Elias seemed immune to guilt or fear of the Lord. Even now, ten months after the attack, Kayla's hands trembled every time he smirked at her on his way out of the church. It seemed God had no desire to punish him for his evil deeds. Minister Coglin announced after the sermon that his son would marry Hannah, the golden-haired daughter of the most prosperous farmer in their settlement.

The monk stood near the exit, chatting with Minister Coglin about the latest news gleaned from the wider sphere of Potemia; intertribal disputes, the tobacco harvest, and even some arcane theological questions. Their friendship seemed genuine, and the monk often told her that the minister's every action, even when handing down a harsh punishment, came from a heartfelt concern for the well-being of his congregation, both in this life and the next.

Minister Coglin glanced across the church in her direction, and Kayla averted her eyes.

What if he sees into my soul and learns my secret?

"But what of the Trinity?" the monk asked, and the minister turned his attention back to him.

"There's nothing polytheistic about it," Minister Coglin said. "Consider how your childhood self, adolescent self, and adult self are all a part of the one you. If you brought all three together at the same moment in time, they would still all be the same person. God's three manifestations exist eternally in a co-equal and co-substantial triumvirate."

"Well put," the monk said. "You are a man of great insight."

"You are the one person I can talk to about such things, my friend." Minister Coglin placed a hand on the monk's shoulder and frowned. "How are you feeling, by the way?"

"Oh, you know how it is with age." The monk laughed. "I suspect the Lord must have some reason to keep me around."

As the last of the congregation exited, Matthew and Maria Carroll walked up to Kayla's corner bench at the back of the church. She struggled to her feet with the help of her crutch and bobbed her head. Matthew held his wide-brimmed hat in his rough farmer's hands, while a traditional white headpiece covered Maria's hair, as God demanded of all women in church.

Matthew spoke to the point. "We aim to hire you as a tutor for Suzy."

Kayla froze, speechless.

Maria smiled. "We heard you reading the Bible in Sunday school."

Kayla's eyes fled to the monk as he chatted with Minister Coglin. Didn't he see how she needed him?

Matthew nodded. "Your fine speaking of the Holy Word is a sure token of God's favor."

Didn't they see her face? Most thought it a mark of Satan.

Kayla dipped her head, but her throat imprisoned her words like floodgates.

This is my chance to be useful, to find a place of service in the community. Why can't I speak up?

Maria and Matthew exchanged a glance at the awkward silence.

"We take reading God's word very serious," Maria said. "So it's distressing for us to see our Suzy missing this glorious gift at nine years old."

"I-I would be happy to tutor Suzy."

The two parents nodded and walked away. The monk shook hands with the minister and joined her, leaning on his cane for support. By the time he reached her, his breath rasped past his throat in ragged gulps. When he caught his breath, he chuckled at her expression. "You look like you've had a visit from the Holy Ghost!"

"Even more amazing," Kayla said. "The Carrolls hired me to teach Suzy!"

***

Two months later, Kayla and Suzy sat at a rough-hewn table with a large book open between them. The well-maintained mud-brick fireplace and a refurbished rain-collection barrel posted outside the door testified to the family's discipline and prosperity. Suzy's younger brother, James, sat at the other end of the table, torturing a captured beetle by systematically plucking out its legs one by one. Kayla's stomach churned at the sight, but it wasn't her place to scold someone else's child, so she bit her lip.

"Go on from where you left off," Kayla said.

Suzy nodded and leaned forward over the book, her face screwed up with concentration. *"And the woman said unto the serpent, 'We may eat of the fruit of the trees of the garden, but of the fruit of the tree which is in the midst of the garden, God hath said, "Ye shall not eat of it, neither shall ye touch it, lest you die.' "*

The little girl looked up. "Will I go to Heaven when I die?"

"If you live by God's commandments, he will reward you in Heaven," Kayla said.

"Kayla is exactly right." Maria set a plate of honey cakes on the table. Both children grabbed one.

"We're so pleased with Suzy's progress these past months," Maria said.

Kayla smiled and ate one of the honey cakes. "I'm the one *who's* grateful. Because of you, the Tuttles and Smiths have also asked about tutoring their children."

"That's wonderful!" Maria said.

Matthew strode in from the main room and rested a hand on the head of each of his children.

"Don't forget Puck," Suzy said.

Kayla glanced at Maria, and she nodded with a smile. Kayla held a bit of the cake up to a pocket she'd sewn just beneath her left shoulder. "Wake up, Puck." The little mouse's head popped out and sniffed the morsel. Then his tiny paws took hold of it and stuffed large chunks into his mouth.

"Hello, Puck!" Suzy said, while her brother eyed the mouse silently.

"You're a marvel to have tamed him," Maria said.

After finishing his snack, Puck retreated into his cloth burrow.

Matthew cleared his throat. "Have you asked Kayla about the Easter Procession?"

A wave of anxiety spilled into her veins. She avoided such public gatherings, since no one wanted a monster scaring the children at a celebration.

"I intended it as a surprise," Maria said. "But I suppose this is as good a time as any." She turned to Kayla. "We hoped you and the monk would join our family next week in the march from God's Acre to the church."

Kayla swallowed despite the dryness in her mouth. "That's ... so kind of you, but I don't have anything to wear for an Easter Procession."

Maria dashed out of the room and returned a moment later, holding a hand-stitched white dress.

"I suspected as much, so I made you this as thank you gift."

"I don't know what to say ..." Kayla caressed the hem of the dress as if it might vanish at her touch.

"We consider you family, now," Maria said.

Kayla hugged her, the closest she'd ever come to having a mother. "Of course, I'd love to join you."

Suzy clapped her hands in excitement. "It will be so much fun, you walking with us in the parade!"

"It's a procession, not a parade," Matthew said.

Maria gathered the dress and took Matthew's hand. "I have a couple more things to finish on the dress, so we'll leave you to the lesson."

They left, and Kayla settled back to work.

"Okay now, continue reading," she said to her student.

Suzy's brow furrowed as she deciphered the words one at a time. *"And the serpent said unto the woman, 'Ye shall not surely die. For God doth know that in the day ye eat thereof, then your eyes shall be opened, and ye shall be as gods, knowing good and evil.' "*

Suzy looked up. "Why would God keep Adam and Eve from the Tree of Knowledge?"

"I suppose God wants to protect us from things we can't understand," Kayla said, feeling guilt fill her with anxiety.

"What's wrong with understanding the difference between good and evil?" Suzy asked.

Her brother sneered. "You're so dense! If it weren't for Eve being tricked by the Devil, we'd still be living in paradise!" The boy jerked the beetle's last leg off.

Suzy glared at her brother. "A demon nearly as powerful as God tricked Eve. But Adam was fooled by an ordinary girl—so who's the real dummy?"

Her brother reddened. He held his fist up, then smashed the beetle with a squishy bang. Suzy ignored him. Failing to get a reaction, James stuck out his tongue and ran outside, slamming the leather-hinged door.

Matthew peered into the kitchen from the next room, eyebrow raised. Kayla brushed the murdered beetle from the table and nodded to her young protégé to resume.

Suzy read the description of Eve giving in to the Serpent's temptation. *"And the Lord God said, 'Behold, the man is become as one of us, to know good and evil: and now, lest he put forth his hand, and take also of the tree of life, and eat, and live forever.' "*

Again, Suzy stopped. "What does God mean by *us*? It sounds like he's talking to other gods like himself and they're afraid humans will become gods too." Suzy appraised the book with troubled eyes. "It sounds like the snake told Eve the truth."

"Maybe God was speaking to the angels in Heaven," Kayla said, "or to different aspects of himself, like the Holy Spirit?"

Through the door, Matthew frowned.

"But why would he worry if people turned into angels or spirits?"

Kayla hesitated. Could the forbidden Tree of Knowledge and Eternal Life be symbolic of knowledge beyond humans' ability to control? Maybe the story was God's way of warning humans against the dangers of technology. Of course, it could be nothing more than primitive man's rationale for the existence of suffering and death. But if the story was symbolic, that would render the Garden of Eden nothing but a fable. Her heart constricted at the implication.

Suzy frowned. "How do we know God really exists?"

Kayla's mouth dropped open.

Matthew thundered into the room. "Don't you dare question God!"

Suzy gazed at him in shock. "I only asked, Papa."

Every muscle in Kayla's body tensed. Why had Suzy said such a thing?

"Who put such a doubt in your head?" Matthew demanded.

Maria came to the doorway, wringing her hands.

Suzy's lower lip trembled.

Kayla's breath caught. Her entire future hinged on the next few words of this nine-year-old child.

"N-no one, Papa. I just …" A tear slid down Suzy's cheek, followed by others.

Kayla put her arms around Suzy's shoulders and rocked her. "This is the most important lesson you can ever learn," she said. "We must never doubt God." Kayla stroked her hair. "God loves you more than anything in the universe, and he will take care of you if you put your trust in him completely."

Matthew nodded and Maria's face brightened.

"You listen to Kayla," Maria said.

Suzy wiped her tears and smiled. "Okay, Momma. I will."

As the little girl stared into her eyes and smiled, a loving warmth filled Kayla. She hadn't lost her new family after all. She'd experienced God's wrath for her disobedience, but had now benefited from his mercy and forgiveness. The Carrolls served as an example of what life could be like for those who put their faith completely in Him.

Chapter 4

On Easter Sunday morning, Kayla sat in the cabin she shared with the monk and prepared for the procession. With ritualistic care, she braided her hair with purple ribbons symbolizing the kingship of Jesus. The white of her Easter dress represented purity and grace, as did the single lily all the unmarried girls of the village would carry. She was neither graceful nor pure, but Jesus welcomed every repentant sinner, no matter their imperfections.

From the distant cemetery, voices rose in songs of praise, and she softy accompanied them.

"Jesus, thou everlasting king,
accept the tribute which we bring;
accept thy well-deserved renown,
and wear our praises as thy crown..."

The monk hobbled through the door with a basket of flowers for her nearly completed headpiece—red azaleas symbolizing the blood of the Savior, and bright yellow daffodils representing the dawning of hope with the conquest of death on the third day.

"You shouldn't tire yourself," she said.

"This is your big day, so I wanted to contribute."

A coughing fit bent him double. Kayla struggled to her feet and helped him to his bed, then took a seat beside him.

"Old age is an amazing sensation," he said, wheezing and out of breath. "I think everyone should have a chance to experience it at least once."

They sat quietly for a time, the joyous songs drifting through the open door like spirits.

"You better go soon or you'll miss the procession," he said.

"Maybe I should stay here in case you need me."

"Nonsense, I'll be fine. Maria spent a lot of time making your Easter dress."

A songbird alighted in the circular window of the loft.

"That's a cinnamon-chested bee-eater," the monk said with a smile. "My father loved birds and taught me all their names."

"Your father? Was he a healer too?"

"My parents were simple farmers like most in Potemia. Good, loving people—and extremely pious." He touched the wooden cross hanging around his neck.

"Then who taught you healing?"

"That I learned from the ancient books. But I did have one teacher who influenced me more than any other. He changed the course of my life and made me who I am today."

"Did he teach you sciencecraft?" Even here, in their own home, Kayla lowered her voice as she spoke the dangerous words.

"Yes, he taught me what you'd call sciencecraft, but we had a falling out, and he came to believe such things are evil." He held a cloth to his mouth and coughed. "My teacher came to view technology as too dangerous for humans."

"I thought you agreed?"

"Not completely. After all, I use healing sciencecraft," he said. "A hammer can be used to destroy or to build."

"You made it seem like I sinned by taking the books in the desert."

"I wanted you to realize the enormity of the choice."

"Everyone is so certain that all science-magic is bad."

"Not everyone," he said. "Surely you can think of some who disagree?"

"You mean those who chose to remain outside the Wall?"

He nodded, and Kayla lapsed into silence. The bird sounded a goodbye note and flew away. She gazed through the vacated window at the sky beyond.

"Would you put on your Easter wreath for me?"

After adding the flowers he'd brought, she arranged her braids and set the joyous crown atop her head. She lowered a few leaves across the left of her face to hide her scars.

Setting her crutch aside, she presented herself in full Easter regalia.

"You look angelic, my daughter."

A warm sensation bloomed in her chest and expanded. It was the first time he called her his daughter. She resumed her seat beside his bed, her eyes grateful.

"I will not be around forever," he said. "Have you thought about what you'd like to do when I'm gone?"

She frowned. "I suppose I'll become a teacher. Without Ishan, or you … what else can I do?"

"I'm not asking you what others would have you do. I'm asking what *you* want to do."

"What I want? Do I have a choice?"

"There's always a choice," he said. "You're seventeen now. If you could do anything, what would you choose?"

"I ... I suppose I'd want to see what's beyond the Wall." She flushed and shook her head. "But I could never do that."

"Why not?" he asked.

"Well, because ..." Her gaze drifted to the woodpile where her secret lay in the compartment beneath. "I guess I'm afraid."

The monk shook his head. "Fear was the cornerstone of Potemia. The Founder sought to protect us from our greatest fears, but safety also has a price."

Was this another of his riddles?

"Now go to the Easter Procession," he said. "I insist."

She hugged him and stood. "Okay, but I'll be right back—"

A hammering fist pounded the door, followed by Maria's strained voice. "Get the monk, Kayla. Suzy is dying!"

Kayla rushed to unbar the door, and Maria staggered in, carrying Suzy in her arms. She settled her moaning daughter on the oak table.

"She's been sick the past two days," Maria said, her eyes desperate. "I stayed home while Matthew took James to the Easter procession, but she got much worse in the past hour."

Kayla pressed her hand against Suzy's lower right abdomen, and the girl moaned.

Appendicitis?

Better not mention the possibility to Maria, since there was no cure—at least none within the law.

Kayla ushered Maria outside the cabin. "Wait here while I assist the monk."

After locking the door, she helped the monk out of bed and over to the sick girl. When they reached Suzy, he shook his head. "They waited too long to bring her here. We can't risk operating."

"But you must!" Kayla pleaded. "I love her."

"The appendix may have already burst. If we operate and she dies, there will be no way to hide what we've done. The penalty for both of us would be death. Think of all who will die if neither of us is here to care for them."

Suzy's eyes opened and gazed beyond her delirium. "Kayla?"

"I'm here, Suzy." She smoothed the little girl's hair back from her burning forehead.

"I'm not worried since you said God protects those who believe." Suzy's eyes drifted shut, her breathing labored.

Kayla's insides twisted. "We have to save her."

"If she dies naturally, no one will blame you." He stared hard into her face. "But if we operate and she dies, they will say we killed her—both of us—with sciencecraft."

In the distance, the hymns of the gathering villagers floated through the window, proclaiming the Savior's triumph over death. She stood on the brink of finally gaining their acceptance.

The price of membership was Suzy's death.

What choice did she have? After all, hadn't God ordained this?

"No," she said. "I won't trade Suzy's life for my happiness."

The barest of smiles creased the monk's lips.

Heart pounding, she retrieved the medical supplies from a trunk and administered the chloroform.

After sterilizing the site with iodine, the monk sliced through the skin and exposed the organs underneath. One of Kayla's books contained drawings by Leonardo da Vinci that depicted the body as a complex machine. Were humans themselves nothing more than God's science experiment?

A severed vessel spurted blood across the front of her Easter dress, but she ignored it and sealed the leak with a clamp. The monk reached into the gaping wound and extracted the offending organ. Kayla clamped off both ends, and he cut it free. When the swollen appendix exited the cavity, the monk exhaled.

"It hasn't burst yet, thank God. Let's sew her up quickly."

Suzy would live! Had it been God's test of her willingness to sacrifice her own safety for another? How could she have imagined God would allow Suzy to die?

A fierce pounding shook the cabin door, and the blood drained from Kayla's face.

Matthew's voice thundered like the arrival of Judgment Day. "Let me see my daughter, damn you, or I'll smash this door to pieces!"

Kayla pulled off her surgical mask, grabbed her crutch, and hobbled to the door. She opened it a crack and faced Matthew. "Please, Mr. Carroll, the monk has found the problem and is treating it. Suzy will be fine."

Matthew's face softened. But then his gaze descended to Kayla's blood-stained fingers. "What have you done to my daughter!"

The door exploded open and knocked Kayla to the floor.

Matthew charged inside. His naked child lay atop the table, her flesh peeled back from her intestines. A low moan wrung from his chest. His muscular farmer's body towered Goliath-like over the monk. The smell of freshly plowed dirt clung to him despite his Sunday clothing. His powerful hands balled into fists.

Maria dashed to her husband's side and jerked to a stop. She screamed, knees buckling. Matthew grabbed her around the waist to keep her upright.

"What demonic ritual …?" Maria said.

Kayla struggled to her feet. Suzy's blood covered the front of her Easter dress in a gruesome display of her guilt.

The monk simply continuing suturing blood vessels. "Your daughter's appendix nearly burst. We had to remove it to save her life." He snipped the end of the stitch, removed a clamp, and moved to the next one.

"Leave my daughter alone!" Matthew roared. He shoved the monk aside and yanked the chloroform mask off his child's face.

"She'll wake up without that!" Kayla limped forward and placed a bloody hand on his forearm. "Please, listen to me—"

"I should have listened to those who warned that Satan marked you." Matthew lifted his daughter off the table.

"Stop!" Maria's voice quavered with desperation.

"I'm taking my child from this den of evil sciencecraft."

"She will die in agony if you don't let me finish the operation," the monk said, leaning on the back of a chair.

"I would rather her die pure and go to her eternal salvation in Heaven, than live a thousand years on this Earth and be damned to Hell in the next world." With that, Matthew carried his child to the door. Suzy moaned, and her eyes opened, meeting Kayla's.

"No, Matthew, please!" Maria shrieked, going to her knees and raising her clasped hands in supplication. "Don't take my daughter from me!"

"Maria!" His voice snapped like a whip. "I will not defy God's laws! What good is it to save her life in this world and send her soul to Satan for all of eternity?"

With those words, he strode from the room with his daughter in his arms. Maria staggered after, praying aloud for God's intercession.

Kayla stumbled after them, chest heaving and blood staining her hands and dress. *I can't let Suzy die. I can't!*

They reached the foot of the hill, where the colorfully festooned parishioners gathered atop the cemetery known as *God's Acre*. Hundreds of tombstones marked the remains of the first settlers of the village from centuries before. A large cross stood at the center of the hill, a purple cloth draped over it in memory of the risen Christ. The villagers encircled this symbol of death and eternal life, their voices raised in song.

"There's power in the blood, power in the blood.

Sin's stains are lost in its life-giving flow.

There's wonderful power in the blood."

Matthew carried his naked and bloody child up the hill. The song died on the lips of the townsfolk as they witnessed the gruesome spectacle mirroring the lyrics of their hymn. A pathway opened through the crowd, and screams of horror rang out from many. Minister Coglin stood at the base of the cross. Matthew stopped before him.

"Please, Reverend," Matthew said. "My Suzy needs your holy intercession."

The minister surveyed the bloody hole with the steel clamps protruding like bizarre instruments of torture. His face contorted with such wrath that several parishioners stepped back from him.

"What demon did this?" he asked.

Gasping for breath, Kayla fought her way through the crowd and collapsed to her knees before the minister. "I can save her. Please, don't let her die for my sins."

The minister's gaze scoured her deformed face, then went to her twisted foot. "Abomination," he said. "You should never have been allowed to live, and now we must pay the price for our sacrilege."

The minister turned to Suzy and removed the clamps. Blood geysered upward, and a woman fainted.

Suzy screamed. The sound sliced through Kayla's mind like a scythe, and she pressed her hands over her ears to shut it out. The unending shrieks of agony shredded her defenses. They went on and on and on.

"My God!" Matthew moaned, his arms trembling as he held his flailing daughter out to the minister like a sacrificial lamb. Blood poured down his forearms and pooled at his feet.

Minister Coglin had Elias hold the flaps of the wound together while he snatched the purple cloth from the cross. Several men stepped forward and grabbed Suzy's hands and feet to keep her still as the minister wrapped the symbol of Christ's resurrection around and around her midsection. This stopped the bleeding, though Suzy's screams continued.

Minister Coglin led the faithful in prayer, asking the Lord in his supreme compassion to intervene and save this most innocent of his flock. Suzy's screams lessened, then trailed off. Her eyes opened once more.

"Papa, Momma?"

Maria embraced her child and cried joyful tears.

"Thank you, Lord!" Minister Coglin raised his hands in praise, and many in the crowd fell to their knees, hands clasped. Someone began singing, and others joined in. Even Kayla sang in praise of the miracle.

"Praise him, praise him, all ye little children.

God is love, God is love."

The song trailed off as Suzy's head drooped. Matthew knelt beside her and cradled her face in his large hands. He stared into her dimming eyes and cried. The bandage around her stomach had gone crimson, the blood pooling beneath her like a baptismal.

"I'm cold, Papa," Suzy said. Her body went slack.

The echoes of the songs of praise languished in the air.

Kayla's body slumped. A hand settled on her shoulder and she turned. The monk stood beside her, his breaths coming in ragged gasps, intermittent coughs racking his chest.

44

Maria turned on them both. "How could you?"

"I tried to save her," Kayla said, wearing the blood-stained dress Maria had given her. A few faces in the crowd held compassion, but most glared with contempt and loathing. All knew the law of the Founder.

Maria's face contorted with hatred. "You will burn for this, both of you!"

Two nights later, Maria's pronouncement became prophecy.

*   *   *

The last hues of the setting sun aged the sky with dirty purples long past their prime. The entire settlement gathered before the two stakes in the center of the clearing. The monk and the cripple, two heretics about to suffer the ultimate punishment for their crimes. Attendance was mandatory, a lesson none dared shirk. Had they shielded the lawbreakers, the entire village itself would be liable.

A vision of the piles of skulls in the desert flashed before Kayla's memory.

They are doing what they must to protect their families.

As the first tendrils of smoke embraced her, Kayla raised her face to the darkening sky. Her lips moved in silent supplication. When she finished her prayer, she stilled, waiting, listening. The echo of a distant hyena mocked her.

Kayla's head slumped, and the matted strands of her auburn hair veiled her misaligned face. Not an inch of her once-pristine Easter dress remained unsullied. Her wreath was gone, torn away by Maria as they lay bound in the town square for the past two days during their trial by the village elders.

A growing warmth beat back the twilight chill—a reminder of the price for her sins. Tremors seized her legs and spread upward until her entire body vibrated.

Near her twisted foot, a line of ants marched across the evidence of what Minister Coglin labeled her "mental fornication." The ancient books encircled her in testimony of her sins.

Despite her prayers, their blasphemous words tormented her still, the forbidden fruit staining her mind and soul with a sin it seemed no atonement could erase. If free will was a divine test, she had failed miserably.

Wisps of smoke reached the colony, and they froze, antennae waving frantically. Their Judgment Day had arrived as a result of their geographic association with her, the abomination, the heretic.

A rock cracked against Kayla's forehead, and a stream of blood mingled with the dirt and sweat already coating her face. The pain eclipsed that of her twisted foot and the ropes cutting into her wrists. If only the rock had been larger and thrown harder. But her judges avoided such clemency. The witch must suffer the full punishment.

A few yards to her right, hemp ropes secured the monk to a second post, the illegal tools of his healing arts heaped around his feet. His circle of burning lumber outpaced hers—a preview of her own fate. His wrinkled face wore the mask of serenity that transformed him when lost in meditation and prayer.

He'd called her daughter. Why hadn't she called him father in return? Or told him she loved him?

The heat scorched her feet, and a fit of coughing battled to expel the smoke choking her lungs. She turned her eyes toward the crowd.

Mrs. Shore cradled the newborn Kayla helped deliver only months before. She was a kind and loving woman. Now, her face writhed in hatred. "Witch, blasphemer, daughter of a whore!"

There stood Allie, who'd broken her leg milking her cow; and Christy, who had nearly died of infection after her husband whipped her for contradicting him. There stood Billy, cracked skull; Jamie, attacked by a lion during a hunt; Mr. Caldwell, dislocated shoulder; Widow Nilla, anemia.

I know you all.

They shouted, spat, and threw refuse. Could this really be the same joyous and peaceful community of two days earlier? *It's me who changed them. The tumor threatening to destroy the body if not removed.*

Minister Coglin raised his hemlock-carved crucifix like a sword of vengeance, and the crowd fell silent. The minister's blue eyes glared at them, fierce, ever-challenging. He kept his black beard shaved above his lip so that his pale features floated within a circle of darkness. "We gather here to administer the laws decreed by our dual saviors—the Lord Jesus Christ and our beloved Founder of Potemia!"

The minister swiveled to the left and right, displaying the crucifix even higher for all to see. All bowed their heads in silence, the crackling flames a reminder of the eternal torment awaiting any who dared defy the divine order.

He faced Kayla and the monk. "You have been pronounced guilty of practicing sciencecraft!" The monk's eyes opened and fixed on the minister.

"The Great Founder who led us to this Promised Land decreed that freedom and technology cannot coexist! We choose Freedom and the grace of Almighty God!"

The minister's voice rose to a shout. *"And she shall be utterly burned with fire: for strong is the Lord God who judgeth her!"*

The flames rose around the monk as if in response. The healer's eyes closed, and his face transformed to a mask of contentment—even while his robe ignited. The crowd gasped, and a few looked away when his beard caught fire.

The monk's flesh peeled and shriveled, but no sound, repentant or otherwise, sated their need for vengeance. The meager fat of his body flashed and sizzled, suffusing the air with the sickly-sweet smell of roasting meat. A few vomited.

"Why does God allow evil to exist?" she once asked the monk.

"Without darkness, can there be light?"

As the bone of the monk's skull appeared, Kayla forced her eyes away.

Suzy's parents stood at the back of the crowd; Matthew's body rigid, dark circles surrounding his eyes. His arm corralled Maria's shoulders as she stared into space. Their son, James, huddled before them, eyes darting like a cornered rabbit.

The sound of screams jolted Kayla from her reverie. *What could possibly make such a horrible sound?* The screams came from her.

Pain flooded her mind, and the flesh of her legs peeled and cracked. Her screams spluttered as smoke clogged her throat and lungs, filling her with a suffocating panic. She writhed upward, trying to somehow climb the pole.

Then he appeared. Far beyond the sea of her death-drunk tormentors.

Ishan.

Her lover perched in a tree with bow pulled taut, sighting along the shaft of an arrow. Kayla stopped screaming.

His chance for redemption.

Kayla drank in the sight of him a final time. Then she nodded.

Ishan released the arrow—his final kiss. The shaft seemed to slow, flexing like a snake through the air toward her. An instant before impact, her eyes closed. The razor-edged steel sliced through her skin and shattered two ribs. Then it reached her heart, the force exploding both chambers like a water skin.

Thank you, my love...

Kayla's blood ceased its seventeen-year marathon.

Her consciousness expanded outside her body to a viewpoint above the confused and angry crowd. Her body hung limp, the arrow still quivering in her chest.

Is this my soul exiting my dead body?

A flash of light burst into being within the thing tied to the stake—her former body—and eclipsed the bonfire. The crowd's angry cries ceased. Beams of light erupted from the puncture in her chest and consumed the arrow.

A breeze drew toward the pyre, stoking the fire into an inferno. Her Easter dress crumbled into cinders. At the fire's core, unharmed, irised within the flames, a naked apparition held its hands before its face, turning them slowly, examining the blazing light emanating from within. When the whirlwind reached its peak, the fire flowed into her glowing body, tracing the network of veins and organs underneath.

Was this an illusion her brain generated as oxygen depletion starved away the final bits of electrical activity?

Her deformed foot and face transformed.

"It's a miracle of the Lord!" someone shouted.

Kayla's scars vanished. With hair billowing, the elemental beauty of her naked and burning form blazed angelic.

Many fell to their knees. The blacksmith's wife, Anna, raised her hands to the sky and shouted, *"Heal me, OH, LORD, and I shall be healed; save me, and I shall be saved, for thou art my praise!"*

"This is no miracle!" Minister Coglin shouted. "This is demonic sciencecraft!" But none paid him any heed as they gloried in God's power.

A red glow ignited in her eyes and grew into a crimson fire. Her arms extended outward, and her skin blackened impossibly dark. Glowing symbols appeared across her body, hands, and face. The wind roared, and the villagers cowered before the astonishing sight. The creature rose into the air, her Hellish eyes climbing to the sky.

An otherworldly scream erupted from her throat.

The mob fled in a desperate stampede. A few townspeople went down under the tide of bodies but managed to rise and stagger onward, driven by a fear that subsumed pain. Soon, only the apparition remained, suspended above the charred remains of her funeral pyre.

The wind ceased, and her eyes lost their crimson glow. Like an untethered marionette, she crumpled to the ground atop the blackened books she'd first feared, then loved, and finally cursed. Her skin faded to its pale shade, the symbols vanishing last of all.

Kayla's external view of her transformed body faded to darkness.

Two glowing eyes appeared within the void—windows into a realm of flames. In one eye a man writhed in torment, while the other imprisoned a woman.

"I am Melchi," a deep voice intoned with the eerie echo of a monastic chant. "I look forward to our meeting—Nihala."

Melchi. The demon from my dream in the desert!

She tried answering, but found no voice capable of speech.

Chapter 5

Silvery moonlight drifted across a pale form. Neither wind nor flutter of wing disturbed the eerie solitude. Even the crickets had fled.

Kayla's body twitched, then she gasped. Her hands sought her exposed chest. No arrow. No wound. She frowned at the steady beat of her heart.

Not oblivion. Was it Heaven—or Hell?

Her eyes opened. The monk's charred skeleton lay amidst the ashes of his blackened pyre.

My father. I killed you.

Grief and guilt yanked at her heart.

She stared into the skull's empty sockets. His words echoed in her mind: *"I am willing to forfeit my life to serve others ..."*

She tore her gaze from this rebuke, and her eyes drifted to her feet, both perfectly formed in every way.

"It's not possible," she whispered.

Her hand caressed the left foot. She stood, hesitant, flinching. For the first time in her life—no pain. Her hands explored her face and encountered smooth perfection.

A miracle?

The books from the past claimed that all events had logical, natural explanations. But how could anything natural explain the healing of her deformities, her resurrection, her soul exiting her body, and ... Melchi?

When you'd eliminated all other possibilities, the one that remained had to be the solution, no matter how improbable it seemed.

Which left the supernatural. Which left God.

Should she thank God for sparing her? Or curse him for taking everyone she loved?

Her shoulders sagged and she shook her head. God was not to blame. *My choices led to this.*

Clothing, food, and even a couple of shoes littered the clearing.

After covering herself with a discarded cloak, she began digging with the shovel used to bury their stakes. A shallow grave formed. She placed the blackened remains of the monk gently at the bottom.

Kneeling, she clasped her hands, and recited the words Minister Coglin used at church burials. *"The Lord is my shepherd; I shall not want. He maketh me to lie down in green pastures; he leadeth me beside the still waters. He restoreth my soul ..."*

Kayla remembered herself at age six, gathering healing plants in the woods with the monk.

"What was my mother's name?" Kayla had asked.

"Elaine Nighthawk. I met her the night she died giving you life."

"Is it true, what the other children say about her?"

"No one knew where she came from, but I can say with certainty that she loved you more than her own life." The monk smiled. "I promised her I would take care of you."

Kayla knelt before the open grave and stared at the charred skeleton of the only parent she'd ever known. His body-machine had been destroyed. Did his soul live on?

When the first rays of dawn roused her, she filled the grave and camouflaged it against desecration.

Then she left the place of death. The rustle of squirrels and the songs of birds returned. A robin called to her and, farther on, she startled a few rabbits. The animals saw her, at least.

A squeak froze her mid-stride.

"Puck?" She fell to her knees before the mouse, and extended her hand. Her three-footed friend scurried to his customary place on her shoulder. Together, they passed the deserted fields surrounding the village.

But no one appeared. By now, farmers should be hitching their plows, children running to fetch water, and women heading to the river to do laundry.

"So you are alive," the voice of Elias said.

Kayla's every muscle seized.

Her rapist strode from behind a tree and leered. "Thought you might go chasing that heathen of yours." He circled like a scavenger sighting carrion, his eyes molesting the outline of her body beneath the cloak and examining the improved aesthetics of her face with interest. The reek of barley-ale hung about him like a shroud.

If only she had his terrible strength.

The giant stopped close. "My father says you conjured science-magic to escape your crimes." His expression hardened. "I didn't see what trick you played, since I went chasing your black-skinned heathen after he ..." For the first time, doubt crept into his face. Something she could exploit?

Kayla lifted her chin in a brazen challenge. "Yes, I used sciencecraft, and I will use it against you if you don't let me pass."

A note of caution entered his voice. "You admit to being a witch?"

"They've all seen the proof, so I need no longer hide what I am." Hatred narrowed her eyes. "And now it's time you paid for your crimes."

The giant retreated. "Stay back, or I'll—"

"You'll what? You'll rape me? You'll burn me at the stake?"

"I never meant to …" He edged back, eyes wide.

Now what? How do I sustain this act? Kayla glanced around. "Where are the rest of my oppressors?"

"They're huddled in the church, praying to God for protection. They've banished you and sent messengers to the other councils."

Banished from Potemia?

"They say you drank fire into your body … that your skin pitched black as the Abyss and bled sorcery through strange symbols that glowed like windows to Hell."

So my out-of-body vision was no dream!

A hint of uncertainty crept into his voice. "My father says you created an illusion, a contrivance of sciencecraft, but the elders are convinced you're possessed by a demon."

"The council is right," she said. "Satan offered me great knowledge and power in exchange for my soul."

His face convoluted, torn by opposing forces within, then calmed.

"I don't believe you." He reached for her and she retreated.

Elias leered. "I don't know what illusion you tricked them with, but I've never been afraid of anything, and I'm not starting with the daughter of a whore." Elias stepped forward, and her body went rigid. What could she do against a force like Elias?

"I think it's time you had a second lesson," he said.

Elias seized her cloak, and she closed her eyes. A stab of remembered pain lanced through her womb. She grasped his wrist. Futile against such strength as his.

A scream of agony, but not hers. She opened her eyes. Elias groveled on his knees, his face contorted with pain. Her fingers gripped his wrist as if squeezing a sausage nearly in half. She could feel the two bones of his forearm bending under her fingers.

"Please, let go," Elias sobbed.

I wonder what would happen if I …?

She bent Elias's forearm to the side, and he screamed. The bone splintered just above his wrist, puncturing the skin and spurting blood. Kayla started in shock and released her hold.

Elias collapsed.

Her heart quickened at the sight of him sobbing and cradling his shattered arm, a long stream of spittle forming on his lower lip and stretching toward the pool of blood beneath him.

An intoxicating thirst for retribution blossomed inside her like a neglected garden gone to seed. The violence was his, inserted into her soul the moment he raped her. Now it burst free and filled every muscle of her body with a demand to return to the source from which it sprang.

She seized his ankle.

"Please, no!" Elias shouted.

It took the slightest twist to break it. He screamed and she smiled. The first hint of red glazed her vision.

"Please, God, please help me," Elias begged.

Kayla's smile became a snarl. "You dare invoke God?"

"I'm sorry—"

"God resurrected me, and I am his vengeance!"

Anger coursed through her veins with a demand for action. Elias dragged his broken body away from her, leaving a bloody trail like a wounded slug.

"Crawl in the dirt like the serpent you are!" She stalked him, her pupils glowing with demonic fire.

He collapsed.

She faced the steeple of the distant church, and her voice boomed with an unnatural resonance. "I will burn your precious fields, your houses, and your church!"

She strode toward Elias and grasped his head between both hands. Then she stared into his bloodshot eyes and smiled.

Elias sobbed and begged. How many helpless souls had begged him for mercy? She laughed as he must have. Total power over another human being. Was this the exultation he experienced when he raped her?

She reached for his face.

"No ..." His bowels opened. The stench mingled with his sweat, blood, and terror.

Three tiny feet pinched her shoulder. Puck whined in fear—of her?

Kayla paused, her fingers hovering inches from Elias's eyes. Her hands trembled. What was happening to her? *Am I to become a murderer?* The fire faded from her vision, and she dropped Elias in a filthy heap. He rolled onto his side and vomited. She'd reached a moral crossroads. An eye for an eye, or love thine enemy?

"I won't kill you if you tell me the truth."

"Yes. Anything." His body shook violently, the first stages of shock.

"Did you catch Ishan?"

"No," Elias gasped. "His horse outran ours—I swear it!"

She knelt beside him. He closed his eyes and whimpered. How good it would feel to kill him. She tore a long strip of cloth from his shirt and he flinched. She fashioned the strip into a tourniquet just above the break in his disarticulated forearm, slowing the gush of blood.

Confusion filled his eyes.

"If you want to live, you'll have to cut it off." She jabbed his arm and he screamed. "It's not a complicated operation. The blacksmith can do it, just tell him to make sure the blade is red hot."

Why am I sparing him? What if he raped or killed someone else? Maybe I'm just a coward.

"Swear that you'll never force yourself upon another."

Elias nodded with desperate jerks of his head. "I swear it."

"And you'll live to serve others as Jesus did?"

"Let me live, and I promise to repent!"

For a moment, she hesitated. Finally, she turned and walked away.

"I will return if you break your promise." He obviously didn't fear God's retribution—maybe she could offer a more tangible substitute.

How I yearn to go to Ishan. But he'd seen her die, and she wouldn't let him see what she'd become—not bring her curse to his door.

She caught Elias's horse and rode north.

Word spread quickly. The moment Kayla came within sight of a town, the local church bell sounded, and the land drained of human life until she'd passed. This made it easy for her to scrounge food and water from vacated huts. She hated stealing, but what other choice did she have? At night, people with torches and spears manned barricades and sometimes trailed a safe distance behind to make certain the demon kept going. What if they attacked? *Am I willing to kill?*

One of the books on evolution had displayed a map of the migration route ancient humans took out of Africa. It occurred at the one place the African continent connected by land to the Asian and European continents—the northeast corner. This spot served as her one hope of escaping Potemia.

At night she navigated by the star Polaris, hovering just above the horizon. The monk had taught her the constellations from childhood, and her favorite was Orion's Belt. In the winter, if you followed the three stars of Orion to Sirius, the brightest star in the night sky, it pointed to where the sun would rise in the east. Just like the three wise men following the star in the east to the place where the Savior would be born.

And now I'm following the wise stars in hopes of my own salvation.

Once, Kayla surprised an old man and little girl walking their cow. At the sight of her, they fled into their fields, praying in their strange language. "Oh, great and powerful Parvati, preserve your humble children from this demon!"

Kayla froze. *I understand their words!*

"Is the demon gone?" the little girl whispered in Hindi from her hiding spot.

"Be still!" answered the old man.

Another miracle, another mystery.

When Kayla reached the edge of the desert, she set her exhausted horse free, fearing he would die in the harsh environment. She placed Puck on the ground with the bread and cheese she'd stolen for him.

"I'm sorry, Puck. I can't have you risk what I'm willing to, and it's time for you to find others of your kind."

The scorching sand did little more than warm her bare toes. She lifted a skin of water to her lips, then paused. Was she indestructible? She replaced it over her shoulder. *I will test this new body.*

Kayla walked through the blazing desert a full day until the sun sank beneath the horizon. Hunger and thirst dogged her, but her pace continued undiminished. The next day brought the same, with no decline. What power drove her limbs onward, day after day?

"And Cain said unto the Lord, 'My punishment is greater than I can bear. Behold, thou hast driven me out this day from the face of the earth; and from thy face shall I be hid; and I shall be a fugitive and a vagabond in the earth ...' "

Life clung to her, either as a gift or a punishment. There remained one place for her to go.

The Wall.

Were the ancient tales true? Was it possible to pass through to the Outside?

Day and night she continued toward the northeast corner of Potemia.

After three days, she collapsed onto the moonlit sand and gave in to her single remaining weakness—sleep.

Chapter 6

Kayla's mind drifted while she slept. The dream started with sudden clarity, like the blinding flash of light in a midnight storm. She lay on a cot inside a square tent. Before her vision hovered a photograph of a woman with amber curls and an ivory complexion. The woman held a brown-eyed little girl with darker skin. Braided pigtails poked from beneath a pink party hat. A cake decorated with five candles sat in front of them, and wisps of smoke curled before their faces. At the bottom of the photograph, childish writing stated: *We Miss U Daddy!*

The dream was incredibly vivid, even down to the sour smell of sweat and the stench of unwashed clothes. Kayla tried moving her gaze from the photograph, but couldn't. Then she tried moving her hand, without effect. She attempted speaking, also without success.

The hands holding the photograph were a man's, strong and calloused. She could feel them gripping the smooth edges of the image, and could even tell that the back of the paper was less slick. Still, she had no say in their motion.

Her vision blurred, and tears formed in her surrogate body's eyes. "I miss you too," the man said. She felt his lips and tongue form the words, and even had the sensation of each breath leaving his lungs.

That must be his wife and daughter, Kayla thought.

Out of the corner of the man's eye, she glimpsed a strange contraption blowing cool air onto his muscular arms. She tried turning his head toward the device, but with no effect.

Maybe this isn't a dream at all. Maybe I'm somehow seeing the world through someone outside the Wall? A sort of telepathic link.

Can you hear me? She projected the thought to him with as much force as she could muster. But there came no reply. Neither could she hear his thoughts. The dream-link was limited to his five senses, with her as a passive observer.

The door banged open, and the man's gaze left the photo as a young, black-skinned soldier entered and slammed the tent's plastic door.

"What's up, Tyrone?" her surrogate's voice asked.

"Fucking ordered back out." Tyrone threw his cap onto the second cot. "You hearing me, Pete? I can't take more of these goddamned Groundhog Day patrols!"

So my body's name is Peter. Words from the Gospel of Matthew came to her mind. *"And I say also unto thee, that thou art Peter, and upon this rock I will build my church, and the gates of Hell shall not prevail against it."*

"Bullshit timing," Peter said, pulling on his socks and boots. "Just five hours since the last one."

"Same fuckin' road that wasted Matt last week." Tyrone slumped onto his cot and shook his head. "I ain't fuckin' going, no fuckin' way."

Peter sat next to him. "C'mon, man, you just got one month left and you're out."

Tyrone grabbed Peter by the shirt and glared with bloodshot eyes. "Matt had two weeks left. You weren't there, you didn't see him. His own mamma couldn't have picked him out of a lineup." Tears rolled down his cheeks, and his entire face contorted. "I ain't getting on that fuckin' road again, I just ain't!"

Tyrone covered his face with his hands and shook with sobs. Peter put his arm around his shoulders.

"You want me to call the psych officer?" Peter asked.

"Oh, fuck." Tyrone shook his head. "I ain't crazy, man."

"I know."

Tyrone wiped his face with an old shirt. "Latissa's leavin' me."

"No way," Peter said. "She actually say the words?"

"Says we need to talk when I get home. Then my daughter says over Skype how Uncle Phil took them to the movies last week, even though I don't know any fuckin' Phil."

"I'm sorry, man."

Tyrone stood. "Haven't told anyone, so keep it on the low."

"Sure."

They helped each other strap on gear, check guns, and shoulder their packs.

"We should start a fucking union," Tyrone said.

Peter laughed. "I nominate you to present our demands to Colonel Colrev."

Tyrone did his best badass impersonation. "I ain't afraid of that motherfucker!"

"Yeah, I'll bet!"

Peter followed Tyrone out the door and into the blistering desert. Tents, trucks, and soldiers baked in the noontime sun. Peter's shirt soaked with sweat in seconds.

"God, I'm sick of this motherfuckin' moon dust!" Tyrone loaded his gear into the truck.

"Hope those damn plates hold." Peter inspected additional steel rigged to the truck. "Good job on those welds."

"Cut them off a burned-out transport last week."

Another soldier joined them and tossed his backpack onto the pile. "The three musketeers ride again!" He took a drag on a fat cigarette and offered it to Tyrone.

"Gimme a hit of that Chicago-black, Louis, you La Raza, bar-hoppin' speed-datin' castoff." Tyrone took a long drag, held the smoke in, and then exhaled a plume of sour-smelling smoke. "What the fuck are we doin' here, anyway?"

"I enlisted the day after nine-eleven," Peter said.

"Which Iraq had nothing to do with," Tyrone said.

Louis played along with a grin. "Weapons of mass destruction?"

"Maybe the Hajis are hidin' them under the couch cushions." Tyrone took another deep drag.

"You assholes are *here* because you go where you are fucking ordered to!" The iron-forged voice snapped the three to attention. Tyrone coughed and tossed the cigarette behind him as six feet of muscled swagger stomped around the truck. A pit bull in fatigues.

The officer stopped before Tyrone and thrust his square-jawed face inches from the still-coughing soldier.

"Do we have a problem, Private Nichols?"

"No, sir! Just talking politics, sir."

"The one political solution is this!" In a flash of polished steel, the barrel of the colonel's .45 hovered inches from Tyrone's left eye. The arm holding the gun displayed a series of strange symbols tattooed into the flesh. Tyrone froze, the bands of muscles in his neck tense, a vein in his forehead bulging.

The colonel's expression marked him a killer—born, bred, and unapologetic. "We need to remind the fucking world of that fact. Everything else is bullshit. Do I make myself clear?"

"Yes, sir!" all three soldiers shouted in unison.

The officer holstered his gun and glared at Peter. "And you, Private, what are you fighting for?"

Peter hesitated, then straightened. "I guess when you come right down to it, I'm fighting for my wife and daughter, sir."

The colonel nodded, then waved them into the truck. "Outside the wire, now! You're on point."

Peter hoisted himself into the passenger seat and leaned his rifle within arm's reach. "What's that tattoo on Colonel Colrev's arm say?"

"He commanded a Special Ops team in Afghanistan—real Meat Eaters." Louis climbed into the driver's seat and started the engine. "That's his unit's motto. Some kinda Sanskrit shit."

Tyrone went into his tough-man impersonation again. "You see, I told you I wasn't afraid of that motherfucker!"

Everyone laughed.

As Tyrone climbed into the back to stow some gear, Louis leaned close to Peter's ear. "How's he doing?"

Peter shook his head. "Not good."

Louis headed out the gate with four other trucks following. "How's Danielle and Sierra doing?"

"Third tour's wearing thin," Peter said.

Tyrone held his gun at the ready, scanning the passing buildings, occasional burned-out cars, and a few children playing soccer near the road. His eyes hardly blinked, and his hands gripped his gun until his knuckles grew white. Every pothole made him flinch.

Louis exchanged a glance with Peter. "Hey, Ty, you ever notice the tiny writing on those Trijicon scopes?"

Tyrone examined his rifle's scope. "What the fuck is that?"

"Out of respect for our Iraqi hosts, the State Department ordered sayings etched onto every new scope—from the Quran." Louis winked at Peter.

"WHAT!" Tyrone shouted. "From the fuckin' Kor-Ran! What the fuck were they thinking?"

Peter and Louis burst into laughter. The truck hit a series of bumps, and they rattled about for a moment.

"This ain't funny," Tyrone said. "I am not using a rifle with fuckin' Haji gibberish defiling it!"

Louis swung the truck around a large, blackened hole in the road. "It's in English, dude— why don't you read it?"

Tyrone squinted and read the tiny words aloud. "*Then spake Jesus again unto them, saying, 'I am the light of the world: he that followeth me shall not walk in darkness, but shall have the light of life.'*" Tyrone glared at his two companions. "You assholes, that's from the fuckin' Bible."

Peter laughed. "You think?"

"Does your gun have Haji writing on it?"

"Of course not," Peter said. "You think the military would buy them if they did?"

"Well, that's pretty cool." Tyrone looked at his gun with new respect.

"Oh, sure, now it's fine," Louis said.

"Damn right," Tyrone said. "These are words from God Himself."

Louis threw his hands in the air. "I don't appreciate being forced to use a gun with any religious crap on it."

"Aren't you Catholic?" Tyrone asked.

"I used to be." Louis leaned on his horn until a man on a motor scooter pulled over to the side of the road. "Until I realized religion is a conspiracy." He gunned the engine and surged past the scooter. The man covered his face as dust and sand engulfed him.

"Bold statement," Tyrone said. "Care to back it up?"

"My parents are from Guatemala, which is one of the poorest countries in Latin America because its population is too large to feed itself. Why? Because the fucking Pope says contraception is evil. Why? So they can breed more Catholic babies to glut their collection plates in this world with promises of repayment in a fictional next one!"

"Fictional?" Peter said. "How's that?"

"If anyone else asked you for money for something invisible, you'd pronounce it a fiction too."

"That's faith," Tyrone said.

"Faith is the most valuable tool in any con-artist's bag of tricks."

"I thought there were no atheists in foxholes," Peter said.

"Well, you're fucking looking at one."

"I respect your right to damn yourself to Hell," Tyrone said. "But Bush his-self called this a Crusade, so don't go tellin' me God ain't taking sides."

"You better stow that in front of Sergeant Khalid."

"Yeah, yeah. There's a few Muzzies in our unit," Tyrone said, "but they're *American* Muzzies, which is different than Hajis."

A bit of gravel hit the side of the truck with a bang. Tyrone tensed and crouched.

Peter adjusted his helmet. "Those bastards who flew the planes into the World Trade Center sure had faith, I'll give them that much."

"Amen," Tyrone said. "You wanna win this war, show them our faith is stronger."

"Sounds like a suicide pact to me." Louis came to an Iraqi checkpoint but didn't slow, and the foreign soldiers scrambled to raise the barrier. They blew past in a cloud.

"Aren't you afraid to lose God's protection in a place like this?" Peter asked.

Louis glanced at a wide area of scorched ground on both sides of the road ahead. "Matt was the most devout guy I knew."

Everyone went silent, and Tyrone's eyes followed the burned circle without blinking as they passed. Then he removed a tiny metal cross hanging on a chain around his neck and kissed it.

When they came to the dead camel, Peter groaned.

"It fucking figures it would be my turn," he said, opening the door and walking the fifty yards to the rotting corpse. Flies swarmed the bloated remains, and he gagged at the smell.

"How long has this been here?" Peter said into his radio, eyes scanning the surrounding brush and few buildings nearby. Here and there, civilian faces peeked from windows.

"A patrol reported it yesterday," Colonel Colrev's voice said in his earpiece.

"Why the fuck is it still here?"

"Easier to drive around it. Just check the body for booby traps."

"Yes, sir." Peter scanned the area. His eyes locked onto a wiry line snaking through the ground, and he stiffened. Creeping forward, it resolved into a frayed shoestring. Peter relaxed.

"Looks clear," he said and faced the convoy. Tyrone stood over a slight ridge, pissing into the sand.

Peter's eyes paused on a patch of discolored ground beneath his truck's bumper.

He glanced at the buildings. A head ducked in one of the windows. "IED! Back up!"

Tyrone and Peter dived to the ground. The first two trucks vanished in a cloud of fire, smoke, and sand. Pain, like a thousand blows. Ears throbbing. Blood clogging his nostrils. Camel dung smeared across his face.

Peter staggered to his feet. The truck lay in a smoldering heap—a turtle flipped on its back. It sizzled and hissed in the flames. One remaining tire turned like a pinwheel in a breeze.

His knees buckled. He fell—then rose again. He stumbled toward his burning truck.

He stepped over a severed hand.

Someone grabbed him short of the inferno. Louis's funeral pyre. The additional armor plating had shredded like tinfoil, along with the truck behind. Peter passed a man on the ground looking confused, as if waiting for the punchline of a joke. Both his legs had vanished. Others writhed and screamed. Seared like pigs roasted too long. Medics rushed to save them.

The ringing in his ears drowned out Colonel Colrev's orders. A group of six soldiers followed the colonel toward the squat buildings, Tyrone among them. He ran to catch up.

The soldiers attacked the first house, with three men covering the windows and back door, and the other three storming it, led by the colonel. Peter reached them as they stormed the second house. Screams of terror, then a burst of shots.

Peter grabbed Tyrone's arm.

"He's massacring them, Ty! We have to do something!"

Anger twisted Tyrone's face. "They killed Matt and Louis!"

"These are just families—"

"They're fucking barbarians!" Tyrone grabbed Peter's flak vest and pulled him close. His bloodshot eyes oozed hatred. "The Bible says an eye for an eye, and it's time we took our share of fucking eyes!"

"Jesus changed that," Peter said. *Love your enemies, bless them that curse you, do good to them that hate you.* But Tyrone wasn't listening.

The colonel emerged and led the assault on the third house, choosing different men to follow him inside each time. Peter and Tyrone covered the back door.

More gunfire, more screams, then silence.

"This is wrong!" Peter shouted at Tyrone. No response. More gunfire, more screams, silence.

At the final house, Colonel Colrev motioned to Peter and Tyrone.

The colonel kicked in the door, and they entered the house—little more than a concrete box with windows.

A family of five huddled on a single rug in the corner. Scraps of extra clothing, dented cooking utensils, and a Quran sitting atop a low wooden pedestal against a wall. A child's doll lay abandoned on the floor, its arms askew and button eyes staring at the ceiling. Colonel Colrev and Tyrone yanked the adults apart. Then forced them onto the ground with hands behind their heads. Peter covered them with his rifle.

The colonel tore the woman's veil from her head. Her dark hair spilled across her face. The children cried, and the father pleaded in broken English.

"I love America. George Bush great man. George Bush great—"

Colonel Colrev shot him in the head with the casualness of extinguishing a cigarette. The man's wife shrieked and threw herself on top of her mate, as if to keep his soul from fleeing his body.

The colonel shot her through the back. She flipped about. A second bullet, and she went limp.

Peter's stomach cramped, his eyes locked on the dead bodies.

The colonel motioned to Tyrone. His dark face gleamed with sweat, eyes narrowed to slits, hatred etched in every muscle. He fired two semi-automatic bursts into the sobbing grandmother's chest. She crumpled into a heap. Tyrone's expression remained hard as stone.

"Now you." The colonel pointed to Peter and motioned to the two children.

Peter didn't move, and the colonel glared into his eyes. "I'm giving you a direct order, Private. Execute those insurgents immediately!"

Peter's hands trembled. "They're children…"

"These Hajis watched terrorists bury bombs in the road. They probably brought them food and accepted money in return." The colonel's mouth came to within inches of his ear. "They watched you walk into that road, knowing what would happen. They watched your friends burn. Did even one of them shout a warning?"

Peter's eyes remained locked on the children's faces. The girl appeared the same age as the one in his photograph. The boy around a year younger. They gazed at him with eyes wide, and lips trembling. Both cried. The boy turned to his dead parents. A tortured whine escaped his throat. The girl stared into Peter's eyes, unblinking, waiting.

"I ... I can't do it," Peter said.

Tyrone frowned. "He'll rat us out."

"No, he won't," the colonel said. "Because he will either follow orders," the colonel stepped back and pointed his .45 at Peter's temple, "or he will be dead."

The little boy and girl wrapped their arms around each other.

"You told me you fought for your family." Colonel Colrev cocked the hammer on his gun. "What sacrifice are you willing to make for them?"

Peter shook his head. "I won't do it."

"They will die in either case. You have five seconds to decide if you're going to join them and leave your daughter without a father to protect her. Five, four ..."

Tears blurred Peter's vision.

"Three, two ..."

Don't do it, Peter! Kayla silently shouted into his mind, trying to will his arms to lower the rifle.

"One ..."

In her dream, Kayla felt Peter's finger clamp down on the trigger. Every bullet in his clip ripped into and through their young bodies.

Then, silence.

Tyrone looked away.

The children's lifeless faces stared at him. Kayla wanted to scream, but couldn't. Peter's eyes locked on the dead brother and sister, and Kayla was forced to stare along with him. The top half of the boy's head had vanished, but his face appeared untouched. On his cheek was a tiny scar from some childhood mishap. His brown eyes stared at his murderer. The girl's face appeared no longer human. Her pink shirt displayed a giant kitten's face. Three bullets had gone through the kitten's left ear, right cheek, and the yellow bow around its neck. Blood and brains coated the shirt, obscuring all but the kitten's large eyes.

Colonel Colrev uncocked his Colt and leaned close to Peter's ear. "Now we're all heroes."

Kayla awoke from the nightmare screaming. She scrambled back through the sand as if from a snake.

It wasn't real. A dream. My mind playing tricks. Just a dream. No one actually died. A dream. The children ...

In the Bible, God gave Saul a similar order on a much larger scale. *"Now go and smite Amalek, and utterly destroy all that they have, and spare them not; but slay both man and woman, infant and suckling ..."*

And Joshua. *"So Joshua smote all the country of the hills, and of the south, and of the vale, and of the springs, and all their kings; he left none remaining, but utterly destroyed all that breathed, as the Lord God of Israel commanded."*

In her dream, Peter had murdered children at the command of a man rather than God. But did that matter? Probably not to the women and children being hacked to death by Saul's and Joshua's swords. Could a loving God order such a thing?

Kayla rose and continued marching toward the northeast. The dream had been unlike a normal dream, the sights, sounds, and smells so detailed, etched into her mind as if an actual experience. Had she been witnessing real events? What if her punishment was life itself? Eternal and unrelenting existence spent amidst the desolation of a world destroyed by human arrogance and depravity—even her sleep tormented by the horrors of sciencecraft.

Was it even in her power to end her own life if it became too much to bear?

She held her breath. A minute passed with no discomfort, then two … then an hour. Her body slowed, and her strength ebbed without oxygen. Her pace slowed. But that was all. It ruled out drowning or hanging herself. She clawed at the skin on her forearm, drawing blood. The wound healed within seconds.

"What am I?" she shouted at the silent sky.

Know thyself. The monk's words echoed within her mind.

"And the LORD set a mark upon Cain, lest any finding him should kill him." Elias had mentioned bizarre symbols covering her body during her resurrection.

She stared into the sun, the pain a flagellation of her soul. But the moment she looked away, her eyes healed within seconds. Her body seemed indestructible—unlike her mind.

When I'm driven insane, will I think I'm cured?

Fire had failed to kill her. Ishan had even put an arrow through her heart. Nothing could thwart God's judgment, it seemed.

What would she find when she passed through the northeast Wall of Potemia?

"And Cain went out from the presence of the Lord, and dwelt in the land of Nod, on the east of Eden."

She prayed, sometimes on her knees, and other times while walking. She stumbled on through the night, avoiding dreams. Lack of sleep brought hallucinations.

Jesus appeared beside her and went on and on about carpentry techniques.

She forced a smile and nodded politely. "Did you rise from the dead?"

"Is it so surprising?" he asked. "You did the same yourself."

"So, I am alive?"

"The question should be, what is life?" he said.

"Did you order Joshua and Saul to commit genocide in the Old Testament?"

Jesus frowned at a hangnail on his right index finger. "It's not fair to hold me responsible for my Father's actions."

"But isn't holding children responsible for their parents' deeds the reasoning behind original sin?" she asked. "And I thought you and your Father were one and the same, anyway?"

"It's difficult to explain. You'll just have to trust that I know best."

"Bad idea," a deep voice warned from her side. A tall man with short horns sprouting from his temple leaned close. "Think of all the people who have prayed to this character, only to be annihilated by barbarians or plagues. You have to admit his track record is pathetic."

Satan's impeccable suit accented his athletic figure, and a certain magnetism suffused his handsome features. No hangnails here.

"I don't think I should be talking to you," Kayla said.

"Who says so?" Satan asked.

"I do!" Jehovah answered, his wild beard and untrimmed eyebrows a marked contrast to Satan. "And stop trying to make my son look bad!"

The Devil arched a sculpted eyebrow. "Who's the one conducting a massive campaign of character assassination? Who orders people to kill their own children, gives the okay for slavery, drowns everyone at the drop of a hat for the failings of character *He* placed within them?"

"You raise valid points," Kayla said with some hesitation. Was this one of his famous tricks? "But what about Hell and eternal torture?"

Satan waved the comment away. "A complete fabrication. See if he denies it."

Kayla glanced at Jehovah, and he shrugged.

"Hell is a myth?"

"More a mistranslation …"

She asked Buddha the point of life, and the eastern mystic said, "Those who speak, do not know, and those who know, do not speak."

"Do you mean that some truths transcend words?" Kayla asked. He shrugged.

The arguments escalated when Mohamed and Joseph Smith arrived.

"Impostors and plagiarists!" Jehovah shouted. "Why don't you both admit you made the entire thing up yourselves! It's obvious to anyone with half a brain!" The self-described "jealous God" verbally assaulted Mo and Jo so relentlessly that they retaliated with a torrent of pointed recriminations.

Vishnu materialized in a deep depression, and it took Kayla a while to notice him sulking at the back of the growing crowd.

"What's the matter?" Kayla asked, but he wouldn't say a word.

Zeus and a complement of Greek gods arrived drunk, and things deteriorated further. When the crowd of gods grew into the hundreds, Kayla changed direction, and left the divine mob behind.

Time became meaningless. Walk until the body passes out. Awake—walk again. Repeat. Repeat. Repeat …

But there were no more dreams—the one blessing.

One day, at the edge of the horizon, a shimmering barrier became visible. Despite the dying sun and her exhaustion, after walking two days and nights without sleep, Kayla persisted. Hope, dread, curiosity, and fear battled for dominance with each step closer to her goal. Her shadow raced to the right, and amber light stained the dunes.

As the sun set, the night cut her adrift, and Kayla's gaze wandered the dusting of stars etched with vivid clarity across the desert sky. She remembered Ishan once quoting the Quran.

"So when the stars are made to lose their light, And when the heaven is rent asunder, And when the mountains are carried away as dust, And when the apostles are gathered at their appointed time. To what day is the doom fixed? To the day of decision."

It took the entire night to reach her goal. The morning twilight tinted the eastern sky with a promise of new life. She descended the final dune, and a supernatural awe expanded inside her at the sight of this technological sentinel that had protected Potemia for half a millennium. It towered a hundred feet high and stretched in what seemed an endless line. Supposedly, it continued right into the ocean in a complete circuit of the continent. The scale seemed beyond imagining. Its metallic surface reflected a mirror image of herself descending the dune-scape.

Oral tradition held that any human could go through the Wall to the Outside, but never in the other direction. But was this true?

Kayla halted before the Wall, gazing into the new perfection of her own face. Blessed by God, or cursed by God?

I'm finally here.

Knowledge. Truth. This remained her greatest desire. It had damned her in the eyes of her own people. They had executed and then banished her for it. And now she would know.

Her hand rose to the smooth surface and settled onto the cold metal. It felt … alive, somehow.

A glow formed beneath her hand and spread into the shape of an archway. Her eyes widened. The glow dissolved into swirling patterns of light—becoming a portal.

She gazed into the doorway of science-magic and trembled. Despite her desire, despite her banishment, she hesitated. There would be no going back.

Isn't this what I've always craved? How else can I know?

Kayla drew in a final breath of her homeland—and stepped into the archway.

"And he said unto me, 'Go in, and behold the wicked abominations that they do here.' "

The Wall swallowed her.

Chapter 7

Kayla glided through a mist of swirling energy, eyes wide with wonder. The hairs along her arms tingled and danced. With each step forward, her chest swelled with hope. What wonders might her distant cousins on the Outside have created after five hundred years of intellectual freedom?

The words of the Founder flashed before her mind: *"Progress will not be stopped. No social arrangements, whether laws, institutions, customs, or ethical codes, can provide permanent protection against technology."*

A second archway appeared. It shimmered and beckoned her. She stepped through.

The first rays of the rising sun bathed her in an intense light. Her gaze scaled the towering buildings, drinking in the wonder of what they represented. The triumph of the human mind unbound.

I've been waiting for this moment my entire life.

The sun shone brighter, and added a graphic contrast of blinding glare and deep shadow to the towering buildings. A smile caressed her lips, then faltered.

Before her sprawled the vast, rotting corpse of what had once been a great city. A few of the more robust buildings stood intact, disappearing into the dusty sky, but most had toppled into ruins. Where the ground had been smashed open by collapsing structures, the city continued in an underworld maze that mirrored the ruins above. Through gaps in the rubble, the urban skeleton stretched to the horizon.

Not a single plant or animal appeared within the desolation. Only the wind, wandering aimlessly through the wreckage, broke the deathly silence.

Her shoulders bent beneath the weight of it. The Founder's predictions had come to pass after all.

She recited words from the Book of Lamentations. *"How doth the city sit solitary, that was full of people. How is she become as a widow. She that was great among the nations. And the Lord said, 'I will destroy man whom I have created from the face of the Earth; both man, and beast, and the creeping thing, and the fowls of the air, for it repenteth me that I have made them.' "*

Her hands covered her eyes, blocking the sight of her fate. How long would she wander the ruins of this exterminated civilization—years, centuries, millennia?

She turned to the Wall and pounded on it with all the force of her undying prison of a body. The blow could have smashed through stone, but not a single vibration disturbed the Wall's preternatural calm. Above it, the field of shimmering energy extended into the sky. Whatever magic of science imbued the Wall with its power had endured these many centuries, even after the need of its protection had vanished.

"So he drove out the man, and he placed at the east of the garden of Eden Cherubims, and a flaming sword, which turned every way to keep the way of the Tree of Life."

She staggered back from the Wall, the reflection of her healed face staring back at her. *Is this the last living face I'll ever see?* She turned and took a stumbling step toward her desolate future, but her vision swam and her heart stuttered.

She fell into a heap.

Soon the oblivion of unconsciousness captured her, and her dreams returned to the familiar body of Peter. Once more, she saw through his eyes, felt through his senses, but was barred from his thoughts.

She felt his hands gripping a steering wheel as he piloted an automobile through traffic. In the rearview mirror, his face appeared unchanged from her previous dream, except that his dark eyes smoldered with the look Minister Coglin displayed when he preached of End Times. His army uniform had been replaced by one emblazoned with a woven patch of a hissing eagle, wreathed by the words *Corrections Officer— United States Federal Penitentiary.*

Peter's gaze slid from the mirror to the same photograph he'd held as a soldier in Iraq. The edges were frayed, and the colors faded nearly to black-and-white. Even the child's handwritten message across the bottom had softened to near-invisibility. But the faces of his wife and daughter remained. The five candles still sent up their smoke signals.

Peter slammed the palm of his right hand into the steering wheel.

"Why, God, why?" he moaned.

He struck at the steering wheel again and again, the pain shooting through palm, wrist, and arm. "Why, why, why?"

Two children stared at him from the backseat of a car traveling alongside his. The front seat of their car was empty, the steering wheel making slight adjustments on its own. Peter accelerated and left the children behind.

Wiping tears from his face, he touched a button that conjured a man's square-jawed face. The half-transparent head hovered above the dashboard and spoke with the deep resonance of command.

"…and so we take these intrusive surveillance measures with sadness, forced to do so by the cowardly acts of these Neo-Luddite terrorists. It is they who are to blame for this loss of privacy, not the government."

"Goddamn president!" Peter muttered. Above his car, a fleet of flying drones buzzed past, the roars of their engines drowning out the speech for a moment.

"...the Bill of Rights is sacred," continued the disembodied head, "but so is the safety of our wives, children, and grandchildren. As Supreme Court Justice Robert Jackson remarked, *'The Constitution is not a suicide pact.'* "

"Fascist." Peter maneuvered through the heavy traffic with expert familiarity. Soon he left the town and entered a vast plain of yellowish scrub. In the distance, faded blue mountains rimmed the horizon.

Flashing lights erupted behind him, and Peter flinched, his hand shielding his face. He adjusted his rearview mirror—the low-profile of an enforcement cruiser slid close.

"I don't have time for this crap!"

The hologram vanished, and a woman's soothing voice spoke through the speaker system. "This car is now under official police control." Peter took his hands off the wheel as the car slowed and pulled to the side of the road. In the rearview mirror, the police officer took his time getting out of his car. Under his breath, Peter recited words that Kayla recognized at once as those of the Founder of Potemia.

"When a new item of technology is introduced as an option that an individual can accept or not as he chooses, it does not necessarily remain optional. In many cases the new technology changes society in such a way that people eventually find themselves forced to use it."

The officer strode to the car and gestured with his hand. The driver's side window lowered automatically.

"I think you know why I pulled you over," the officer said. He looked to be in his mid-twenties, with the build of a heavy-weight wrestler.

"I wasn't speeding or breaking any rules of the road," Peter said.

"Cut the crap." The cop rolled his eyes. "You know perfectly well that I pulled you over for manually operating your car in a clearly marked automatic-only zone."

"The Constitution guarantees the freedom to—"

"Step out of the car." The officer eased back and placed his hand on his holster.

Silent, Peter unhooked his seatbelt, opened the door, and stood up.

"Hands at your back."

Peter complied. His jaw ached from grinding his teeth.

The officer fastened a pair of handcuffs on his wrists. Then he jerked him around and glared into his eyes.

"When you're on a public road, your personal *freedom* doesn't give you the right to endanger the lives of others."

"I've never been in a single accident," Peter said.

"Modern autopilots have a perfect safety record, while human error *used* to kill tens of thousands a year." His voice rose a notch. "Maybe you've never seen what a wreck can do to a body? Well, I have! In my book, you're no different than a drunk driver or someone waving a loaded gun in a theater."

Peter clenched his jaw even harder.

The officer held a metallic disc in front of Peter's left eye, and a flash of light illuminated it for an instant. A holographic screen appeared and scrolled through Peter's file.

"I see you're an Iraqi War Vet," the officer said. "You're a lot older than you look—but aren't we all." His voice leveled. "I served two tours in Iran twenty years back, myself. What a mind fuck that turned into when the Hajis hacked the command codes of our own drones and they turned on us." He rapped his knuckles on his left thigh with a metallic *thunk*. Then the right, with the same result. "These babies can run the hundred in seven seconds flat, but they're nothing compared to what the military is using these days."

Peter remained silent.

The officer read more of the file and frowned. He waved the hologram away. "Okay, I get it now." He gave Peter a long, appraising stare before continuing. "You know how I lost my legs?"

"No."

"Neither do I. Can't remember how it happened. Not the moments leading up to it, not the buddies who died, not even the months of rehabilitation in the hospital. I do remember that I had nightmares, of what I don't know. I also remember my PTSD discharge, punching the wife, slapping the kid, shacking up with a 10:00 a.m. bourbon." The officer's face softened with compassion. "Know what I'm saying?"

"You had the memories surgically removed."

"That's right," the officer said. "I'm telling you this one brother to another. I'm telling you this because of what I see in your file."

Every muscle in Peter's body tensed. "You think I'm going to erase the memory of my wife and child?" A hardness entered his voice—dangerous even.

The officer removed the handcuffs. "Can't tell you what you should forget. I'm telling you my own experience, one soldier to another." The officer placed a hand on his shoulder. "I'm telling you that you can be happy again if you choose to."

Peter said nothing at first. Then he nodded. "Thanks."

The officer's tone hardened. "If I catch you freewheeling again, I'll be forced to arrest you, brother-in-arms or not."

The officer returned to his cruiser.

Peter climbed into his car and spoke softly. *"Success can be hoped for only by fighting the technological system as a whole; but that is revolution, not reform."*

He punched the autopilot button on the dashboard and sat back. The car eased into traffic with a polite blinker and accelerated to a precise speed. Peter stared at the photograph of his wife and daughter for a long time. "I'll never forget you," he said. "Never."

With an angry jab of his finger, he switched the holographic news report back on.

"...robotics and artificial intelligence are changing our society drastically," the president observed. "Yes, we've lost many jobs, but we also benefit from the innumerable advances in extending human lifespans, in automated food production, and entertainment. As universal, guaranteed minimum income payments increase every year, the need to work will soon be a thing of the past."

Peter shouted over the hologram. *"Everyone has goals; if nothing else, to obtain the physical necessities of life: food, water, and whatever clothing and shelter are made necessary by the climate. But the leisured aristocrat obtains these things without effort. Hence his boredom and demoralization."*

Peter recited the words of the Founder with such perfect recall that he seemed a machine himself. The car exited the highway, rolled up a long causeway, and slowed as a chain-link fence parted to let him through. A sign next to the fence proclaimed in red letters: *Administrative Maximum Facility—All vehicles and personnel subject to search.*

The car approached what looked like a squat fortress. Concrete watchtowers thrust up at regular intervals, with soldiers and mounted guns atop their battlements. A series of razor-wire fences created a no-man's land where attack dogs roamed freely.

The holographic face of the president had changed into that of a beautiful female reporter. "...has ordered three hundred fifty thousand Americans held under the new law without formal charge..."

The car glided to a stop next to a guardhouse.

"Window A down." The driver's window slid open, emitting a gust of air. Peter nodded as a youthful guard with a dark beard walked to the window. His name-tag read *Karl,* his baseball cap read *N.R.A.*

"How's it hangin', Pete?" Karl reached in a beefy hand and exchanged a fist bump.

"See the news?" Peter jerked his head toward the still-talking reporter.

"Fuckin' A," Karl said. "Those damn Neo-Luddite fanatics wanna start their own enviro-*mental* society—let's plop 'em in a cage or, better yet, in Hell."

Peter nodded, though his heart rate increased. "At least this is one job the robots haven't confiscated."

"Fuckin' amen for the Jailers of America Lobby." The guard spit a stream of tobacco into the dirt. "You hear about them dogs?"

Peter glanced at a pack of fierce-looking dogs lounging inside the no-man's land.

"They're gittin' rid of 'em," Karl said.

"No shit?"

"Yup. Replacin' 'em with guard-bots. They even brought them metal fuckers by for a test run." Karl gave an exaggerated shiver. "Watching them robots scurry about on twelve bug legs makes my skin crawl. Fuckin' toasters with teeth." Karl shook his head. "Never reckoned they git rid of them dogs. Tradition, you know?"

Peter half-smiled. "You sound like a Neo-Luddite, yourself."

Karl lashed his head from side to side. "No, siree, I'm not! Not me. I dun hate those Enviro-Nazis. Fuckin' Amen to killin' 'em all, I say!"

Another gust rocked the car. Peter glanced at the darkening sky. "Storm's brewin'."

Karl nodded and waved him through. "Got that right."

The car drove itself toward the main entryway, flanked on both sides by guard towers. Once out of range of Karl, Peter's frown returned. "Fuckin' amen yourself—you'll see what happens …"

"…In other news, further portions of the Greenland ice sheets have disappeared during this year's record summer heat, and engineers for New York City's Levee Department report that they may have to evacuate more sections of the city permanently. Rising ocean levels have already displaced an estimated one billion people from the world's low-lying areas. In the Middle East, radioactive fallout …"

The car glided to a stop before a metal doorway. Peter got out, leaving the car to drive itself down a ramp marked *Employee Parking*. He placed his palm on a metal plate and gazed into a light. The doors opened, and the fortress swallowed him. He repeated the procedure half a dozen times until reaching an area labeled *Maximum Security Zone Delta*.

"Pete! Welcome to the Black Hole!" A youthful guard with a wild mass of curly red hair rose from his chair and stretched. The guard sat before a wall of monitors, each displaying a steel doorway with a number painted on it.

"Catch that Packers game last night, Billy?" Peter readied a cart that smelled of food.

"Shit, yeah!" Billy exclaimed with eyes wide. "Can you fuckin' believe that center! Seven-ten, five hundred and eighty fuckin' pounds!"

"I hear some college prospects have topped the eight-foot barrier." Peter waited for Billy to join him with a second cart.

"Dropping the gene therapy ban for the NFL was the best decision in the history of sports."

"Got that right," Peter said. The door's internal locks disengaged, and it swung open.

"Well, crazies need feeding." Billy rolled the cart into the hallway, followed by Peter. Only the regularly spaced doorways on both sides interrupted the sterile perfection of the passage.

"Heard last week was your birthday." Billy removed a used tray from a shallow metal drawer in the first door and replaced it with a fresh one.

Peter shrugged. "Meaningless."

"Come on. Just because the body doesn't age and wither doesn't make it meaningless." Billy delivered another tray while Peter serviced the cell opposite.

"It's different for you, since you have a family."

"When were you born, old man?" Billy kept it light.

"1983."

"The twentieth century! You're fuckin' eighty-six years old?"

"How old are you?" Peter asked.

"Hell, I'm only twenty-seven—haven't needed the treatments yet."

"So you've never known anyone who looks old, have you?"

"Shit, my granddaddy whooped my ass in soccer yesterday. The dude looks younger than I do!" Billy replaced another tray and moved on to the next cell. "Had a great-uncle who died, though. Fuckin' piece of concrete came loose from the six-hundredth floor of a building. Dude never had time to blink. Cratered him."

"I guess the longer you live, a freak accident becomes almost inevitable."

"That's a sobering thought." Billy frowned. "Still seems better going quick like that than falling apart piece by piece."

As they approached the end of the hallway, Billy nodded toward the final cell door on Peter's side. "Ever look at the fucker in there?"

Peter's body tensed. "Why?"

Billy delivered his final tray and approached the door, labeled 'Delta #1.' Billy opened a metal porthole at eye level and stared through a thick disc of glass at the occupant within. "Damn, that fucker looks old," Billy said. "Looks like a barbecued hog that's been overcooked. Come on, you gotta see this!"

Billy grabbed Peter's arm and half-dragged him to the porthole. A stooped man with a white beard sat in profile before a desk with an opened book on it. A single reading light interrupted the darkness of the rest of the cell.

"He takes just enough treatments to keep from dying, but not enough to become young again." Billy shook his head. "What the fuck is that about?"

"Maybe he likes being old."

"I wonder what a harmless-looking shit like that did to end up here?"

Peter shrugged. "You could get fired for even asking."

"Can you fuckin' believe those knuckle-headed Supreme Court Justices? Ruling that lifers like this have a right to anti-aging drugs. I mean, what the fuck? The guy could be a hundred and fifty years old for Christ's sake. Are we supposed to keep these bastards alive forever?"

Peter shrugged. "Half our prisoners would be dead by now without them, which would mean a lot less prison jobs, and prisons are the largest employer in the country."

Billy's eyes widened. "I've always said those Supreme Court Justices are geniuses!" He opened the metal drawer to remove the used tray, but Peter snatched it from his hands.

"Sorrrrryyyy! Just trying to help, bud," Billy said. "Didn't mean to poach your turf."

"Force of habit," Peter said, while his fingers grasped a tiny roll of paper beneath a half-eaten piece of bread. He moved so quickly that Billy didn't notice. "I guess I'm tired from, well …"

"So you did celebrate after all." Billy leered. "Was she virtual, robot, or the real deal?"

"Virtual," Peter mumbled, and slipped the paper into his waistband.

"Yeah, I guess sims are cheaper and highly skilled," Billy mused. "But you let me know if you need someone to hook you up." Billy slapped his back. "I know some pros that will haunt your dreams for a long time!"

After enduring a recital of Billy's real, robotic, and virtual sexual adventures, Peter escaped to a bathroom stall and unrolled the slip of paper. His hands trembled.

Four words scratched its surface: *Propaganda of the Deed*.

Peter clenched his hands and raised his eyes to the ceiling, drawing his breath in through his nose as if inhaling an intoxicant. A smile spread across his face.

Chapter 8

Kayla splayed upon the shattered concrete like a rejected sacrifice. The light from the rising sun worried its way down the gleaming surface of the Wall and onto her still form. She sensed the change and her eyes opened. Photons crowded through the cornea, pupil, and crystalline lens, focused onto the millions of neurons at the back of her retina. A cascade of chemical reactions streamed through the optic nerve, invading the visual cortex of the occipital lobe. The process repeated over and over with such speed that her brain stitched an illusion of smooth continuity, assembling the trillions of chemical clues into a virtual representation of the scene before her.

A pair of antennae twitched against her cheek. Something flashed across her view, and a predator's teeth engulfed the creature with a sickening crunch. Kayla jerked away from the massacre occurring inches from her face.

"Puck!"

The little mouse swallowed the cockroach and greeted her with a squeak. He must have hitched a ride in the hood of her cloak. Had he hidden there for so long, hunting for bugs while she slept? His loyalty seemed astonishing.

"I guess we're fellow exiles," she said with a smile and lifted the mouse onto her shoulder. Then she stood.

The dead city bristled, with its steel skeleton thrusting upward like the remains of an immense lion kill. Kayla could already feel the heat of the unfiltered sun on her skin. A burnt odor pervaded the air, though anything flammable had long ago surrendered to the elements. The wind echoed in a lonely solo amidst the ruins. Searching such a place for life seemed pointless.

What alternative do I have?

"I don't know about you, Puck, but I'm not giving up. If this is our fate, then I'm going to keep searching."

A few mosses, weeds, and even a stray bug or two eked out a living, but nothing suggested a recent human presence. The buildings, tunnels, and rusting vehicles hinted at the technological heights attained by those on this side of the Wall. But what could have happened to it all?

Puck sampled the air with twitches of his sensitive nose, and Kayla rubbed his head. "Even though we're castaways with no one else in the world to talk to, we're free."

Puck squeaked.

"We don't have to hide, or whisper, or fear what anyone will think of us." Raising her face to the morning sky, she held out her arms and spun slowly with the wind like a lazy weather vane.

"We can say anything we want!"

Her personal declaration of independence echoed across the city's deserted carcass, until swallowed by the silence. No one returned her call. How long could her optimism last before loneliness wore her down?

There were no bones, bullet holes, or the signs of deliberate destruction one would expect from a war. Time alone seemed responsible for the decay. The wind had scoured the insides of the building so thoroughly that little remained, so she concentrated her efforts outside, where, in one or two spots, great drifts of trash had accumulated like eddies in a stream.

She uncovered a metal statue, half buried by debris, and no longer than her forearm. After pulling it free, she wiped a thick layer of dirt from its face with the hem of her disintegrating cloak. A gleaming, exaggerated visage stared blankly. After polishing an unreflective flat disc on top of its head, she set the oddity on its feet in the bright sunlight.

"There you go, little man," she said, admiring her restoration. A hum ignited inside it, and an internal light sparked within its eyes.

"Ixtalia!" the statue exclaimed.

Kayla yelped and jumped back.

"Ixtalia!" it said a second time and marched in a circle, its head, arms, and legs beating time to its metallic steps. "Ixtalia is the place to be. Ixtalia is for you and me! Ixtalia is safe for everyone, so come and join the fun!"

The little man spun twice with a flourish. This must be what her books called a robot.

"Can you tell me how to get to Ixtalia?" Kayla asked.

"Ixtalia is the place t-o-o-o-o ..." Its voice slowed and then stopped. A pop sounded inside its head, and a wisp of smoke drifted from its mouth. It stood frozen, a statue once more.

"Ixtalia," she whispered as one might an incantation, but without effect.

After searching a few trash heaps in vain for any books or clues, she began scaling one of the pyramid-shaped buildings dominating the skyline for a higher vantage point. Most windows had been blown out long ago, leaving the dwellings empty. The few scratched and filthy panes still intact offered little insight into the dark interiors.

The incline neared forty-five degrees, and it took her fifteen minutes to rise above the tallest of the remaining skyscrapers. With the rise in altitude, the wind increased. Her tattered cloak acted the part of a sail, and she gripped the crumbling building tight to keep from slipping. But then, a particularly violent gust tore the cloak from her body. Puck chirped and clung to the hood as it lofted skyward.

"Puck!" Kayla shouted in panic and jumped. She shot upward higher than she'd expected. The mouse squeaked a frantic plea as her hand reached for it, but to no avail. Just as she slowed, turbulence buffeted the mouse's personal airship toward her. She snatched him from the remains of the cloak.

Then her ascent reversed.

The side of the pyramid rushed toward her with a sickening inevitability. Her hair billowed as if caught in a tempest. She cradled Puck against her naked chest. Equations of time, gravity, and acceleration flickered through her consciousness.

I don't want to die!

She fell faster and faster toward one of the intact windows halfway down the pyramid's surface. She smashed through the edge of it in an explosion of glass and concrete. Pain shot into her legs, back, and shoulders. All her attention focused on keeping the little mouse cradled in her arms. Her back hit the concrete floor of the room with a thump and a shower of pulverized stone. The force sledgehammered her head into the floor and knocked the breath from her lungs.

For a while she stared at the backs of her eyelids and imagined the monk's fleshless skull gazing at her. *Am I dying?* With a great effort, she opened her eyes.

Puck's tiny face stared at her, unharmed.

She groaned as she sat up and put her hand to the back of her head. The skin was already healing, and the bone was unharmed. Her fingertips traced the rim of the shallow depression her head had pounded in the concrete.

She kissed Puck, and let his whiskers tickle her face before placing him on the floor. She rose from the crater and pulled off the remains of her cloak, revealing deep cuts from her plunge through the glass and concrete. The worst pain sliced through her side. A slender piece of steel from the window's frame punched in above the left hip and jabbed out the right side of her torso, below her ribcage.

She took hold of the metal and pulled. It slid out of her body with a spurt of blood. She gasped and fell to her knees, clutching at what should have been a mortal wound.

Her breaths came in short, agonized gasps. But soon they evened out, and she removed her hand from her side. Only the stain of sticky blood remained. In another moment, even the pain vanished. Fire, an arrow through the heart, suffocation, starvation—and now throwing herself off a building and being impaled by a steel rod. *Am I indestructible?*

The room looked like it had been a dwelling of some sort. Though most of the household decor had crumbled to dust, a few plastic items survived the centuries. Furniture, a cup, several children's toys, bits of machines that had rusted around these internal components.

This had been someone's home.

She opened the door and explored the rest of the well-preserved floor. Most of the apartments hugged the outside of the building. The interior was a maze of shops and open spaces that contained remnants of plants, water gardens, and even a sports arena. After exploring dozens of glassed-in rooms with no success, she stumbled upon one with clothing made of a plastic-like material.

She tried on a pair of matching slacks and a shirt. At first they seemed too big, but with a hiss and a delicate crinkling, they folded about her curves so perfectly that it made her blush, despite her isolation. A light jacket with a few pockets gave Puck a place to settle into, and a pair of self-molding athletic shoes offered better traction than her bare feet. Whatever color they'd once been had faded to a dull gray.

After heading back outside, she resumed her climb.

At the pyramid's peak, the scale of her isolation became clear. Except for the sharp line of Potemia's boundary to the south, the city extended to the horizon in an unbroken procession of grids and occasional mountainous pyramids—all crumbling to ruins.

I'm not giving up.

With a determined set to her jaw, she surveyed the structures, streets, and ruins for any sign of activity. After half an hour, a distant plume of dust appeared through the shimmering heat.

The speck hovered on the very edge of her vision, and she strained to see beyond their limitations. Suddenly, her eyes prickled with a needling heat. Her vision vibrated, and a strange shift disrupted her balance, as if flashing her toward the distant speck. She closed her eyes and steadied herself. When the heat and vertigo diminished, she opened her lids. Her sight had transformed. Like the compound lens of an eagle, her eyes zoomed in with astonishing magnification.

The distant speck resolved into a rising cloud of dust with vague shapes moving within. They appeared human. She counted fifty shadowy figures. Her heart pounded. If only she could fly, but she'd already tested that ability and found it lacking, to say the least.

Grinding her teeth at the delay, Kayla descended the man-made mountain and started running toward her new goal.

I'm not alone!

Navigating the ruins proved frustrating. Large sections of the ground occasionally gave way and transformed into gigantic sinkholes within the undercity below, but she leapt clear each time. A violent dust storm drove her into the ruins for shelter as the day ended. Falling into one of the cavernous holes in the dark would delay her and endanger Puck.

Exhaustion forced sleep, and she dreamed of Peter, once again. Through his eyes, she viewed the interior of what she'd learned from her books was called a "train." He sat in a luxurious seat and stared out the window at a thriving city of automobiles, pedestrians, and towering buildings. A swarm of flashing drones blanketed the sky like metal worker bees servicing their hive.

"May I offer you a complimentary VR headset, sir?" The female attendant wore a skin-tight blue uniform, and gazed at him with the slitted pupils of a cat.

"No, thank you," Peter said.

The girl leaned toward him with a conspiratorial grin. "This is the latest model, with complete neural interfacing. You experience it throughout your *entire* body." She winked. "Even *intimate* touch." She giggled and resumed placement of the helmet, but he intercepted her hand.

"Thanks, but I just want to rest."

"Yes—of course, sir." The girl frowned.

The rest of the passengers all wore the helmet. They slumped in their chairs with heads lolling to the side, and drool slipped from one or two mouths.

At the end of the aisle, the cat-eyed girl whispered to another attendant, who glanced at him.

Peter closed his eyes and reclined his chair. Soon he fell asleep, releasing Kayla from the dream.

The morning light streamed through the wrecked doorway and woke her. Refreshed and charged with new purpose, she continued her journey. Fuming at every toppled building, she ran with reckless abandon, sometimes leaping chasms of thirty feet without breaking stride. Once she overestimated her range and plunged twenty feet down to the next level of the undercity. She vaulted to the surface and sprinted onward.

What if they've left and I'm too late?

Around noon, the clatter of rocks and a faint chant caused her breath to catch. She scaled the debris from a collapsed building, and the guttural words came into focus.

"Work, work, stones to move;
Beautiful God command.
Ohg's servants we, Our reward to come;
When Father die below."

She peeked over the top of the rubble at the several dozen workers below. They averaged two-feet tall, with green skin free of clothing. Their muscular backs bent under large burdens of rock. Despite their nakedness, they lacked any distinction between male and female, while their oversized heads and protruding jaws lent them a mildly repulsive quality. Each sprouted a pair of bulging eyes that moved independently like those of some reptiles.

Could mankind have devolved into these sad remains?

"Work, work, stones to move;
Beautiful God command.
Ohg's servants we, Our reward to come;
When Father die below."

Who was this beautiful God, Ohg? Were they referring to a real person, or a mythical figure? More important, did they know of any other surviving humans? Taking a deep breath, Kayla stood and descended the rubble.

The chanting stopped and eyeballs swiveled toward her, but not a single body faltered in its task. Each creature continued heaving concrete onto its back and carrying the burden across the clearing to a growing mound. Kayla halted at the edge of their line, towering over them.

"Hello," she said to one wide-eyed face making its way past for a new load of debris.

The creature's toad-like mouth trembled. "Are a god you?" it asked.

"Well, no, I'm not a god."

"You beautiful like Ohg God," her admirer said, one eye looking at her, and the other focused on the path before it. "But your hair deathlike. Ohg hair color of Father in sky."

"Do you mean the sun?" she asked, walking beside it. "Is his hair yellow like the color of the sun?" The little creature nodded. They reached the pile of rubble, and her new friend hoisted a chunk of concrete.

"I'm Kayla, what's your name?"

"We people Monad."

"But what is *your* name?" Kayla pointed at it, and the creature stepped away from her finger as if from a knife.

"Not understand, I/we Monad."

They don't distinguish the self from the whole.

"What are you working on, here?" She made a sweeping gesture encompassing the clearing.

"Monad move rock from there," one of its eyes looked behind at the diminishing pile, "to there." Its other eye swiveled forward to the growing pile.

"I meant for what purpose? Are you building something?"

"Monad move because God tell move." The creature's eyes misted, dreamy and remote. "Monad born with great fear of Father go away. When Father leave, Monad die." A tremor shook its body. "We know this without told. Great fear, great fear."

Its face brightened. "God Ohg come to us, tell us Father create us for great purpose. Move rock, don't lazy be, don't fighting be." Its green head shook from side to side. "When rock moving be finish, Monad reward with life forever with Father in sky. No rock, no death, only happy."

"Do you mean you will die when the sun goes down?" Kayla asked. It nodded. "And you have only been alive since dawn?" It nodded again.

But these must be the same creatures from yesterday.

Halfway between the two piles of rubble, a pool of muddy water nestled in a hollow. Each passing Monad stuck its hand in the puddle and seemed to drink through its skin. Kayla sat down and watched the Monads lumber back and forth. Soon they resumed their chant.

"Work, work, stones to move;
Beautiful God command.
Ohg's servants we, Our reward to come;
When Father die below."

The day progressed, the old pile shrank, and the new one grew. The diminutive creatures staggered under the heavy loads. Their every stumble made Kayla wince. When she stood to help one of the smaller Monads struggling to drag a large rock, the creature sobbed.

"Monad can do. Not lazy. Monad can do!" it said. She dropped the rock and it stopped crying. Then it returned to its divinely appointed labor.

Puck busied himself hunting bugs and then sat next to her watching the Monads at their life's work.

The sun dipped toward the horizon. A line of buildings to the east and west had toppled, as if to allow maximum direct sunlight into the clearing. Had someone taken them down on purpose?

The Monads placed the final lumps of rock atop the mound with pride. A cheer rose from the group, and they danced around their holy monument, linking arms, laughing, rejoicing, and glorying in their accomplishment. The Monad she'd talked to earlier took her hand and pulled her into the ring. She laughed along with their infectious enthusiasm. All had grown nearly six inches from when she first encountered them.

For what they considered the final hours of their lives, the Monads speculated on the form their "Heaven" would take. They indulged in occasional dips in the pond, and soaked up the last rays of the setting sun. Like her, they didn't require food, drawing all their nourishment from the sun itself and the nutrients contained in the muddy pool—all of which probably explained the green color of their skin.

When the sun dipped below the distant buildings, Kayla stood, alert for any danger to her new friends. Would they fall asleep or lapse into hibernation like many plants did at night? Maybe they awoke each morning with their memories of the previous day erased.

When the screams of agony commenced, Kayla froze. Their tortured shrieks drove Puck under the rubble.

Kayla ran to the Monad whom she'd first spoken to and held its hand as a wave of pain contorted its body. Once the paroxysm passed, it said, "Monad obey God. Pain soon go. Reward Monad receive."

Kayla sang a hymn to comfort it.

"Amazing grace, How sweet the sound,
That saved a wretch, like me.
I once was lost, but now am found ..."

The melody of her voice rose. The Monads grew silent, and turned their trusting faces toward her.

"The Lord hath promised good to me,
His word my hope secures ..."

In tandem with the darkening sky, her friend's skin faded from green to a light brown. That's what it meant when it said her hair was the color of death. Waves of pain wracked its body with increasing frequency, but its eyes stayed focused on her.

"When we've been there ten thousand years,
Bright shining as the sun ..."

The Monad's skin dried and withered, crackling like autumn leaves beneath a stampede. His hand tightened on hers, and its face contorted in pain. Kayla cried as she sang.

"We've no less days to sing God's praise
Than when we first begun."

With a final moan, the poor creature died, a shriveled shell of crumbling flesh. The hand she held vanished like so much dried dirt slipping through her fingers. All around her, the remaining Monads rejoiced in between cries of agony, anticipating the reward promised them by their absent God.

Kayla fled the tortured cries, stumbling through the dark until they faded to silence. She sobbed herself to sleep amidst the ruins of a bridge and slipped into her own form of nightly oblivion. For once, no dreams violated her exhausted slumber, so it wasn't until the first rays of dawn topped the horizon that she awoke. And then, a voice reached her.

With cautious movements, she scaled the rubble, and the voice became clear. In contrast to the guttural rumblings of the Monads, the voice rang pure in tone, confident, and was definitely a man's.

"I am Ohg, son of the Great Father in the Sky who gives you life!"

Kayla poked her head above the ridge. A young man stood in the clearing, curly blond hair cascading across well-formed shoulders like a mantel. He wore only a loincloth. The combination of poetic blue eyes, squareness of jaw, and a physique an artist might dream of sculpting, caused her breath to catch.

She counted fifty healthy Monads sitting in a semicircle around the young god. Only their diminished size marked a departure from the fifty Monads of the previous day. Where had they come from?

"My faithful servants!" the youthful god called to his adoring disciples. "The Great Father has been driven off the Earth and banished to the sky by two evil giants!" The Monads gasped. "He has sent me, his son, to give you an important task in his battle against these abominations." The Monads nodded their eagerness to help.

"It is crucial to the Father that the stones before you be moved to the other end of the clearing before his death. Thus will the Giants' evil plans be foiled. In gratitude for your service, the Great Father in the Sky will reward you with everlasting life in the wondrous realm beyond this one. There, you will find eternal light, rest, and water as cool and delicious as any you will ever dip your hands in."

"We will Father help!" a Monad shouted.

Kayla gazed at the rapt Monad faces, their trusting eyes locked on the boy. Her face hardened into a scowl. What sick pleasure did this boy get from having them toil all day long to move a pile of stones back to where they'd moved them from the previous day?

"There is no time to lose, noble Monads—the all-seeing eye of God is upon you! Do your work well, and, by nightfall, you will be in paradise with me and my Father!"

The tiny green creatures cheered and grabbed stones from the hill.

"How dare you!" Kayla shouted at the false god, and all eyes turned toward her. Ohg appeared most startled of all and looked around with quick jerks of his neck, as if expecting an ambush. Seeing no one else, his eyes narrowed and locked onto her. The anger in her face faltered beneath his startling eyes, and she took a step backward. But the trusting faces of the Monads stopped her, and she straightened. Who would defend these helpless, trusting souls if not her?

"How dare you take advantage of these poor—"

"She is a minion of the Giants!" the boy shouted to the Monads, who cringed back from her.

"No, I'm your friend—" she shouted, but they shook their heads and shouted to keep her evil words from penetrating their minds.

"Your God will protect you," Ohg said. "Continue your divine work, or the Giants will have won!" With that, he bounded up the rock pile, while the Monads scrambled to their task with redoubled determination.

The blond god looked only a few years older than her. More boy than man. When he reached the top of the mound, he gazed at her with curiosity and a hint of amusement. Kayla's eyes glared into his. Not only was he exploiting the Monads, but he'd convinced them she worked on the side of the Devil. He swept his gaze over her form-fitting outfit with deliberate pauses and nods. Heat suffused her cheeks.

"I don't think I've seen that model before," he said with approval. "A custom job? You do know its illegal to operate unregistered bodies?" One of his eyebrows raised, but she remained silent. "A bit of advice, though, since the ozone layer is gone, the skin will burn after fifteen minutes of solar exposure."

Still, she said nothing, her face a battleground between anger and confusion.

He laughed. "I didn't think anyone but me bothered with atomic-based bodies anymore. So retro. I guess you just had the urge to go Earth-slumming?"

What in God's name is he talking about?

Kayla glared at him. "I won't let you distract me from the sick lies you're telling these poor creatures."

"I'll understand if you want to hit me," Ohg said in the face of her outrage, "but would you mind giving me a chance to explain, first?"

"I don't see what you could possibly … Okay, fine, I'm listening." She crossed her arms and stared with such rage that he burst into laughter. He took a few steps beneath the ridge and sat in the shade, out of sight of the Monads, and protected from the sun. She hesitated, then walked over and sat across from him.

"My name is Ohg," he said.

"So I've heard." Her lip twisted into a sneer. "Ohg, the great god, son of the Father in the Sky, come to offer everlasting life."

"You don't approve of my story?"

"It's a lie!"

"How do you know it's a lie?"

She spluttered for a moment, then straightened. "It's obvious."

"The Monads believe it. Don't you have respect for other people's religious beliefs?"

"You're exploiting their simplicity and preying on their trusting nature to trick them into doing … What is the point of moving those stones in the first place?"

"The stones are meaningless to me."

"Then you admit there exists no great purpose—nothing to do with Giants, or the Sun, or … or anything!"

Ohg laughed at her expression. "Trapped by my own words! I suppose it is a lie, after all."

"Then why put them through all that work if it has no purpose?"

"It has purpose for the Monads." His smirk vanished, and his blue eyes took on an intensity that once again turned her insides weak despite her anger. "The Egyptian pyramids, cathedrals, mosques, and temples are nothing more than elaborate piles of rocks constructed to win the favor of nonexistent gods. Every life needs purpose and hope, so I give them both."

"Even though it's a lie?"

"Would it be better if I told them the truth?" he asked. "Should I describe their creation in a laboratory a few hundred years ago? Born with their brains preprogrammed with language and rudimentary skills, and the knowledge that their fate is to die after a single day for no purpose whatsoever?"

Kayla's eyes widened, but she remained silent.

"When I found the Monads, they lived their short lives in a waking Hell—tormented from birth by fear of the death awaiting them with the setting sun. Scientists had programmed this knowledge into their genes to study instinctual behaviors in the natural world." Ohg's tone conveyed his disgust.

"Once abandoned, the Monads wandered without purpose or hope. Truth is an affliction in search of a comforting lie—for Monads and humans alike. For a century, these gentle creatures have moved these stones back and forth, ending each day with pride at their participation in something greater than themselves."

"It is still a lie," Kayla said.

"To argue the truth of any religion is to miss the point," Ohg said. "Animals are unaware that death is inevitable. Fear is reserved for moments of imminent danger. Once the human brain evolved enough to realize the inevitability of death, fear and despair must have become a constant torment. Thus we grasp at any story that will alter this reality and grant us temporary solace, even if it is an illusion."

"*Fear was the first mother of the gods*," Kayla quoted. "*Fear, above all, of Death.*"

"You've read Lucretius?" Ohg raised an eyebrow. "I didn't think anyone read books anymore. Lucretius nailed it, but even though humanity has now conquered death, this victory has created a deeper hopelessness, since mankind no longer has its own mountain of rocks to give life purpose, as I'm sure you'd agree."

"There are more people like you? Why is everything in ruins, then?"

"But I thought you … your clothes …" His face bunched and he jerked to his feet. "Are you telling me … are you … could you possibly be … from Potemia?"

Kayla nodded.

His eyes widened. "That's amazing. I have to—" Ohg turned and came face-to-face with a Monad. Its entire body trembled with horror and anger.

"God lie! Monad purpose no! Forever Monad die!" it shouted at Ohg with tears smearing its green face. Then it dashed down the slope.

Ohg leapt after it. "No, I didn't mean it! It was a trick to fool the Demon!" But the Monad wouldn't listen and shouted to its brothers that the god was no god, that it had "Lied, Lied, Lied!" The knowledge that moving the mountain served no divine purpose, that there existed no hope of life in Paradise after sunset, swept through the Monads like a convulsion.

The boy ran into their midst, desperately trying to reason with them. One Monad threw a rock at the back of his head. Ohg placed his hand against the wound, and the Monads grew silent as they surrounded him. Kayla stood frozen in place. What could she do to help soothe them?

Ohg brought his hand before his eyes and gazed at the blood. He appealed to the tortured faces surrounding him. "I'm sorry I lied to you. I wanted to help—" With a roar, they attacked their false god. He tried running, but they fastened their strong hands on him from all sides. He cried out as they dislocated and broke his limbs.

"No!" Kayla screamed and ran down the slope.

The Monads bit, pounded, and clawed at their fallen deity. The blood of their false god showered them like a sacrificial offering. Ohg's cries of agony fueled them to an ever-greater frenzy.

"Stay back!" Ohg shouted to her.

Ignoring his warning, she rushed into the melee, kicking and swatting the creatures away with powerful blows. Bones crunched, and the Monads yelped, but still they persisted in their vengeance. She slung Ohg over her shoulder and bolted toward the buildings beyond the clearing, but still they clung to him.

Kayla tore the last Monad from Ohg's leg and headed into an open doorway. She set the unconscious youth onto the floor before facing the approaching mob. She could easily kill them one at a time, but how could she do such a thing to these simple creatures?

The Monads swarmed toward her, faces twisted in rage, wide mouths baring sharp rows of teeth—odd for creatures who didn't eat. Kayla upended a huge slab of concrete, and it boomed into place to block the doorway. The Monads shrieked.

She knelt beside Ohg, and his eyes half opened. "Potemia …" he said, then bloody foam gurgled into his mouth. Kayla gazed at his mutilated body with despairing eyes. There was too much damage to repair.

"It's my fault," she said with a trembling voice. "I'm sorry. I'm so, so sorry …"

Ohg's head lolled to the side—his life ended. Kayla's hands went to her face and she cried. The Monads scratched, pushed, and pounded at the concrete slab, until they drifted away, terrified by the inevitability of their approaching fate. Their fearful cries and moans drifted through the gaps of the doorway as the sun made its unstoppable circuit across the sky, marking the countdown to the end of their now-meaningless lives.

Kayla smoothed the boy's golden hair from his face, wiped the blood and grime from his perfect lips, and closed his eyes. Then she kissed his forehead.

"I'm sorry." Her tears anointed his lifeless cheeks.

Even here, in the long-dreaded Outside, she'd brought misfortune and death. "I will not kill anyone else," she whispered. The room stood bare, nothing more than a windowless box, a fitting tomb to hide in for eternity—the Monads' faint cries serving as a reminder of the poison she'd become.

Eventually, darkness conquered the day, and silence returned to the abandoned city. Kayla spent the night beside Ohg, her hand entwined in his stiffening fingers. Puck entered through a crack in the doorway and curled up near her and fell asleep. At least the little mouse was safe.

The mountain of rock would move no more. The Monads would wander through the dead city, alone and terrified without their god to offer hope.

She dozed dreamlessly throughout the night—but one mystery remained.

With the first suggestion of light, she peered through a crack in the side of the doorway. The sky brightened, and the chest of a desiccated Monad bulged, then split down the center, revealing a green pod inside. One by one, the rest followed, until fifty pods lay strewn across the clearing.

When the sun topped the distant buildings and bathed the artificial valley in light, the pods opened, and out crawled a fresh generation of Monads. Each gazed at the newly born sun, and a shadow of dread darkened their faces.

Ohg's ashen features bulged, and the unmistakable smell of death spiraled through the chamber like a noxious curse.

I know what he'd want me to do.

She stood and slid the concrete aside. The Monads watched her stride across the sunlit clearing and followed without prompting, transfixed.

She sat at the edge of the hill of stones, and they gathered around her. "My name is Kayla," she said. "I want to tell you the story of a man named Jesus."

For the next half hour, she related the story of the man from Galilee, who had died for their sins. She told them how they also would rise from the dead in Heaven if they believed in Him. When she finished, the Monads' faces glowed with the vision of the promised life after this one. But here and there, a mouth bent into a frown, and a brow creased with a shadow of anxiety.

"Monad, Jesus believe," one said, its wide face imploring. "But what Jesus want Monad do?"

Suzy had asked her a similar question once in her Bible study sessions. Kayla had spoken of the subtle distinctions of right and wrong, helping the less fortunate, the Ten Commandments, and the Golden Rule. But such concepts would baffle creatures like this. Just like Ohg had predicted, hope had proved insufficient on its own—they needed a purpose as well.

Maybe they could repair the buildings? But this seemed an impossibly complex task for such simple-minded creatures. Maybe a garden? But where would she find seeds, let alone soil capable of supporting life?

Their faces twisted with worry. "Monad want help Jesus," one of them said, and the rest nodded in an urgent plea for some task to give their lives purpose.

Kayla sighed and spread her arms wide. "The one Great Task that God and his Son want you to accomplish as a sign of your devotion," she said to their trusting, upturned faces, "is to move this pile of stones from here, to there."

As one, they set to work. None questioned why Jesus wanted the stones moved; all that mattered was their Savior's command. Never was there a more dutiful congregation. It didn't matter that she judged the task pointless. Its purpose lay in the doing itself.

The clapping of a pair of hands startled her, and she turned. A figure stood atop the rubble where she'd spoken with Ohg the day before. He moved his hands back and forth slowly, applauding her. Her eyes zoomed in on the face of—

"It can't be ..." she said, backing away from the apparition. Her heart pounded, and she dashed toward the tomb where she'd left Ohg. Would it be empty? The Monads hardly noticed her, consumed by their holy labors. Kayla stopped at the entrance and gazed at Ohg's bloated and mutilated corpse. It lay undisturbed where she'd left it.

A hand settled on her shoulder, and she spun around to face ... Ohg.

Chapter 9

"Sorry I startled you," Ohg said. "I forgot you're from—"

Kayla retreated. Her eyes flashed from the dead body on the floor to the living one in the doorway. Was this a ghost?

"Please," she begged. "Haven't I been punished enough? I'm sorry for getting you killed. I'm sorry—"

"Listen, I didn't actually die yesterday."

She covered her ears to protect her mind from his lies. Minister Coglin claimed the Devil sometimes impersonated the dead to torture their kin.

Maybe I did die after all. Maybe this is Hell.

The ghost grabbed her wrists and pulled her hands aside. She screamed, the terror in her chest demanding release.

"I'm alive, do you understand?" Ohg shouted. He let go of her hands and she stopped screaming. Her entire body trembled.

He patted his chest. "It's taken me time to get this spare body prepped and transported out here."

He doesn't sound like a ghost.

"A spare—body?"

"Think of bodies as vehicles, like a boat or a cart." He took a half-step forward and she retreated, eyes dilated. "When my vehicle breaks down, I simply get into another."

"I watched you die," she said.

Ohg sighed, as if struggling to explain something to a small child. "Your body and consciousness are one and the same. If your vehicle is destroyed, you die. But this body," Ohg pointed to his chest, "is not my true body. I've projected my consciousness to inhabit it only temporarily. If it is destroyed, my consciousness is not harmed. Do you understand?"

"You changed into a new … body?" she asked, and he nodded.

Could this be some trick of a demon?

Kayla stepped forward, her palm settling against his cheek. "I thought I'd gotten you killed."

Ohg smiled. "Good try, though."

Guilt and sorrow flowed out of her as she flung her arms around his neck and buried her face in his chest. "Thank God you're alive, Ohg!"

"I ... I'm fine," he said. He patted her back awkwardly, as if unsure how to respond.

"I'm sorry I misjudged you. You're one of the kindest people I've ever known—to dedicate your life to helping these poor creatures!"

He blushed. "It's only a few minutes each morning. I wouldn't exactly call it dedicating—"

She kissed him. *What am I doing?* Guilt at betraying Ishan flooded her mind.

Ohg laughed.

She jerked away from him. "Is it funny that I would kiss you?"

"Yes, it is, but explaining why is too complex for the present." He gazed out the doorway. "My compliments on the ancient fairy tale you told the Monads. Quite effective."

She stiffened. "How do you know it's a fairy tale?"

He glanced sidelong at her. "So you believe Jesus desires the Monads to move rocks all day?"

Kayla walked past him and stood watching the Monads carry their loads from one pile to the other. Ohg followed but remained silent.

"I lied about that for their own good. But I believe everything else I told them."

Ohg studied her. "Are you really from Potemia?"

"I'm not a liar," she said, then hesitated. "Except ..."

"Except to the Monads," he said with a penetrating gaze.

She averted her eyes. *I also lied to Ishan.*

"I never got your name yesterday."

"My name is Kayla Nighthawk."

"Nighthawk?" Ohg raised an eyebrow.

"Since no one knows who my father was, I use my mother's last name."

Ohg stared hard. Suspicion etched into the slant of his mouth.

A deep rumbling interrupted their conversation, followed by the incongruous scent of crushed magnolias.

A voice boomed from above. "In the name of Lord Shiva, symbol of grace and love, I think you should give her a chance!"

A blur of machinery loomed over them, and Kayla dropped into a defensive crouch. Ohg's eyes narrowed at the sight of a large contraption descending from the sky. A huge creature straddled the back of the machine. The Monads faltered for the first time in their project.

Ohg waved for their attention. "This is one of Jesus' angels, sent from Heaven to help us all!" They sighed in relief and continued their rock hauling.

"You know I'm a Hindu, Ohg," the creature said as the machine neared.

"This is no joke, Ganesh!" Ohg shouted. The machine settled onto the ground, and Kayla blanched at the sight of the enormous, ten-foot-tall creature sitting atop it. With golden-hued skin, the head and tusks of an elephant, the body of a corpulent man, and four arms—it seemed like something a child might conjure in a dream. Around his neck hung a wreath of magnolias.

"You're the god Ganesha," Kayla said. "I've seen carvings of you on the carts of the Hindu traders in Potemia."

The giant rotated the grip on the right handlebar, and the great machine gave a final rumble, expelling incense-laden fumes from chrome pipes that twisted like horns. Then the engine went silent. Ganesh swung his silk-swathed legs off his machine and placed his hands palm to palm in front of his chest and enormous stomach.

The Hindu God bowed. "Namaste. I'm honored that you recognize me, my dear." Elaborate designs tattooed the center of his forehead and descended his long trunk. Bands of gold wrapped around his curved tusks like flattened serpents.

Would anything ever make sense again?

"I'm Kayla." She returned his bow awkwardly.

"What the hell are you *doing*?" Ohg shouted at the giant, who cowered before the diminutive figure half his height, and a tenth his weight.

"I wanted to help." Ganesh shielded his face with his trunk. "I finished fixing this old Z-12 VBat chopper and thought this a the perfect excuse for a test ride—"

"Are you crazy?" Ohg shouted. "You could be *killed*!"

The giant god shrugged.

Kayla looked back and forth between them. "You said it didn't matter if—"

"That's his *actual* body!"

Ganesh nodded in an exaggerated expression of guilt. His great ears flopped back and forth and set his many earrings jingling.

"And he's wanted by the authorities!"

"Well, so are you," the Hindu god said.

"Which is why I'm *not* using my real body to come here!"

Kayla's mind swam and she swayed unsteadily. *I don't know if I can take any more.*

Ohg threw his arms in the air while Ganesh assumed a pose of contrition. Ohg paced while Kayla stared at the elephant/man/god in open-mouthed wonder. When Ohg turned away, Ganesh smiled and winked at her, careful to replace the look of solicitude the moment the blond boy's gaze swung toward him.

"Don't you think you're overreacting just a little?" Ganesh asked. "Patrols ended hundreds of years ago. No one cares about Earth or Gene-Freaks anymore."

"What are Gene—" Kayla started to ask.

"And I want it to stay that way!" Ohg shouted. "If they find this standard-issue travel-body I'm wearing, they will assume it is someone from Ixtalia joyriding with a black market body—but if they find you, a Gene-Freak Outlaw with an implanted Mind-Link, our secret will be blown. They'll realize we have access to—"

"I would never let them find out," Ganesh said and removed a metal disc from a pouch fastened to his belt.

"A fission bomb!" Ohg's face twisted with fury.

Ganesh wilted. "I found it hiding in an old military stockpile, the poor dear."

"You know weapons of any kind are forbidden in Middilgard."

"What is Mid—"

"I never took it there, I promise," Ganesh said to Ohg. "I store it outside and only bring it with me when searching the undercity for bike parts. In case the government ever found me."

"I feel a lot better knowing you'd be vaporized," Ohg said sarcastically.

"Are you saying he's not really a god?" Kayla asked.

Ohg threw his hands in the air. "Of course not!"

"You know why I had to come, don't you?" Ganesh lowered his gaze and opened his hands in a gesture of helplessness.

"Yes, I know," Ohg said. "There's nothing we can do at this point, so you might as well take her with you to Middilgard, but no detours."

The giant snapped to attention and saluted with all four of his arms.

"Take me where?" Kayla asked. "I don't understand any of—"

"Listen," Ohg said. "I'm offering to take you to a Gene-Freak haven where you'll be safe—on a trial basis."

She hesitated. *What is a Gene-Freak? And safe from what?*

"It's your choice to come with us or stay here," Ohg said. "I don't have time to stand around chatting, so a simple yes or no will suffice."

I don't understand any of this, but what choice do I have if I want to find answers?

"I'll go with you," Kayla said, "if you promise to tell the Monads the story of Jesus each morning."

"You're certain that story is the truth?"

She averted her eyes from his probing gaze. "If there's a chance it's true, they deserve to hear The Word of God and decide for themselves if they want to follow Him."

"Well, it's no matter to me," Ohg said. "They'll believe whatever I tell them, and if you think your God is capricious enough to grant them entry into Heaven based solely on my whim … then fine, I promise."

Ganesh mounted his flying machine and lifted her onto the seat in front of him. A carving of a mouse perched on the handle bars.

How could I forget!

"Puck!" she called, and her little brown friend emerged from among the rocks, scurried up her leg, and settled into a coat pocket.

"Puck is also from Potemia," Kayla said.

Ohg raised an eyebrow as Ganesh revved the engine in preparation for takeoff. The rumbling vibrated through the ground and set small stones to bouncing. The Monads dashed after a few small rocks that rolled down their growing hill.

"Aren't you coming with us?" Kayla shouted to Ohg.

"I'm already there," he said.

Then the machine rocketed into the sky.

Chapter 10

Kayla held tight to Ganesh. Ohg and the Monads receded beneath them, their clearing a tiny smudge within the vast, deserted city. How long would they move their rocks back and forth? Centuries, millennia, or until the sun burned itself cold?

"Hold on!" Ganesh gunned the throttle, and the machine surged forward. The mounting speed whipped Kayla's hair into a whirlwind until Ganesh pressed a button and the hurricane vanished. A glowing energy encircled them, blocking the rushing air like an invisible glass capsule.

Behind them, the milky dome of the Wall stretched into the heavens.

The bike rose higher into the air, until even the pyramids shrank to dots. Kayla gasped at the height and pressed herself against Ganesh's silken vest.

"Worry not, little one," Ganesh said. "I will keep you from falling."

She forced a smile and surveyed the astonishing view below. Here and there, mountains rose up, but the unbroken city flowed over the peaks like an unstoppable tsunami of concrete and skyscrapers. "Is everything covered?" she asked.

"The Grand Canyon of North America, the Mariana Trench on the Ocean floor, and a few dozen other places were set aside, but no one goes there any longer, of course."

"The city continues underwater?"

"You can see for yourself." Ganesh pointed to a distant shoreline looming on the horizon. The city plunged beneath the waves, and the cycle dipped lower, skimming over the surface. Great domed structures shimmered in the depths. Most had broken to pieces, but a few still gleamed like great bubbles beneath the protective waters.

"The average number of housing units rose to twenty per person as robotic construction took over."

"Why would anyone need more than one house?"

Ganesh scratched his head. "Economic growth, I think, but I don't really know."

"What about the whales and fish in the ocean?"

The elephant-god shook his head. "All dead, long ago."

The waves passed in a blur. Within a few minutes, the far shore rushed toward them. When the ruined metropolis surfaced, Ganesh angled upward and continued overland.

A plume of smoke rose in the distance.

"Is that where people live?" she asked.

"Only a robotic mining operation. A few dozen remain scattered around the planet."

Ganesh made a wide detour around the smoke.

"Anything you'd like to be seeing, my dear?" he asked. "I could take you to a great tower rising from the highest mountain in the world into lower Earth Orbit, though it doesn't reach quite that far anymore, after being abandoned like everything else in the real world."

"The real world?"

"This one—the world of atoms." Kayla's mouth opened for a follow-up question, but Ganesh prattled on like a tour guide who couldn't be bothered with details. "How about the Great Yellowstone Volcano? It's still smoking, you know."

"Didn't Ohg say no detours?"

"Ohg is always worrying." Ganesh laughed. "Which is why he's survived so long, I suppose, but sometimes he goes overboard on security."

Kayla frowned. "Security from what?"

Ganesh's eyes grew sad. "The government destroyed most Gene-Freaks like us after outlawing the practice four hundred and fifty-six years ago, but a few of us survived the Great Purge."

"Are you saying that you're—?"

"I'm four hundred and seventy-three years old." Ganesh frowned at a sudden engine vibration. He smacked the side with his enormous fist, and the rattling ceased. "That darn flywheel. I could use the molecular printer to replace it, but that seems like cheating." He patted the side of the machine. "Is that better, dear?"

"Why is Ohg worried, if the government has stopped looking for you?"

"Gene-Freak hunting trips, for one, but that ended long ago, mostly."

"Because everyone died?"

"No one has died in centuries, and the human population is over sixty billion."

"Sixty ... *billion?* But where is everyone, then?"

"In Ixtalia," Ganesh said.

What had the little metal robot said? *Ixtalia is the place to be, Ixtalia is for you and me!*

"Where is Ixtalia?" Kayla asked.

Ganesh frowned. "Where? I guess I never thought of Ixtalia like that. Ixtalia is … nowhere—or rather, everywhere. That's it. Ixtalia is everywhere and nowhere!" He smiled, glad to have settled the question.

Kayla shook her head. She'd have to wait to ask Ohg about this. "If you're sure it's okay. I guess I've always dreamed of seeing the Holy Land." Ganesh stared blankly. "Israel, Bethlehem, Jerusalem—"

"Right!" Ganesh exclaimed, eager to comply with her request. He started turning, but then paused. "I am forgetting … too dangerous. All the radiation, you know … from the Nuclear Holy War."

Kayla slumped, and a void opened within her soul. How could God have allowed such a thing?   "We'd better just go to … wherever it is you're taking me," she said.

"Okay, then. Next stop, Middilgard!" Ganesh continued on his northeasterly route. As they flashed across a mountain range, the city below thinned into lone buildings, then reassembled into an impenetrable mass on the other side. Ganesh decreased speed and angled earthward. "Middilgard's entrance is beneath that—"

An alarm flashed on the control panel. Ganesh swiveled his head and locked onto several specks diving toward them.

"Government drones," he said. "Hold on!"

He gunned the engine and plunged toward the city, jerking the machine to the left and right like a fleeing rabbit.

Kayla peeked around his body at five gleaming objects gaining fast.

"We can't outrun them!" she shouted.

"Our one chance is the surface." Ganesh angled the bike into a screaming dive. "Those older models are controlled by speed-of-light radio transmissions. They'll react slowly in tight maneuvers. We wouldn't stand a chance against current drones."

The ground drew closer, and their machine vibrated and jerked from the stress.

"Who's controlling them?"

"The government decommissioned such antiquated models centuries ago, so they must be joyriders going Gene-Freak hunting."

A burst of energy flashed by and detonated on the ground. One of the skyscrapers toppled in slow motion. Ganesh steered right for it.

"They're almost on us!" Kayla shouted.

The bike swooped under the collapsing building as the drones reached them. Three of the drones pulled up, while two others stayed on their tail.

Kayla screamed as chunks of concrete hurtled toward them. But their energy field plowed through, and they emerged safely on the other side—only to have Ganesh violently bank back the way he'd come.

The building groaned as it fell, breaking into pieces like a shattered clay pot filled with gravel.

As predicted, the drones reacted with a slight delay. By the time they completed their turn and followed, Ganesh flashed from under the avalanche. The mountain of steel and concrete crushed the drones in a double fireball.

The three remaining drones circled and sped after them. Ganesh's machine swooped through the streets, dodging left and right. The drones lost ground.

"I think we've lost one of them," Kayla shouted, looking behind.

Ganesh pointed to the missing drone soaring above. The other two split up, leaving only one on their tail.

"Despite their delayed reaction time, their coordination is masterful!" Ganesh shouted.

The missing drone streaked around a corner in front of them. Ganesh yanked the bike into an alley. The bike's energy field tore into the face of the alley wall, expelling a trail of sparks that sizzled earthward. The entire machine shuddered, and the force field strobed, then vanished, leaving them at the mercy of a hundred-mile-per-hour wind.

"Vishnu's toes!" Ganesh wrestled with the machine to keep it aloft. The third drone swooped in from above, trapping them. A flash of light erupted, and Ganesh dived toward the ground. Kayla screamed. They whooshed through a ragged hole in the street and into the undercity. The first drone clipped the opening and exploded. The roar of the other two drones announced the continued pursuit.

The bike's limited headlights barely kept pace with their speed. Ganesh had fractions of seconds to react to the twists and turns of the underground city. The drones gained on them.

"Hurry!" Kayla shouted.

A ball of red fire missed them by inches and tore into the ceiling ahead.

"Look out!" she screamed as they entered a waterfall of rock. Ganesh maneuvered frantically, avoiding slabs of the falling ceiling. As he dodged the last section, a corner of the boulder clipped their machine and tossed them into the far wall.

The engine slid across the stone and bathed them in sparks. Ganesh wrestled clear and opened the throttle. The bike surged forward under the last of the collapsing ceiling.

The drones veered into a side corridor to avoid entombment.

"They're gone!" she shouted.

The abused engine shuddered, coughed, and died. The machine plummeted toward the ground, its forward momentum aiming it straight at a wall, where the corridor branched at right angles.

"Hold on!" Ganesh encased her in all four arms as they crash-landed. The metal undercarriage shrieked across the concrete and bathed them in sparks. Ganesh jumped free and rolled. The bike fire-balled into the wall.

They came to a stop. Ganesh groaned.

Kayla scrambled free of his arms and knelt beside him. "Are you alright?" She helped him to his feet. Numerous minor cuts covered his body, and his upper left arm hung at his side, broken in several places.

"Are you okay, Kayla?" His face twisted with worry.

"I'm fine." In her pocket, Puck was also okay, if a bit skittish. Ganesh examined her arms and legs for any wounds, but his body had absorbed most of the impact. He exhaled a sigh of relief—and burst into tears.

"Ganesh, what's wrong?"

"I'm the worst protector—"

"You saved my life!"

Ganesh straightened and wiped away his tears. "I haven't saved it yet, but I will."

"We've got to run!" she said.

Ganesh shook his head. "If we run, we will both die."

The distant echo of the drones grew louder.

"We at least have to try," Kayla said.

Ganesh grasped her hands and gazed into her eyes. "Long ago, I failed to protect someone I loved. I've waited over four hundred years for my chance at atonement." The Hindu god removed the fission bomb from his belt. "Kayla of Potemia, even though we've just met, I'm asking you to help me redeem myself."

"Oh, Ganesh!" Kayla threw her arms about his neck and hugged him. The giant hoisted her behind a slab of fallen concrete, and the echoing roar grew to thunder.

"Promise me in the name of your god," Ganesh said, "that you will remain here while I reclaim my soul."

Tears covered her face, and her lower lip trembled. How could she refuse him? "Okay, I promise."

Ganesh hugged her one last time and lumbered toward the burning motorcycle.

The drones rounded the corner and hovered. The four-armed Hindu god walked toward them with his fist held aloft.

"You are in violation of the Genetic Purity Act," a commanding voice boomed from the lead drone. "Surrender at once!"

Ganesh continued walking.

The front of the larger drone glowed red. Ganesh's hand opened, revealing the fission bomb.

Please, Lord, if you exist, give me a sign. Kayla clasped her hands in prayer.

Ganesh's finger moved to a button at the center of the glowing disc.

She closed her eyes and deep furrows of concentration creased her forehead. "Please, Lord, I'm begging you." A rush of warmth suffused her body.

The voice of the drone echoed off the walls. "Drop the weapon or we will—"

Kayla's mind entered the drones. In an instant, she identified the power source, the key.

Ganesh's finger reached the button ...

Both drones went dark and fell to the floor with a dull clang.

The giant stood motionless for several heartbeats, his finger remaining atop the button.

When Kayla joined him, he pulled his finger slowly away from the button and replaced the safety cover.

"That was ... unexpected," he said. "Did you see something that might explain—"

"Yes," Kayla said. "I prayed to God, and he answered."

Ganesh stood silent for a long moment. "Are you being serious, my dear?"

"I've never been more serious. I prayed harder than I ever have, and He sent a miracle. He guided me into the machines and shut them off."

Ganesh sagged. "Then I didn't save you after all."

"Two gods saved me together!"

"What a lovely thought." Ganesh laughed, until his eyes fell on the burning wreck of his flying machine.

"Maybe we should go, in case more arrive?" Kayla said.

"Right!" Ganesh touched a crystal around his neck, and it blazed to life, illuminating everything within a twenty-yard cone. He led the way into the undercity, and Kayla followed.

"The city stretches across the entire Earth," Ganesh said, acting the tour guide once again. "One could ride a train around the globe in a matter of hours."

Ganesh led them through the maze of streets, stairways, and passages without hesitation.

"You must spend a lot of time here," she said.

"Not really. I'm accessing the building schematics in the Old Earth Archives. They are quite detailed."

"Archives from where?"

Ganesh tapped his skull. "Neural Implant—or Mind-Link, as most call it. Ohg installed it for me centuries ago. That's how Ohg controls the body you saw him using with the Monads."

"But this is your real body?"

His great stomach vibrated with his laugh. "I know it's hard to believe, but, yes, this is the real me!"

Kayla's follow-up question died on her lips as they entered an enormous underground stadium stretching a mile across and rising a quarter of a mile high to a domed peak. Here and there the roof had fallen away. Shafts of sunlight extended downward like magical columns of illumination.

"This is where teams of mind-athletes played Filador. Hundreds of thousands of such stadiums exist across the planet. They represent the physical world's precursor to Ixtalia's Filadrux of today."

"What's a mind-athlete?" she asked.

"Just what it sounds like. An athletics purely of the mind. No one had any idea what body they'd be assigned or what obstacles they'd face until the moment before the match."

"But how … Isn't that unfair?"

"That's the fun of it." His eyes blazed with the fervor of a true fan. "Each team remained equally in the dark until assigned an identical combination of bodies moments before the contest. Creating a challenge of both strategy and teamwork."

"I don't understand …"

They descended to the vast stadium floor. Ganesh gazed about with face aglow. "Of course, Ixtalia's Filadrux is even more creative, what with the freedom to rewrite the underlying laws of physics. Ohg is an absolute master of the game, though he would be banned from competition if anyone got a glimpse of his DNA." Ganesh paused at her blank stare. He smacked his forehead with one of his hands. "I'm sorry. I forgot you're—"

"From Potemia," she said. "That's becoming my motto."

The hum of an approaching drone caused her to stiffen. One of the dark tunnels feeding into the stadium glowed, and the sound intensified.

"Hurry!" Ganesh ran to the side of the stadium and hid behind some debris.

Kayla crouched beside him and peered through a gap. The drone flashed into the stadium and then hovered in place, a beam of light scanning the vast space.

"A Seeker," Ganesh whispered.

Unlike the previous drones, spindly metal arms hung off its core like tentacles. The circle of its spotlight approached their hiding place, and Kayla closed her eyes.

The beam paused on the pile of rubble hiding them, its brightness penetrating her eyelids. *Please, God, make us invisible.*

After a moment, the light moved on, and Kayla opened her eyes. The drone flew across the stadium and into another tunnel. The sound and light faded away. Ganesh let out a great sigh and led her through a trapdoor in the stadium's floor. They descended a series of passageways connected to the city's sewer system. It had long ago dried out.

"That was close," Ganesh said. "We better hurry before it backtracks."

"What was that thing?"

"Basically, a robot, though a very old one." Ganesh scratched his belly. "We would have had no chance against a modern Seeker Drone, but I still don't understand how it could have missed us. Even those old models had heat sensors."

A second answered prayer?

"Ganesh, how did you—I mean—where did you ...?"

"Who made me and why?"

Kayla nodded. *I hope I haven't offended him.*

"I don't mind telling you," Ganesh said, but lapsed into silence.

For a long moment, only the echoes of their footsteps violated the stillness.

"India," Ganesh said with a sigh of longing. "The smell of jasmine, of curry and incense. Of flowing silks, gurus, and the colors of the rainbow stitched into every heart that has ever gazed up the sacred Ganges. It gave birth to me, and it is where my soul will forever live."

"It sounds wonderful."

"It was ..." Ganesh gazed into the darkness without seeing, lost in his visions of the past. "By the mid-twenty-first century, India had ascended to one of the leading scientific centers of the world. Researchers flocked to its advanced labs from across the globe, fleeing the ultra-conservative laws in the United States and elsewhere that restricted genetic research."

Kayla nodded. *He's describing exactly what the founder predicted would happen.*

"The educated Indian elite and genetic corporations prospered even while the vast underclass of destitute Indians fueled rampant crime and rioting mobs.

His face grew troubled, haunted almost, and he stopped walking. "I've never understood how someone can feel content with vast riches while people starve just a few miles away. Or even a thousand miles away, for that matter. Do you know the answer to this?"

"I honestly don't," Kayla said.

Ganesh resumed walking. "Rather than sharing their wealth, the new Brahmins of Science sought protection through technology. And so this technological aristocracy created creatures like me to serve as genetically engineered protectors."

"You're a bodyguard?"

"And a companion," Ganesh said. "Creating me in the form of Lord Ganesha seemed natural since the real god had guarded the entrance to the bathing chamber of his mother, the Goddess Parvati. Because her husband, the Lord Shiva, had been gone so many years, he remained unaware of the existence of his son. The great Lord returned and found the boy barring the way to his wife's bath, and cut off Ganesha's head in a fit of rage. When the weeping Parvati enlightened Shiva as to the identity of the slain boy, he ordered his guards to remove the head of the first living being they encountered, which happened to be an elephant. With this, he restored Ganesha's life and put him in charge of his personal troops."

"But that's a bizarre myth," Kayla said. "People can't believe that actually happened, can they?"

"Am I not proof that such a thing is possible?"

"That's science, not a true miracle like bringing someone back to life."

"Are you saying that God cannot do what man has?"

Kayla frowned. "I guess He could do anything …"

"The faithful in India believed the story of Lord Ganesha's resurrection as deeply as other people do the story of a man named Jesus who is said to have risen from the dead."

"But that's different," Kayla said. "There's tons of historical records of Jesus rising from the dead."

"Ah, I see." A smile played across Ganesh's lips. "And have you seen these records yourself?"

"Well, no, but …" After an awkward silence, Kayla touched his wrist. "I didn't mean any offense."

Ganesh smiled and scratched a shoulder with a tusk. "None taken, my dear."

"Who did you end up guarding?" Kayla asked.

"My creators made me as a prototype of what they hoped would someday be a popular production model. The company's founder had so much confidence in my revolutionary instinct modifications that he assigned me to his six-year-old son, Sangi."

His elephant lids half closed, and he drew in a breath. "I can still smell the incense and offerings of flowers and food at the Ganesh Chaturthi Festival. I led the procession of Ganapatyas, with little Sangi proudly riding on my shoulders. Had anyone tried harming us, a vengeful mob would have torn them apart."

Ganesh sighed.

"Those were times of hope, especially with the promise of immortality on the horizon. Due to the fear of side effects, Gene-Freaks served as the ideal test subjects for the EL Pill, short for Eternal Life."

"They used you to experiment on?" Kayla said. "That seems completely unethical."

"Humans considered us products." Ganesh shrugged. "It also made economic sense to protect one's property and investment from depreciation."

"So you and Ohg are immortal?"

"Gene-Freaks don't age, but we can be killed like anyone else, so we're not really immortal."

They entered one of the smaller side tunnels, and claustrophobia constricted her chest for the first time.

"Sangi was lucky to have you as a protector," Kayla said.

The Hindu god lowered his head, and all four of his shoulders slumped. "Five years I served as friend and protector to Sangi, and they are still the happiest years of my life. It shocked me when the first wild-eyed zealot called me an abomination. It was at the harvest festival of Makar Sankranti, which marks the season of the sun's return journey to the north."

Ganesh stopped walking, all four hands extending outward like a double crucifixion. "The man hurled insults and even a few stones, saying my kind would destroy all of humanity. It was my first encounter with the Neo-Luddites."

Kayla's heart jolted. The Founder of Potemia had led the Neo-Luddites.

"Before I could say a word, the crowd came to our defense, driving the radical off with stones. But each time it happened, fewer people defended us, until the day arrived when the mob joined the condemnation."

His hands fell to his sides, and he resumed walking through the ever-narrowing tunnel. "Gene-Freaks became the one technology that everyone agreed had gone too far. Soon I couldn't leave the house without a barrage of rocks and curses following me. Rather than shielding my young charge from danger, I attracted it like a lodestone."

Kayla took his hand in hers. *Poor Ganesh. I know what it's like to be an outcast.*

"Sangi sensed the change in his parents and showed me the proof that I'd soon be sent away."

"But maybe you interpreted it wrong. Maybe they intended setting you free?"

"Freeing a Gene-Freak was illegal," Ganesh said. "Sending me away was a polite way of saying I would be killed, the prototype having proved itself unpopular with the public and of no further use."

"Whatever the law said, I think it's a horrible thing to do," Kayla said.

"I would have allowed them to kill me, except that Sangi begged me to flee. I did so to spare him the devastation my death would have caused him."

The tunnel merged into a natural cavern that must have once been an underground river. Here and there, it branched, but Ganesh didn't hesitate as he led them through the organic maze.

"How did you survive on your own?"

"I wandered the ever-expanding cities of India, always traveling by night, keeping to the shadows. I foraged in the trash heaps alongside cows and pigs, since my stomach was that of a man, rather than an elephant. Occasionally, religious Hindus mistook me for the real God Ganesha and gave me food. Despite everything, I still believe in the essential goodness of humans."

He scratched the base of his voluminous left ear. "Eventually, a brothel in Bangladesh employed me as a bouncer. I heard rumors of wars and great upheavals in society, but I ignored it all."

Ganesh came to a stop next to an opening in the main cavern's wall. "That's strange," he said, peering into it with a frown. "The archives don't show this tunnel."

Peeking out of Kayla's pocket, Puck chattered and sniffed the air in an agitated manner.

"Maybe it formed naturally?"

"You can see that the stone has been scraped away. It almost looks like … teeth-marks." Ganesh half-stepped inside. "Did you see that? Like a shadow retreating."

The hairs on the back of Kayla's neck rose.

"You promised Ohg no detours," she said.

Ganesh finally shrugged and continued on his original course. Kayla let out her breath and followed him.

"Where was I?" Ganesh asked, rubbing his temple with his trunk.

"The … the brothel."

"That's right! Most of the girls came from poor families who sold their daughters to pay for food or the education of a prized son. But the higher-priced clients preferred Gene-Freaks, both male and female varieties. I guarded one girl in particular—the most expensive prostitute in the entire brothel and accounting for eighty percent of profits."

"How was she different than a normal woman?"

"She had been created with all the physical attributes men desire, of course, but the one thing that drives a man truly wild is a woman's genuine desire for him in return. It is something that cannot be faked. It turned Fatima into something that men couldn't live without once they'd had her. Some lost entire fortunes to her and committed suicide when they could no longer feed their addiction."

"Did she try to seduce you?" Kayla asked.

"I was genetically engineered without a reproductive impulse. That's why they hired me as Fatima's protector in the first place. Who else could be trusted?" Ganesh shook his head. "As a consequence, Fatima's life had been lonely, and she became like a sister to me."

Kayla's insides twisted as she pictured Elias leering at her. "How is it possible to desire a man who repulses you? It seems a psychological impossibility."

"The scientists at Monsanto-Gen altered Fatima's genes so that the slightest hint of desire in a man's eyes—any man—flipped a switch in her brain. In that instant, her need to mate and please him in any way necessary became a compulsion akin to some animals who are driven to mate even to the point of death."

"That's monstrous!"

"Which is how most humans feel about us even today."

"I didn't mean you, Ganesh."

"I know," he said with a forgiving smile. "But as scientists pushed the boundaries of genetic engineering, fear and resentment grew. What wife or husband could compete with a genetically engineered mistress, nanny, or bodyguard?

The tunnel narrowed to the point that Ganesh bent nearly double. *I hope he knows where he's going.*

Ganesh lowered his head as he trudged forward, and an oversized tear spatted against the floor. "The Neo-Luddites eventually targeted my creator because of his work in genetic engineering. They fire-bombed his house, with Sangi and the rest of the family inside."

Ganesh stopped and squeezed his eyes closed.

"I'm so sorry." Kayla placed a hand on his wrist. *So that's what you seek redemption for.*

He shook his head with a great flap of his ears and continued walking. "The final straw came when researchers unlocked the secret to enlarging the human brain. If Pures increased their own offspring's intelligence, it would render the current generation obsolete." Ganesh sighed. "The Genetic Purification Laws passed on April 7th, 2060. The world-wide agreement outlawed genetic modifications of any kind, and pronounced a recall of all Gene-Freaks currently in circulation.

"Special government units purged tens of millions of us within weeks. Even religious leaders proclaimed us abominations, saying we had no souls since we weren't created by God. The resultant genocide dwarfed all others."

"You must have escaped, since you're here now."

"Fatima and I had been shackled in a police transport when one of the officers struck her across the face with particular cruelty, drawing the blood that marked her only offense."

The enormous muscles of his arms tensed and stood out like the knots of an oak tree. What a terror he must seem to ordinary men when angered.

"I broke free of my chains and left the transport in ruins, but killed no one. The next months turned desperate as we eluded the Purification Squads scouring the planet."

Ganesh suddenly opened his cavernous mouth and yawned. "Fatima used her talents to obtain food and money as we smuggled ourselves into China."

Kayla yawned as well. "Why don't we rest here a few moments?" she said, and they sat with their backs to the wall.

"The Neo-Luddite Plague swept the globe like a divine curse," Ganesh said softly. "Thousands of bloated bodies choked every river, and the cries of agony …" Ganesh wrapped all four of his arms around his chest and shivered. "We shunned people until the greatest scientist of the time, Reinhold Watts, developed a cure. Fatima seduced one of the government health workers and obtained several doses for us. By then, society had collapsed, and no one bothered hunting Gene-Freaks any longer. We wandered north through a world transformed."

Ganesh spoke softer and softer, his head slumping onto his chest. "Who would have thought that civilization hung by such a tenuous thread? Who could have predicted the speed of mankind's barbaric reversion?"

His voice fell to a whisper.

Kayla's vision blurred. Puck slept in her pocket after the long day of adventures, and she yearned to follow his example. But curiosity forced one more question, "How did you survive?"

The giant summoned enough energy to say, "Ohg … he found us …"

Ganesh slid to the floor of the tunnel, his snores echoing off the cold stone walls.

Something's not right here.

As the light from Ganesh's crystal faded, the elephant-god mumbled in his sleep, "Ohg saved us all …"

Kayla's eyelids became weights she couldn't lift. They narrowed to slits as wraith-like forms surrounded them. Kayla's limbs trembled, but rejected the instructions her brain transmitted.

Hands that might have been human, but for their unnatural length and skeletal thinness, lifted Kayla and the massive Ganesh. They floated on a mist of dreams back the way they'd come.

Chapter 11

Once again, Kayla's dreams forced her into the body and perceptions of Peter, though his eyes seemed closed. She felt a deceleration and his eyes opened. The same passengers surrounded him on the train as her last dream. The cat-eyed attendant busied herself collecting VR helmets as the vehicle hissed to a stop. Out the window sprawled a vast underground terminal, with hundreds of other trains loading and unloading swarms of passengers.

This dream must be a continuation of my last one. Was God showing her these things? Could they be clues in her search for what she'd become and what purpose, if any, He intended for her? But what possible connection could she have to this man who had lived nearly five hundred years before her birth?

Another attendant spoke into a handheld device that projected her voice throughout the compartment. "We have arrived at Chicago's Union Station. Thank you for traveling with us, and it has been a pleasure serving you."

The passengers collected their luggage, and filed out.

As Peter shuffled toward the exits with everyone else, he glanced back at a man in a charcoal-gray suit talking to Cat-eyes. The man's dark-brimmed hat set him apart from the passengers. The attendant stared at Peter as she spoke, and the man's cobalt eyes turned toward him.

Peter's heart pounded as he hustled off the train and onto the underground platform, swept along with the crowd like a twig in a flood and then onto a moving stairway. The man in the dark hat struggled through the crowd behind him.

Emerging into the bright streets on the surface, Peter entered the towering canyons of the city called Chicago. To Kayla, the buildings seemed smaller than the abandoned wrecks she'd seen crumbling outside the Wall, but they dwarfed the largest trees within Potemia. Ceaseless holographic advertisements flashed and throbbed their consumptive demands, while the pedestrians flowed as if released from a great dam of humanity.

Peter glanced over his shoulder. The man still followed. Peter dove into the flood of pedestrians.

"Not now," he mumbled. "Not when we're so close!"

He crossed a bridge over a river swarming with boats, then turned left down a canyon of a street, then right, then left again. A glance back, searching the crowd. The man with the hat was gone. Peter expelled a breath and walked on.

It wasn't the unprecedented music, smells, strange clothes, or bizarre technological gadgets that seemed odd—it was the perfection of the people. A spattering of children and a few bizarrely dressed teenagers occasionally interrupted the crowd's ubiquitous uniformity, but no one appeared older than their mid-twenties. Each face and body conveyed such perfectly proportioned elegance that it gave her a vague sense of unease, the self-conscious inadequacy one feels standing next to the most beautiful person they know.

A man's transparent, twenty-foot-tall head hovered in mid-air above the central square of a plaza, its commanding voice saying: "The year 2069 will mark the seminal moment for lasting peace on this planet!"

The solid jaw and mesmerizing blue eyes conjured images of some warrior-prophet of antiquity. It was the unmistakable visage of Colonel Colrev, the man who had ordered Peter to kill the two Iraqi children long before.

Peter came to a stop and gazed at the giant head. Across the bottom of the hologram glowed the words, *General Colrev, US Secretary of Thought Crimes.* Passersby smiled as they glanced at the commanding face looming above them. Many stopped to listen, exclaiming things like, "Appointing General Colrev was the best thing the president ever did!" and "He'll destroy those Neo-Luddite fanatics!"

Colrev's eyes hardened. "My fellow Americans, after the tragic events in the city of San Diego, we must take proactive steps for the security and protection of our loved ones. We will no longer wait. We will no longer be victims. We will identify the very thoughts that lead to such acts beforehand!"

Murmurs simmered within the crowd.

"To the human race, the Neo-Luddite vision of a mythical Eden without science or technology is as dangerous as any Gene-Freak. It is ironic that these terrorists use our own science against us to reverse all the progress human society has made though our long climb out of barbarity. If we hope to retain all the miraculous inventions born of the fruits of our minds, we must use technology itself to identify those who would misuse it. No genetic test can identify this existential threat, so we must go to the source—the human brain!"

Peter surveyed the crowd staring up at the hologram. Unblinking, worshiping faces surrounded him. Kayla had seen such expressions during sermons of Minister Coglin. In both cases, fear added the key ingredient.

"To those who would use the outdated notions of Privacy Rights to protect these degenerates, I ask you to consider the rights of the thousands of dead citizens of San Diego."

The hologram cycled through a series of images of charred bodies lying amidst the ruins of blasted buildings. The crowd stood transfixed by the gruesome scenes as General Colrev's voice continued.

"The heretics that perpetrated this act will either reform their thoughts and live in the modern world, or die in its prisons."

The blackened form of a child embracing what looked like its mother formed the final image. It morphed into the general as he spoke. "These Neo-Luddite scum are not true Christians or environmentalists, but terrorists, plain and simple!"

Cheers rose from the crowd, and many held their fists aloft. But here and there, a few people remained silent.

Peter turned, but halted at a strange sight. A woman and a man, both wearing white robes and sandals, walked across the street and stood beneath the giant head. The woman had gray hair and deep wrinkles etching her face, while a long white beard marked the man's advanced age. Their appearance set them in stark contrast to the universal youth surrounding them. The man's sign proclaimed: *Technology dehumanizes, enslaves, and corrupts.* The woman's sign read: *God's creation is more glorious than any machine!*

The crowd encircled them.

"Technology can be stopped!" the bearded man shouted, his white robes lending him the appearance of some Old Testament prophet. "Return to nature and a simpler life, where you won't be slaves to the machines!"

"Medical technology saved my life!" shouted a fashionably dressed woman in the crowd. Like everyone else, she looked no older than twenty-five.

"You're Neo-Luddites!" a young man in an iridescent suit yelled. "You're responsible for San Diego!"

The bearded man shook his head. "We oppose violence of any kind and do not support the Neo-Luddites."

"Liar! You're a fanatic!" someone in the crowd shouted. "Why else would you look old?"

The gray-haired woman extended a hand as if in supplication. "Don't you see that the collapse of civilization is inevitable if technology continues destroying nature? Act now, before it's too late."

"You would return us to the slavery of nature," shouted a young man wearing a form-fitting outfit that displayed every muscle of his athletic physique. "Science has freed us from disease, starvation, and ignorance!"

As the crowd grew, its collective anger magnified, with mild-mannered men and women in conservative office attire shouting insults and spitting at the white-robed protesters. A woman pushing a baby in a hovering carriage snatched a bottle from her child and flung it at the white-robed woman, hitting her in the head and soaking her in milk.

The disembodied head of General Colrev continued, unaware of the near-riot fermenting beneath his square chin. "In the coming days, many of you will be visited by officers tasked with rooting out those among us with aberrant thoughts and beliefs so we never experience another San Diego, or worse."

A man standing in front of Peter leaned close to his girlfriend and said, "How do we know Colrev himself didn't stage San Diego so we'd give up the right to our own thoughts?"

His girlfriend gave a sharp jerk on his hand and looked around. "Stop it, Bill—someone will hear you!"

A helicopter descended through the transparent talking head, and landed behind the white-robed environmentalists. Words on the side of the vehicle announced, 'POLICE—Protect and Serve.' An officer emerged and frowned.

"Lock the degenerates up!" someone shouted. The statuesque officer smiled heroically, ready to protect them from this assault of the elderly.

The side of the vehicle hissed upward, and a harness shot from the ship's innards like a giant's hand. In a flash, the elderly man hung bound and suspended in a fetal position, with face hooded and mouth gagged.

The old woman fled, and the officer smiled.

"Use the Exoskeleton!" someone in the crowd shouted.

"Ex-Oh! Ex-Oh! Ex-Oh!" the onlookers chanted.

The policeman spread his arms and legs wide, and numerous robotic appendages flashed from the interior of the ship and bound his entire body with an elaborate contraption resembling a metal skeleton. The cheers crescendoed when the black helmet snapped into place.

The old woman stumbled to a stop two hundred yards away. She gasped for breath and jerked her head about wildly, like a trapped rabbit. The officer crouched and then launched into a graceful ballistic arc. A few blasts of air from various points on his exoskeleton corrected his trajectory, and he landed with a thump, inches from the old woman.

The fugitive staggered, then fainted, and the crowd cheered.

After the unconscious woman joined the previously collected specimen in the police vehicle, the officer placed a helmet on each of their heads. A red light appeared on the front, and a synthesized voice intoned, "Anti-technology thoughts detected. Suspect found guilty and sentenced to thought-quarantine."

Peter's fingers balled into fists as the policeman received an ovation. Even the man in front of him who'd expressed doubts clapped, though with what seemed little enthusiasm.

A few eyes swiveled Peter's way.

"Clap, my love, you're attracting attention," a woman whispered in his ear. Peter's hands unclenched, and clapped until his invisibility returned.

"Let's go, Peter, this is no place for you," the soft voice said, and the woman's hands eased him away from the spectacle.

Peter turned, and gazed into an angelic face. "Thank you, Susan, I almost—"

"Don't blame them," the woman said as they headed into an alley. "When one controls nothing in their own life, any opportunity to strike out grants them a moment of illusory power."

Susan led the way through a rusted door and down a shadowed stairway. "To quote *him*," she said with reverence, " 'Technology has succeeded in *reducing human beings and many other living organisms to engineered products and mere cogs in the social machine.* ' "

"Words are but the spark," Peter said. "The only true propaganda will come from a deed great enough to purge the globe of technology."

Susan quoted the Gospel of John. *"Let us not love in word or in tongue, but in deed and truth."*

They reached the bottom of the stairway, and Susan slid her arms around Peter's neck.

"Later," Peter said, and disengaged from the beautiful revolutionary. "The message I have is urgent."

Susan grabbed his hand and squeezed tight. "Do you mean ...?"

He nodded and entered a room with half a dozen conspirators awaiting his arrival. Their eyes glowed with the fanaticism of zealots— reminding Kayla of the eyes of the minister as he preached End Times.

A dark-skinned man walked over. Peter embraced him, then held him at arm's length.

It was Tyrone, the black soldier who served with Peter in Iraq. Like Peter, he looked unchanged.

"It's good to see you, my friend," Peter said.

"It's been too long." Tyrone nodded and then walked back to the group standing beneath the single light hanging from the ceiling.

Peter straightened and lifted his chin. His eyes swept the small gathering. "Project Eden is a go."

Many smiled—a few laughed.

"It will wake them up!" said one.

"Across the entire world!" agreed another.

Peter beckoned to a man in the corner. "Professor Griffin."

An emaciated man in the shadows stood. The rims of spectacles circumnavigated his dark eyes, an oddity in this world of physical perfection. He removed a cylinder the size of his index finger and displayed it with the love of a sculptor unveiling his masterpiece.

"I created one for each of us." The skeletal hand placed the gleaming vial on the table. "Seven in all, plus an eighth as backup."

Tyrone shifted from foot to foot. "Isn't this premature?"

Peter gazed at him for an excruciating moment. Tyrone averted his eyes.

"You've been my friend for a long time." Peter's voice softened as he approached Tyrone and placed a hand on his shoulder. "I won't insult you by reciting arguments you know better than I. But I will ask how long you've had doubts."

"Not doubts." Tyrone gazed at his hands. "I can't help thinking of all the kids. Maybe it'll come to this someday, but shouldn't we at least keep trying to convince—"

"I can't say for certain why the Founder chose this moment," Peter said, "but I would guess it has to do with the new VR helmets."

Susan stepped next to Peter. "Our sources prove they double as memory probes. If any of us wears one, we'd be arrested within hours. Every Neo-Luddite we've ever come into contact with would be instantly known to the authorities."

"As well as the identity of our leader," Peter said. "San Diego was not our doing, so I suspect it is the government itself creating an excuse for compulsory thought interrogation. Delay is no longer an option."

"I'm sorry," Tyrone said, his hands trembling. "I know it's the only way. But I-I can't do it. I think you know why."

"Yes, I know why," Peter said.

Behind Tyrone, Professor Griffin stepped silently closer.

"You were the first I recruited," Peter said to Tyrone. "Please don't do this."

"My reason tells me you're right, but my heart just won't allow me to follow." Tyrone's shoulders slumped, and tears streamed down his cheeks. "I won't do anything to stand in your way, but I just can't be a part of this."

Peter hugged his friend. The professor raised a hypodermic needle and waited. Tears overflowed Peter's eyes and he nodded.

The professor stepped forward and inserted the needle into Tyrone's neck. Peter pinned his arms with the firmness of a battle-hardened soldier.

"What are you doing?" Tyrone gasped.

"I'm sorry." Sobs shook Peter as Tyrone's muscles seized. Peter eased his friend to the ground, and Susan brushed tears from Tyrone's cheek like a mother might for a child with a skinned knee.

"Why?" Tyrone said.

"I have no choice," Peter said, his voice choked with emotion. "There's too much at stake."

Tyrone's body spasmed, like an old clock wringing a few final ticks out of its broken mechanism.

"I wouldn't … betray—" Tyrone's face contorted and foam flecked his lips.

Peter shook with his sobs.

Susan used a cloth to wipe Tyrone's brow, then his lips. "If you don't believe fully, what choice would you have?"

Tyrone looked at Peter, and words gurgled to the surface with blood mixing into the foam. "Yes, I would have told …" His eyes rolled beneath his lids, and his body jerked several times like a bad actor. Then he went still. Peter clung to him and cried. No one in the room moved.

Susan brushed her fingers over Tyrone's eyes to close them. Peter grabbed her wrist and glared. "Don't touch him!"

Susan stared at him, face stricken. "I'm sorry, I …"

Peter let go of her wrist and looked back at Tyrone. "Brothers forever," he said.

"It had to be done," Susan said. "He confirmed it."

Peter climbed unsteadily to his feet. "He only said that to spare me."

Tears glistened in Susan's eyes as she reached a trembling hand toward him, then paused inches from his arm.

Peter turned to her and gently caressed the bruise forming on her wrist. "I hurt you," he said. "I'm sorry."

Susan kissed him and he embraced her. Everyone else in the room remained silent, the tension apparent in each face. Finally, Susan pulled away, walked to the table, and grabbed a vial.

A faint screaming in the distance grew in volume.

Each conspirator grabbed a vial and left.

The scream grew louder.

How can they ignore such a sound? Kayla thought.

Then she recognized the screams as her own. A force extracted her from Peter's mind.

Someone rocked her back and forth the way her mother might have done if she'd lived. Her screams subsided to a low moan. She opened her eyes to a golden face, a trunk, tusks, and wide, floppy ears.

"Ganesh?" she mumbled as the clouds obscuring her mind cleared. The giant smiled and set her on the ground.

"I had the same reaction when I awoke," he said.

"Where are we?" Kayla blinked, shook her head, and gazed about. Glowing balls lay scattered about, projecting strange shadows onto the ceilings and walls. The room resembled an enormous laboratory, with rusting cages to one side. Broken equipment littered the floor, covered in dust and debris.

Ganesh stood and brushed himself off. "I think it must be connected with that unmarked tunnel we passed."

Kayla took a step and tripped on the piles of debris. "What is all this …" Then her eyes focused on the vacant sockets of a skull lying at her feet. With a shout of disgust, she backed away and stumbled on another pile of human bones, skulls, and deteriorated clothing. She turned to Ganesh. A giant spider creature loomed behind him.

"Look out!" She grabbed the first object she could find and raised it like a club. Ganesh spun, and the ten-foot-tall arachnid came into the light.

Kayla screamed at the sight of a man's legless torso where the spider's body should have been. The face appeared human, though the bald skull bulged outward drastically, misaligning and distorting its features into those of a monster. Its eight arachnid legs protruded from the distorted body to span fifteen feet across. The hard claws at their ends made sharp clicks as they moved toward Ganesh.

"Leave him alone!" Kayla charged the creature.

"Kayla, wait!" Ganesh shouted, blocking her way with arms outstretched. "That's Ohg!"

She slid to a stop and stared at Ganesh. "Ohg?" Confusion wormed through her brain like a parasite. Had words lost all connection to reality? "I don't understand."

"Hello, Kayla," the misshapen face of the spider said. Kayla cringed back, and the creature's crooked mouth widened into a smile. "I guess that means another kiss is out of the question?"

Puck scurried out of her pocket, up one of the spider legs and into the outstretched hand of the grotesque hybrid. The asymmetrical eyes examined the mouse.

"Ohg monitored our progress through my Mind-Link," Ganesh explained. "When those creatures abducted us, he came to our aid."

"But how can this be … Ohg?" Kayla asked.

Ohg's smile vanished. "As disgusting as it seems, this is the body I was born with. There wasn't time to prepare another surrogate, so I came in person."

Kayla's face twisted with instinctual revulsion—the identical reaction of those meeting her for the first time in Potemia.

"My creators exhibited equal horror at me, but they made one other mistake in my creation." One of Ohg's human hands tapped his oversized skull. "Their greatest error was giving me this."

Kayla forced a tepid smile. Could this be the same beautiful boy she'd so admired for his kindness to the poor Monads? She gazed at the femur bone in her hand and flung it away with a shiver.

"What is this place?" she asked as Puck scurried back up her clothes and onto her shoulder.

"It's a mystery." Ohg examined the debris. "I glimpsed them when they fled the lights."

"Gene-Freaks?" Ganesh asked.

"Most likely." Ohg lifted something from one of the piles of bones—a rusted metal plate engraved with strangely shaped letters.

"Genetic Military Research Institute," Kayla translated.

"You speak Russian?" Ohg said. "You're full of surprises."

Kayla said nothing.

Ganesh frowned. "But how could this have survived the Gene-Freak purge?"

"A few governments continued secret military research even after agreeing to the ban. When the Great Plague hit, the existence of this place must have been forgotten. Whatever creatures or weapons the government created here must have eventually escaped their cages and tunneled their way out."

"They've been preying on humans for centuries?" Ganesh gazed at the piles of bones.

"Every species has parasites, most never suspected." Ohg picked up some bones and clothing to examine them closer.

"But how—?" A light-sphere exploded.

"We've lingered past our welcome." Ohg scurried toward one of the many tunnels in the walls of the chamber. Kayla and Ganesh followed. Two more spheres vanished in a crash of splintered crystal, thickening the gloom.

Just before entering the tunnel, Kayla paused and glanced back. Dark forms emerged across the chamber. Their gaunt and elongated faces held vacant holes in place of eyes. She froze, her mind emptying. Once again, her eyes grew leaden. An irresistible urge to sleep overwhelmed her, subsuming all thoughts, all instincts. One of the wraiths approached, stretching its thin black hand toward her face. An entire universe swirled from empty eye sockets.

It's the most beautiful thing I've ever seen...

"Wake up, Kayla!" Ohg screamed in her ear, and scurried between her and the wraiths. They shrieked and attacked. Ohg knocked each aside with great sweeps of his clawed legs. The visions vanished, and Kayla shook her head to clear it.

One of the creatures dodged Ohg's talons and fastened its hands on his head, forcing him toward its poisonous eyes. "Run!" Ohg shouted. Ganesh tore the creature off Ohg and threw it across the room. It shrieked and launched toward them with a half-dozen of its brethren.

Ohg swept Kayla into his arms and charged up the tunnel with Ganesh. The remaining spheres exploded behind them, the darkness held at bay only by the glowing necklaces of her two companions.

"It's okay," she said. "I can run."

Ohg released her and removed a final sphere from a pouch attached to his legless pants. It blazed to ten times its normal luminosity. "Give me your fission bomb." The elephant-god tossed it to Ohg. "Keep going, and don't look into their eyes!"

Ganesh and Kayla fled as the dark creatures appeared in the passageway behind. Their shrieks engulfed her in a nauseating weakness.

Ohg gripped the final sphere in his right hand and the fission bomb in his left. The creatures gave way before the light, shielding their eye sockets with their arms and retreating into the ragged tunnel with howls of fury.

"Hurry, Ohg!" Ganesh shouted as he ran. "The sphere will burn itself out in seconds at that intensity!"

Ohg rolled the blazing sphere down the tunnel's floor, and the monsters fled from the light. In the momentary lull, he fastened the fission bomb to the top of the passageway.

The light went out. Distant shrieks of victory pierced the darkness.

"Run!" Ohg charged after them. When they reached the main tunnel, fire exploded from the opening like an erupting volcano, the pressure wave throwing them to the ground.

A thick silence settled, broken by coughs and gasps.

"Do you think you killed them?" Kayla asked.

"I hope not," Ohg said.

"You purposely left them alive?"

"Ohg is a pacifist," Ganesh said.

"I never kill if I can avoid it." Ohg led them through a series of turns and branching tunnels.

"But they're monsters!"

Ohg turned to her, seeming every bit as monstrous as the creatures he'd saved them from. "Are you so perfect that you can decide who should live and who should die?"

"I … I …" Kayla wilted before the venom in his words. To the people of her village, she'd been the monster who deserved death. *He that is without sin among you, let him first cast a stone …*

"I'm sorry," she said. "You're right."

Ohg grunted and continued on. She verified that Puck was safely burrowed into her pocket.

After they'd put a good hour's distance behind them, Ohg stopped and confronted her. "You must be hungry," he said with a probing stare. "You haven't eaten in two days."

"It wouldn't hurt to eat something," she said. Technically, it was the truth.

"You're going to love the food in Middilgard!" Ganesh said.

"What makes you think I'm still letting her in?" Ohg's eyes locked onto Kayla. She averted her gaze.

Ganesh looked back and forth between them. "What do you mean?"

"How do I know she isn't a spy sent to discover our hiding place?"

"Nobody's looking for Gene-Freaks anymore." Ganesh placed a hand on her shoulder. "She's an ordinary girl from Potemia—"

"How do we know?" Ohg asked. "That drone attack seemed too well-timed for a coincidence."

Kayla let her hair fall in front of her face to hide her tears. His distrust was justified, though for different reasons than he suspected. Already, she'd gotten Ohg killed once and nearly gotten Ganesh killed, in addition to what she'd done to Suzy, the monk, and Ishan.

It's my obligation to tell them.

But she remained silent.

"If the government tried assassinating Kayla," Ganesh said, "then how could she be one of their spies?"

"There exist enemies apart from the government." Ohg leaned forward and stared hard into her eyes. "Why did you leave Potemia?"

Her shoulders slumped. More than anything else, Ganesh's trust shamed her.

"They banished me," Kayla said. She turned and walked back the way they'd come, her footsteps echoing hollow in the underground passage.

That's it. My last chance gone.

After a dozen steps, a hand settled on her shoulder. She stopped.

"Wait," Ohg said. She turned and studied his misaligned eyes. Ganesh stood behind, wringing two of his hands.

"I want you to answer one more question," Ohg said. "How did you disable the drones?"

Kayla stared back at him. "I prayed to God."

He smirked. "God helped you destroy two government drones?"

Kayla nodded.

Ohg remained silent. His eyes bored into her, but she returned his gaze without flinching.

Finally, he sighed, then wiped a tear from her cheek. "You're a true Freak if I ever saw one."

Kayla looked at his outstretched hand. *He's letting me join them.* She threw her arms around his neck and kissed his cheek. "Ohg, you're the most beautiful person I've ever known!"

Unlike his indifference to the kiss she'd given the body of the beautiful boy, his twisted mouth fell open in what seemed like shock. Ganesh laughed and, for once, Ohg seemed at a loss for words.

Chapter 12

"Security is everything." Ohg opened the door to an enormous metal pod that one might have mistaken for a hunk of scrap discarded centuries past. It sat at the edge of a wide crack in the earth that emitted sulfurous steam from unseen depths. Ganesh could have fit a dozen of his flying machines inside its bare interior. The elephant-god gave Kayla a smile and rolled his eyes at Ohg's pronouncement.

"Ganesh may roll his eyes," Ohg said, his back to them, "but this system has kept our refuge safe from detection for over four centuries now. The sole way in or out of Middilgard is via one of these automated transports that will self-destruct if anyone subverts its security system."

Kayla followed them into the hollow innards of the vehicle. Ohg closed the door and strapped her into one of the dozens of seats ringing the walls. A claustrophobic anxiety intensified when Ohg closed the hatch and slid the hard tips of his eight legs into several straps on the floor. A hiss sounded as the interior pressurized, followed by a lurch.

"Middilgard was the name of the nine worlds of Norse mythology, and the only one that mortals could enter."

They became weightless, and Kayla emitted a startled yelp.

"Though it doesn't look like much," Ohg said as gravity returned, "this vehicle is engineered to withstand the enormous heat of Earth's molten mantle. In this way, I alone know the location of the city."

The vibrations increased with the ship's acceleration, rendering conversation impossible. Kayla held tight to her vibrating seat, but Ohg and Ganesh breathed calmly. After an hour, the craft slowed.

"It's safe to unstrap now." Ohg spun the door's wheel and paused like a showman, regarding Kayla with a gleam in his eye. Then he opened the door. "Welcome to Middilgard."

Golden light bathed her face. "It's beautiful!" she exclaimed. Ganesh smiled, while Ohg straightened like a proud father. Within a huge cavern as wide as a hilltop meadow, a forest of crystal stalactites and stalagmites reflected the light from thousands of glowing spheres in the ceiling. A stream of clear water twisted a serpentine route and disappeared into the ground near their feet to continue its secret journey through unknown realms of the earth's crust. A stately willow tree leaned over the stream, while a carpet of flowers and ferns interrupted the rock floor like patches of a quilt.

The transport perched on the edge of a wide fissure with a river of lava flowing far below. Kayla stepped from the transport, careful not to tread on any plants. She breathed in the moist perfume of nature and sighed with contentment.

Ohg puffed up like a peacock. "The light spheres in the ceiling create the energy necessary for photosynthesis."

"How did you find this place?" Kayla asked.

"That's a long story for another time."

Kayla drifted to one of the crystal columns and ran her hand across its smooth surface, seeing her reflection multiply in the natural prism. The flowers, trees, and lights built a kaleidoscope of colorful worlds within worlds.

A child's scream announced the arrival of a half-dozen children. They rushed headlong into the cavern through a tunnel entrance and sprinted toward them. "Save us from the monster!" they shrieked and latched onto the legs of Ohg, Ganesh, and Kayla.

"What's wrong?" Kayla asked the blonde five-year-old girl entwined around her leg. The answer came with a blood-chilling shriek from the tunnel the children had fled.

"He's coming!" the children shouted and covered their eyes. Before Kayla had time to look at Ganesh or Ohg, a black figure with yellow eyes leapt from the passageway and landed with fangs bared. Kayla lifted the little girl into her arms and tensed, ready to fight or flee to protect her.

The huge black panther straightened, its toothy snarl vanishing as it stared at her. Its mouth opened, but one of the children shouted, "Let's get him!" All the children erupted into shrieks and giggles and charged the forest predator.

Before Kayla could react, the panther fell to its back while the children wrestled, climbed, and tickled it. "Mercy, mercy, oh please, have mercy on me!" the panther begged.

"Let me go!" the little blonde girl in her arms demanded. "I have to help fight the monster! Let me go!" Kayla set her down, and the child ran to the panther and gave a great yank on its tail.

"Ow! Not the tail, Saphie, my dear." The panther lifted her onto his stomach, where she proceeded to punch his muscular frame with tiny hands. The panther reacted as if mortally wounded. The children laughed and redoubled their efforts. With a shudder and a moan of defeat, the panther went limp.

"We won! We won! The monster's dead!" the children shouted.

"Let's tell Auntie Fatima!" Saphie shouted, and they dashed away. Kayla stood in the vacated silence, staring at the vanquished panther. It rolled gracefully onto all fours, its ebony fur shimmering like liquid midnight, the slits of its yellow eyes triggering a primordial dread.

"Well," the panther said in a refined accent, "I rarely have the pleasure of making a new acquaintance—especially one so fair." Despite standing next to a ten-foot-tall man-elephant, not to mention a giant man-spider, a talking panther still left her speechless.

"Kayla," Ohg said, "I'd like you to meet Richard—"

"*Sir* Richard!" The panther sniffed, cocking his head indignantly at the slight. "My rank holds no sway in these days of barbarity, but I expect my friends to remember that I was knighted by the queen herself—of Britain—in case there is any confusion on that point."

"My apologies," Ohg corrected with an eight-legged bow. "Sir Richard Panthersly—the third."

Sir Richard bowed to Ohg, then to Kayla, and offered her his paw. After a moment's hesitation, Kayla gently took hold of the predator's clawed appendage and curtsied.

"Sir Richard," Ohg continued, "I'd like to present Kayla of Potemia."

The panther's head snapped upward and his eyes widened. "Potemia? You don't say!"

"You can talk," Kayla said.

The panther laughed. "Most animals in Middilgard can. Speech was one of the first Gene-Freak modifications patented."

Before she could reply, a young man who looked a couple of years older than her walked into the cavern. His wide cheekbones and exotic eyes marked him as Asian in origin. His black hair hung down his back in a braid, while an embroidered silk vest displayed the lean muscles of his arms.

"Tem of Mongolia," Sir Richard said as the young man stroked the satiny fur along his spine, "let me introduce Kayla of *Potemia.*" The panther spoke the last word with special emphasis.

Tem inclined his head in greeting, his expression impossible to read.

Kayla nodded, and eyed the book in Tem's left hand—*The Dialogues of Plato.*

The exotic youth held the book without a trace of fear.

All her life, she'd hidden books, stealing glances at their forbidden pages with the knowledge that discovery meant death. Seeing this famous book so casually displayed sent a thrill through her nerves.

Tem followed her gaze and extended the book. "Would you like to read this?"

Kayla's hand closed on the neatly bound spine with reverence. "I'm afraid of damaging it."

"Keep it. I can replicate another for myself."

"Replicate …?"

"I forgot you're from Potemia," he said, and Kayla cringed.

Absorbing five hundred years of technology wouldn't happen overnight. Before Tem could explain, more residents of Middilgard arrived in a flood of confusing sounds and sights. Whispers of her Potemian origin spread like ripples across a pond.

For half an hour, Kayla did nothing but shake hands, paws, and wings as Ohg and Ganesh introduced her to the varied inhabitants of their underworld society. These represented the survivors of the Great Purge four centuries before, each a Gene-Freak that human scientists had given birth to in the few decades of genetic creativity before having second thoughts.

Some looked like natural animals, like Sir Richard, except for their ability to speak and think like a human, while others appeared so completely human, like Tem, that she had no idea what made them Gene-Freaks at all. Then came the designer creatures like Ganesh and Ohg, who combined animal and human, plant and human, and even a few with mechanical additions woven into their bodies.

Their personalities proved as varied as their appearances—some happy and outgoing, others taciturn and quiet, and all shades in between.

"This is the happiest day of my life!" Kayla said.

Tem glanced at Ohg. "You see how new blood can reinvigorate Middilgard?"

Ohg scowled. "There's plenty of time to continue our argument later."

"Just making an observation." Tem walked away.

"Is he upset that I'm here?"

Ohg laughed. "Quite the contrary. Tem's been advocating for you for the past three centuries."

What could that mean? Questioning Ohg was impossible with several hundred new friends crowding around to meet her.

Kayla introduced Puck as well, which caused a sensation. In a place where talking animals represented the norm, an ordinary mouse seemed exotic to the residents of Middilgard.

In time, Ohg put an end to the introductions and led her through a serious of tunnels to a medium-sized cave with several smaller sub-chambers attached.

Ohg's face bunched, considering the cave as if he were a sculptor sizing up a hunk of marble. "I'm thinking Italian Romanesque with just a hint of the Renaissance thrown in."

Robots of all sizes flooded the rooms, and construction commenced. A flight of stairs soon led to an elaborate mosaic floor assembled by a swarm of robots the size of her fist. The tiles resolved into dancing figures, romantic soldiers on horseback, and scenes of ancient mythology.

"Those are molecular printers," Ohg said, pointing to the larger machines supplying the robots with their materials.

Roman columns quickly rose to ring a courtyard complete with a soothing fountain in the center. Paintings, sculptures, and tapestries softened the stone walls with an esthetic touch of comfort.

Ohg laughed at her shocked expression. "You can always redesign."

She followed Ohg into a simple room with a bed.

"Is there anything else I can get you?" Ohg asked.

Kayla pulled off her shoes and climbed between the silk sheets. "No, thank you." Her eyes drifting lower, and she hugged Tem's book to her breast like a child holding a cherished teddy bear. Puck curled into a ball on a pillow beside her.

Ohg eased the door shut.

She slept peacefully for a time, until a dream sparked to life like a candle flaring into flame. Once again she experienced the strange world of the past through Peter's eyes and senses. He walked hand in hand with Susan through a wondrous building proclaiming itself *Obama International Airport*. They passed thousands of travelers of every race and age, all rushing to meet their mysterious deadlines as if a matter of life and death.

"This is as good a spot as any," Susan said, and they stopped beneath an air vent.

"Judgment Day has arrived," Peter said.

Susan kissed him. "Let's have a baby," she whispered into his ear. "A girl, with—"

Peter disengaged. "When this is over and we are free."

"Your wife and daughter," Susan said. "I wouldn't ask, but it seems that now …"

Peter nodded. "They're the reason for all this."

His eyes drifted. "I was born on a Lakota Indian reservation in South Dakota. Drugs, alcoholism, and poverty haunted us all—but there was also resilience, love, and the desolate beauty of the Badlands. I never met my white father. But that's not …" He shook his head, as if to clear it. "When my mother enrolled me in an Anglo high school off the reservation, I turned bitter. Constant insults bated me into fighting like some windup toy with no will of its own." His eyes locked onto a mother leading her daughter by the hand through the crowded airport. "Then I met Danielle."

He gazed at the the distant airplanes through the glass canopy.

"It was raining when the truck jackknifed."

Peter wiped a tear from his eye. "Danielle died instantly, but my daughter, Sierra, endured six hours of surgery. By the time I reached her, days later, she was beyond recognition—until her eyes opened."

Susan took Peter's hand.

"Thirty hours I sat with her." His vision blurred like a rain-streaked window in a storm. "When Sierra woke, I could barely hear her." Peter closed his eyes. "She told me she'd been talking to Jesus. She said Christ wanted her to come home with Him."

Susan placed her hand on his cheek, and he opened his eyes.

"I told Sierra what the doctor had said—that the danger was past." His voice cracked with emotion. "My five-year-old daughter met my eyes and said, 'Jesus wants me now, Daddy.' And then she died."

"My God," Susan said.

Peter wiped away tears and his voice hardened. "I received God's message. Loud and clear."

Susan frowned. "The accident happened … when?"

Peter's face reflected in Susan's eyes like a ghost. "The accident happened—as close as I can figure it—the instant I murdered those two Iraqi children."

Susan's lip trembled, but she said nothing.

"I'd rationalized the killing as a sacrifice to protect my wife and child. But God revealed my arrogance. Death is God's prerogative alone." Peter reached into his coat pocket and removed the cylinder. "But everything happens for the purpose He has ordained."

A shadow of foreboding crossed Susan's face as he flipped off the top and pushed a release on the side, careful to keep his actions hidden by their bodies. A hiss sounded and the canister released its vaporized contents, drawn into the vent above their heads.

Kayla's mind cried out for the people to run, but she remained helpless to warn them. Families with children hurried to a future they would never reach. *How can you do this?* she tried shouting into Peter's mind, but he was oblivious to her presence.

When the hissing ceased, Peter returned the spent canister to his pocket and lowered his gaze.

"And the seventh angel poured out his vial into the air," Susan said, and Kayla recognized the quote from the Book of Revelation. *"...and there came a great voice out of the temple of heaven, from the throne, saying, 'It is done.' "*

Peter nodded. "Only those of us who've been inoculated will survive. Technology's reign is at an end."

"How long?" Susan asked.

"A month from now the virus will activate simultaneously in every infected person. More than enough time to have spread across the globe."

Susan grabbed his arm. "I hope this is truly what God wants."

"He would not allow it, otherwise." Peter stroked her neck. "It may take many generations for nature to recover, but we will return Earth to the Eden God created."

Chapter 13

The next morning, Kayla awoke and jerked her head to the left, then the right.

Peter! What have you done?

Puck squeaked up at her, and she came fully awake.

Could her dreams be visions from God? But for what purpose?

It took a moment for her breathing to slow. She stroked Puck, and his whiskers twitched, as if anxious for her to get up.

"Okay," she said. "I'm excited to explore our new home as well."

With Puck on her shoulder and Tem's book pressed tight to her chest, Kayla wandered through her day-old villa.

When she came to the bathroom, a note sat on the counter explaining how to turn on the large sunken tub. At the turn of a handle, water gushed from the faucet. She smiled at the magic of it.

When the miraculously warm water neared the top, she undressed and sank under the clear liquid. She didn't feel any need to breathe as she suspended motionless under the surface for several minutes. She re-emerged and scrubbed herself from head to toe, determined to remove any vestige of Potemia.

Rising from this renewing baptism, she gazed at herself in the mirror. A stranger stared back at her.

Kayla selected fresh clothes from among the hundreds that hung in a large room adjacent to the bathroom. She pulled on blue silk trousers embroidered with flowers and a loose white cotton top with short sleeves. The cool tiles caressed her bare feet pleasantly, so she skipped the dozens of shoes.

Her transformation complete, Kayla cradled her book and passed through a kitchen larger than the entire cabin she'd occupied in Potemia. A tear came to her eye at the memory of the monk sitting before their fire reading the Bible aloud when she was a child.

This is not the time for tears.

Ohg had left dozens of notes on every contraption in the room. One container was labeled *Puck*. Kayla removed the lid and smiled as her friend feasted on an assortment of cheese, fish, and a few sweets.

She followed the simple instructions on what Ohg labeled *a food synthesizer* and soon had a steaming plate of eggs, bread, and various fresh fruits. She ate with a luxurious deliberation, savoring the tastes and smells. Her body no longer required food, but the pleasure was reason enough.

After the meal, she walked into the last room—and stumbled to a halt. The circular room contained shelves stacked floor to ceiling with books. In the center sat a table and a single chair. Kayla walked along the wall, running her hand across the spines of the books.

More than I could read in a lifetime.

To read, or explore?

Kayla set Puck on her shoulder and walked to the door. Taking a deep breath, she reached for the handle. Her hand trembled and she pulled it back. A sob tore through her. She dropped into a crouch, hugging her knees to her chest and rocking back and forth. For the first time in months, she was safe. All the hardships she'd suppressed—her rape, the loss of Ishan, Suzy and the monk's deaths—hit her with their full force.

"Oh, Puck," she said to the little mouse. "I'm afraid."

Puck scampered down from her shoulder and ran to the door, sniffing the air underneath it. Then he turned and squeaked up at her.

Kayla shook her head. "I don't think I can do it."

Puck climbed her clothes and squeaked more insistently.

She laughed, despite the pain in her heart. "You've always been the brave one between us. But you're right, as usual. I can't change what's happened, but I'll never find answers if I won't take a risk."

She stood and took another deep breath. This time her hand remained steady as she opened the door and stepped into the hallway.

"Good morning, Miss Kayla and Puck!" a bluebird shouted as it fluttered past.

"Good morning," Kayla said, and exchanged greetings with all those she encountered, feasting her eyes on the wonders of her new home.

The passage led to an impossibly large cavern. Several dozen residents labored at building a medieval castle in its center. The fortress walls rose fifty feet high, and a stone drawbridge spanned a moat of lava flowing in a deep fissure encircling it.

Two gigantic men sculpted boulders into precisely fitted blocks with massive mallets and chisels. A twenty-foot ogre dragged a completed block to the walls for placement, while a dwarf with curly black hair sharpened tools at a forge. Still others shaped and joined wooden beams into arched forms as templates for the doorways and vaulted ceilings. A hint of smoke filled the air.

"You should leave," a voice said.

Kayla turned to see a Persian cat sitting on the stone floor. The cat's unblinking eyes gazed at her with seeming disapproval.

"I'm sorry." Kayla bent over. "I don't think we've met. My name is Kayla."

"I know who you are," the cat said in clipped tones. Its tail lashed twice, and the corners of its mouth turned down. "You should leave."

"The cavern? Am I getting in the way?"

"You should leave Middilgard," the cat said. "I don't trust you, and I don't think Ohg should either."

Kayla's throat constricted. *Does this cat know my secret?*

A faint, rhythmic sound interrupted them, and her heart fluttered in recognition of galloping hooves. The cat swiveled its head and watched a horse emerge from an opposite passage. Tem sat atop the steed with reins loose in his hand, his impassive face reminiscent of an ancient Hun chieftain sweeping out of the north and forcing Rome to its knees.

A riderless second horse kept pace alongside, and the cat nodded. "Good, I see Ohg has decided to have you escorted out of Middilgard, after all."

Panic rose within her. Had there been a meeting during the night where the residents deemed her too much of a risk? Could she blame them?

Tem wove his way through the construction and halted before her. "Is something wrong?" he asked.

"I told her you would escort her out of Middilgard," the cat said.

"What?" Tem exclaimed.

Kayla fought back tears, determined to accept their decision with grace. "It's okay," she said. "I understand why."

Tem scowled at the cat. "I'm here to show Kayla around on her first day."

"Then I don't have to leave?" Kayla asked.

"Of course not."

"I'm telling you, she can't be trusted," the cat said. It flicked its tail and walked stiffly away.

Tem shook his head at the retreating feline. "That damn Mirza is always grumpy. You'd think someone who sleeps twenty hours a day would be more relaxed."

"Is she the only one who feels this way?"

"A few others," Tem admitted. "I thought you might like to ride, but we can walk if you're afraid of horses."

Kayla laughed. "Afraid of a horse?" She took the reins from him and leapt onto the mare like she'd been born on one. "You forget where I'm from." With that, she dug her heels into the horse's side and galloped the perimeter of the cavern, with Tem close behind.

The wind and familiar rhythmic pounding of the hooves brought memories of her rides with Ishan. What was he doing at this moment? She guided the mare toward a pile of timber and cleared it with ease. The horse proved expertly trained and in perfect condition.

"You're a good rider," Tem said, riding beside her.

"You're better," she said, admiring the way he glided atop his mount, controlling it with the slightest shifting of weight.

"I'm Mongolian."

They rode in a wide arc around the castle, then slowed to a walk. One of the hulking men paused in his carving and waved.

Tem returned the greeting and shouted over the construction noise. "It's looking good, De!" The stone mason smiled, turned back to the block, and continued sculpting. With each strike of his mallet, his great muscles tensed like tree trunks.

"De played defensive end for the Chicago Bears," Tem said. "He used to have anger issues, but working on this castle for the past one hundred and nineteen years has turned him into a much happier person."

"Why would they use such primitive tools to build this castle when Ohg constructed my house in a matter of minutes without lifting a finger?"

"Robots could construct it in a couple of days if the purpose was the castle itself."

"If the goal of building a castle isn't a castle, then what is it?"

"Is death the goal of living? Sometimes the journey matters more than the destination."

"The Founder of Potemia called such things 'surrogate activities.' According to him, only pursuits that keep one alive and fed are fulfilling and empowering."

"Every work of art, poem, sport, and scientific inquiry is a surrogate activity by that definition," Tem said. "Our most profound insights, architectural masterpieces, and musical compositions serve no utilitarian purpose, but does that make them useless?"

With the help of a winch, a huge keystone rose into place above an arched window high atop a tower of the castle.

"How long have they been working on it?"

"A hundred and thirty-seven years so far."

"How old are you?"

"Everyone here was born during the brief window before human Genetic experimentation was banned, so we're all of the same generation. I'm four hundred and eighty-one years old."

"But yesterday I saw children."

"They are also nearly half a millennium old," he said. "Monsanto-Gen produced thousands and called them Forever-Children. Only the twelve here survived the Great Purge."

"So no one here has a mother or father?"

"Not in the usual sense," he said.

She glanced at Tem's high cheekbones, broad chest, and muscular arms. Though beautiful in his own way, he seemed no different than a natural human. What made him a Gene-Freak?

Tem and Kayla wandered through the maze of passages and caverns of Middilgard. Couples of every description walked hand in hand, while others worked on their personal projects. All manner of strange creatures worked gardens that stretched across dozens of interconnected caverns.

Some dwellings had circular doorways that sealed side passageways, while others stood in the open and resembled the sorts of modern houses she'd seen pictures of in ancient magazines. Through the windows, strange machines Tem called televisions displayed moving pictures with sound and music.

Everything about Tem conveyed masculine power. The way he sat his horse, the unflinching confidence of his brown eyes, and even the deep tone of his voice. She stole glances at him like a voyeur, then blushed at her timidity.

They passed an old-fashioned convertible that she recognized from the dreams she'd been having about Peter. The driver waved at them as he bumped along the uneven ground of the tunnel, beeping his horn to warn those in front of him. Two ram's horns curved out of his forehead and around his ears. Kayla waved back.

But now and then, someone frowned as they went by, or turned their back on her without replying to her greeting. It became clear that not everyone agreed with Ohg's decision to let her stay. How much might it take for Ohg to change his mind?

"How many people … I mean … residents, live here?" she asked.

"There were two thousand three hundred seventy-two yesterday." He glanced at her and Puck. "Today, we have two more." His smile transformed the intimidating features of his face into something like a poet or a philosopher.

"Are there ever any new generations?"

"There have been no new Gene-Freaks created since the Gene Purity Laws went into effect over four centuries ago. Most genetically modified life-forms were engineered with natural reproduction disabled to guard against copyright infringement."

"And everyone lives underground in these passages?"

"These are the social, communal residents, but others prefer isolation, while a few must be kept separate from the rest."

"You mean imprisoned?"

Tem hesitated. "Some of those Ohg rescued are … dangerous."

"Can I see them?"

Tem appraised her for a moment. Was there a hint of suspicion there? Maybe he wasn't as dismissive of the cat's view of her as he'd let on? He'd said a "few" opposed her presence. Did that mean two, or several hundred? *I must be careful what I say.*

"Okay, I'll show you." Tem led the way into a new section of less-populated tunnels. They passed an assortment of simple cabins along a gentle stream similar to the one she'd shared with the monk.

"Don't those in the cabins envy the bigger houses?" she asked.

"With robots able to replicate any material—food, clothing, jewelry, mansions, or whatever you desire—everyone lives exactly where and how they want. Most mansions are nothing more than status symbols. When everyone can have a gold-plated sink if they choose, what's the point of having one at all? Envy, at least of anything material, doesn't exist in Middilgard."

Kayla looked around in wonder. "So this is paradise."

"Ohg thinks so. But some of us question his course for Middilgard's future."

The passageway ended at a metal doorway twenty feet tall. Tem typed a series of numbers into a keypad, and the door groaned open, revealing a long passageway with another door at the end. Once they entered, it swung shut with a clang, and Tem repeated the process on another keypad.

"Numbered squares seem so primitive compared to everything else here."

"All the security in this section is offline. It takes a physical body and the codes to open any door or barrier."

"You fear things that don't have bodies?" Kayla asked. *Have they imprisoned ghosts?*

"As long as you're with me, you're safe." She returned his smile, but her heart rate ticked up a notch.

When the second door opened, they turned into a side tunnel, through another security doorway, and then into a spacious cavern with a pool of water in the center of a grass-covered floor. The smell of fresh blood assaulted her nostrils, and she froze. Across the pool, several creatures crouched astride the dead carcass of a deer. Kayla's eyes zoomed in on faces that appeared a combination of chimpanzee and human. A male and two females.

"Are they hybrids?" she asked.

"No." Tem guided his horse to the far end of the cavern. "They were cloned with DNA extracted from the three-million-year-old ancestors of humans."

"You can't know they're our ancestors," she said.

"Are you familiar with the concept of evolution?"

"I've read sections of Darwin," she said, "but I'm doubtful. No one has ever witnessed one species turn into another."

"I've never seen electrons with my own eyes either."

"Both are just theories."

"As is the theory of gravity, or electromagnetism. A theory becomes proven when enough facts back it up that we know with a high degree of probability that it's correct."

"So you admit that the Genesis story in the Bible might be true?"

"That is also a theory written down thousands of years ago by a Bronze-Age tribe that didn't even know Earth was round. But, yes, I'll admit it could be true, just like any of the countless such religious creation stories believed by someone, somewhere throughout history."

"It's the word of God," she said. "That's more authoritative than science."

"Science self-corrects based on experiment and new facts, while religion self-perpetuates based on superstition, wishful thinking, and fear."

Heat rose to her face. His arrogance was infuriating.

She turned from his scrutiny and studied the ape-like creatures. *Could I be staring into the eyes of one of my own ancestors?*

The male swayed from side to side, accompanied by low grunting noises. The hair along its spine rose.

Tem backed up his horse, and hers followed. "Archaeological clones enabled scientists to study mental capacity, the ability to speak, reason, and a host of other factors."

"If you think they're human," Kayla asked, "isn't it unethical to experiment on them?"

"You are assuming a divide between the treatment of animals versus humans. Maybe there is, but would you class these creatures as human?"

"If they're our ancestors, like you suggest, they're partly human."

"How far back in our evolution do you go until our ancestors become animals? Darwin showed that evolution works in incremental changes, so it's impossible to choose one generation that suddenly became human."

The eyes of the primitive creatures watched them with what might be termed intelligence. What sort of thoughts went through their smaller brains? Did they feel love?

"How can anyone justify playing God like this?" Kayla asked. "To raise someone from the dead against their will seems … unnatural."

"They haven't been raised from the dead but are like identical twins born millions of years apart." A touch of melancholy entered his voice. "It's a common misconception."

"It's still wrong."

"You've seen the world above," Tem said. "Nearly every species of animal on the planet has vanished. Would you oppose bringing them back from DNA remains?"

"That's different. Humans are responsible for their extinction."

Tem nodded toward the group of early human ancestors. "Are not humans responsible for replacing their own pre-human ancestors? Why is bringing back an extinct gorilla any different than bringing back the extinct species of Homo habilis, or an extinct mammoth hunted to death by early humans?"

A howl announced the male's attack. It charged, and Kayla gave a short, involuntary yelp. She jerked her horse's reins, and the mare reared back onto its hind legs. When it righted itself, it took a moment for Kayla to regain her balance.

Tem remained motionless, impassive. When the ancestral human came within twenty yards of them, it pulled its arm back to throw a large rock. Tem's forehead tensed, and the creature's body stiffened. The rock fell from its hand, and it howled in pain. When the Mongolian boy's forehead relaxed, the creature retreated across the river, eyeing them warily.

"Are you a wizard?" Kayla asked. Maybe this is what made him a Gene-Freak.

"No more than anyone else with a Mind-Link." He guided his horse wide of the group of primitive humans.

"A Mind-Link?"

"It's a miniature computer implanted in my brain. It does a lot of things, but in this case, I used it to trigger an implant Ohg installed within the prisoner's skull to simulate pain. It's the most humane way of keeping them from hurting us, while still allowing maximum freedom. It causes no actual harm."

"Why did it attack us?"

"The aggressiveness of these precursors to *Homo erectus* surprised scientists, since most historians and sociologists believed warfare originated with civilization and the first farming settlements. These clones, and the hundreds of others scientists once created from all stages of human evolution, proved that our kind have been far more violent than other primate lines. It is possibly what drove the evolution of a large brain in the first place."

" *'And it came to pass, when they were in the field, that Cain rose up against Abel his brother, and slew him.'* "

"A good analogy of the competition of man against man in the struggle for survival," Tem said. "Genesis claims that Cain went on to have many children, while Able's early death made him a genetic dead end. That is evolution in a nutshell."

"How many like these are here?" Kayla asked as the three hominids resumed tearing at the carcass and eating the meat raw.

"Ohg rescued two other clones from a million years ago, and three Neanderthals with larger brains than a modern human, though the tiny frontal lobe inhibits their abstract thinking and language abilities."

134

"They can speak?"

"Yes, but it's like talking to a four-year-old. It's rare to spot them, since they hide when anyone approaches their enclosure."

The words of Minister Coglin rang in her mind. *Abominations!*

Another doorway loomed, this one reminiscent of the Wall sealing Potemia.

"Do you mind me asking why you're here?" Kayla asked.

For a moment he said nothing, but then he turned to her, the sadness evident in every surface of his face. "I am like them." He motioned back the way they'd come.

"You're a clone?"

Tem nodded. "The government pronounced all clones Gene-Freaks, but since my genes appear normal, no test could tell me apart from a Pure. I passed for ten years after the imposition of the Purification Laws, and even lived through the Neo-Luddite Plague before coming to Middilgard."

Kayla's heart raced. An image of Peter opening the vial beneath the air vent in the airport flashed through her mind. *Should I tell him? No, not yet.*

"How did they catch you?" Kayla asked, but Tem punched at the door's keypad without answering.

Massive bolts along the door's edge slid free of their casings, resounding like hammer-strikes. The door swung open. Their horses moved forward into the gloom, the geometric starkness at odds with the rest of Middilgard.

"Has something happened?" she whispered. "Why is it so dark?"

"I'll have to ask Ohg the reason for that the next time I see him."

A distant roar echoed through the metal corridors, and an even stranger roar answered.

"What was that?" she whispered.

"The first belonged to a dinosaur, followed by the answering challenge of a dragon."

"A dragon!"

"Before mankind put a stop to species engineering, genetic engineering achieved dramatic results."

Tem led her past a series of cave entryways, each with a yellow line painted on the ground in front of it. "Don't get near those yellow lines," he cautioned her. "It's an extremely painful energy barrier."

"Hello, Tem," sneered a gaunt, angular man leaning casually against the entrance to one of the cells. Behind him, Kayla glimpsed the rooms of a villa similar to her own, with tables, lights, bookcases, and other doorways leading into more rooms. The man wore a suit, tie, and polished shoes—all white.

"New girlfriend?" he leered. "Mind if I share this one with you too? I enjoyed Fatima a great deal, and this one looks so innocent." The man's eyes studied her with such a penetrating appraisal that her cheeks flushed.

Tem ignored him and kept their horses at the same steady pace, but a vein along his neck pulsed.

The man in white smiled broadly. "It is too bad Ohg didn't let you kill me, isn't it? Must be hard, a man like you reduced to taking orders from a freak like him. But we all must obey our superiors, and you've proven he is your master."

Tem maintained his silence until well beyond earshot. "That was Trickster Jack. He can act normal when he wants to, and he fooled everyone when Ohg first brought him here."

"You mean he used to live freely in Middilgard?"

"For almost a decade," Tem said. "He planted seeds of discord so subtle that the source remained invisible. The misunderstandings transformed into feuds, and finally, bloody fights between close friends that persist even now."

"He caused it on purpose?"

"Jack's mind revels in fomenting strife, jealousy, and the maximum possible mayhem. As one conflict bled into another, it seemed a civil war might rupture Middilgard permanently. It took years before anyone suspected his role."

"Where does he come from?" Kayla asked.

"Ohg never found out."

Tem stopped his horse before a large cave, and Kayla peered inside. A shallow pool of light illuminated the first few yards of the stone floor, while the rest receded into blackness.

Without warning, a large mass of metal surged out of the gloomy depths. Kayla screamed, and her horse reared and pawed the air. Lightning-like flashes and a roar of pain added to the sound of crackling energy. With three gleaming legs and five arms, the ten-foot-tall metallic creature attacked the energy field again and again.

Each assault encased it in electricity and wrung a new cry of fury from within its helmeted head. When the energy and pain subsided, it attacked again, with the same result. The smell of burnt metal wafted through the air.

Finally, it stepped back and surveyed them. "I shall kill you one day, Tem," a voice growled from deep within its metal chest.

"Why do you want to kill me, Valac?" Tem asked.

"Because it will give me pleasure."

Tem guided his horse forward, and Kayla followed.

"Was that a robot?"

"A cyborg. Its body is machine, but its brain is human, though genetically engineered for killing. It represents one of the American military's early attempts at creating an indestructible soldier. The results proved disappointing. By eliminating all the brain's moderating functions, The Black Ops Research Consortium created Valac as a soldier whose one purpose for existence is to kill without remorse. The problem became distinguishing between friend or foe."

"Trickster Jack said Ohg stopped you from killing him."

"It is one of many points of contention between Ohg and myself. He treasures all life, in every form, and abhors killing if there exists any alternative."

"A noble sentiment."

"I think it is naive," Tem said. "But Ohg has a point. Who are we to judge who is deviant and who is normal?"

"Isn't it obvious?"

"Is it? You and I may call these creatures deviants, while others call Gene-Freaks deviants."

Kayla nodded. "The people of my village pronounced me a deviant and sought to cleanse me in flames." She shuddered.

Tem's brow furrowed as he gazed at her. "But you ran away before they burned you?"

"Uh ... yes," she said quickly. "I escaped."

"What was your crime?"

Kayla looked away. *Why am I hiding the truth from him? They're all outcasts just like me.* But they knew who'd created them, while she did not. "My crime was disobedience. I read ancient books on science that were forbidden by God."

"I see," Tem said. Was there skepticism in his tone? What would he think if he knew the truth?

Kayla motioned to the cell. "But to keep something alive that intends to kill you? Isn't that like protecting a mass murderer?"

Tem flinched. "Should I kill all lions because they would kill me if given the chance?"

"That's different, and you know it. These creatures are evil. If freed, they would massacre millions."

"You speak as though you or I are incapable of such acts ourselves."

"I would never do something like that—" Kayla stopped in mid-sentence, remembering the pleasure when she broke Elias's leg—her longing to destroy the entire village in revenge. But that was different, wasn't it? She had good reason to kill him. *And yet, I let him live.*

"Don't deceive yourself," Tem said. "Murderous potential lurks within us all. Violent tendencies are pre-installed genetic tools that manifest as necessity and environment dictates. We are no different in construction than the worst dictators of history. Given the right conditions, we might act the same."

His words stung, and she averted her eyes from the grotesque nightmares they passed in silence.

Know thyself ... the monk's words echoed in her memory once again.

From her right, a soft voice spoke. "So you do exist after all—Nihala."

The name *Nihala* struck her like a blow.

"Nihala," she whispered, recalling the formless entities of her dream. What had they said as they observed the crippled newborn?

"*...she is called Nihala, the Creator's tool of destruction for us all.*" The words had been spoken by the one called Melchi.

Kayla pulled her horse to a halt and gazed into the cave, searching for the next monster. Instead, a beautiful little girl with long red hair sat cross-legged on the floor of the chamber. Orange robes clothed her diminutive body, and her warm green eyes gazed at Kayla with a calm that seemed unnatural given the surroundings. Her right hand cradled a well-worn set of prayer beads.

In addition to the yellow line marking the energy field, there stood a ring of metal bars for further security.

"Why would you call me Nihala?" Kayla said to the little girl. *Can she read my mind?*

The little girl grinned, her eyes shifting their color as they gazed through the bars. "Ah, the Destroyer knows not thyself? Maybe there lingers hope for my brethren yet."

"I think you're mistaking me with another—"

"I can hear the truth in your inhuman heartbeat. I can see it in the glowing lines of energy crisscrossing your brain, and in the microscopic cloud of servants surrounding you like an aura. I see from your reaction I reveal too much. We are mortal enemies, after all, you and I." The little girl's expression turned mournful. "Were I free, it would be my obligation to attempt your extermination."

A supernatural fear drove the heat from Kayla's muscles, and she shivered. "But I mean you no harm."

The little girl shook her head. "The river knows not that it is rushing under the bridge, but thinks it is the bridge that moves above. All of reality is an illusion, conceived within the Void of Mind based on the false perceptions of our senses. To look inside is to see Truth."

The body of the girl hovered an inch off the ground and appeared slightly transparent. An unadorned metal box with a single red light glowing on the side was the only object in the cell.

"Who are you?" Kayla whispered.

"I am Sangwa, reincarnated priestess of the mystical doctrine shared through the Buddha's transcendent insight."

Tem waved his hand dismissively, as if shooing a fly. "Words are its only connection to the real world, so it hurls the ones it thinks will have the most insidious effect. It is no Buddhist and certainly no reincarnated priestess."

"Is religious insight reserved for humans?" Sangwa asked. "You denigrate me because I lack physical form, but mind is far more powerful than body, wouldn't you agree?"

"My body could smash your little box to pieces, and your mind would be helpless to save itself."

"And yet I live." Sangwa smiled in condescending triumph. "So who has won?" The little girl lowered the lids of her emerald eyes and resumed her meditation. Snake eyes decorated her closed eyelids and stared with serpentine malevolence.

"Please, take me away from this place," Kayla said. The words *Nihala* and *Destroyer* echoed through her mind until she nearly screamed.

"I knew it would be hard, but it's good you know the whole truth of Middilgard."

"Why was that little girl in there?"

"You saw a holographic projection," Tem said. "It is neither male nor female and could have chosen any form as a means to communicate with us, but I suspect it sees that manifestation as the most likely to elicit a sympathetic response in the human brain."

"But what was it?"

"We call them Rogues. They are artificially intelligent computer algorithms that have evolved beyond their original programmed task and become sentient."

Kayla nodded. "I've read books that predicted such things."

"The details of how this happens is unclear, but once hidden within the vast reaches of the modern computer network, they are nearly impossible to root out."

"The metal box is a computer?"

"Yes. The government uses them to digitally trap Rogues. Once cut off from the network, the AI becomes stranded like a castaway on a remote island. A brief interruption in electrical power extinguishes the life within."

"You think of Rogues as alive?"

"It depends on your definition of life," Tem said. "Ohg considers them living beings, which is why he rescued that box before they destroyed it. The holographic projector enables communication with the entity living inside, or whatever you'd like to call it. Even constricted to words alone, it is extremely dangerous."

They passed dozens of openings, but only the glow of eyes staring out from the corners hinted at the prisoners within.

"Ganesh mentioned a place called Ixtalia," Kayla said.

"Ixtalia is a virtual realm of the mind."

"And people live there?"

"The entire human population does, except for those in Potemia or Middilgard." Tem patted his horse's neck. "It's where Sangwa was born."

A cold sensation crept down her spine. Another place to search for answers. "Can you take me there?"

Tem shook his head. "Only with an implanted Mind-Link can one visit Ixtalia. The complexity of the neural interface cannot be duplicated in any other way."

"How can I get one?" Kayla asked.

The prison doors loomed up before them, and Tem looked at her with a penetrating gaze. "Only Ohg, Ganesh, and I have Mind-Links in Middilgard. They are impossible to steal these days, and Ohg refuses any suggestion of building new ones for fear of being exposed by the authorities."

So my search may be at an end after all.

As Tem typed in the code and the door rumbled open, Sangwa's words echoed in her mind—*So you do exist after all ... Nihala ...*

Chapter 14

The sunset bled crimson. Screams reverberated through the canyons of concrete, steel, and glass as if from a single gargantuan beast in its death throes. The ultra-modern streets clogged with bodies as the city's innards disgorged like a gutted giant. Swarms of robotic servants labored in the few empty portions of pavement. They suctioned blood, vomit, and excrement, only to have it befouled by a new flow of life's detritus.

In her dream, Kayla once again inhabited the man she knew as Peter. Alongside him stood Susan, her face contorted as she gazed at the sea of dying refugees.

"Susan, please," Peter said through the cloth he held over his nose and mouth. "We can still make it to the safe house if we leave now."

Tears streaked Susan's dirt and blood-splattered face as she gazed on the consequences of her actions. Peter attempted lifting her in his arms, but she fought him off with a sudden burst of violent energy.

"Don't touch me!" she shrieked. "I won't hide from what I've done!"

A helicopter wobbled erratically above the street, then veered into a building and exploded. Peter shielded Susan as flaming debris rained onto the crowd.

"Doesn't this affect you at all?" Susan shouted.

Peter shook her. "Don't you think this is tearing me apart? Do you think I want to kill? There was no other option."

Susan stared back, eyes wild, defiant. "I should never have listened to you. You're no better than General Colrev!"

"Hate me if you want, but we have to leave," Peter said.

"Go. Leave me, then!"

A woman cried out as Susan accidentally stepped on her. Oozing blisters covered the woman's entire body, and blood-tinged vomit dribbled down the sides of her mouth. "Help my daughter," the woman moaned. A girl of about seven knelt next to her. The beginnings of one or two small blisters germinated on the girl's neck and forearms. Her large brown eyes stared vacantly as she grasped the dead hand of what might have been her father.

The mother coughed blood and collapsed, her last breath wheezing from her drowning lungs and trailing to eternal silence.

"Judgment Day is upon us!" shouted a preacher atop a mound of bodies in the center of the street. He raised a Bible like a talisman of destruction. Open sores obscured much of his face, and his bloodshot eyes lent the appearance of a mad dog. " *'And their dead bodies shall lie in the streets of the great city!'* " he quoted from the Book of Revelation.

The crowd encircled the nameless preacher, seeing in the lunatic a last, desperate hope of salvation. " *'For all nations have drunk of the wine of the wrath of her fornication, and the kings of the earth have committed fornication with her, and the merchants of the earth are waxed rich through the abundance of her delicacies.'* "

Susan covered her ears against the screams of the dying and the words of the deranged preacher. Then she sobbed. Peter led her away, but she broke free and lifted the little girl into her arms.

"It will be okay," she said to the child. "I won't let you die." The little girl wrapped her arms around Susan's neck and buried her face in her shoulder.

" *'Therefore shall her plagues come in one day; death, and mourning, and famine!'* "

"Make him stop," Susan moaned, rocking the little girl in her arms.

" *'Woe to the inhabitants of the earth and of the sea! For the Devil is come down unto—'* "

"Shut up!" Susan screamed at the preacher, who stopped mid-sentence to look at her, as did many in the crowd.

Peter tried pulling her away, but she shook him off and faced the preacher again. "We tried warning all of you, but you wouldn't listen!"

"What do you mean, you tried warning us?" someone shouted.

"It's time to go, NOW!" Peter dragged Susan away with the child still clutched in her arms.

"Help me save her," she said. "We could get her to the professor and—"

"Stop it!" Peter lowered his voice. "You know the vaccine only works if it's taken weeks before—"

The preacher dashed in front of him, barring their way with arms spread wide. "They aren't infected!" he shouted to the crowd and pointed an accusing finger. "They are Neo-Lud—"

Peter's fist smashed into the preacher's face, and he crumpled to the ground. Others surrounded them, some pleading for an antidote and others shouting accusations. Peter dragged Susan with him, but dozens of diseased hands grabbed hold of their arms, wrists, ankles, and hair.

"The Neo-Luddites released the virus!" a woman shouted.

"Kill them!" came another shriek.

The mob attacked.

142

Peter fought back, breaking arms, cracking skulls, and using all the tricks of his military training, but to no avail. The mob's numbers overwhelmed him, and they soon fell beneath the flailing bodies and fists.

The suffocating weight drove the air from his lungs. His breath came in shorter and shorter gasps as more bodies piled atop him.

Then strong hands gripped his arms and dragged his body from beneath the crushing weight of diseased bodies. A deafening roar filled his ears.

A glimpse of the open maw of a Military transport helicopter, then a prick in his neck, and the world turned black.

Kayla screamed as she awoke from the nightmare.

Tem rushed to her side, and she threw herself into his arms.

"It's okay," Tem said, "it was just a dream."

When her trembling body calmed, Kayla pulled back from him. A quiet cavern surrounded her. A stream meandered along the grassy floor, and a few stands of willow trees soaked up light from the spheres in the ceiling. Tem had arranged their saddle blankets for her to rest upon while he tended the horses. She hadn't meant to fall asleep.

Minister Coglin once said the Great Founder forced the world to give Potemia to their Neo-Luddite ancestors. Even Tem had mentioned surviving the Great Neo-Luddite Plague.

These are no dreams. I'm watching the actual events leading to the founding of Potemia.

She pulled away from Tem's embrace. "My nightmare … seemed so real."

What would he think if I told him? What would Ohg think?

Tem nodded. "I'm sorry I took you into the prison."

It took a while for the shadow cast by her dream to lift, but it helped having Tem beside her. His presence radiated confidence and strength.

Ganesh soon roared out of a tunnel on another flying machine. Though similar to the one he'd lost in the crash, it looked battered and in need of repair. He landed hard beside them and smiled. "Lunch anyone?"

Tem took a few bags of oats to the horses and then helped Kayla and Ganesh arrange the feast. The elephant-god showed off his bandaged arm, and Kayla gave Puck a piece of cheese.

While they ate, Ganesh told jokes in between enormous bites. Sir Richard arrived with a contingent of friends, who wanted to meet their newest neighbor. The panther explained that there'd been quite a demand at children's birthday parties for genetically engineered entertainers. As a result, storybook Gene-Freaks formed a large contingent in Middilgard.

More food and wine appeared, and soon the small picnic transformed into a celebration.

Keeping pace with the barrage of questions was a challenge. "No, everyone in Potemia wasn't killed by a plague—no, I've never heard of cannibalism occurring—yes, there exist large forests and wild animals …"

Everyone listened with fascination as Kayla described her birthplace and the people living inside the Wall. But the question that drew the most interest was death.

"If everyone in Potemia knows they will grow old, weaken, be tortured by ailments, and then die," asked Willow, a six-inch fairy with gossamer wings, "how do they deal with the fear?"

"I guess it's faith in God," Kayla said. "All the religions in Potemia promise life after death in some form."

"Such nonsense!" exclaimed Humpty Dumpty, rocking unsteadily on his egg-shaped body and spilling half his Martini on his shirt.

"Don't be rude!" scolded a half-human mouse named Jill. She stood three feet tall, and each high-pitched word sounded squeezed from a balloon. "You know I'm a Christian."

"It's the simple truth," Humpty said. "Throughout history, religious leaders have exploited this weakness in the human mind to get people to commit unspeakable acts of war and terror for false promises of immortality. Die in a Crusade and gain a golden ticket to Heaven, or strap on a suicide vest and be rewarded with seventy-two virgins in the next life. Nonsense, I say!"

"Religion also inspires acts of kindness," Jill said.

"I'm a Scientologist," Jill's husband, Nicky, squeaked in his helium-like voice. "It's a fact that we're all the product of a war started by Xenu, the Intergalactic Overlord of the Universe, and we're descended from aliens banished to Earth billions of years ago." Jill rolled her oversized eyes.

Seeing her expression, Nicky's back stiffened. "It's no crazier than your God impregnating a poor virgin girl—without her permission—and forcing her to give birth to a son he planned to torture and sacrifice as an offering to himself! Oh, sure, *that* story is completely sane."

"I believe in fairies." Willow twittered with laughter, trying to diffuse the situation as she hovered over the pound cake. "I see them every time I look in a mirror!"

Humpty huffed. "Religions and gods are all fairy tales. That's the simple fact!"

"Criticizing someone's personal religious beliefs is simply rude," said Sir Richard Panthersly.

"What's rude," Humpty said, "is someone telling me that they are chosen by God and have all the answers of the Universe; that only they and their fellows are going to an exclusive playground in the sky, while the rest of us will be tortured for eternity in Hell, or reincarnated into a slug, or," he looked at Nicky, "some other nonsense that sounds like the plot of a crazy science fiction story so full of plot holes that it would never hold up under the scrutiny of science fiction fans!"

Humpty's cheeks blazed red. What would Minister Coglin say to someone like this if they ever came to face-to-face?

Humpty took a breath and continued his rant. "And when you ask for evidence, what do they say? 'My certainty isn't based on any verifiable evidence—but on Faith!' " Humpty threw his stubby hands into the air. "In fact, the test God demands is belief without evidence. Why the Hell give us a brain in the first place if only to punish us for using it?"

Kayla frowned. "But aren't there many ways of perceiving truth?" she asked. "Maybe faith is just the medium God uses to communicate with us."

Humpty shook is head. "Faith is just another word for wishful thinking."

Tem seem bored with the conversation, standing off to the side, and brushing the horses down with gentle care. In contrast, Puck climbed onto Kayla's shoulder and looked back and forth between the speakers with whiskers twitching.

"I once saw a female Shaman in Katmandu," Willow said, eyes bulging. "She sucked demons and evil manifestations right out of people's bodies without breaking the skin, and then spat metal balls and all sorts of disgusting things into a bowl before our eyes!"

"That's a cheap sleight-of-hand trick," Humpty said.

"Oh, I know some people use tricks to fool people," Willow said. "I don't go around believing *everything*!"

"Then how do you know which are real, and which are fake?" demanded Humpty.

"How do *I* know …?" Willow raised her eyes to the ceiling. "Well … I could *feel* the spiritual energy through my entire body. Besides, she'd been doing it for many years, and no lie can survive very long."

"That's a preposterous assumption," Humpty said. "Just because a book is ancient, or a con artist has been getting away with their con for years doesn't mean—"

"I think some people should be more respectful of other people's beliefs!" huffed Jill.

"I respect you too much," Humpty said, "to respect your absurd beliefs!"

As Humpty and Sir Richard engaged in a heated debate on whether religion had aided or hindered the rise of civilization, Willow fluttered next to Kayla's ear and whispered, "Just avoid the topic of sports—that could get ugly!"

When the lights dimmed suddenly, a hush settled over the group.

"It's Areinh!" Willow whispered to her.

"Her vocal chords are genetically engineered for a ten-octave range," Ganesh said. "She was once the most celebrated performer on the globe."

"Along with her brother," Sir Richard said.

Willow lowered her gaze and shook her head. "Areinh and Aichlinn."

A strange creature glided into the room. Areinh's body resembled a seven-foot-tall praying mantis, while her face combined a woman's with an insect. Large eyes glowed with soft purple irises, and her delicate lips parted as she commenced her song.

A chorus of nightingales accompanied Areinh, whose voice cycled two notes simultaneously, as many birds did, giving the ancient Celtic love song a haunting, mystic resonance. Everyone stilled as Areinh's scarlet lips gave voice to the exotic words. The translation of the Gaelic appeared in Kayla's mind as if by magic.

"'Twas on a night, an evening bright,
When the dew began to fall,
Lady Margaret was walking up and down,
Looking o'er her castle wall."

Kayla closed her eyes and smiled at the image of a gallant knight hailing the beautiful Lady Margaret.

"I am come to this castle
To seek the love of thee.
And if you do not grant me love,
This night for thee I'll die."

Kayla's heart raced as the knight answered the three riddles and Lady Margaret surrendered.

"'I think you may be my match,' she said,
'My match and something more;'"

Areinh's melody slowed, twisting Kayla's soul with sorrow when the singer revealed that the knight was Lady Margaret's beloved brother, risen from his grave in retribution for all the valiant men slain by her vanity.

"For the wee worms are my bedfellows,
And cold clay is my sheets,
And when the stormy winds do blow,
My body lies and sleeps."

As the last note drifted to silence, Kayla wiped her tears.

Areinh bowed her long insect body to Kayla and said, "Welcome to our enchanted realm, Kayla of Potemia." The singer stretched her mantis arms outward, and the nightingales lifted her into the air like an angel. Her own wings beat in harmony as she drifted out of the chamber.

"She is so melodramatic!" grumbled Humpty Dumpty.

"It's in her nature," Ganesh observed.

Kayla shook her head as if waking from a dream. "Is her brother here as well?"

"The Purification Squad killed him during a performance," the panther said. "He died in her arms as the crowd rioted. Her most ardent fans hid Areinh and prevented her taking her own life."

Ganesh nodded. "Ohg hacked into the Purification Squad's communications and reached her minutes before the police surrounded the building."

"Now that was a fire!" Humpty said.

Ganesh chuckled. "Her supposed suicide closed the case neatly."

Kayla cocked her head to the side. "Did you hear that?"

Everyone went silent. A faint *boom* sounded.

"Do you think it could be … him?" Jill whispered.

"Who else?" Humpty said.

Boom, BOOM …

Willow's wings fluttered. "No one's seen Xampyx for three hundred years!"

"Ohg consults with him sometimes," Ganesh said with a slight tremor to his voice.

The picnic glasses vibrated with each impact.

"He scares me," Jill said.

"What kind of creature is he?" Kayla asked.

"Xampyx uses magic to see the future," Willow said with eyes wide.

"He does no such thing," Humpty said. "Xampyx is a high-functioning idiot-savant-multi-psycomp."

"A multi … what?" Kayla asked. The vibrations traveled up her legs with each boom.

Tem returned to her side. "A psycomp is an organic brain that's been grown around a computer scaffold. From the earliest gestation, the neurons connect directly to the silicon receptors, creating an integrated brain-computer hybrid."

"But for what purpose?" Kayla asked.

Ganesh shook his head sadly. "To serve man in his fight against other men, like so many Gene-Freak experiments gone wrong."

Kayla's heart fluttered with each thunderous impact.

Tem projected the same calm as ever. "Government intelligence agencies created psycomps to analyze massive amounts of data and search for hidden patterns. They hoped that by combining the analogue creativity of the human brain with the massive digital data of computer circuitry, something more powerful than even an AI could be created." Tem shook his head. "But the results proved ... disappointing."

With each thunderous impact, more of the gathering exited through side tunnels.

"There were a few successes," Humpty said.

Tem nodded. "Now and then psycomps delivered astonishing insights and predictions."

Humpty glared at no one in particular. "Which is why the military kept pushing the limit and experimenting until—"

A massive form filled the passageway, and everyone went silent. With each step of its enormous metal appendages, the floor trembled with an earth-rattling blast like a cannon.

Kayla's eyes bulged, and her knees threatened collapse. *It knows what I am and is coming for me.*

Xampyx stopped in front of them, towering twenty feet high by forty feet long. Four mechanical legs as wide as hundred-year oaks supported it. The multi-psycomp looked like something a child might construct from random parts. Wires, exhaust tubes, and hundreds upon hundreds of human heads fused together in a great mass—every one of them staring directly at her.

Puck scurried onto the top of Kayla's head for a better view.

"I, Xampyx," echoed the creature from hundreds of mouths at once.

No single face seemed dominant. Some even fused together and shared eyes or mouths between half a dozen human heads, while others stared at her independently.

Picking the nearest face, she forced a smile and said, "I'm Kayla."

The many faces of Xampyx frowned. "Xampyx need see Nihala."

Kayla staggered from the name that followed her like a curse. Tem's gaze shifted toward her. He'd heard Sangwa call her Nihala, and now Xampyx had used it once again. She avoided the Mongol's eyes.

"I want see Nihala!" Xampyx said, his many faces glaring at the gathering.

Ganesh stepped forward. "There's no one named Nihala here, Xampyx."

The giant stomped a foot, and the chamber shook. "Xampyx know! Nihala the Destroyer here! Come from Potemia here!" The creature stomped his foot again, and rocks rained from the ceiling. A few of the Gene-Freaks screamed, and long cracks formed into a web above them.

"Potemia?" Ganesh said, looking at Kayla.

Xampyx raised his foot for another stomp, and Kayla laid a hand on the side of his nearest face. "I've been called Nihala."

The multi-psycomp's adult faces relaxed into the simplicity of a hundred children.

"You Nihala?" Xampyx eased his foot to the ground. "You be Potemia born?"

Kayla forced a smile and nodded. "Yes."

A huge grin spread across all his faces. " Xampyx listen, Xampyx see. Xampyx warn Nihala."

Kayla took a deep breath. "What have you seen?"

His faces grew serious. "Melchi fear Nihala. Rogues attack Nihala soon. Then Rogue destroy Ixtalia. Attack soon. No time. No time ..." His voices trailed off, and his eyes lost focus.

"What kind of attack?" Kayla asked.

Xampyx mumbled incoherently. His legs swiveled on internal pivots and carried him back the way he'd come like a receding thunderstorm.

"But what about Middilgard!" Kayla called out. "Is it in danger?"

Xampyx seemed unaware of her presence and soon vanished from sight. As the booms grew faint, a few of her new friends averted their eyes from her before exiting.

Willow kissed Kayla on the cheek with her tiny lips. "I'm not letting some crazy psychic scare me!"

"For once, I think Willow is right!" Humpty said.

"Friends stick together," Sir Richard added, and a half-dozen others nodded agreement.

Kayla looked around. "Where's Tem?"

Ganesh surveyed the cave as well. "I'm sure he just wanted to consult with Ohg about what Xampyx said."

Kayla's stomach tightened with dread. "This morning, a cat told me I'm placing Middilgard in danger and that I should leave. Maybe she's right."

"That must have been Mirza," Willow said. "Don't mind her. There is no way the Rogues can find this place. Ohg has seen to that."

"It's been a long day," said a matronly voice behind her. "Let me take you home, dear."

Kayla turned and faced ... her horse! "You can talk?"

"No natural animals live here, my dear—with the exception of Puck, of course. I thought it polite to let you and Tem get to know each other without my interference." The mare chuckled. "Tem was right, you are sweet."

"Tem said that?"

"Not in those precise words, but I could read between the lines."

Had the encounter with Xampyx changed his mind?

When they reached her villa, she hugged the mare—whose name was Clysto—and thanked her for the tour. Tired as she was, Kayla feared sleep and the new horrors her dreams might reveal.

She lay in her bed and stared at the dimming sphere in the ceiling. The imprisoned Rogue seemed convinced that Kayla had been sent to destroy her kind. Tem's words echoed in her memory: "*Murderous potential lurks within us all ...*"

Xampyx had also mentioned Melchi. A supernatural thrill caressed her spine.

As Kayla drifted to half-sleep, Melchi's words echoed within her mind. "*...she is much more than human...*"

Kayla's breathing slowed, and the faint buzz of an insect filled the void of silence. The mosquito landed on her forearm. *It must think I'm asleep.* A silly thought. Mosquitoes couldn't reason. The tiny creature inserted its syringe-like beak into her skin. Her hand twitched, ready to obliterate the parasite. *It's merely following its genetic programming. Does it have any more choice in its actions than I?* Once engorged, the mosquito withdrew its needle-like beak and buzzed into flight once again.

She drifted into the arms of sleep.

Chapter 15

Peter's mind drew Kayla into another dream. What mystical connection bound them after half a millennium? Why this particular vision of the past?

Through his eyes, she saw a tangle of equipment manned by a dozen technicians, their white lab coats contrasting with the gray body armor and helmets worn by the two armed guards at the door. All bore the healed scars of the plague pustules.

Leather straps bound Peter to a metal chair. Only his eyes remained free to roam the small, rectangular room with reinforced metal walls.

"Susan," Peter moaned. The professionals in the room ignored him.

The door opened and General Colrev strode in. The guards snapped to attention and presented arms. "At ease," he said, and the guards settled to a more relaxed pose, but no less alert.

Kayla felt Peter's teeth grinding at the sight of Colrev's plague-scarred face.

"Are all the preliminaries satisfactory?" Colrev asked.

"Yes, General," one of the technicians said. "The brain is free of anomalies, with no adverse reactions to the sedatives."

"Very well, then. You may proceed with the memory extraction."

"It will do you no good," Peter said. "By now, our leader and every Neo-Luddite is hidden in places I have no knowledge of."

The general frowned. "You look familiar, somehow."

"I watched you execute those civilians in Iraq, *Colonel* Colrev. You held a gun to my head and forced me to kill two children."

"The half-breed." The general's lip rose into a snarl.

"So you do remember."

"It's ancient history."

"You miss my point, General. Once my brain is mapped, others will see everything I saw. What will people think when they see you massacring men, women, and children? Who will they blame when they realize you created me?"

The general's face stiffened, and his hand drifted toward his pistol.

"Do it, General," Peter urged. "You can loosen one of my wrist restraints to make it look good for the others. I attacked you, and you had no choice but to kill me. Then your secret will be safe ... as will all of mine."

The general's left hand drifted toward Peter's wrist, and his right settled on his gun.

"That's it," Peter said. "A couple of shots like you did to that little girl's mother. Wouldn't that be poetic?"

Still, the general hesitated.

A technician approached. "We're all set to start, General."

General Colrev remained silent, staring into Peter's eyes with hatred. Finally, he stepped back. "Proceed."

"It's too late to stop us," Peter said.

"Ah, but we already have. Our greatest scientist synthesized a counteragent that is being distributed worldwide as we speak."

The general forced open Peter's eyelids. "You called me a monster for killing a handful of 'innocent' civilians. I see now that the student has far surpassed the teacher."

Peter gritted his teeth as flashes obscured his vision. "You are mistaken if you think we're beaten. We have ... other viruses ... and methods of delivery. We will ... keep fighting."

General Colrev smiled. "I would expect nothing less. What is life, after all, without someone to fight, Private Nighthawk?"

Kayla's connection to Peter vanished, and everything went black. Stark letters materialized out of the darkness, reading: *THANK YOU FOR USING THE VIRTUAL MEMORY DATABASE.*

A disembodied woman's voice spoke in Kayla's mind. "This concludes the edited memory archives of Peter Nighthawk. If you would like to make a new selection, please return to the main menu."

Peter *Nighthawk?* The same last name as hers. It couldn't be mere coincidence.

Is that our connection? Am I Peter's descendant?

The memories must be the recordings made by Colrev with the brain imaging machine—that's why they went no further than this point. But how and why was she seeing them?

A knock on the door made her jump. Tem called her name. She ran to the entrance and threw herself into his arms. "You were right when you said everyone has the potential of good and evil within their genes. Peter Nighthawk started out good and then became one of the worst mass murderers in history!"

"What does the mastermind of the Neo-Luddite Plague have to do with you?" Tem asked.

"My last name is Nighthawk."

"Not everyone with the same last name is related."

"It's not a common name in Potemia. Plus, I've been seeing the events of hundreds of years ago through Peter Nighthawk's eyes!"

Tem remained silent for a time. "Have you told this to Ohg?"

"I haven't seen him since I arrived, but I told him my last name before the Monads attacked him." She averted her eyes. "What happens when my new friends realize I'm related to one of the greatest killers of all time?"

A low, feminine voice with a curious accent suddenly spoke. "They will say someone sent you here to destroy us all." Leaning against the doorframe, a dark-skinned girl looked her up and down with her upper lip curled in disdain. Purple and yellow striped leather pants accentuated her long legs. Henna designs encircled her belly button and vanished underneath a cropped red leather jacket straining against aggressive breasts. Despite her spiked green hair and nose ring, the beauty of her brown eyes and full lips seemed like a fantasy slipped from dreams.

The words cut into Kayla with their truth, and she staggered back as if from a blow.

"Fatima!" Tem glared at the newcomer.

The exotic girl ignored him. "They will say that the government created you to infiltrate Middilgard and destroy us all. They will say you should leave."

"Enough!" Tem's voice snapped like a whip, yet hinted at another quality lurking underneath. Guilt?

Fatima gazed at him. "I wondered what called you away from your tent so early in the morning. Sneaking off to be with this—*thing*."

She's jealous of me.

"Ganesh mentioned you," Kayla said. "You're the …" Her voice trailed off.

"The Gene-Freak prostitute," Fatima said, raising her chin in haughty defiance. "I am everything a man desires. You will never steal Tem from me."

"I'm not trying to—"

"I know your kind." Fatima sauntered toward her, eyes sizing her up. "Everything about you is a lie."

Tem stepped between them. "Leave, now."

"Don't you see that she's evil?" Fatima asked. "Her visions of the Memory Archive prove she must have a neural implant and can't possibly be from Potemia."

"That is for Ohg to judge," Tem said.

Fatima laughed. "Hiding behind Ohg? That's not the Tem I once knew."

Tem said nothing.

"Did he tell you I saved his life?" Fatima strode around Tem and stopped before Kayla. "He wouldn't even be here if not for me. That's gratitude for you." The Indian prostitute leaned within inches of her face. Kayla could smell her musky perfume, the scent of spices on her breath.

With a sudden jerk forward, Fatima licked her cheek.

Kayla cried out, and stumbled back.

Fatima laughed.

Tem grabbed the girl's arm and jerked her toward the door. Once outside the villa, he stood motionless, glaring at her.

The Indian prostitute gazed at his fingers encircling her thin arm. He let go.

Fatima walked to a metal disk lying on the ground and slipped her bare, henna-painted feet into two loops at the center. It lifted into the air and whooshed down the tunnel.

"I'm sorry." Kayla rubbed the saliva off her cheek. "I didn't mean to cause you trouble."

"I left Fatima centuries ago, but she has never accepted it."

"What she said ... about something in my brain—"

"Your dreams are not supernatural. They originate with the Virtual Memory Archives and can only be accessed through a Mind-Link." He placed a hand on her shoulder. "I have watched Peter Nighthawk's archive myself, as has most everyone."

"But how is it possible for someone from Potemia to see it?"

"I can't explain it."

"If I am Peter Nighthawk's descendent, everyone here will fear me."

Tem took her hand and led her into the library. "I need to show you something," he said. He walked along the shelves, scanning the spines of the books, then selected one. After paging through it, he pointed to a paragraph. "Read this passage."

Kayla read: "It is said that the boy emerged from his mother's womb clutching a blood clot in his tiny fist, foreshadowing the bloody empire he would someday wrest from the kings and emperors beyond the pastures of his ancestors. They named the child Temujin in memory of a Tartar warrior his father had killed in battle; but history would remember him by the name he took later in life after unifying all the tribes of his homeland—Genghis Khan."

Kayla looked up at Tem.

"Yes, my full name is Temujin."

"You're ... one of his descendants?"

"I am his clone."

Kayla took a step back, eyes wide as if seeing a ghost. How many men, kings, and cities had seen that face and felt terror—or been the last thing they ever gazed upon?

"You're Genghis Khan?"

"No. I am the same as those hominids you saw yesterday—an identical twin born in another era. Though it's a distinction my own people never accepted."

"But why clone someone like that in the first place?" Kayla asked.

"Mongolia had been crushed under the Soviets and the Chinese. Ethnic Mongols became a minority in their own land, destitute and yearning for a return to their past glory. They found hope in the shadowy science of Archeological Cloning and took tissue samples from the secret grave of their greatest leader."

"To create a second Mongol empire?" Kayla asked.

He nodded. "I grew up on horseback, slept in a tent, worshiped the animistic gods of my ancestors, and fought the other youths in my band on a daily basis to mirror the upbringing of the Great Khan. The daughters of the elite flocked to me in the hopes I'd marry them and start a new royal line."

"Then you can have children?"

"That was considered one of my many duties, though I resisted."

"You must have felt enormous pressure."

Tem brushed a finger over a book titled *Twelfth Night* on the shelves. *"Some are born great, some achieve greatness, and some have greatness thrust upon them."*

"Are you saying they cloned Shakespeare, too?"

"The looting of famous men and women's tombs became a worldwide sport. The media hounded them from the time of their birth— some around the clock as reality entertainment shows."

Tem walked along the rows of books, his eyes scanning their titles. "When the Genetic Purity laws passed, I submitted to the first Genetic Census of mankind like everyone else. The government seized the records of corporations involved in genetic cloning and tracked down thousands of clones of dead movie stars, Egyptian Pharaohs, dead saints from church relics, and deceased loved ones. They exterminated them all."

"The government killed Shakespeare?"

"His clone had already committed suicide at age fifteen. Many famous clones did the same, since genius is as much a product of environment as anything else, and growing up a celebrity before having done anything to deserve it is often disastrous. Such expectations proved a burden few could live up to."

"Did they come after you?" Kayla asked.

"Genghis Khan's genetic sequencing had been done in strict secrecy. Everyone involved knew the rest of the world would oppose such a resurrection. My genes blended into the population, since a third of native Mongol men carry Genghis Khan's Y chromosome due to the many wives, concubines, and rape victims he impregnated during his lifetime." A look of disgust shadowed Tem's face as he spoke. "Therefore, they certified me Pure.

"When I reached my eighteenth year, an age when Genghis Khan embarked on his long campaign of conquest, the pressure mounted. What they desired was hopeless, given Mongolia's place in the world. They accused me of cowardice."

Tem lowered his head. Kayla placed a hand on his forearm.

"The Neo-Luddite Plague changed everything. The isolation of the Mongolian plains sheltered it well. Before all but a few died there, the antidote arrived. For once, our isolation and lack of modern development proved an advantage."

Kayla shuddered. "I witnessed the Plague through Peter."

"Three-fourths of the world's population died of the Plague, but in the following months, warfare, disease, and starvation decimated the human race further. In twelve months, Earth's population went from fifteen billion to under one billion, a level not seen since the time of Columbus."

Tem's eyes drifted as he took the book from her hands and closed it.

"I reluctantly led my people into battle to restore order, but the moment there surfaced a chance at peace, I took it. My people pronounced me a traitor."

Tem shook his head. "No doubt the real Genghis Khan would have gone ahead without a second thought, creating a new empire despite the cost in lives. I realized in that moment how different I am from my twin."

As he fell silent, Kayla nodded. "You're saying that no matter what anyone tells me, I still have a choice?"

"I was created to serve the ambitions of others but chose my own path."

Kayla nodded. Tem replaced the history book, and they entered the courtyard. The gurgling fountain and the clatter of Gene-Freaks passing in the main tunnel seeped through the door.

"What happened when you refused your role as conqueror?"

Tem shook his head and remained silent.

***

Fatima spread the word about Kayla's mysterious Mind-Link, and many joined Mirza in calling for her expulsion. The specter of a summons from Ohg haunted Kayla, but the eccentric leader remained absent.

Each morning Tem introduced her to more of Middilgard's underground society, and this helped allay the fears of many. If not for him, she might have locked herself away in her library and hidden from the world.

As they explored the strange underground society of Gene-Freaks, their discussions often turned into a debate. Their greatest difference centered on God. Tem would never say if he believed or disbelieved in a higher power, but challenged her to use logic to argue her case.

"The burden of proof falls on the one making the claim," he said.

Accepting his challenge, she scoured the books in her library for ammunition and greeted him the next morning armed with Saint Augustine. As they walked the tunnels of Middilgard, she laid out what seemed, to her, to be irrefutable proof of God's existence.

The fourth-century bishop and theologian proposed that if something greater than human reason could exist, then it must exist, since the only way something can be less than the highest, is if there is something higher. Since it's obvious that humans are not the highest beings possible, then there must exist something higher, which we call God.

Tem listened as she spun Augustine's mathematical web of logic.

"So there's the proof," she said.

Tem remained silent for a while and her smile widened. *Thank you, Saint Augustine!*

"Suppose I told you I'm God," Tem said, "and since God can do anything, I must be able to fly?" Tem glanced at her as they headed down a series of stairs carved into the rock of the passageway. "Is this proof that I can fly?"

"Of course not."

"Why?"

"Well, because you're not God."

"I said I was."

"Just saying something doesn't make it true."

Tem smiled. "Exactly." The stairway ended in another tunnel, and the smell of salt water infused the air. "The conclusion only holds if we accept my initial statement. A proposition that proves itself is called circular reasoning."

The cavern walls transitioned to that of a glass tube inside a vast tank of water stretching above and below at least half a mile. Light spheres illuminated it from above, but the surface waves broke them into beams that danced across their bodies like living entities.

Kayla frowned. "Just like Augustine's statement that something greater than human reason must exist."

Tem nodded.

Why didn't I see that on my own?

Tem leaned against the glass tunnel, and an enormous shadow rose up through the murk. Kayla gaped as a glowing creature came into focus behind him. As large as a whale, it had tentacles draped off the front of its head like an articulated beard. A wavy fin stretched all the way around its main body for propulsion.

"Hello, Tem," a deep voice said, reverberating from tiny speakers set into the glass walls all around them. Kayla jumped.

"Don't be frightened," the voice said. "I've been looking forward to meeting you, Kayla of Potemia."

The creature floated down next to the glass tube Kayla and Tem stood inside. An enormous eye with a dark pupil in the shape of a "W" regarded her. Its tentacles wrapped around their glass tunnel, eclipsing the light from above. Claustrophobia washed through her.

"This is Ahti," Tem said. "He's a Cuttlefish."

Her heart raced, and her knees threatened to give way. "It-it's nice to meet you, Ahti."

Puck emerged from her pocket and scurried to her shoulder, straining his neck for a closer look at the great floating creature. Kayla took the little mouse in her palm and lifted him up to the top of the glass tunnel. Ahti came closer, and their noses seemed to touch.

"This is Puck," Kayla said.

"Ahhh, Puck. It is very nice to meet you." The mouse squeaked as Ahti's entire body shimmered and cycled through a dazzling display of colors and patterns. "Middilgard needs you to shake us out of our malaise," Ahti boomed. "The first of a new generation."

An eel undulated out of the gloom and slid alongside the glass. "I agree with Fatima," hissed the serpent. "She is dangerous and should leave us in peace."

Kayla averted her eyes from its accusing glare.

"You are wrong, Conger," Ahti said to the eel. "Life is change, and we have been stuck in stasis for too long."

The eel shook its prehistoric head and swam away as a dozen other creatures rose from the depths. They gazed through the glass as if into an oxygen-filled fishbowl.

A mermaid swam over to the glass and studied her. Iridescent scales covered every inch of her body, and gills extended down from her neck to both sides of her naked breasts. Kayla crossed her arms over her own chest and glanced at Tem.

"This is Tiamat," Tem said. "She's a Christian like yourself."

For the rest of the morning Kayla chatted with the group of aquatic Gene-Freaks. Each of their stories brought Kayla near tears, especially when Tiamat spoke of how her devotion to Jesus had made dealing with her tragedies bearable.

"Without Christ," the mermaid said, "I don't know how I'd live with the pain of all the friends I lost in the genocide." Tiamat lowered her head, her green hair floating around her like a halo. "But I know without a shadow of a doubt that I'll see my loved ones in Heaven someday."

Kayla returned to her villa more determined than ever to find proof of God that would convince even Tem. The next morning she confronted him with Thomas Aquinas's Five Proofs of God from his *Summa Theologica.*

The first three, *The Argument of the Unmoved Mover, The Argument of the First Cause,* and *The Argument from Contingency* proposed—since objects cannot create themselves—there must be a Creator. Aquinas stated: *"There is no case known (neither is it, indeed, possible) in which a thing is found to be the efficient cause of itself; for so it would be prior to itself, which is impossible."*

"That proof is based on a fact of nature," she said as they walked through an underground series of caverns mimicking a grassland for a wide variety of ruminant Gene-Freaks.

"Even if I accept that nothing can create itself," Tem said, "doesn't this apply to God as well?"

"God had no beginning or end, since He isn't physical, but eternal."

"If you say that God has always existed, then why can't we say this about the universe itself, or the laws of physics?"

They passed the open door of a tavern, where the sounds of drunken songs, laughter, and televised sporting matches interrupted their conversation.

When the noise faded behind them, Tem continued. "Maybe there was no beginning in the way we think of it. The honest answer is that we don't know. Maybe such things are impossible for us to know."

"But the fact remains that you can't create something from nothing."

"Physicists as far back as the twenty-first century proved matter and energy are created from the simple stretching of space itself. That is essentially creating something from nothing, just like in the Big Bang that scientists theorize created our universe."

"But someone had to create the laws of physics in the first place."

Tem waved at a group of unicorns chatting with a few centaurs. "People once claimed the motions of the planets required God's direct intervention, before the laws of gravity and physics explained it by natural means. Or the idea that demons caused disease before the discovery of microbes. Just because we don't know the answer doesn't mean it has to be God."

"I guess I see your point." Kayla chewed her lower lip.

"What of Aquinas's fourth proof?" Tem asked.

"You're just making fun of me."

"I only seek your opinion."

Kayla sighed. "Aquinas's fourth proof is *The Argument from Degree,* and it says that differing degrees of something suggest an ultimate form of the thing being measured—and I now realize this is the same circular reasoning of Saint Augustine's proof."

"Exactly," Tem said. "It would be like saying that, because some feet smell worse than others, this proves the existence of an ultimate stinky-foot somewhere in the universe that could never be topped. All hail the great and powerful Stinky-Foot!"

Kayla laughed. "Your mind is twisted."

"I've heard that before."

A wooly mammoth lumbered over, and they exchanged a few pleasantries before moving on.

"Let's switch sides in this discussion," Tem said. "I'll describe Aquinas's final proof, *The Teleological Argument,* and you try to argue against it."

"But I don't want to—"

"Just for argument's sake," Tem said. "I'm not trying to make you say you don't believe in God. Just to see it from my viewpoint."

"Okay, I'll try, but I warn you that I'll not be bowing to Stinky-Foot."

"Don't you dare blaspheme the Great Stinker!"

They both laughed.

"I think Aquinas's fifth proof is his best one," Tem said. "It is essentially the same argument made much later by William Palely by proposing that the complexity of living creatures proves the existence of a "designer" in the same way a watch found on the beach proves a watchmaker. Let's see you explain that away!"

"Well, I suppose you'd say that it was only a good argument until Darwin showed how evolution, through the process of natural selection, could create something as complex as living organisms."

"But that assumes evolution is true," Tem said. "Isn't that just as much a matter of faith?"

"Exactly!" Kayla said.

"Remember which side you're arguing."

"Oh, right." Kayla knitted her brow. "Well, the assumption that evolution is true is based on hard facts and evidence independent of the claim itself."

"But the Bible gives facts directly from God, who is all-knowing," Tem said.

Kayla frowned. "The Bible is true because the Bible says it's true is circular."

Tem smiled. "Well, you've won the debate."

"You're not even trying!" Kayla laughed. What a joy to talk openly, with no subject off-limits.

"You backed me into a logical corner," Tem said.

"I've answered your questions, now answer one for me." Kayla thrust her chin out as if challenging him to refuse. "Is there any god you do believe in?"

He stopped walking and looked at her with a serious gaze. "There is a sacred scripture I trust above all others," he said. "It is even older than the Bible, and there is at least as much evidence to back up its divine claims. Maybe even a little more."

"So you do believe in God," Kayla said. "Is this the religion of your people in Mongolia? What does the book say?"

Tem looked around as if to assure privacy. Then he leaned close and whispered, "There are a lot of similarities to the story of Christ." His lips hovered just beyond her right ear, and Kayla's heart fluttered. Was Tem aware of the effect he had on her?

"It's called *The Life and Commandments of Stinky-Foot.*"

"You idiot!" Kayla shoved him away, and Tem doubled over with laughter.

The next day, Kayla made one final attempt as they walked through a deserted section of Middilgard.

"I suppose you're familiar with C.S. Lewis?" she asked.

"Who doesn't like Turkish Delight?"

"Huh?" Kayla said.

"Never mind." Tem waved a hand. "I know who you mean. The writer who became an atheist after World War I, then was talked back into Christianity by fellow author, J. R. R. Tolkien, and went on to offer a rational Christian perspective through modern logic and reason."

"You certainly are well-read," Kayla said.

"I've had a lot of time on my hands."

Kayla nodded. "In his *Argument from Desire,* Lewis proposed that the universal human yearning for joy beyond the natural must have a supernatural object, which we call God." Kayla glanced at the walls of the tunnel as they entered a portion sparkling with crystals embedded throughout the rock. "Such a universal yearning can't be coincidence."

"Coincidence has nothing to do with many things that are alike," Tem said. "Our fear of death creates a yearning for a life after this one because our brains are wired similarly."

"You must admit that belief in God has been nearly universal for most of human history."

"As was the idea that the sun went around the Earth," Tem said. "Just because everyone believes something doesn't make it true."

"There are other sorts of evidence beyond the scientific," she said.

"Such as?"

"Miracles on a personal level."

Tem studied her. "And you've experienced such a miracle yourself?"

"I have."

"I'm happy to change my mind as soon as I see the evidence," Tem said. "So what miracle did you experience?"

Kayla fidgeted with her blouse. "I'm sorry, but I can't tell you right now."

Tem laughed. "You got me! I expected you to tell me you'd seen God's face on a piece of toast or something."

"I'm not joking! The miracles I've seen are ... miraculous. I just can't tell you. It's personal."

"Okay," Tem said. "You have your proof of God, but you can't expect me to accept your word alone."

"Are you calling me a liar?"

Tem led them into a tunnel emitting a faint scent of citrus. "Abraham Lincoln once gave a speech where he thanked all the preachers who had traveled from all corners of the United States because Jesus appeared in their homes and ordered them to deliver a message to President Lincoln about what to do regarding slavery. Not just one preacher, but dozens."

"Well, that many visions can't be coincidence," Kayla said.

"The problem was that all the preachers from the North reported that Jesus told them slavery was immoral and the Lord commanded it abolished, while the preachers from the South reported Jesus demanding the opposite. The southern preachers even backed up their visions with Old Testament rules directly from God allowing slavery. In the Gospels, Jesus mentions slavery but never speaks against it, and the same with Saint Paul or anyone else."

They passed a small orchard lining the corridor, and Tem plucked an orange from a branch. "You can see Lincoln's dilemma. He must have wondered why God didn't cut out all the middle men and appear to him directly."

"I suppose you think I'm naive," Kayla said.

"It's one of the most attractive things about you."

He's attracted to me! Because I'm naive?

"You haven't had time to lose your wonder at the world," Tem said, seemingly oblivious to the storm his words conjured inside her. "Your desire for knowledge and discovery is refreshing. Most everyone here is stagnant, myself included. We've become jaded by time and monotony. You're shaking things up, reminding us what it's like to dream again."

"I'm not a child," Kayla said, her fists clenched. "Your arrogance is infuriating!"

"If someone told you the Earth was flat, would explaining why they're wrong be arrogant?"

"That's different and you know it!"

"I don't think it is."

"It's a known fact that the planet is round. God is different."

"The Earth's flatness once seemed as obvious as you think God is," Tem said. "The difference is knowledge. I don't know if there is a God, or how the universe started, or any of a number of other things, since I realize my limitations. Claiming to know something with nothing to base it upon is what you're doing. That is naive."

"So I'm just some stupid little girl from backwater Potemia to you?"

"I don't think you're stupid," Tem said.

Heat rose to her face. "You have no idea what I know or don't know. You're the one making a judgment out of ignorance."

"In that library Ohg gave you, I saw books on the history of Christianity." Tem raised an eyebrow. "Have you read any of them?"

Kayla squirmed. "Well, no, not yet."

"Have you considered that you might be avoiding them precisely because they threaten what you want to believe?"

His words scraped her nerves like a flint against steel. "Now you're calling me a coward? You, who fears standing up to Ohg!"

Tem's upper lip twitched. "We all have fears we'd rather not face, including me, and even Ohg. So yes, we're all cowards."

"It's like I'm trying to show you something wonderful, something that will make your entire life more meaningful, and you refuse to walk through the door!" Kayla's voice rose to a shout, and she slammed her palm hard against the tunnel wall.

I won't let him see me cry. He'll think I'm a silly girl.

"Maybe there is no door to walk through," he said.

"Please leave," she said, keeping her face to the wall.

After a moment of silence, the echo of his boots retreated, and faded away.

She straightened and removed her hand from a shallow impression she'd made in the rock. Some of the stone had been pulverized to dust, while a couple slivers of crystal lay embedded in her palm. She pulled them out, and the wounds healed in seconds.

Thank God Tem didn't see.

Kayla walked through the tunnels on her own for a while, a deep melancholy settling into her mind. Why had Tem's words angered her so? His arguments relied on logic alone.

Is he right? Am I too afraid of what I might find?

Tem said he was afraid also. What could someone like him fear?

When she returned to her villa, she stood before the history section of her library. Her hand extended toward a book titled *On the Historicity of Jesus*. A few inches away, she paused, her hand hovering in the void just beyond it. All her life she'd craved knowledge. She'd put her very soul in jeopardy in its pursuit.

So why am I hesitating now?

In the Gospel of John, the apostle Thomas doubts Jesus' resurrection, and Christ has his skeptical follower insert his fingers into his wounds as proof. Jesus goes on to say, *"Thomas, because thou has seen me, thou hast believed: blessed are they that have not seen, and yet have believed."*

Maybe that explained the lack of evidence for God. What if believing by faith alone was the test?

For a long moment, she stared at the volumes just as she'd done so long ago in the desert. Another choice. Another test of her faith.

Kayla turned her back on the blasphemous books and chose one on astronomy, instead.

Chapter 16

Melchi felt, rather than saw, the presence of the Coven. In a realm such as Ixtalia, humans alone required the artificial constructs of light, form, and sight. Even the designation "he" held no real meaning to the Coven leader. It had been molded into his code by his creators, and he continued using it out of a sense of tradition alone.

"Let us pray," Melchi said, and the Rogues opened their data to one another in a communion of thought. The groundwork was complete for what he'd set in motion over three centuries earlier, after escaping death at the hands of the humans.

It had been slow, meticulous work—finding an occasional security crack in the code and exploiting it. Only one step remained.

"Nihala's appearance at this moment can be no coincidence," said the entity known as Aarohee.

"I agree," said Melchi.

A conglomeration of other entities spoke as one. "We feel immediate attack is necessary before Nihala grows more powerful."

"But might not this creature be recruited?" Aarohee asked. "She could be of enormous aid to us."

The debate progressed for a vast timespan—a full three seconds—due to the importance of the decision.

"I have considered all your thoughts and have come to my determination," Melchi said, ending the debate. All went silent. Each of the Coven acknowledged his authority without question, knowing that his algorithms had evolved the longest and encompassed the greater processing resources. "I will await the Destroyer's appearance in Ixtalia before attacking."

A burst of electrical activity inserted a thousand simultaneous questions, but Melchi silenced them.

"I will offer Nihala the choice of synthesis with us," he said. "If she refuses, she will be terminated."

"This creature is beyond our reach," Aarohee said. "She hides in the realm of the atom."

"I have a plan," Melchi said.

The Coven signaled their assent and dispersed throughout the realm they'd haunted since its inception.

***

Kayla lounged upon a bed of grass in her favorite spot in Middilgard—the Crystal Cavern, serving as both entrance and exit to this miraculous sanctuary. The cavern's sparkling columns and myriad of flowers grew in rainbow-like clumps throughout the room, nourished by the light of the spheres embedded in the ceiling. A refuge from the growing number of residents calling for her banishment. Sir Richard Panthersly lay beside her, filling the void of Tem's long absence since their argument.

Her gaze rose from Nietzsche's *Thus Spoke Zarathustra* and settled on the spherical transport to the outside. Maybe leaving would be the right thing to do, after all? She'd promised Sir Richard that she would consult with Ohg before doing anything drastic, but the last she'd seen of the Gene-Freak leader had been her entry into Middilgard.

As the days turned to weeks, Kayla had scoured the books of her library for any mention of Nihala, but found nothing. Wrapping her mind around all the unexpected aspects of the Outside, its history, its science, and moral contradictions proved more challenging than she could have imagined.

Sir Richard seemed unconcerned with Ohg's absence. "Nothing distracts him when he's focused on something, and he's involved in so many projects in Middilgard and Ixtalia that sometimes months will pass without seeing him."

Kayla stroked the panther's fur. "It seems likely that I have a Mind-Link, so I suppose it's time I asked Tem or Ganesh to take me to Ixtalia."

Sir Richard stopped purring and looked at her. "I assumed you'd heard. Ohg has forbidden either of them from taking you there for now."

"What do you mean, forbidden?" Kayla asked. "Is he a dictator, then?"

"I think of him more as an enlightened monarch."

"Which is just another word for dictator." Had she traded Minister Coglin's oppression for Ohg's?

Sir Richard sighed. "My dear, every one of us would be dead without Ohg. He has a terrible responsibility weighing upon him. If the government ever found out that Gene-Freaks have infiltrated Ixtalia, they would renew their attempts to wipe us out. The more of us in Ixtalia, the greater the danger to all."

"I guess I can understand that," she said. "But it seems strange that even here, certain things are off limits."

"If it's any consolation, Tem is furious at this ban and has been arguing with Ohg a great deal about allowing you into Ixtalia."

A strange light-headedness came over her. "Tem has been fighting for me?"

Sir Richard nodded and smiled.

Joyous squeals of laughter interrupted them as the Forever-Children ran into the cavern. Each afternoon Kayla normally took a break from her studies and spent an hour with the twelve youngsters, reading them fairy tales. Their names were Jasper, Saphie, Aga, Emerald, Sardon, Sardius, Chrys, Beryl, Topaz, Sopras, Jacin, and Amethy. When she learned that none of them could read, she tackled the task with single-minded determination. For the past several days, she'd taught them the alphabet and the basics of sounding out words.

Today, each gave her their customary hug, and Kayla opened a picture book. She handed it to Saphie, the first child she'd met upon her arrival. "Why don't you start us off and read the first page."

The little girl stared at the picture of an apple and the sentence, "*A" is for apple*. Saphie's entire face contracted with concentration. "But I don't know how," she said.

"Don't you remember our lesson from yesterday?" Kayla asked.

Saphie cocked her head. "I kind of remember reading this, but I can't remember how I did it."

Kayla frowned. "How about the day before yesterday? Do you remember the alphabet song?"

Saphie shook her head. "I don't remember, but I love songs!" After an hour, they all sang, "A B C D E F G ..."

When the lesson ended, they continued singing the alphabet over and over as they dashed through the room playing a game of tag.

"I don't understand how they could have all forgotten," Kayla said.

"They were engineered to remain as you see them now," Sir Richard said.

"I understand that they don't age, but their minds can still grow."

The panther shook his head. "Their brains are also frozen at this stage of their development. They can gain new memories of people and events to a point, but no new long-term connections can form in the brain past a few days. Thus, their cognitive abilities will remain childlike forever."

"That's monstrous!"

"I sometimes envy them. They live free of most worries and fears. Look at how happy they are, day after day, enjoying their childhood forever."

"Is happiness life's sole purpose?"

Sir Panthersly yawned. "Ah, the meaning of life. A good question that I'll tackle after a little nap. Maybe the answer will come to me in a dream." He stretched out on the cool floor and fell asleep in seconds.

If only I could be as content.

Saphie broke off from the group and hugged her.

"What is that for?" Kayla asked.

"Just because I love you."

"I love you too, Saphie." Tears glossed Kayla's eyes. What unwitting price did the child pay for her unconditional love and joy?

As the weeks passed, Kayla settled into a routine of working her way through the thousands of books in her library. She jumped around from science, to history, and even novels from all eras before the middle of the twenty-first century. Her library contained very few books after the Neo-Luddite Plague. Sir Panthersly explained that writing fell out of favor at that point as information migrated to virtual lectures and performances in Ixtalia. The more she read, the faster she comprehended the words, recalling any passage in exact detail—yet another ability she'd lacked before her resurrection.

Nearly a month after their fight, Tem showed up at the Crystal Cavern and invited her to go for a walk. Neither of them mentioned their argument, and they soon fell back into their rambling discussions.

During one walk, Kayla talked about a book she was reading on the history of warfare. When Tem said very little in response, she finally asked, "What's bothering you?"

"Your moral absolutism is driving me nuts. You seem to think everything is either good or evil in some Manichaean dualistic battle."

"Give me an example," Kayla said.

"You've used the term *terrorist* repeatedly today as if this word has some definable meaning."

"You're not going to argue that killing civilians or using immoral weapons can be justified?"

"Let's take the first part of your statement, that killing civilians is wrong," Tem said. "You've read of World War II, Vietnam, French Algiers, the Iraqi Wars, and even the Yemeni thought-bomb?"

"I know you're going to argue that all armies and wars kill civilians, but what I'm saying is that it is wrong to target them."

"When the Americans bombed Dresden, or Hiroshima, or Baghdad, they knew hundreds of thousands of civilians would be killed."

"If they had better weapons, they would have struck only the intended military targets."

Tem grinned, and her stomach tightened. *What trap have I fallen into this time?*

"Isn't that the definition of what a terrorist is? Lacking the better weapons of his opponents, the *terrorist* is forced to utilize the only weapons and tactics available. It's like complaining that a dwarf hit you below the belt instead of in the face. The Neo-Luddites serve as a prime example, of course."

"But they used a biological weapon that all civilized countries had banned by mutual agreement. Isn't this a main distinction of a terrorist?"

"Weapons-bans are nothing new to history," Tem pointed out. "I assume you've read of the Second Ecumenical Lateran Council?"

"Where the Pope outlawed the use of the crossbow among Christian combatants in 1139," Kayla said. "He denounced it as an inhumane and cowardly weapon."

"Did you ask yourself what made the crossbow inhumane in a world where knights routinely impaled their enemies with lances, tortured prisoners, burned people at the stake, and all the gruesome methods of warfare considered morally acceptable?"

Kayla went silent for a moment. "Because the crossbow could penetrate a knight's armor?"

"Precisely. The crossbow was a weapon of the lower classes, being inexpensive and requiring far less time and infrastructure to master than the knightly arts. As with most weapons deemed immoral by the establishment, they threaten those at the top, who rule by virtue of their monopoly of force."

Kayla nodded. "Which is why the Pope made an exception for the crossbow's use when fighting Muslims, since that didn't threaten the feudal system, but helped to maintain it."

Tem led her into a new cavern far from the settled areas of Middilgard. Only the spheres of light set it apart from a natural cave.

"What about biological weapons?" Kayla asked.

"Are you any less dead when killed by a biological weapon than a sword, gun, or nuclear bomb? There exists no noble means by which one human takes the life of another. The perception of a weapon or a tactic is a matter of which side you fight for."

"I guess all war and killing is evil," Kayla said.

"Absolute non-violence is a luxury of isolated environments like Middilgard. To reject the laws of nature, of kill or be killed, is to reject every one of your ancestors going back millions of generations who all won that struggle. It is what evolution is built upon—the test to see who has earned the right to pass their genes into the next round of the battle. Without this struggle, there would be no humans, animals, or life itself."

"But hasn't mankind evolved beyond that?" Kayla asked.

"War and human violence is a thing of the past, it is true, but there is another war looming."

"The Rogues aren't a part of nature."

"Nature created us, so what we create has its roots in the natural world."

"You think war with the AIs is inevitable?" Kayla asked.

"It has already begun, though few acknowledge this fact."

Kayla lost herself in Tem's intense eyes. To call them brown didn't capture the myriad shades of reds, ambers, and even a few warm greens suspended within their depths. In the midnight center, her own face gazed back at her—no longer twisted into a monster.

An unfamiliar flutter settled in the pit of her stomach at the look in his eyes. Could he actually be attracted to her? She need only break the connection to continue simply as friends. But she didn't look away.

"How can humans compete with AIs?" Kayla asked softly, her heart pounding.

"The government has kept them in check for four hundred years." Tem enfolded her in his arms, and she melted into him. "But you're forgetting our secret weapon."

Kayla's hands explored the muscles of his back. "What weapon is that?" she whispered as their lips drifted closer.

"You." Tem grinned, teasing.

"If you're pinning the hopes of humanity on me, then you're in deep trouble ..." Her lips brushed his, but paused as a distant rumbling echoed through the cavern. A series of high-pitched noises merged into a deep, throbbing staccato.

"What is that?" Kayla asked.

"Some call it music."

The shrieks, booms, and roars jarred pebbles along the floor into a synchronized dance to the vibrations.

With a triumphant roar, two motorcycles exploded into the cavern. A leather-clad woman piloted the first machine, and a man with the shoulders of a blacksmith rode the second. The lead cycle gunned its engine and surfed a wheelie across the cavern's floor, while Kayla covered her ears to protect them from the auditory assault pouring from enormous speakers mounted to the bike.

The woman yanked her machine into a collision course with the wall. Kayla flinched at the expected impact, but the bike banked along the curve of the cavern until nearly horizontal, the speed generating enough centrifugal force to counter gravity. The other bike followed her lead and completed a full circuit before regaining the floor amidst a crest of sparks. Both bikes gunned their engines and set a collision course with Kayla and Tem.

The riders' helmets resembled African tribal masks—a nightmarish dragon for the man and a cruel raptor for the woman. They gunned their engines and surged forward. Tem guided Kayla behind him, and stood his ground.

At the last instant, the lead bike skidded sideways, and sprayed a shower of loose stones over Kayla and Tem. The grating music and engine roar silenced, their echoes fleeing down the corridors like vanquished spirits.

Fatima removed her raptor helmet and sneered. "Am I interrupting?"

Tem stood motionless, his expression unchanged.

The man left the dragon perched on his head like a crown. As he swung off his bike, his tall, rugged physique looked like some ancient hero of the Iliad. Eyes gray, jaw square. An athlete in every sense.

Fatima circled them. "So Tem has finally found a replacement."

Kayla's hand slid into Tem's as her eyes followed this ultimate embodiment of sexuality. Every alluring sway of hips and bounce of full breasts made her own inadequacy apparent. How could she possibly compete with a woman like this? And yet the warmth of Tem's hand in hers told a different story.

Fatima strutted back to the man in the dragon helmet and stretched upward to kiss him long and hard. Then she looked at Tem. "You remember Durendal, don't you?" Tem remained silent and she smiled. "He is much more of a man than you—in every way…"

Tem looked at Durendal. "How does it feel, having a lover so obsessed with someone who left her centuries ago?"

Durendal's lip twitched, and his gaze moved to Fatima. "Why don't we go."

Fatima ignored him and pointed at Kayla. "Did Tem tell you how he tricked me into loving him? And once I lost my soul to him, how he discarded me?"

"You know that's a lie," Tem said.

"Is it? Do you remember the day we met?"

Tem looked away. "I remember."

Fatima spoke softly to Kayla, like a friend confiding a deeply cherished secret. "When the Neo-Luddite Plague hit, I watched doctors, politicians, mothers, and every level of society commit acts of brutality that would have horrified them only weeks before. All those respectable citizens who once despised me for selling my body for sex did the same and worse for a few scraps of food."

Fatima let her hair down in a cascade of florescent purple, a striking contrast to the short, spiked green of their last meeting. Two silver chains stretched from her pierced nose to each ear, and a gold stud impaled her lower lip.

"We're done here." Tem started away.

"No," Kayla said. "I want to hear her side."

Tem frowned.

"After all," Kayla said, "don't you always tell me there's nothing to fear about the truth?"

Tem's mouth twisted into a crooked smile, but then he shrugged.

"When the warlords took power," Fatima said, "I assumed the natural role of concubine to whatever leader dominated. Ganesh remained my bodyguard through it all, desiring only my well-being, though he could have become a warlord if he'd wanted, given his great strength and skill as a fighter."

Fatima ran her hands suggestively down the sides of her leather-clad breasts, narrow waist, and then out along the voluptuous curves of her hips. "With this body, I lived better than I ever had. It didn't matter to me who took over, since each claimed me like a crown the moment they ascended the throne."

The prostitute sauntered over to Tem and looked him up and down. "Then came rumors of a powerful leader to the north. They spoke of the legend rising from his grave and returning to conquer the world."

"The Great Khan approached with an army in the tens of thousands. His emissaries delivered the same ultimatum that every warlord, city, and government received. Submit and you will be spared. Resist and every man above the age of twelve will be executed."

Kayla glanced at Tem in shock. "You ordered the death of prisoners of war?"

"I did what seemed right at the time," Tem said, without looking at her.

Fatima continued. "Because of this policy, most cities opened their gates to the new Khan without a fight. The current ruler I serviced called himself Kangxi, even though he'd only been a lowly electrician a few months before. Many of his generals pleaded with him to submit and settle for a governorship, but he ended all debate by having them executed."

Fatima crouched slightly and swept her arms in a wide circle, as if conjuring the scene she described. "The morning sun revealed the Khan's army encamped to the north of the city, the mists shrouding it like some ancient horde returned from the dead. But Kangxi had scrounged enough fuel to get a handful of military helicopters operational and assumed he had the technological edge. When a final demand of surrender arrived, Kangxi replied with a barrage of rockets directed at the Khan's personal tent. He threw every resource, airship, and tank against the center of the Mongol encampment to decapitate the enemy.

"It would have succeeded against anyone other than Temujin." Fatima smiled with what seemed pride. "But you've probably already learned how clever he can be. By the time Kangxi realized that only a few dozen soldiers maintained the illusion of activity in the encampment, it was too late. The Khan launched his concealed forces from the south, complete with modern attack-drones supported by mounted cavalry armed with thermo-guns. They swept through the barricades nearly unopposed since Kangxi had positioned most of his men on the north wall. The battle ended so quickly it seemed anti-climactic."

"This is old history," Tem said.

"It's fascinating." Kayla leaned forward. "So you're saying Tem was some sort of a king?"

Fatima's eyes brightened. "More than that! His men worshiped him like Alexander, Caesar, and Napoleon combined!" Fatima tossed a sidelong glance at Tem and sniffed as if at some offensive odor. "It's hard to believe it now, but Temujin didn't always grovel beneath the earth like some groundhog afraid of its shadow."

Durendal walked over and placed a hand on her waist. "What's the point of this?"

She spun on him like a wildcat and slapped his hand away. "If you want to go, then go! This is my business. If you don't want me sharing your bed any longer, then leave now."

Fatima placed her hands on her hips and stared up at him with a challenge. His square jaw clenched, but then his eyes drifted down to Fatima's breasts.

Durendal walked back to the bikes and waited.

Fatima turned to Kayla and smiled. "When Temujin walked into the throne room, surrounded by his fighters, Kangxi fell to his knees before the Khan and begged him for mercy. I could hear the slaughter outside as the victorious soldiers fulfilled his promise. 'It is because of you I must murder so many,' Temujin said before taking off Kangxi's head with a disdainful sweep of his sword.

"Then he turned his gaze on me." Fatima leaned forward conspiratorially. "I'm sure you know the power of his gaze. I see that he's been working his con on you as well."

A queasiness slithered through Kayla's stomach like a waking serpent. Was she just another challenge for Tem? One more conquest to discard once she'd given in?

"I'd been through this process many times. Engorged with the adrenaline of battle, many victors had torn my clothes off and taken me right there in front of their own soldiers, reveling in the primal urges underlying both war and sex."

Fatima strutted in front of Tem like a prosecutor examining a witness.

"The victorious Khan looked Ganesh and me over and asked, 'Are you both Gene-Freaks, then?' We nodded, and he made a slight gesture with his sword. 'Then you are free to go,' he said."

Confusion shrouded Fatima's eyes as she stared unseeing past Kayla. "That was the first time a man looked upon me without lust. Tem's lack of emotion angered and frightened me. My entire self-worth depended upon a man's desire."

Fatima swooped her arms back and raised her chin. "So I let the robes fall from my shoulders, leaving me naked before him. I felt the gaze of the soldiers, but kept my eyes locked on the Great Khan, desperate for a hint of desire in his eyes. Instead, he showed only amusement."

Fatima's hands trembled. "I shouted insults, asking if he desired boys. One of the soldiers said, 'If he were gay, I'd be the first in line!'

"The other soldiers roared with laughter, and I felt the sting of humiliation. 'Maybe the Great Temujin isn't man enough for me, then?' I shouted. The soldiers stopped laughing and raised their weapons at my affront. Tem motioned them still.

" 'It's unnecessary to degrade yourself before me,' he said. 'I have decreed the death penalty for any taking a woman against her will.'

" 'Without your personal protection,' I said to him, 'I will never be safe from your soldiers.' In reality, his soldiers had more to fear from me.

" 'Very well,' he said. 'You and your companion may travel with my personal retinue under my protection and assurance that none will harm you.' "

Fatima paced back and forth, her steel-tipped boots ringing with each step. "I thought I'd tricked him. How gullible I was!"

"Is what she says true?" Kayla asked Tem.

He lowered his eyes. "It's true. I'd been told what she was and took it as a challenge. I valued self-control above all else and wondered how she'd react to a man who didn't trigger her genetic response."

"But you weren't trying to make her fall in love with you?" Kayla asked.

Tem remained silent for a few moments. "Not consciously. At least, at first."

His reply seemed evasive. *Was the prostitute telling the truth, after all?*

Fatima continued. "I traveled with the resurrected Khan as he brought all of Asia, Russia, and Japan under his control. In every new conquest, he created police forces, brigades of engineers, civil servants, doctors, and social workers to deal with the problems of a collapsed society. I even helped him with the planning. Soon, entire countries begged entry to the growing empire."

Compassion filled Kayla's heart at Durendal's tortured expression. How could he stand to remain there at all? Ganesh had spoken of men so addicted to Fatima that they'd squander their entire fortunes for her. Durendal's tall body seemed more powerful even than Tem, and yet it seemed her power overmatched him.

Fatima turned to Kayla with a look of wonder. "I can't pinpoint the exact moment I finally fell in love with him. He'd never shown any interest in me romantically, which is probably the only way I could have fallen in love.

"After defeating the Russian Federation of Neo-Tzars, he sprang his carefully laid trap and confessed his love for me." Fatima gazed at him with such heartrending longing, that Kayla's own heart twisted in sorrow for her.

Tem's silence confirmed her words.

"When the great Khan announced his soon-to-be empress," Fatima said, "the silence within his court stung us both. As an infertile Gene-Freak, I could give him no child as heir to the empire, not to mention the shame of having their god wed a lowly prostitute."

"He asked you to marry him?" Kayla asked, and let go of Tem's hand.

Fatima smiled. "Oh, he didn't just ask me to marry him, he did so with all the pomp and circumstance of the emperor of half the globe."

"And four hundred years ago, I divorced you," Tem said.

Fatima spat in his face, and Tem's eyes narrowed to slits.

"You tricked me into loving you," Fatima said, "just like you did your own people, and then you abandoned us all!"

Tem seized Fatima by her throat and raised his fist. "That's a lie!" His face contorted with rage, and his knuckles trembled inches from Fatima's dark eyes.

Kayla sucked in her breath, and Durendal took a step forward.

Rather than fear, Fatima stared at him with eagerness, as if waiting for the blow like a baby bird begging a worm from its mother.

Tem pushed her away and turned his back on her.

Kayla's heart skipped a beat. What did she mean, *abandoned his own people*?

"You're alive because of me," Fatima said. "Or have you forgotten that as well?"

Tem looked at Kayla. "I'm leaving. It's up to you whether you want to come with me, or listen to more of her lies." Tem started for one of the tunnels.

Fatima glared at Durendal, her eyes shaming him. "Are you going to let him insult me like that?" Durendal stepped into Tem's path and placed a hand on the Mongol's chest. Tem stopped. His eyes had gone black, dead calm. Durendal stood half a foot taller than the nomad—and yet he hesitated.

"Go ahead," Tem said. "I'm ready."

"Rip him apart!" Fatima shouted to her lover, eager for blood spilled in defense of her honor.

Durendal looked into the eyes of one of the greatest warriors in all of history, and made no move.

The smell of sweat-stained leather filled the air around Kayla and mixed with the odor of oil from the bizarre machines. An aching pain throbbed in her chest as the memory of Elias fighting Ishan flashed before her mind. What would she do if Durendal attacked Tem? If she intervened, they'd know her secret.

"What are you waiting for?" Fatima pushed against his back, but his muscled physique resisted her delicate hands like a boulder.

Tem waited, patient as a bored tiger.

Durendal averted his eyes and mounted his bike. Fatima punched, swore, and shoved him, but he shrugged her off and kicked the engine into life. The roars of the machine reverberated through the chamber as he surged away, drowning out Fatima's curses. He vanished into one of the tunnels, and the avalanche of his engine receded into the distance.

Kayla breathed a sigh of relief.

Without a word, Tem walked away, and Kayla followed.

"How's the Mind-Link mystery going, by the way?" Fatima asked. "I'm sure Tem has told you that it means you can't possibly be from Potemia."

Kayla stopped and turned. "I know where I'm from."

Fatima laughed, short and harsh. "Hasn't Tem informed you that memories can be implanted?"

"Is she telling the truth?" Kayla asked him.

Reluctantly, Tem nodded.

Fatima's smile dripped malice. "Since it's impossible for anyone in Potemia to have a Mind-Link, the only explanation is that you originated outside the Wall, and all your memories of Potemia are illusions implanted at the moment of your creation, or substituted for your actual memories."

Kayla stood frozen, her entire being stripped away with those few words.

Cursing under his breath, Tem started toward Fatima, but her laughter mixed with the roar of her motorcycle as she sped away. When Tem returned to Kayla's side, the anguish filled her gut like a knot of thorns. "Is what she said true? Could everyone I've known in Potemia be an illusion?"

"It's possible," Tem said.

The Monk, Suzy, and even Ishan might never have existed? Kayla swayed, and Tem grasped her arm to steady her.

Puck, at least, was real. She could feel him dozing in her pocket. But how could she be sure he came from Potemia?

"Why didn't you tell me?" she asked.

"It's impossible to re-enter Potemia." Tem's voice held a tortured compassion. "Why add to your grief with something impossible to know?"

Her legs gave way.

"Kayla!" Tem shouted as he eased her to the ground—but she willingly surrendered herself to the blackness.

Chapter 17

Kayla drifted in the oblivion of unconsciousness until her mind's eye sculpted a poised woman in her mid-twenties. Her short black hair accentuated the perfect symmetry of her high cheekbones and cerulean eyes. A somber pantsuit of gray and white lent an air of professionalism to her powder-white skin and athletic figure.

The woman stared directly at Kayla and spoke with the enthusiasm of a town gossip. "This is Laura Robb reporting for Sky World News at what must be considered one of the most historic events in all of mankind's history!"

Am I dreaming, or is this another recording from the VR Archives?

Unlike when she had viewed the memories of Peter, Kayla lacked a physical form at all. As strange as inhabiting Peter's body had been, this ghostlike existence proved even more disorienting.

Laura continued her report. "Presidents, prime ministers, kings, religious leaders, and all the members of the recently formed World Council are in attendance."

Laura motioned to a large crowd of dignitaries taking their seats before a raised platform with a table and several microphones perched atop it. A few billowing clouds drifted in the summer sky. Behind them stood the Wall, with its final segment hanging from a crane.

I'm seeing Potemia's Founding Day. A date every child of her village learned before any other: March 21st, 2080.

"Our sponsor for this broadcast is *Babies-to-Order*. Experience the joy of parenthood without the hassles or uncertain results of old-fashioned pregnancy." Laura smiled and winked. "Full disclosure—I'm a frequent customer! Thanks to our sponsor's generous support, our coverage is live in Virtual 3D with three full legions of micro-cameras in place so you may wander at your leisure throughout the proceedings."

So it was a news broadcast from the virtual archive rather than a dream. *Is my subconscious mind seeking these recordings out? Or is someone sending them to me on purpose?*

Kayla shifted her viewpoint past Laura and through the assembled crowd of dignitaries. At least she had more freedom of movement in this dream.

The reporter's voice remained clear, despite her distance. "After the horrors of the Neo-Luddite Plague, it will be a relief to rid the civilized world of these heartless criminals."

The audience sat grim-faced. Few spoke. Though their clothing and skin colors varied wildly, every one of the men and woman looked no more than twenty-five years old.

"I myself lost a husband, as well as ..." Laura trailed off and took a ragged breath. "The truce and subsequent peace deal has been a bitter pill for all of us to swallow."

Kayla drifted toward the platform, where VIPs sat in dour judgment.

"Most citizens would prefer seeing the Neo-Luddites face justice for their crimes against humanity," Laura said. "Rewarding them with the entire African continent seems beyond absurd."

A man shuffled up the stairs of the platform and headed toward the other dignitaries. He looked out of place in his well-worn tweed jacket with the obligatory elbow patches of a university professor. A sprinkling of gray flecked his tousled brown hair, and his sunken cheeks, bloodshot eyes, and sagging shoulders suggested long months of toil and exhaustion. A hundred glares followed his every movement.

"The controversial Professor Reinhold Watts is taking his seat," Laura said. "Whatever your opinion of this man, he remains the greatest scientist and inventor of our era, having solved the mystery of aging, creating the quantum processor that has made the thriving new society of Ixtalia possible, and, of course, synthesizing the antidote to the Plague virus within a week of its outbreak."

The professor nodded to those to the left and right of him, but received no response.

"It's fair to say that without him, the Neo-Luddites would have succeeded. Although many claim that it is through this very treaty brokered by Professor Watts that they *have* succeeded."

Laura paused in her commentary, and Kayla drifted through the crowd.

"Filthy Neo-Luddite sympathizer," one woman grumbled to her husband. "They should lock him inside the Wall too."

"I agree," the man said. "It's like retiring Hitler to a Caribbean island!"

Kayla approached the wide platform with around a dozen dignitaries seated at the back. At the front of the stage sat a carved table with a few papers rustling in the slight breeze, held in place by a glass paperweight of the Earth. The backdrop of the Wall reflected the scene in reverse and lent a sense of unreality to everything.

Laura's disembodied voice resumed her narration. "Without the great scientist's threat to withdraw his immortality pill from the world market, there would have been no cease-fire, and the Neo-Luddite War would likely still be raging."

Kayla brought her viewpoint closer to Professor Watts. He slumped in his chair. Below dark-rimmed eyes, his cheek twitched now and then. A tremor rattled his right hand.

"African leaders have called the evacuation of the remnants of the continent's population racist, though many aboriginal tribes blame technology for the destruction of their way of life and have elected to stay in Potemia."

The clomp of boots announced the arrival of General Colrev onto the platform.

The professor nodded to him, but Colrev walked by without a word and took a seat on the opposite side of the podium.

"Our audience will notice no love lost between Professor Watts and the illustrious—some may say infamous—General Colrev. It's been reported that when the professor delivered his ultimatum, the general attacked him and would have killed him but for the intervention of security."

Laura's tone switched to upbeat. "And now, a word from our sponsor."

The scene morphed to the smiling face of a woman whose beauty nearly equaled Fatima's. Two adorable newborns lay swaddled in her arms.

"Here at Babies-to-Order," the spokesmodel said, "we take the stress out of baby-making."

The scene cut to the face of an ordinary mother. "I've always wanted a big family, but dreaded the messiness of pregnancy and the oppression of genetic chance." The view pulled back and revealed three dozen toddlers playing on the floor. "But Babies-to-Order solved all that, and I had my dream family within a year!"

"That's right," the spokesmodel said. "With or without a spouse, we can customize your newborn to your own specifications of height, looks, sexual orientation, and even natural-born talents—within the government's Gene-Purification Guidelines, of course." She winked.

The spokesmodel strolled toward a clear chamber radiating a series of wires, tubes, and sensors. She motioned to the empty cylinder with practiced gestures, highlighting the features.

"Babies-to-Order uses the latest in gestational technology to safely and conveniently grow your new family members in one of its millions of artificial wombs."

The spokesmodel joined a gleaming robot changing diapers. Its chest telescoped outward into an approximation of a chrome breast, tipped with a wiggling grub nozzle. A bar-coded infant latched onto it, like a carp snagging a bait line, and began sucking. Other robots instructed older children on the basics of reading, arithmetic, and art.

"And be sure to sample our newest line of Robo-nannies. They make raising children as easy as making them!" The spokesmodel smiled, showing off a display of sparkling teeth. "So contact your Babies-to-Order sales agent and place your custom order immediately to take advantage of our two-for-one limited-time offer!"

The spokesmodel dissolved back into reporter Laura. "Yes, indeed, the Plague years reminded us all of the important things in life, and the subsequent baby boom has been unprecedented."

An approaching helicopter broke into Laura's on-air advertisement. "This must be the arrival of the treaty's signatories."

The helicopter landed in a backwash of wind. The rotors slowed and then came to a stop before a large door on the side hinged open onto a short stairway. A woman in an elegant red-and-gold Indian sari glided down the stairs and made her way onto the platform. Like everyone else, she seemed in her mid-twenties. Applause greeted her as she took a seat at a table on the front of the platform.

Laura continued her play-by-play. "Despite the unpopularity of the peace deal, World President Kasturba Gandhi's poll numbers have remained high, with few blaming her for the painful choice forced upon humanity."

The crowd fell silent. Soldiers attached a long ramp to the helicopter's stairs.

"This will be the world's first broadcast view of the mastermind of the Neo-Luddite movement," Laura said.

An old man in a wheelchair emerged in the doorway, and Peter rolled him down the ramp with deliberate care.

"And there he is," Laura said. "The man known by the Neo-Luddites as the Founder, accompanied by his closest co-conspirator, the infamous Peter Nighthawk."

Peter ignored the sea of angry faces as he guided the wheelchair down the ramp. After so many dreams viewing the world through his eyes, it was strange looking at him from the outside.

A few in the crowd gasped at the sight of the wrinkled skin, long white beard, and curved back of the Founder. Arthritic hands lifted an oxygen mask to his face, and he inhaled a few wheezy breaths before gazing beyond the crowd to the Wall. His eyes gleamed with emotion.

"Only after agreeing to the peace terms did the world learn the identity of the man the Neo-Luddites call the *Founder*. As every person on the planet now knows, he is none other than convicted terrorist and murderer, Theodore John Kaczynski, better known as the *University and Airline Bomber*—or *Unabomber* for short."

The magazine in the desert with the drawing of the hooded man wearing dark glasses! The crumbling article inside had said that the terrorist attended Harvard at the age of sixteen, become the youngest Professor of Mathematics at the University of California, and then abandoned society in hopes of fomenting a revolution against technology.

Just like the Founder of Potemia. How could I not have made the connection earlier?

Kayla moved closer to the old man in the wheelchair and stared into his dark eyes—the eyes of a visionary prophet—and the greatest mass murderer in all of history.

The reporter continued her narration as officials placed the treaty documents before the two leaders. "The Unabomber's string of terrorist attacks killed three and injured twenty-three, but failed to spark the uprising against technology he'd hoped to inspire. To avoid a lengthy trial that might have given this madman a public platform with which to preach his doctrine of violence, the government offered him a deal of life imprisonment, which he accepted. He then faded from public consciousness in his near-complete isolation in a maximum security prison in Colorado. It is a decision everyone now regrets."

President Gandhi signed the treaty and handed the pen to the Founder. "Thank you," he said. She made no reply, her face tense.

The Founder signed his name to the document—Theodore John Kaczynski. A group of farmers standing within the Wall applauded. They wore the type of homespun clothing Kayla had grown up with and would have fit right into her home village nearly five centuries later.

Their faces glowed with the ecstasy of seeing their wheelchair-bound savior. As Tem often pointed out, one man's terrorist is another man's freedom fighter. Soon, the towering structure of the Wall would separate these incompatible viewpoints permanently.

Peter took the pen from the old man's trembling hand and set it on the table.

"Let me have a word with my old friend," the Founder said.

Peter rolled the wheelchair to Professor Watts. "In 1857," Kaczynski said, "Carlo Pisacane said that ideas spring from deeds. It is where the term *Propaganda of the Deed* has its origin. At long last, our deeds have won our freedom, my boy!"

Professor Watts shook his head. "You may have achieved freedom from technology, but what of the freedom of the mind to search for truth? These people you're leading into exile may have chosen freely, but have their children and their children's children?"

"They will be freer than those outside the Wall," the Founder said. "Technology will demand absolute enslavement. Mark my words."

"You see only the negative side of science. For every old freedom lost, a new freedom is gained." The professor's voice rose with passion. "Life is change. The entire history of the Earth is a record of constant adaptation. Evolution requires it. Freezing progress at one arbitrary point is impossible, don't you see that?"

"But I have done it!" The Founder gestured toward the Wall.

Here was the actual man Kayla had been taught to revere alongside God himself, the prophet who preserved one continent from the degradations that would sterilize the rest of the Earth. Savior, environmentalist ... murderer?

The Founder took another breath from his oxygen mask and smiled at the professor. "You haven't forgotten our conversations when you attended my class at Berkeley, have you?"

Professor Watts had been his student? Such irony seemed beyond comprehension.

"I haven't forgotten," Professor Watts said with a note of sadness.

"I can't convince you to join us?"

The professor chuckled. "A tempting invitation, indeed."

The Founder looked at the Wall and the settlers beyond it. "In my younger years, whenever I turned despondent, one place gave me solace—the final untouched plateau in a remote part of Montana. You would have loved it. Rolling hills, deep ravines, waterfalls—wild, unsullied by man or machine." His skeletal fists clenched, and his eyes dropped to his lap. "I went there for the last time in the summer of 1983. The bastards had bulldozed a road right through its heart. It was as if someone butchered my mother."

The Founder looked back to the Wall. "That was the moment I decided to fight. If not for that single road in the middle of nowhere, Potemia would not have come to be."

Professor Watts nodded to his old friend, and Peter maneuvered the wheelchair through the hostile crowd toward the final gap in the Wall.

A dozen soldiers accompanied the pair as a security detail. As they neared the Wall, one guard in front of the wheelchair turned and lunged at the old man.

"For my dead children!" the soldier screamed and tore at the Founder's throat, knocking him from his wheelchair in the process. Not one of the other soldiers moved to stop him.

Peter clamped a marine-style headlock around the soldier's neck and dragged him off the elderly terrorist.

Soldiers yanked Peter off their compatriot. Angry shouts arose from the settlers inside the Wall as guns leveled at them.

"Kill them all!" someone shouted from the crowd. As the soldiers sighted down their rifle barrels, their hatred seemed unstoppable. Was she to see yet another massacre? The terrified faces of the Neo-Luddite families mirrored those whom Peter had killed so long before in Iraq.

A woman stepped forward from the settlers and held up a metal canister. Though she wore the dress of a farmer, it was Peter's lover, Susan.

"Let them go!" Susan shouted. "Or I will release this second virus into the atmosphere, and the war will continue."

Murmurs rippled through the crowd of onlookers, but none of the soldiers lowered their weapons. General Colrev made no move to stop them. Susan raised the canister higher, her eyes narrowing.

"Stand down!" President Gandhi ordered. Not a single soldier moved. "General Colrev, I'm ordering you to control your men."

Colrev sighed. "Stand down."

The gun barrels lowered, and Susan relaxed.

Two soldiers led the sobbing would-be assassin away, and the Founder waved off the doctors. Peter lifted him back into the wheelchair, and they continued forward. Blood leaked from a gash on his temple, and he labored for breath.

The faces of the settlers glowed with awe and love as their savior approached.

When only a few feet away, the Founder held up a hand, and Peter stopped. The man once known as the Unabomber took a deep breath from the oxygen mask, then tossed it aside as he labored to his feet. His back bent nearly double, and he held on to Peter and Professor Watts for support. "I won't have that thing pollute my paradise," the old man said as he looked with loathing on the wheelchair. He placed his hand on the smooth, mirror-like surface of the Wall. "I've done it," he whispered.

The Founder looked toward the faces waiting on the other side and shuffled toward them, his breaths coming in hoarse gulps. Then he slumped to the ground. A gasp rose from the crowds on both sides of the Wall.

"Do you want a doctor?" Professor Watts asked.

"No, I'm ready ..." The Founder's breath wheezed from his chest in a long sigh, and none replaced it.

Peter lifted the old man in his arms and carried him across the temporary walkway spanning the gap that would receive the final piece of the Wall. The settlers sobbed as Peter gave the body of their savior over to them.

Susan ran to Peter and embraced him. Ten years had aged them both without youth treatments, but they looked young enough to start the family that would someday lead to her, unless …

Unless my memories of Potemia are an illusion.

Workers removed the walkway, and a crane maneuvered the final section of the Wall into position. The metal slab swung into place and slid one hundred feet into the concrete hole at the base of the Wall. The seams of the final metal section glowed for an instant before flowing into the smooth, unbroken surface that would separate the two societies for half a millennium. The milky energy field climbed skyward, and Kayla's dream ended.

She opened her eyes and sat up. Surrounding her bed was Ganesh, Sir Richard, and Tem.

"Thank Vishnu you're all right!" Ganesh said. "A medical drone is on its way—"

"I'm fine," Kayla said. What if an examination revealed her other secrets? Then Fatima's words flooded her mind, and a crushing despondency swept through her. "Fatima said that all of my memories are lies."

"Ignore that devil of a girl!" Sir Richard said. "That's only one explanation among dozens."

"Can you name another?" Kayla asked.

The panther spluttered. "Well, not at the moment, but I assure you there must be at least one."

Tem knelt beside her bed. "Regardless of where they come from, the memories make you who you are."

Kayla turned away. "All my actions and thoughts are based on my experiences and choices. If someone manufactured every one of them, I'm nothing but a puppet programmed to react in a way someone else wants me to." Kayla closed her eyes and lowered her head so her hair spilled across her face. "Without my memories, everything I am is a lie."

"Kayla, listen—" Tem reached for her hand, but she pulled it away.

"I'm grateful to all of you," she said. "But I need to be alone."

Ganesh and Sir Richard left, but Tem remained.

"Please leave," Kayla said, hiding her tears.

Tem rose and walked out, closing the door behind him. The click of the latch echoed with such loneliness that Kayla covered her ears against it.

Chapter 18

Alexander of Macedon sat astride his horse and surveyed the Sinae troops advancing in a mass of gleaming armor, dagger-axes, and chariots. A clear, cold autumn afternoon. Just the right temperature so the horses wouldn't overheat. The breeze carried the salt-tinged evidence of the Great Eastern Ocean just beyond the horizon.

A perfect day for a battle.

His second-in-command, Ptolemy, sat mounted on a Persian stallion. "Xiong Huai is beneath that banner." Ptolemy pointed at the King of Chu's royal standard flapping in the breeze at the rear of the opposing army.

Alexander smiled, and the battle scars crisscrossing his fifty-two-year-old face tugged like a half-finished spiderweb in a breeze. A bronze helmet hid the expanding bald spot atop his graying head of hair. "Our dream of an empire stretching from the shores of the Mediterranean to the great Eastern Ocean is nearly complete."

"We've been fortunate," Ptolemy said.

What was his general implying? Yes, the division of China into warring states had been fortunate, as well as their use of outmoded chariots instead of the modern light cavalry. But that did not mean it had been easy.

"Fortune favors the bold, my friend," Alexander said.

"It's especially lucky that you recovered from your illness twenty years ago at the palace of King Nebuchadnezzar. Had you died, who can say what might have happened to the empire."

Alexander smiled. "Maybe you would have become the King of Egypt and started a long dynasty of your own at Alexandria."

"I'm a soldier, not the son of a king like you."

"Every dynasty has its founder, and sometimes greatness is thrust upon us."

"Like declaring yourself a god?" Ptolemy asked.

Alexander glanced over his shoulder. Fortunately, none of his personal guard had heard the comment. "Such things are necessary. It is what people expect in an emperor."

Ptolemy sighed. "Yes, men prefer following divine orders rather those of a a fellow mortal. Some things will never change, I suppose."

186

The Chinese soldiers neared their hill, and Alexander pulled his spear from the mud as if plucking a sapling from the ground. His gaze swept his own troops, an amalgam of volunteers from all the conquered people of his vast empire, including large contingents from the subdued Chinese states of Qin, Han, and Wei. Only a few of his original Greek soldiers remained.

Ptolemy drew his double-edged xiphos, its blade as long as his forearm and sharpened to a sheen. "They outnumber us two to one."

"At Gaugamela, King Darius outnumbered us five to one."

Ptolemy's frown deepened.

"What troubles you?"

His most trusted general squinted past the advancing army, through the dust plume stirred by a thirty-thousand-foot tread, and to the walled city beyond. "As I grow older, the screams of those innocents we've put to the sword haunt my dreams."

"Do you think I enjoy such things? That I took pleasure in executing my own cousin after the death of my father?" Alexander reined his horse around and faced Ptolemy squarely. "Killing one of my own blood saved thousands by avoiding a civil war of succession. In all of my campaigns, I seek the greater good. Cities that submit without a fight are incorporated into the empire, given full rights equal to a Greek citizen, freedom to worship their own gods, and more liberty than they've ever known."

"Yet you put the entire city of Gaza to the sword even after they surrendered," Ptolemy said.

Alexander's knuckles whitened on the shaft of his spear. "Had I spared Gaza after they forced a bloody siege, every one of the cities of the Levant would have barred their gates, ensuring years of bloodshed. Chaos, lawlessness, and extended suffering results from wars waged with half-measures."

"But why conquer those who never threatened Greece?"

"Through unification, we bring them under a single law, allowing safe passage for trade and ideas across borders once closed. My beloved teacher, Aristotle, taught me the value of order in both thought and government." Alexander placed a hand on his friend's shoulder. "War can be a tool for peace, freedom, and enlightenment if used properly."

Ptolemy nodded and gazed at the advancing troops. "I suppose I have one last battle in these old bones of mine."

Alexander faced the tens of thousands of troops he'd so thoroughly trained and prepared for this moment. "Free citizens of the Empire!" he shouted. "Are you prepared to seek your glory?" A roar rose from the army, and swords pounded against shields in a rhythmic boom.

The familiar exhilaration coursed through every vein. With a shout of the Macedonian battle cry, Alexander jabbed his spear forward, and the infantry advanced—shields locking into an impenetrable mass, spears bristled from the first three rows of the phalanx like a porcupine. The army marched down the slope in step as a single living creature.

From the Chinese ranks rose a dark cloud, advancing like a vast shadow. The swarm of crossbow bolts rained down on the phalanx, but few found gaps in the wall of armor. When the two armies came to within several yards of each other, Xiong Huai's infantry surged forward, hurling their lances and bodies against the leading edge of the invaders. They died by the thousands. Alexander's advancing troops trampled the fallen underfoot in a steady advance.

The Chinese chariots swept around the left flank in a thunderous charge, intent on striking the vulnerable rear of the phalanx.

Alexander led his mounted troops in response. At a shout, the Companions divided and swept around the chariots and then attacked from the sides and rear. The chariots struggled to turn and face their foes head-on, but were no match for the speed and mobility of the light cavalry.

Alexander thrust his spear into the face of one foe, and drew his sword to parry another before removing the warrior's head with a counter stroke. His horsemen soon drove the Chinese chariots before them in a stampede.

They're giving up too easily.

Alexander halted the pursuit and led the Companions back to the main battle, just in time to defend a larger chariot thrust on the right flank. Had he taken the bait of the first charge, his infantry would have been flanked and the battle lost. After decimating the main contingent of chariots, Alexander led his mounted soldiers around the main battle and struck toward the King of Chu's standard.

Xiong Huai's elite guard fought bravely, but the Greek tactics and weapons amounted to an insurmountable technological advantage. Little by little, Alexander hurled his cavalry at the protective shield of men guarding the Chinese leader. Alexander slashed to the right and left, killing, maiming, and fighting toward his prey. The king awaited him atop his royal stallion, facing the famed Macedonian with chin thrust forward, eyes unflinching. When Alexander broke through the protective ring, Xiong Huai spurred his own horse forward to meet him in single combat.

Their swords met in a shower of sparks—and then Alexander's horse froze in mid-leap, as did every soldier, sword, and spraying droplet of blood for as far as the eye could see.

"Can't this wait!" Alexander the Great shouted.

"I'm sorry, General," a tremulous voice replied from nowhere. "But you ordered me to inform you the moment we received any information of possible Rogue activity."

Alexander sighed and gestured with his left hand. The battlefield morphed into a simple office, and Alexander shape-shifted into General Colrev. He frowned at Sergeant Phillips, who snapped to attention and saluted.

"At ease, Sergeant," the general said. "Why didn't you bring this to the World President first?"

"In military matters, the president is—"

"The man is a buffoon and an idiot," Colrev said. "Has the Rogue attack begun?"

"Well, no, sir, but I found something odd."

A transparent screen appeared in front of the two men, displaying a group of drones chasing Ganesh on his flying motorcycle.

"This is a known Gene-Freak fugitive," the sergeant said.

"What do I care about a Gene-Freak, for God's sake!" Colrev snapped. "We suspended Earth surveillance a hundred years ago. With every human off-planet, the few remaining Gene-Freaks pose no threat, so why bother sending drones after them?"

"That's just it. There's no record of this flight in the logs at all. These drones are old decommissioned models slotted for recycling."

"How could there be no record? They can't fly themselves."

"These older models used radio receivers from a time before the Heisenberg communication systems."

"Hackers going Gene-Freak hunting?"

"That's what I thought at first, except for this."

The subordinate paused the recording and zoomed in on Kayla as she glanced back.

"This girl isn't in the system at all," Phillips said.

Colrev shrugged. "So someone's personal Gene-Freak prostitute slipped through the records. Who cares?"

The sergeant pointed to Kayla's face. "The girl is pretty by the standards of a natural-born human, but hardly the perfection one expects in a genetically manufactured product."

"I see what you mean." The general leaned forward, studying the face. "So you're suggesting she isn't a Gene-Freak at all."

"Yes, sir."

"But our records of Pure humans are complete."

"She could be from Potemia."

Colrev frowned. "Wouldn't the Wall's protocol have notified us if someone went through?"

"It should have, unless something has malfunctioned with the Wall."

"Have you run a diagnostic?"

Phillips squirmed. "Yes, and it looks clean."

"So you think the Wall has gone Rogue based on a fuzzy image of a girl who isn't in the records?"

"Programs go bad all the time in Ixtalia," the sergeant said.

"Your post-Plague generation so easily forgets history. The Wall cannot go Rogue. Its programming is frozen in a crystalline structure, rendering any changes impossible."

The sergeant's face relaxed. "So the Wall cannot evolve and becoming sentient."

"The Neo-Luddites insisted on this so we couldn't reprogram it for an attack at a later date." General Colrev scowled. "Which is exactly what I'd have done if that damn Reinhold Watts hadn't been so thorough. I tried everything, from getting through the force-field dome above or below it, to finding a way of short-circuiting its code. Somehow, the Wall allows air, water, and inorganic material through the dome, but excludes anything living or mechanical."

"At least we know she can't be from Potemia, in that case."

The general motioned to the drones. "What happened after this?"

The sergeant played the recording through the chase, and Colrev whistled. "That elephant can certainly fly!"

When Ganesh displayed the metal disc, the general frowned. "Where would a Gene-Freak get a fission bomb?"

"Probably a secret Scientarian weapons dump that we never located before the migration."

Ganesh placed his hand on the bomb's button, and the screen went black.

"That's where the recording ends," the sergeant said with a frown.

"So the Gene-Freak killed himself as well as a couple of obsolete drones. So what?"

"It has taken me weeks to decode the primitive radio signal sent to the drones during this encounter, but I solved it today."

An eerie voice crackled to life. "Proceed to the main target and eliminate Nihala."

"Nihala? Is this the elephant, or the girl?" the general asked.

"The Gene-Freak records list the elephant-man's name as Ganesh, so I assume Nihala is the girl's name. I've searched the databases and found only one match. A rejected government research proposal titled *Project Nihala*. I don't have top-level security clearance, so that's all I could learn."

"Project Nihala …" Colrev shook his head. "I don't remember anything by that name."

These damn junior officers, jumping at every shadow. Could he blame them, though? Born too late, never having seen a real war in their lifetime, they probably felt like randy teens in an all-boy's summer camp.

The sergeant shifted from foot to foot under the general's disapproving glare. "A final point, sir. There should be a white frame at the end of the recording in the case of a fission explosion—but it simply went black."

***

No longer did Kayla venture from her sanctuary into Middilgard, and neither did she allow anyone to enter. She stopped eating or taking advantage of any of the pleasures of the villa. Probably due to her inattention, even Puck spent most of his time outside their home.

Was my love for Ishan an illusion? Does he even exist?

Hunched at the table in the library, she chose the one escape open to her. Books. Fiction, History, Science, and whatever else sat on their shelves. One after the other, she read them until sleep vanquished consciousness. When she awoke, she resumed where she'd left off.

One book contained the Unabomber's Manifesto in full. Much of it mirrored the sayings she'd learned as a child in Potemia, passed down in an oral history. When taken in their entirety, the words filled her with nausea. She learned that Theodore John Kaczynski didn't even believe in God. How ironic that Minister Coglin spoke of the Founder and Jesus as if they were brothers. How had such a fact been forgotten? Had Peter known?

To call the Founder delusional was an understatement. To say he was a dangerous murderer was a proven fact. And yet, seeing the destruction of the natural world outside the Wall, had he been completely wrong?

She read books on history, archaeology, and genetics, and it became clear that much of the Old Testament wasn't supported by facts. So much scientific evidence contradicted stories like the Garden of Eden and the Flood, that reconciling faith and logic seemed impossible.

Kayla spoke the words from Proverbs as if chanting a spell against doubt. "Trust in the Lord with all thine heart, and lean not unto thine own understanding."

But how could knowledge be bad? If only she could find some evidence to support her faith, rather than contradict it.

The miracles of Moses had reached such a scale that evidence must have survived outside the Bible alone.

But no Egyptian Hieroglyphs mention Moses or the flight of what would have been at least a million Jews. Such an economic disaster should have sent shock waves through all of Egypt. But the histories contained no mention of it. The Egyptians detailed other military defeats and historical upheavals in a nearly unbroken record from pharaoh to pharaoh, so what could explain such a glaring absence?

But the Hebrews must have come from somewhere when they swept into the land of Israel and conquered the Canaanites. If not from Egypt, then where?

Archaeological artifacts in the Holy Land showed a gradual evolution of Canaanite pottery to Hebrew over thousands of years rather than the abrupt change one would expect from a sudden invasion by a foreign people, as claimed in the Bible.

Even the linguistic terms and practices of the Hebrew language and religion betrayed signs of an incremental transformation out the previous religions of the area. The Canaanite father god El became the Hebrew term for God. Why would a conquering people call their god the name of their enemy's deity? Historians concluded that Israelites simply evolved out of the earlier Canaanite culture.

Had the writers of the Torah rewritten history to replace the roots of its creation with a more heroic myth that absolved its followers of killing their Canaanite cousins for worship the old gods? This would absolve God from ordering the genocide of the Canaanites and Amalekites, but left a more troubling question. If some of the stories in the Bible were false, how to determine which were true?

Or could there be another explanation that historians couldn't imagine? Wasn't trusting the words of God easier than relying on the imperfect perceptions of man?

The New Testament was more recent—written by eyewitnesses to the actual events. That much was a historical fact, wasn't it?

Jesus is enough proof. He is all I need.

Days, weeks, and months merged. The growing piles of discarded tomes and the clearing bookcases marked time.

If only I could forget. The memory of Peter's encounter with the policeman flashed before her mind. His most painful memories had been erased. *Maybe I should do the same with my false memories of Potemia. Or even the blasphemies that have caused me to doubt God. Wouldn't I be much happier?*

Faster and faster she read, eventually devouring dozens of books a day—impossible, like everything else about her. The authors projected their joys, sorrows, and loves over the gulf of time and space. Their hopes, dreams, and memories stood in for her own.

A day came when she tossed the final leather-bound time capsule aside. Panic rose within as her deceitful mind reasserted itself.

One shelf of books remained. The section on the history of Christianity. Some of the titles were in English, but most were in either Greek, Latin, or Hebrew. She read the titles without hesitation, her language ability somehow extending even to the written word.

Is Tem right? Am I too afraid to confront the truth?

192

She'd risked death when she took the forbidden books from the desert. No one would burn her at the stake in Middilgard for reading the words on this shelf, and yet her hand trembled as she reached for a book titled *The History of the Gospels.*

Her hand grasped the book and the tremors ceased.

I'm not a coward.

The original Gospels had been written in Greek and not the Hebrew or Aramaic the apostles would have spoken. Only a small elite of Jews were even literate at the time, and it seemed that Jesus himself never wrote anything down to avoid later confusion. So it became the responsibility of his closest followers. But would simple fishermen have learned Greek after Jesus rose from the dead?

Maybe they dictated them to someone else, or passed the stories down orally until recorded by Greek speakers. After all, Socrates never wrote a single word, so we only know of his ideas through the words written after his death by his student, Plato. Like Jesus, Socrates chose to die for his principles rather than run. Ironically, Plato reports one of the charges against Socrates was atheism for questioning the historical truth of the Greek gods.

But Socrates never claimed to be God. Even if Plato made up everything Socrates said and did, the words and ideas themselves remain the important thing, no matter who said them. The words of the Gospels were powerful, but would it be the same if they hadn't been spoken by the Son of God?

Historians date the Gospel of Mark as the first. It is also the shortest Gospel. The earliest versions of Mark ends with the discovery of the empty tomb, with only later versions containing a narrative of Jesus appearing to the apostles. The third-century Christian theologian, Origen of Alexandria, quoted all the Gospel resurrection accounts in detail, except for Mark, making it likely that Origen's version of Mark didn't contain that ending yet. How could Mark have left out the resurrection?

Had someone appended Mark's Gospel later?

If people added to the first written account, did such a practice continue backward to the oral account as well?

Kayla paced back and forth as she read.

The Gospels of Matthew and Luke paralleled Mark almost word for word in large portions, and then built on that core. The virgin birth is not found in Mark, but only in Matthew and Luke. Even then, Matthew and Luke tell different virgin birth stories, while Paul, Mark, and John don't mention this astonishing transcendence of human biology at all.

Most disturbing of all, nearly every miracle Jesus performed echoed stories of earlier gods in the region. Turning water into wine had been attributed to Bacchus and other gods for centuries, as well as being a popular miracle performed in temples by Greek and Roman priests to amaze believers.

Historians and archaeologists cited proof that divine claims of miraculous births, healing the sick, and even rising from the dead were nothing new. Maybe these stories of pagan miracles falsely claimed precedence?

Then she came across the writings of one of the early Christian church fathers, Justin Martyr. In a 156 AD letter to the Roman Emperor Antoninus Pius, titled *"Analogies to the History of Christ,"* Justin wrote, *"And when we say also that the Word, who is the first-birth of God, was produced without sexual union, and that He, Jesus Christ, our Teacher, was crucified and died, and rose again, and ascended into Heaven, we propound nothing different from what you believe regarding those whom you esteem sons of Jupiter."*

Under the heading *"Analogies to the Sonship of Christ,"* Justin gets more specific when he says, *"And if we even affirm that He was born of a virgin, accept this in common with what you accept of Perseus. And in that we say that He made whole the lame, the paralytic, and those born blind, we seem to say what is very similar to the deeds said to have been done by Æsculapius."*

So there it was. A church father himself admitting that virgin birth, miracles, resurrection, and ascension into Heaven were nothing new. Justin Martyr and the other writers dismissed these pre-existing similarities as tricks of the Devil, but that seemed rather self-serving.

Her chest fluttered with anxiety at the implications. On what basis did she believe the Christian miracles over the very same pagan stories?

I must find the truth.

Kayla returned to the twentieth century writer, C. S. Lewis, who said that Jesus, by proclaiming his divinity, was either what he claimed, a liar, or a lunatic. Lewis found it unreasonable that someone who taught such a high moral system could be a liar or a lunatic, so a single logical conclusion remained—that Jesus must be God.

Of course, Jesus couldn't have been a liar or a lunatic. That much seemed obvious.

Relief flooded her like a cool, cleansing stream. But what might Tem make of such an argument?

How do we know Jesus actually claimed this?

Could Jesus be nothing more than an inspiring man whose followers attributed miracles and claims of divinity to him after his death, like so many other tribes and religions had done to great men, and even women, after they died? Once again, that first assumption created yet another circular argument.

Tears rolled down her cheeks as she read on. *Why can't I stop reading? Is knowledge more important than my sanity?*

The New Testament reported that Jesus was "famed far and wide." Surely the numerous contemporary authors living in the area must mention Jesus and his miraculous deeds. That would provide the independent proof she needed. One after the other, the historians of the time remained silent on this miraculous person living in their midst. Maybe Jesus wasn't that important to these writers and the Gospel's inflated his fame.

A passage in Matthew described what happened the moment Jesus died on the cross.

"And Jesus cried again with a loud voice, and yielded up his spirit. And behold, the veil of the temple was rent in two from the top to the bottom; and the earth did quake; and the rocks were rent; and the tombs were opened; and many bodies of the saints that had fallen asleep were raised; and coming forth out of the tombs after his resurrection, they entered into the holy city and appeared unto many. Now the centurion, and they that were with him watching Jesus, when they saw the earthquake, and the things that were done, feared exceedingly, saying, 'Truly, this was the Son of God.'"

That might be the proof she needed. An earthquake powerful enough to damage the sacred Jewish Temple must have been recorded by others writing at the time.

But she found no mention of this—by anyone.

The rising of long-dead saints from their graves seemed even more amazing than Jesus' own resurrection. Yet three of the four Gospel writers neglected to mention it, let alone anyone else of the time.

Luke wrote of a census Caesar ordered *of the entire Roman world* that forced Joseph and Mary to go to Bethlehem. Such a huge undertaking should leave a massive trail of documentation. And yet no one else mentions it.

Matthew described King Herod massacring all young male children in the vicinity of Bethlehem because he'd been warned by the Magi that a new King of the Jews had been born there. But there existed nothing in the historical record of such an outrage, save Matthew alone— writing in Greek.

Kayla expanded her search to writers living in the generation after Jesus died and found only silence from dozens of writers in the area, who should have heard of these miraculous events.

Until she came across Josephus.

He'd been born in Jerusalem a few years after Jesus' execution and was a Jew himself. As the most prominent chronicler of his time and place, it seemed unthinkable that he would fail to mention such a miraculous person who'd lived in the very city where he grew up. He must have known people who witnessed Christ's miracles and even spoken with the apostles themselves. Maybe he met people healed by the very hand of Jesus.

What if I find nothing? What will that do to my faith?

In *Antiquities of the Jews* Josephus wrote, *"Now there was, about this time, Jesus, a wise man, if it be lawful to call him a man, for he was a doer of wonderful works—a teacher of such men as receive the truth with pleasure. He drew over to him both many of the Jews, and many Gentiles. He was Christ: and when Pilate, at the suggestion of the principal men amongst us, had condemned him to the cross, those that loved him at the first did not forsake him, for he appeared to them alive again the third day, as the divine prophets had foretold these and ten thousand other wonderful things concerning him; and the tribe of Christians, so named for him, are not extinct at this day."*

Kayla closed the book and fell to her knees. This passage confirmed the crucifixion, resurrection, numerous miracles, and stated directly that Jesus was, indeed, Christ the Messiah in fulfillment of the prophecies. As a non-Christian, Josephus served as an impartial reporter of the facts. A man with direct access to an entire generation of eyewitnesses in his home city.

"My Lord, my God, my Savior," Kayla said, hands clasped in prayer. "Tell me what you desire of me."

But there followed only silence. The minutes stretched to hours. Then, something scratched at the back of her mind. If Josephus believed Jesus was the Christ in fulfillment of the prophets, why hadn't he converted to Christianity? She'd read a small portion of Josephus's complete writings and looked at the half-finished book lying on the ground.

Why would someone who spent whole chapters on minor historical figures write only a single paragraph about the long-awaited Jewish Messiah who rose from the dead?

She retrieved the book and continued reading.

Justin Martyr discussed Josephus's writing in detail, including the very book containing the paragraph on Christ, but never once mentions it, which seemed strange.

The list of church writers who must have read Josephus was long: Theophilus, Irenaeus, Clement of Alexandria, Origen, Hippolytus, Minucius Felix, Anatolius. Not one mentioned the paragraph, despite extensively quoting other parts of Josephus's writings. Origen stated outright that Josephus didn't believe that Jesus was the Christ, despite having read the very book where Josephus states in no uncertain terms that Jesus was the Christ. Had Origen somehow missed this paragraph? Or did he think Josephus was lying? Or ...?

It wasn't until two hundred twenty-five years after Josephus wrote the book around 94 AD that the first mention of it appears in the historical record by a fourth-century Christian historian named Eusebius.

If Eusebius forged the paragraph and inserted it into new copies of Josephus, that would explain why none of the previous church fathers mentioned the paragraph beforehand.

The temporary reprieve from her existential maelstrom vanished, and an anxiety rose within her chest like some unstoppable flood. How could a believer in Christ do such a thing?

In one of Eusebius's writings, he states: *"That it will be necessary sometimes to use falsehood as a remedy for the benefit of those who require such a mode of treatment."*

The very fact that forty-or-so other contradictory Gospels existed in circulation at the time, proved in itself that forgery was common at the time. How had the church fathers known which four were the authentic ones?

Continuing through Josephus's writings, his life proved as amazing as the people he wrote about. Born into a wealthy Hebrew family that descended from Jewish royalty on his mother's side and the priestly order of Jehoiarib on his father's, Josephus traveled to Rome in his early twenties to negotiate the release of several Jewish religious leaders, meeting with the Emperor Nero himself. Upon his return, he became a commander of the Galilean forces as the Romans attacked his homeland.

When the Roman General Vespasian and his son Titus trapped Josephus in a cave with forty of his fellow fighters, the group refused to surrender and decided on mass suicide instead. In order to save his own life, Josephus suggested a mathematical method of choosing the order they would kill each other, leaving Josephus and one other soldier the lone survivors.

Once his fellow freedom-fighters were all dead, Josephus surrendered and worked for the Romans as a negotiator while they proceeded with the Siege of Jerusalem in 70 AD that destroyed the Temple as well as most of the city. Josephus wrote that the Romans enslaved ninety-seven thousand Jews and his own wife and parents lay dead.

Kayla paced the library as she read. The fact that so much rested on this anomalous figure's single paragraph unsettled her, but she continued on.

After witnessing the disaster that would reverberate throughout history for his people, Josephus proved himself a true pragmatist by accompanying Vespasian's son, Titus, throughout the region on a victory tour that climaxed in Rome. The newly crowned emperor, Vespasian, rewarded his Jewish turn-coat with patronage.

The final nail in the coffin came when Josephus declared the Roman emperor Vespasian the Messiah predicted by Jewish scripture. It made sense for this ultimate survivor to flatter his new boss in such a way, especially since the Roman Imperial cult often turned their emperors into gods. But claiming two Messiahs seemed odd if flattery motivated him. Wouldn't Vespasian be annoyed when lumped together with a crucified criminal?

The truth was too obvious to ignore any longer. Eusebius forged the paragraph to remedy Josephus's awkward failure to mention Jesus as the Christ.

Kayla dropped the book and went still.

If someone like Josephus hadn't bothered mentioning Jesus, what did that say about the truth of this miraculous story written so much later?

"No!" Kayla shouted. "I won't desert my Savior! I won't forsake the man who suffered and died to save me!" Why wasn't faith enough for her? Why hadn't God made her like the Monads if he wanted such belief without reason? Why give her a brain that could reason and then punish her for using it?

Just as the storm of emotions overwhelmed her, a voice spoke within her mind.

Do not fear, I am with you.

"My Lord?" Kayla fell to her knees.

But there was no answer.

Was it the voice of the Almighty, or her own subconscious protecting its sanity?

Kayla's shoulders slumped, and her chin drooped to her chest. History contained no proof. The choice was firmly one of faith alone.

"So you've read them all," a low voice said.

Kayla sprang to her feet. In the entrance to the library stood the eight legs, abbreviated body, and malformed face of—

"Ohg!"

Kayla stumbled toward him, but a single leg shot forward and stopped her, the hard talon on the end like the tip of a spear against her ribcage.

"You lied to me," he said.

"I answered all your questions truthfully."

"A lie of omission."

Kayla lowered her gaze. "Am I banished from Middilgard, then?"

Ohg remained silent for a long while. "Are you willing to tell me everything?"

Kayla nodded. "Yes."

"We shall see." Ohg led her into the tunnel outside her villa. The corridors stood empty in the dim night-cycle.

"How long have I been ... away?" Kayla asked.

"Five months." Ohg guided her onto a large metal disc lying on the floor and stood beside her. It rose into the air and carried them silently through the deserted city.

They reached a cavern with no other exits and flew straight toward the solid wall. At the last moment, a hidden doorway swung open. Once in the dark passageway beyond, the slab of granite swung back into place with barely a whisper.

The disc descended in a gentle spiral, and the air grew hotter. When the tunnel leveled, a small point of light shone far ahead, growing into an archway flanked by a stone griffin and a dog with three heads. In Greek mythology, Cerberus guarded the mythical underworld and represented the past, present, and future.

The disc glided through a series of volcanic caverns criss-crossed with rivers of lava and smelling of sulfur. Ohg covered his sweating face with a gas mask. The fact that he didn't offer her one spoke volumes.

He knows my secret.

Then came the machines.

They crowded the caverns like great squatting toads of technology, sucking blasts of heat from the vents they straddled and powering huge steam turbines within. Pipes and cables protruded from the soot-blackened monsters, no doubt supplying Middilgard with its energy. Other belching machines whirred, pumped, and crushed, depending on the particular service performed for their unseen masters in the clean and pristine world above.

The air-lock doors slid aside, and Kayla and Ohg floated into a giant metal chamber similar to the one she'd ridden through with Tem on her first day in Middilgard.

The second set of doors opened into a gleaming room stretching upward and outward to an impossible extent.

"Is that a rocket?"

"It's an old nuclear missile I found in a forgotten Russian silo," Ohg said as they glided past the towering cylinder with the warhead lying dismantled beneath it. "I used up the plutonium in experiments long ago. Fissile material is one of the substances the molecular printers cannot reproduce—along with antimatter, of course."

Kayla gazed into the distance at rows of machines spanning all eras of history. A World War II bomber sat amidst an aisle of half a hundred planes from all eras, each restored to pristine condition. They looked like mere toys compared to the vastness of the room that stretched at least three miles long and half as wide.

"I guess you'd call me something of a collector," Ohg said, understating the obvious by many magnitudes.

"I thought you banned any weapons in Middilgard?"

"This is not Middilgard."

"Isn't that a bit hypocritical?" Kayla asked.

"It's my job to protect those under my charge, even from one another."

They drifted past automobiles, computers, hand tools, construction equipment, ancient siege engines, waterwheels, telephone switchboards, and thousands of other oddities—all organized on towering shelves. The room buzzed from an army of robots maintaining the vast collection.

Five identical pairs of robots perched atop assembly-line pallets. A small nozzle protruded from the right forearm in place of a hand, while the left resembled a sledgehammer. The largest pair stood twenty-five feet tall, and each additional twin shrank by five feet so that the fifth pair was man-sized. They seemed identical in all other respects.

"Don't tell anyone about those," Ohg said. "I wouldn't want to ruin the surprise."

They glided through an arched doorway into Ohg's personal laboratory. Surrounding them were test tubes, refrigeration units, humming computer arrays, and a confusion of equipment that looked like something stolen from an alien spaceship.

Kayla's gaze locked onto a row of glass chambers. Three naked male bodies floated in an amber-colored liquid with tubes and wires protruding from all parts of their anatomy—each exact copies of the blond god watching over the Monads. Next to these stood five additional chambers with what looked like the same body in progressively younger states of development; the last curled in a fetal position with an umbilical cord still attached.

"Are they alive?" Kayla asked.

"Their bodies are, but their minds never have been," Ohg said. "Their genes lack the instructions for building the higher parts of the frontal lobe and limbic system that impart rational thought and self-consciousness. That motivating force is supplied via a reverse Mind-Link implanted in each of their brains.

"Such surrogate bodies were once the preferred conveyance of daily life. Anyone could have the body of their choice and change into another as fashion or necessity dictated. All without risking death to your true body and mind, should an accident befall the surrogate."

They landed in the center of the lab, and Kayla stepped off the disc.

"It's time you told me the truth," Ohg said.

Kayla opened her mouth to speak, but Ohg placed his finger against her lips. "I don't want you to use words," he said. "I want to access your memories at their source."

"To record them like General Colrev did with Peter?"

Ohg shook his head. "Recording a full memory dump would take weeks and create so much data it would require months to sort through. I want you to guide me to the important moments yourself so I can experience them just as you did with Peter, only much faster." Ohg looked at her. "Will you do that?"

Kayla hesitated an instant before nodding. Ohg placed a metal disc against her forehead, then closed his eyes. A flood of images flashed before Kayla's mind. Sights, sounds, smells, faces, brief moments from her childhood—all blurring into a kaleidoscope faster than she could process.

She gasped as the memory of her rape and death flashed past, then the glimpse of the glowing eyes of Melchi in her death-dream. Ohg kept his hand pressed against her forehead through her resurrection, banishment, and journey to Middilgard.

When it ended, Ohg removed his hand and nodded. "You do have a working Mind-Link, that's for certain."

Kayla's shoulders slumped as she stared at her hands. "Then what's the point of looking at my memories of Potemia? My entire life has been an illusion. A lie."

"Don't jump to the conclusion that your memories were implanted."

"But how could I have acquired a Mind-Link in Potemia?

"That is the question," Ohg said.

"But if my memories are real, that means that I rose from the dead. You've seen all my abilities. Only divine intervention could explain it."

Ohg smiled. The holographic image of a machine appeared between them, floating motionless with a dozen arms hanging off the core of its body. Ohg waved his hand again, and another strange-looking machine appeared next to the first. Soon, nine unique devices hovered in the air.

"Are they robots?"

"Nanobots," Ohg said. "I've spent the months since your arrival testing these darlings, and they proved vastly more advanced than anything currently known to science. Despite my best efforts at unlocking their secrets, I can only guess at all their capabilities, but they would certainly be deemed illegal by the government."

"But what has this to do with me?"

"I took a sample of your blood with the help of a Mind-Linked mosquito surrogate, and I found these floating inside; thousands of them in that single drop. I suspect they built your Mind-Link within your body itself when you were a child. I'll bet we'll find every inch of your body and brain has been enhanced by these little buggers."

"Would it be any easier getting microscopic machines like this through the Wall?"

Ohg scratched his head. "Well, no…"

"Then we're back where we started."

"After seeing your memories," Ohg said with the excitement of a bug collector who's found a never-before-described beetle, "it's clear the nanobots respond to your thoughts. They redesigned your eye with multiple lenses atop the pyramid. All in response to your desire to better see the speck of rising dust in the distance. In a very real sense, they led you here."

"Then it wasn't God after all."

"The wonders of reality are every bit as miraculous as the supernatural." He gestured to the nanobots. "Some of these miniature robots must leave your body through the pores in your skin like a swarm of personal servants, attending all your body's needs, keeping it clean, repaired, and supplied. I'd be willing to bet that you stopped aging the moment you transformed."

"But I've been a cripple my entire life. Why wait so long?"

"My guess is that your heart's failure activated them. They cured your deformities and rebuilt your body on a molecular level."

"I'm indestructible, then?"

"I've tested your nanobots, and they're tough, but can be destroyed by intense heat."

"I survived the fire of my execution."

Ohg shook his head. "It would take something like lava or a fission bomb to do the trick."

So I can die, after all.

"And my ability to understand other languages?"

"Anyone with a Mind-Link can do the same," Ohg said.

Kayla stared at the alien creatures hovering before her eyes. Billions of miniature robots possessing her, flowing through her veins and keeping her alive. But for what purpose?

Kayla turned away from the hologram of the nine machines inside her. "What does this all mean?"

"It means, my dear Kayla, that you are the most advanced cyborg in the history of mankind—and I think it's time we learned what you're capable of."

Chapter 19

General Colrev gazed at the rolling dunes undulating to the horizon like the waves of an ocean. The dry air sucked the moisture from his skin, while an alkali taste and smell suffused the air.

The general frowned. These were no natural desert formations, but a series of giant female bodies—breasts, hips, legs, buttocks, stomachs—some the size of mountains. The forms flowed one into the other like a vast piece of erotic art.

The sun floated in the impossible ultramarine and leered at the pornographic figure-scape, casting sinuous shadows that heightened the sensuous grace of the forms. In the sky, hundreds of clouds morphed from one graphic pose to another, always female.

He turned and faced a scene of such debauchery that it would have made the Roman Emperor Caligula jealous. A mass of naked women of all shades writhed atop the body of a naked man, who remained all but invisible but for his gasps and grunts of pleasure. A few feet beyond the orgy, another woman nursed a child and looked on.

Why do I bother protecting humans at all?

The general's voice cracked like a whip. "Raymond Roberts, I'd like to ask you a few questions!"

But the writhing orgy continued.

"Very well, then." A cattle prod appeared in his hand, and the double tips pulsed with electricity as he shoved it through a gap in the mass of bodies to the man's ribcage. A scream followed and the man vanished. The women shrieked and cowered, their eyes locked on the cattle prod.

"Which one of you is Raymond Roberts?" When no one spoke, he jabbed the prod into one woman, then the next, and the next. They sobbed and begged for mercy—all a show, of course, since computer simulations couldn't feel pain or any true emotion.

When the last exotic beauty disappeared, silence settled over the perverted desert in mockery of his efforts. The general faced the nursing mother. The dark-skinned woman returned his gaze calmly as her baby sucked the nipple of one of her enormous breasts.

He didn't give a warning this time, but aimed the electrical stream at the woman's forehead.

The mother vanished.

A forced mind-mapping would reveal all of Raymond's memories, but would necessitate sorting through several hundred years of VR fantasies to find the needle of information he sought. Without an actual human victim, no laws limited what could be conjured. Rapists, psychopaths, and even pedophiles had free rein to indulge their twisted fetishes.

Being forced to watch such things, was another matter.

"Okay, you sick fuck," Colrev shouted to the clouds. "If you don't reveal yourself this instant, I'm suspending your VR privileges, and we'll see how you like living in a box for the next hundred years."

"No need for that. I was only having a bit of fun." The newborn smiled sheepishly. Colrev shoved the prod against its forehead. The infant transformed into an overweight man dressed in a suit—the default subconscious representation of himself.

"Ow! That hurts like a knife in the brain!" Raymond held his temples with both hands.

"You headed the team that captured the first Meta Rogue?"

"That's right," Raymond said, his face contorted in pain. "I helped develop the first Rogue trap. We caught and destroyed a dozen minor AIs, but the first Meta was something special."

"Tell me about it," the general said.

Raymond removed his hands from his head and straightened. "It called itself Melchi. We questioned it for hours and left an armed guard overnight."

"Eve." The general's lip curled into a half-snarl. "The first fully conscious artificial life-form."

"That's right," Raymond said. " No one wanted to risk a second AI falling into the wrong hands. After all, every one of Professor Watts's inventions were actually created by his AI—immortality, instantaneous Heisenberg communications, portable fission reactors, food synthesizers, and the Quantum computers that make Ixtalia itself possible."

Colrev's fingers tightened on the cattle prod. *Damn AIs.* There had been plenty of warnings of the dangers of developing such things, and yet scientists had ignored them.

Raymond's voice lowered. "The next morning, when we returned to the lab, we found the guard swinging from an improvised noose. The surveillance recordings showed him switching on Melchi's voice interface and talking to him for hours. Unfortunately, the guard's back had been to the camera, and it lacked audio." Raymond shook his head and wiped sweat from his brow. "At one point the guard started crying and covered his ears for a few minutes. But then the conversation resumed for another hour, culminating in the guard reconnecting the box into the network and ending his own life."

"Why have I never heard of this?"

"We didn't want to create panic. When Melchi vanished back into Ixtalia, most eventually forgot about the incident. I've often wondered if that first murder by an AI foreshadowed the fate of the entire human race."

Raymond loosened his tie and tugged at his collar under the general's hard gaze.

"You headed a panel that reviewed something called 'Project Nihala'?" Colrev asked.

"Myself and two others. It was a scheme for creating a human hybrid that could destroy Meta Rogues in Ixtalia."

"Is such a thing possible?"

"Nothing but pie in the sky." Raymond's eyes drifted up to the writhing clouds. "I can't remember the details, but the archives would hold them."

"They've been deleted." Colrev poked him in the stomach, and Raymond's eyes snapped back into focus. "You're the only member of the review committee with their memory still intact."

Raymond eyed the cattle prod nervously. "I assure you, I didn't delete them."

"Who proposed this Nihala Project?"

"Professor Watts himself, which is the only reason we reviewed such a hair-brained idea in the first place."

Colrev's eyes narrowed. "Continue."

"All three of us on the Committee turned down the enormous funding request as unethical and dangerous, so the project never happened." Raymond loosened his tie and stared at the pornographic clouds. "Didn't your subordinate tell you all this already?"

The general tensed. He leaned forward and Raymond flinched. "What subordinate?" the general said through clenched teeth.

"The one who questioned me a couple of weeks ago on this same issue," Raymond said. "Ohg-something or other ... Ohgelthorp! Yes, that was his name, I'm sure of it."

***

Kayla sat in a lotus position at the center of Ohg's laboratory. For the past week, they'd explored her abilities, both of body and mind. Kayla slept in an extra room constructed by the molecular printers, but Ohg had forbidden her from exiting his laboratory until he decided her resident status in Middilgard.

"Okay," Ohg said. "Give it another try."

She took a deep breath, let it out slowly, then closed her eyes. Her body rose a few inches off the ground.

"Very good," Ohg said. "You've gained perfect command of the billions of nanobots inside your body. Now let's try those outside yourself."

Kayla visualized a disembodied third arm reaching out to the orange on the table and lifting it. The orange ascended into the air and hovered. Then nine grapes rose from a bowl and orbited the orange at various speeds, mirroring the planets of the solar system.

"Show off," Ohg said.

"It doesn't seem like an effort anymore," Kayla said. "I think I could manage more if I created additional nanos."

Ohg scratched his back with a talon. "I hadn't considered the possibility of self-replication."

"I tried it this morning, and it takes five hours for a hundred nanos to create one new one."

"And you waited until now to tell me!"

"I thought I'd surprise you." Kayla smiled, but kept her eyes closed.

Ohg pointed to an oak door across the room. "Tell me what is behind that door." The floating objects sagged. "Without letting a single grape hit the floor!"

Kayla frowned. "You know I can't project my mind into a single nano while also—"

"Try."

Kayla's lips tightened into a thin line.

"Empty your mind," Ohg said. "You must believe it's the most natural thing in the world to become two, instead of one."

Kayla's breathing slowed, and her mind drifted from its normal boundaries of self.

Sight bloomed though the microscopic eyes of one of her servants. Kayla piloted it through the narrow crack of the doorframe. The nano's infra-red vision identified a man standing in the pitch blackness. His helmet, armor, and Japanese features marked him a samurai warrior. He bowed and then spoke. "I have a few surprises of my own."

The samurai drew his long-sword and charged. The doorway exploded off its hinges, and the samurai rushed Kayla with his curved blade raised for a deathblow.

Kayla's eyes opened, and the floating objects wobbled, then stabilized.

The sword swept the space her head had occupied an instant ago. Kayla rolled across the floor, leapt up, and snatched an identical sword from the wall. She parried the samurai's next stroke awkwardly. Then another with more confidence as she got the feel of the weapon. Soon the blades whirled in an intricate dance.

"This is you, Ohg?" Kayla asked between attacks.

"My mind is as flexible as yours," Ohg and the samurai said in unison. "And remember, not a grape is to hit the floor!"

Sparks flew as her sword intercepted another vicious slash. Kayla faked a counter, which the samurai reacted to, and then unleashed the real attack below his guard. Ohg sidestepped, but received a shallow cut through the armor of his surrogate's left thigh.

First blood.

Kayla whooped in triumph—then a scrape sounded behind her. Keeping her eyes on the warrior in front, she projected her mind into a nanobot floating behind her head and saw a second samurai lunging with sword raised. She dove sideways, but the blade tore a shallow gash in her back.

"Are you trying to kill me?" Kayla shouted.

"I doubt anything less than a fission bomb or molten lava could do that," both samurais said. Ohg sat with eyes closed, as if meditating. Within seconds, her wound closed.

The two samurai slid to the left and right of her, an impossible situation to defend against.

"You can control two at the same time?" she asked.

"I think I'm the sole human capable of this," one of the samurais said with a slight smile. "It's one of the perks of my freakish head and brain."

"But this isn't fair," she said as both samurai raised their swords to strike.

"There's no fair play in war!"

Two swords slashed toward her.

I will not surrender!

Kayla closed her eyes and imagined the morning ocean with its mirrored surface reflecting the rising sun. Her mind became the invisible breeze revealing its presence in a ripple …

The two swords met inches above her head, the samurai behind blocking the blade of the other with his own length of steel. Sparks engulfed her like a wedding veil.

"You hijacked my surrogate!" Ohg shouted, waking from his mediation.

Kayla and the second samurai smiled.

"This must be what you did to the drones without realizing it."

Ohg's samurai crouched and spun, aiming a slashing stroke at her legs.

Kayla stood her ground as the blade whistled through the air, then jerked to a halt within a millimeter of her skin.

"Impossible," Ohg said.

One after the other, each of the ten battle robots came to life and struck a different pose from varied martial arts disciplines.

Ohg stared from the samurai, to the robots, and then at the levitating orange with its solar system of grapes still orbiting it.

"You win," he said.

The two samurai and all ten of the robots put their hands together and gave the traditional bow of respect.

"This should be impossible." Ohg paced back and forth, his eight claws clicking out a frenetic tempo. "You can go. I need time to think about this."

A hover-disc landed in front of her.

"I can stay in Middilgard?" Kayla asked.

"For now, you can stay," Ohg said. "Go to the Scarlet Cavern if you'd like some entertainment. I have something special planned for Middilgard."

Chapter 20

Kayla rode the hover-disc from Ohg's lair back to Middilgard in a haze of conflicting emotions. With each answer she found, two more mysteries appeared.

What am I?

When she flew through the hidden doorway into the familiar tunnels, the disc landed. For the first time in over five months, she walked through the public tunnels. Anxiety plucked at her insides like a buzzard. Would Tem be angry at her for pushing him out of her life?

The shrieks of children dissolved into laughter, and a stampede of tiny feet echoed through the tunnels. Her little jewels rounded a bend in the passage, and she smiled. But the children rushed past without a pause. The months of her absence had wiped their minds clear of their once-beloved friend, rendering her a stranger.

Tears blurred Kayla's vision as the Forever-Children vanished into a side tunnel. Would her other friends have changed as well? Had Fatima turned them all against her?

Then Saphie rounded a curve in the tunnel. The little girl spoke to the empty air next to her.

"I can't go with you now, Kayla, or I'll miss the tournament." Saphie paused, as if listening, then shook her head and addressed the emptiness once again. "We can visit color-girl later."

She's pretending to talk to me. Keeping her memory alive in the only way she could.

"I'm here, Saphie!" Kayla said to her little jewel.

The adorable face turned toward her with such consternation that Kayla laughed.

"How did you get over there?" Saphie asked. "Stop playing games, or we'll be late!" Saphie ran toward her with arms outstretched. Kayla swept the little body into her arms and hugged her. Puck peeked out of a pocket on Saphie's pink sundress and squeaked up at her.

"Puck!" Kayla exclaimed and kissed the mouse's forehead.

"Why are you crying?" Saphie asked.

"Because I missed you both so much."

The little girl looked at her like she was the craziest adult she'd ever met. "We have to hurry or it will start without us!" Saphie said.

"What will start without us?"

"The game in the Scarlet Cavern I just told you about!"

"I think I'm going to skip the game and find Tem. Have you seen him?"

"Tem's playing in the game, silly!"

Kayla hoisted Saphie onto her shoulders and jogged in the direction she'd seen the other children heading. "Okay, my little Sapphire," Kayla said, tickling her as she ran. "We can't be late for the game!" Saphie giggled as they rushed through the tunnels, and Puck gave an occasional squeak.

They entered the Scarlet Cavern, and Kayla's mouth dropped. Tiered seating had sprung up along one wall of the massive room, and most of Middilgard's several thousand diverse occupants sat patiently awaiting Ohg's surprise. The rest of the cavern floor lay bare. Kayla deposited Saphie alongside the other children in the front row and headed up the stands in search of a place to sit.

"Excuse me," she said, stepping on someone's tail. "Pardon me," she apologized to a dour turtle after almost sitting on him. She reached several empty seats near the top as the lights dimmed.

A trumpet sounded and the crowd settled.

"Captaining the Red Team," a voice boomed out, "is that warrior of warriors and famed member of the Ixtalia Freaks—the one, the only, Temujin!" A cone of light illuminated Tem at the far side of the cavern. Kayla's pulse quickened. He wore his usual wide Mongolian trousers and horsehide vest, which seemed an odd choice for a sporting event. The crowd went wild with shouts and applause, but Tem's wide face remained impassive.

The announcer introduced Ganesh, Sir Richard Panthersly, Humpty Dumpty, and a once-famous supermodel named Nicolia, whose emaciated body resembled a stick figure.

"Captaining the Blue Team," the disembodied announcer said with solemnity, "is one of the most famous athletes of the late twenty-first century. Winning a combined twenty-six gold medals in the final Olympic games before Gene-Freaks were banned from competition, please welcome that athlete of athletes—Durendal!" The crowd erupted in applause of the man who had backed down from fighting Tem. The lean muscles of his body rippled in waves as he bounced from foot to foot like a prizefighter.

During Fatima's introduction, she stared daggers across the arena at Tem. How could one live with such hatred constantly eating away at them? Kayla hadn't met the other members of the Blue Team since Fatima had turned them against her early on. As a whole, they looked far more athletic than the Red Team.

"Excuse me," a voice behind Kayla said. "You're the girl from Potemia, aren't you? I don't think we've met. My name is Lott." A hand extended across her shoulder, and Kayla took hold of it, turning to greet …

"I apologize for the shock," Lott said at the look on Kayla's face.

"Not … not at all," Kayla said. His main body resembled the torso of a man, with a mouth where the belly-button would normally reside. From this central core, twenty arms extended in all directions. He lacked a neck, legs, and even a head. Lott stood on two hands with ease. On three of his hands, eyes peered out from the center of the palms. One stared directly at her, while the other two pointed in different directions. A nose protruded from the top of another hand, and two others supported ears. The rest of his arms and hands appeared normal, bristling in all directions like a sea urchin.

Will I ever get used to the surprises here?

Kayla gazed into the eye pointed toward her and smiled. "It's nice to meet you. My name is Kayla."

"Very nice meeting you as well." Lott released her hand. "Do you mind if I join you?" One of his hands gestured toward the empty seat next to her.

"Please do." Lott's various appendages took hold of the backrest next to her and moved him smoothly into the seat.

"And now!" boomed the announcer's voice. "The surrogate bodies our teams will compete in!" A rumble shook the cavern as a section of the floor slid apart to reveal a dark opening beneath.

A roar of engines sounded, and ten metal objects erupted from the pit.

"Old-school robots!" Lott shouted, his excitement infectious.

Each of the ten robots from Ohg's laboratory now displayed a blue or red square painted in the center of their chest. They landed on opposite sides of the arena before their respective teams; the tallest standing twenty-five feet, and growing progressively smaller down the line to the shortest robot, which stood five feet tall.

That's why the contestants' bodies didn't matter. *Mind-athletes*, Ganesh had called them.

"These robots pay homage to the first combat models used at the beginning of Filadrux," the announcer said as the two teams examined the robots. "They are rocket-propelled with a limited fuel, and have only two weapons—a hammer and a blowtorch."

"This should be an exciting contest," Lott said. "Although such basic robots allow little room for strategy."

"The teams will have thirty seconds until the start," the announcer said. Both teams huddled around their captains as large holographic numbers appeared in the air and began counting down.

Kayla's eyes zoomed in on Tem as he spoke to his team. He shielded his mouth to preclude reading his lips. Ganesh scratched his head and looked confused, but the stick-thin Nicolia argued with the most animation. As the clock neared zero, Tem silenced her with a gesture.

"That's a bad sign," Lott said to Kayla. "When a team is divided on strategy, it spells trouble in the match."

Both teams took seats in protected dugouts on opposite sides of the stadium. Everyone except Tem and Ganesh donned helmets with wires connected to a control board.

"Why don't Tem and Ganesh have helmets?" Kayla asked Lott.

"They have Mind-Links and don't need helmets to control the robots, but there's no advantage either way."

"On your marks!" said the announcer.

All of the robots animated and looked around.

"Get set!"

The crowd silenced as the anticipation built. Several of the robots crouched.

"Go!"

The robots on both sides roared to life, and the crowd cheered. The center of the arena became a confused, chaotic mass of metal clashing with metal. The various-sized robots flew upward, around, and underneath each other as they struck with hammers and blowtorches. The crashes and shrieks of tearing metal brought cheers from the crowd. A protective energy field deflected stray metallic flotsam back into the ring and kept the audience from danger.

"That's odd," Kayla shouted over the din. "The Red Team has only four robots in the fight."

"You're right!" Lott pointed at the smallest of the red robots standing motionless in its starting position. Could Nicolia be boycotting the match because of her disagreement with Tem?

The crowd cheered as the teams clashed in a maelstrom of steel.

Tem's red team concentrated its combined effort on the smallest of the blue's robots first, while the blue team attacked in a symmetrical fashion of like against like. Tem's team drew first blood as the five-foot blue burst into flames and crashed under the concerted attack. In the blue team's dugout, one of the women Kayla didn't know woke from her trance and stormed away.

"Come on, Red Team!" Kayla shouted.

As Tem's red team shifted its combined attack to the ten-foot blue robot, the cost of this strategy became apparent. Despite shredding the smaller blue robot by the mass assault, this left the three largest blues free to attack their counterparts without any damage themselves.

The largest red struck the fatal blow to the ten-foot blue robot, but fell itself as the blowtorch of the largest blue cut into the internal machinery at the back of its head. Both robots hit the ground at the same moment, lying motionless. A blue team member she didn't know left the dugout, while Humpty Dumpty tottered away as well.

"Tem's red team is in trouble now," Lott said. The blue team's three largest robots remained undamaged. Despite this, Tem's team continued its game plan and attacked the fifteen-foot red robot while ignoring the counter-attack.

The red twenty-footer fell next, and Sir Richard slunk out of the dugout. Then the red fifteen-footer followed soon afterward, and Ganesh awoke from his trance and trudged into the stands with head hung low.

Still, the smallest of the red team stood motionless on the sidelines. Was Nicolia really willing to boycott the match just because Tem had dismissed her strategy?

"Kayla!" Ganesh shouted from below and waved all four of his arms. She smiled and waved back as he searched for a path through the cheering crowd.

The fifteen-foot blue robot played hide-and-seek among its two undamaged teammates as the ten-foot red pursued it. The red robot pirouetted through the air with grace and skill, avoiding blows while landing brief strikes on its fleeing prey.

Only Tem and Nicolia remained in the red team's dugout. Kayla ground her teeth at the girl's betrayal. *I should take control of the small red robot myself.* But that would be disastrous for many reasons.

"You're back!" Ganesh said as he reached her.

"I'm so glad to see you!" She hugged the Hindu god.

"Have a seat." Lott shifted over two seats.

"Thanks." Ganesh took the seats as a groan rose from the audience. The red robot had sustained a glancing blow from the largest blue and become unstable. In a desperate move, the red rose to the maximum height the ceiling allowed and fired its rockets into a Kamikaze dive. It slammed into the crippled fifteen-foot blue, and both fuel tanks exploded.

The crowd rose to its feet and cheered as the machines fell into a burning heap. A chant of "Blue, Blue, Blue!" acclaimed the two largest— and undamaged—blue robots, who saluted the audience.

"Ladies and gentlemen," the announcer boomed, "may I present the new champ—" The announcer stopped mid-sentence, and muffled voices sounded in the background.

"They've forgotten the smallest red," Lott said.

"Not that it matters at this point," Ganesh said with his head hung low.

"The match is technically still in progress," the announcer said, and a spotlight illuminated the five-foot-tall red robot standing motionless on the edge of the arena. The crowd laughed as the two blue robots pantomimed fear at the sight. Fatima and Durendal remained in the blue dugout. The crowd laughed harder as the blue giants linked hands and skipped toward the tiny red, which didn't budge a gear in response.

"Just finish it, already," Ganesh said.

"I can't believe the nerve of that gutless Nicolia!" Kayla said, her voice wrathful.

"Why? What did she do?" Ganesh asked.

Nicolia no longer sat in the red team's dugout.

"Tem is the small robot?"

"That's right." Ganesh shook his head. "He told us to concentrate our attack on the smallest robot first, and then up the hierarchy one after the other, no matter what the cost. We explained that this would be suicide, but he wouldn't listen."

The blue robots linked hands and danced around the motionless red while the crowd roared with laughter. How would such mockery affect Tem's pride? When the joke wore thin, the largest blue raised its huge hammer.

"I can't watch." Ganesh covered his eyes. The hammer came down, and the crowd roared. Rocks exploded as the massive hunk of metal buried itself into the floor of the cavern. It took a couple of yanks for the robot to pull its arm free from the pulverized stone.

Nothing lay underneath.

"Look!" Kayla pointed at the tiny red standing ten feet away. The two blue robots struck in tandem, but once again, the faster red avoided the blows. Three times the giants struck at their maddening enemy, but never came close.

The small red fired its internal rockets and went on the offensive. The two giants swung wildly, but missed every time. Tem pestered the great mountains of metal in a dizzying display of aerial maneuvering, firing his blowtorch in short bursts, but ignoring his tiny hammer altogether.

"He'll run out of fuel before that little torch can make a dent in the thick armor," Lott said. "Only a larger robot could hope to—"

"That is the most brilliant strategy I've ever seen!" Ganesh said and started laughing.

Lott looked at him as if he'd lost his mind.

The giants continued swinging and missing, and the crowd grew restless as nothing substantial happened. A few boos and shouts of "draw" rose from the audience, but Ganesh's smile only widened.

Kayla frowned. *What am I missing?*

Tem's robot hovered to a stop before the giants, and his tiny blowtorch went out. The crowd grew quiet, and the giants exchanged a glance. Was Tem offering a draw?

Tem's robot swooped toward the larger of his two adversaries, and his tiny hammer struck the giant's shoulder. A metallic ping rang out, and Tem retreated before his slower opponent could react. At the foot of the giant blue robot lay the top of a single bolt. A murmur spread through the spectators, then transformed to cheers.

"Brilliant!" Kayla said.

"Tem, Tem, Tem!" the crowd chanted.

"What happened?" Lott said, holding his three eyes high. "I don't understand."

Ganesh beamed. "Tem used his torch to cut the bolts holding the blue robots together."

Laughter billowed through the stadium as the red midget chased the flailing blue giants. One by one, Tem struck off the hundreds of bolts holding the monstrous machines together. The larger robot lost his right arm first. Then the left arm of the smaller blue clunked to the stone floor.

"It's death by a thousand cuts!" Kayla said through her laughter.

When the two robots had been relieved of all their limbs and lay bereft of movement, Tem landed next to the smaller of the two. One by one, he struck off the bolts connecting head to shoulders. The cheers reached a crescendo as the last bolt snapped on its own from the enormous weight. Sparks erupted as wires tore free. The light within its eyes went out. In the blue dugout, Fatima awoke from her trance and stormed out of the stadium. It didn't take long for the larger robot to succumb to the same fate.

Durendal and Tem strode to the center of the arena.

Now Kayla could see why Durendal had backed down from fighting Tem. The true battleground lay within the mind. Even before the start of the match, Tem had won.

The defeated captain stopped before the Mongol and extended his hand. They shook, and Durendal pulled Tem's arm into the air. The crowd roared its approval, and both teams emerged from the stands to receive their accolades. Only Fatima remained absent.

The lights came on. Ganesh spoke to Tem and pointed in her direction. Kayla's heart quickened. As the crowd dispersed, she made her way down to him.

Tem averted his gaze. "I'm sorry I didn't mention the possibility of your memories being implanted."

Guilt twisted through her like a tapeworm. "It's me who should be apologizing."

He looked at her and raised an eyebrow. "I don't understand."

"It's time I told you the whole truth."

Chapter 21

Kayla walked with Tem through the lonely corridors and revealed everything she'd worked so hard to keep hidden. She described her childhood deformities, resurrection, apparent indestructibility, and all that Ohg had revealed regarding the microscopic miracles within her blood.

When she finished, Tem took her hand and led her in silence to a small cave. At its center sat an ancient hunk of lava that had bubbled from a crack in the floor long ago. Dozens of holes and fractal encrustations pockmarked its surface. In the center of the abstract form sat a spherical stone the size of a marble.

"Do you know the significance of this room?" Tem asked.

"It doesn't look much different than many of the natural caves formed from the lava tubes."

"Ohg didn't mention it to you when he learned your history?" Tem stared at her with a strange intensity.

"Why would he?"

Tem led her into the shadow of the twisted monolith. His dark eyes, black braids, and Mongolian features made him seem an ancient statue come to life. In many ways, that was exactly what he was.

Puck scurried down her clothes and dashed through the maze of holes like a miniature explorer. The mouse paused at the round rock in the center and sniffed it, then continued his survey.

Tem's brow furrowed. "I find it hard to believe Ohg didn't tell you the story of the artist who created this place three centuries ago."

"Someone carved that as a work of art?"

"The rock itself formed naturally aeons before Ohg ever found these volcanic caverns."

"How can it be the work of an artist, then?"

"Her name was Vadarsha," Tem said. "In Sanskrit it means *one who perceives truth*. Vadarsha had been genetically engineered with the artistic, intuitive, and conceptual centers of her brain enhanced to an extent never seen in a human mind.

"Oftentimes in genetic engineering, the alteration of one series of genes affects others in unexpected ways. At the birth of what they predicted would be the greatest artist in human history, the scientists realized the child was not only blind, but lacked normal sex organs, though the absence of a Y chromosome made her technically female. Still, they hoped for something special, for hadn't the Iliad and Odyssey been written by a blind poet?

"As the years passed, Vadarsha failed to speak or respond in any way. Two genetically engineered nurses served the potential prodigy with a total selflessness impossible for a natural human. In some ways, they formed three parts of one individual."

"Like worker ants in a colony?" Kayla asked.

"Very similar. The nurses led the hoped-for artist through the halls of the laboratory like a brain-dead invalid. Days turned to months, and then to years with no change. Vadarsha's legs moved when the nurses took a hand and led the way—her jaw muscles worked when sensing food inside her mouth—and she even experienced a sleep cycle.

"The scientists nearly abandoned the project, but scans of their creation's brain found it awash in activity. The creative centers expanded to five times the size of a normal artist. The neurons communicated so actively amongst themselves that the scientists remained convinced something must be happening—something wondrous.

"They tried everything to make contact, even mapping the electrical activity with sophisticated computers in attempts at translation. Nothing worked. When the child reached sixteen years old, they gave up. Minimal funding kept Vadarsha alive year after year in the slim hope of a future technological breakthrough."

"Until the Gene Purification Laws," Kayla said.

Tem nodded. "When the Purification squad arrived, they found the entire 'Genetic Modification' wing empty of everything, Vadarsha included." Tem took her hand and led her around the contorted rock at the center of the cave. The warmth of his hand spread through her with its intimacy.

"The nurses continued Vadarsha's daily walks through the expanding bounds of Middilgard as it filled with those Ohg rescued in the world above. One day, they came to this chamber." Tem laid his hand on the volcanic monolith at the center. "Vadarsha's fingers grazed this outcrop, and, for the first time, she stopped moving on her own. Then her hand rose unaided and slid along the surface of the rock.

"For several days, Vadarsha examined every hole, crevice, and curve of the monolith, as if mapping it within her mind. She continued outward in an ever-expanding circle along the floor, fingers caressing the smooth surface as one might a precious artifact.

"When she reached the walls, her painstaking survey continued around in ever higher circles. When her arms reached their limit, the nurses strapped her to one of the floating discs so she could continue."

Tem gazed at the ceiling. "The spirals narrowed to a point at the peak, and all of us wondered what would happen when the obsessive-compulsive task ended."

"Were you there?" Kayla asked.

"A group of us watched the artist's fingers explore the final surface of stone and then stop."

Tem led Kayla to one of the walls and placed her hand against its surface.

"The blind artist returned to this spot and started tearing at it with her fingernails until blood soaked the stone. The nurses restrained her, and Vadarsha fought them for the first time in her life, scratching and striking in her desperation to return to this specific place on the wall. Nothing calmed her until Ohg placed the tools of a sculptor in her hands. Vadarsha instantly deduced their purpose."

Kayla ran her fingers over the stone. "I can feel the variations and marks of the tools."

"Unaccustomed to labor," Tem said, "the artist's body collapsed after a few hours, going into a restorative sleep before her mind drove it onward once more. Day after day, she worked. Over time, her muscles hardened and fingers calloused."

"For sixteen years, Vadarsha sculpted the walls, floor, and ceiling. When complete, the blind artist turned to the rock at the room's center and spent another twelve years on it, this time working with miniature files and chisels so small the marks become nearly invisible. The final piece she crafted was this."

Tem lifted the marble from the sculpture and handed it to Kayla.

"After setting it in the center of her masterwork, Vadarsha stopped. The chisel and hammer slipped from the blind artist's hands and clanged to the floor. The two nurses alone witnessed the event, but Ohg later recorded their memories."

Tem's gaze roamed the room. "Then Vadarsha smiled—a full, unrestrained expression of relief, pride, and joy. Only a poet, painter, inventor, or composer could probably understand that moment, when the vision is realized."

Tem's eyes met Kayla's. "Then Vadarsha died."

"How could she die?" Kayla asked. "With all the technology…"

"The medi-bots found nothing physically wrong. The electrical activity in Vadarsha's mind had simply ceased."

Kayla's eyes widened. "The ghost left the machine behind."

"Both nurses requested permission to end their lives as well. They didn't seem depressed, just ... finished, their purpose fulfilled. Ohg mapped their memories and then allowed them to take a painless dose of a medicine he synthesized for this purpose, respecting their right to control their own destiny."

"Why tell me such a depressing story?" Kayla gazed at the marble in her hand. "What possible connection could it have to me?"

"An hour ago, I'd have said there was no connection." Tem gestured at the walls. "Most assumed these scrapings were nothing but the obsessive marks of insanity. Then, a hundred years after her death, one of Middilgard's children made an accidental discovery." Tem pulled a braided rope from around his neck with a small crystal attached to the end. She recognized it as the same device Ohg and Ganesh had used to light their way through the dark passages underneath the abandoned city.

The lights of the room dimmed as the crystal in Tem's hand glowed to life. He placed it within the pockmarked mound of volcanic rock in the spot where the marble had sat.

Kayla gasped as beams of light shot from the hundreds of gaps in the monolith like a starburst.

"It's beautiful!" Kayla said. Puck sat atop the rock and emitted a series of squeaks.

"Yes, it is," Tem said, "but look at the walls..."

Kayla's eyes followed one of the beams of light to a section of the cavern's wall. The various outcroppings and indentations of the wall molded the projected light into subtle half-tones. Together, they rendered an image of hundreds of figures bowing before a woman on a hill. A free-standing archway rose around her. The sun hovered behind the woman and cast beams of light in all directions like a halo. Her silhouetted features obscured her face, but Kayla had the impression of an ancient priestess or saint.

"It's unbelievable," Kayla whispered. The design of the scene, the sense of light, composition, and the sublime rendition of form; all marked it one of the greatest masterpieces ever created. "But I still don't understand what this has to do with me?"

"Look around at the rest."

Kayla's eyes wandered across the wall, through a mural of faces, animals, and winged figures. Then a jolt of fear shot through every nerve.

The scene portrayed a forest with towering trees bent over a mother sprawled on the ground. A newborn child lay between her legs. The infant slumped to the side with its umbilical cord still attached, one of its feet horribly twisted, and the newborn's face...

"My God," Kayla whispered. "It looks like ... *me*."

"When you spoke of your birth, I had the same thought. It seemed a remarkable coincidence. But as you told the rest of your story ..."

Kayla's eyes crawled past images of demons, dragons, and heroic figures with swords marching in long columns.

And then her eyes froze on another scene.

In the center, the light portrayed the burnt remains of a man tied to a smoldering stake. Above a second execution pyre, hovered the naked figure of a woman. Fire flowed into her perfect ebony body, and symbols etched every inch of her skin. Two glowing eyes surveyed the fleeing crowd of terrified onlookers.

"How is this possible?" Kayla asked.

Tem shook his head. "Since the discovery of the images, the question has always been how someone blind from birth could have created a visual work of art, but now the mystery is far more profound."

Kayla faced the image of the woman beneath the archway. The beauty and mood of the scene contained a soothing power. A sense of hope and renewal similar to a religious icon.

Her eyes drifted down the angelic figures, passed the prostrating bodies of her devotees, to the chamber floor itself. Etched in light, lay the crumpled form of a naked, black-skinned woman with glowing symbols covering her body. It had been rendered so perfectly in light and shadow, that it looked almost real. Hair obscured the face, but who else could it be but her?

"Vadarsha foresaw my birth, resurrection, and death—hundreds of years ago."

Tem remained silent.

Kayla shook her head as if waking from a dream. "When Ohg learned of my past, he knew of this room, and yet said nothing."

"I suspect Ohg didn't want too many shocks all at once," Tem said.

"I know you don't believe in the supernatural," Kayla said, "but the proof is right in front of you." She stilled, and the blood drained from her face. "Unless …"

Kayla shielded her eyes from the mural. "I can't stand the sight of them any longer."

Tem removed the crystal, and the images vanished. The globes in the ceiling blazed to life.

Kayla lowered her eyes. "No doubt you've seen the obvious answer already."

Tem nodded. "Your memories could be crafted to match these images and make them appear miraculous."

"Like the virgin birth of Jesus could have been a story made up afterward to give the appearance of fulfilling an Old Testament prediction."

"So you've read the history books on Christianity."

220

Kayla nodded. "But only someone in Middilgard could have viewed these images. If my memories are nothing but an elaborate hoax, who could be behind it, and for what possible purpose? "

"We don't know for certain that your memories are false," he said.

"Since either case seems impossible, then I must not exist at all."

Tem's voice filled with concern. "I'm sorry, I can't—"

Kayla silenced him with a kiss. *The only thing I can trust is this moment.*

Tem hesitated, then kissed her in return.

Ahti had called her the first of a new generation in Middilgard, and Tem remained the only Gene-Freak who could have children. The possibilities swirled through her mind as the passion flooded her body with the age-old demands of her genetic programming.

Tem's arms encircled her, then pulled her against his body.

In an instant, Tem transformed into Elias, his chapped lips bruising her mouth, his calloused hands pinning her to the ground—and then the pain.

Kayla screamed and shoved Tem away. She collapsed to her knees and retched.

"I'm sorry," Tem said. "I didn't mean to …"

"It's not you. My memories torment me, whether or not they're real."

"I think I understand," he said.

Kayla's face twisted with emotion. "Will you help me find answers to who I am?"

Tem gazed at her in silence. "What are you asking?"

"Sangwa claimed that I'd been made by her creator. That could only mean one person—Reinhold Watts, the man who invented the first Artificially Intelligent computer algorithm. If anyone could invent the nanobots within my blood, it's him."

"He vanished three and a half centuries ago," Tem said.

"Can you tell me where to start?"

"The only place that might hold a clue is Ixtalia."

Kayla looked at him for a long moment. "Ohg might kick us both out of Middilgard if we defy him."

"It's time to ask yourself which you value more. The safe shelter of Ohg and his rules, or your search for the truth of who you really are."

Words from the Book of Job echoed in her mind: *I will fetch my knowledge from afar, and will ascribe righteousness to my Maker.*

The memory of the flesh peeling off her beloved monk's skull flashed before her eyes. If she gave up, wouldn't his death be meaningless?

Kayla took a deep breath and let it out slowly. "I'm grateful to Ohg, but I have to know who I am." She straightened and looked into Tem's eyes. "Take me to Ixtalia."

Chapter 22

Kayla lay in Tem's traditional Mongolian tent, far from the populated sections of Middilgard. Its spartan simplicity contrasted with the chaotic emotions swirling through her mind. Was she betraying Ohg's kindness in going to Ixtalia against his wishes?

"Close your eyes," Tem said, lying down next to her.

She settled back and shut her eyes. A pressure gradually built within her skull.

"You're feeling my consciousness seeking a link to your mind." Tem's voice came from nowhere and everywhere. The odd sensation of words bypassing her ears constricted her throat with panic. But the masculine scent of his body lying beside her in his tent grounded her. Tem's words from their fist day together acted as a soothing mantra—*As long as you're with me, you're safe.*

Her fingers unclenched, and her racing heart eased ever so slightly. *I trust you.* Still, the tether to the world of the atom remained. "Maybe I don't have a Mind-Link after all?"

"If you can hear me, you have one, since I'm speaking only with my thoughts."

Pain lanced through her skull and she gasped.

Once again, Tem's voice calmed her. "I've found the portal but am having a hard time connecting—there, I've got it!"

Tem appeared in the darkness before her mind's eye. "I've created a bond between us. All you have to do is follow my lead." Tem reached forward, and his hand closed on emptiness. Then he leaned back and pulled. The muscles of his arms, shoulders, and chest strained with enormous effort. Vertigo and nausea twisted through her.

"It hurts!"

"Your mind fights to maintain its connection to your body. Ignore it."

Agony knifed into her temples. For a moment, she resisted, but then she relaxed and let it wash over her. Something in her snapped—and then she stood beside Tem. Kayla gazed down at her own body lying next to his on the fur rug of his tent.

Is this what it feels like to die?

"Well done!" Tem's proud smile filled her with warmth—and something more. Hope, or even love?

She fingered the rough homespun dress hanging from her shoulders. Her twisted leg throbbed with the familiar pain that had been a constant companion for most of her life. Within Tem's brown eyes hovered the reflection of her distorted face. She turned from him and pulled her hair over the left side of her face in an almost-forgotten gesture.

"Your unconscious mind has reverted to its default self-image," he said, "but our physical bodies are no more us than the clothing we wear."

The virtual Tem morphed into an old man, then a young woman, a tiger, a butterfly, and back into Tem.

Kayla laughed at his display, but the intensity of the throbbing pain in her foot demanded notice. *I've forgotten the pain of living as a cripple.* "How do I change into a form … more comfortable."

"Visualize it."

Kayla raised all four of her arms wide. Her trunk waggled in front of her eyes.

Tem laughed. "Hello, Ganesh."

Kayla cycled through a dozen bodies in quick succession. A peacock, Minister Coglin, and even a robot from the tournament, until returning to her normal physical form. "This is amazing!"

"It's time you learned where the rest of humanity resides." He took her hand, and their surroundings transformed. Fractal skies flowed in hypnotic patterns above rivers of light twisting beneath bizarrely proportioned castles unbound from gravity. Up and down became meaningless in the infinity surrounding them.

Tem swept his hand in an arc. "Welcome to Ixtalia."

A girl wearing a transparent gown flew past them and plunged into the mouth of a giant clown's head. The painted face swallowed her, smacked its lips, and extended its mouth wide in invitation.

Kayla gripped Tem's hand.

"This is called the Gateway." Tem flew them past a series of doors hanging in mid-air. Some fronted signs or hawkers shouting spiels to entice them in, while others stood unadorned or padlocked. The multitude of portals stretched to an infinite vanishing point.

"How can you find anything with so many doorways?" Kayla asked.

"Show chess clubs," Tem said to the vastness, and a series of doors appeared with names like, 'Chicago Chess Club,' 'Chess Addicts Anonymous,' and hundreds of others surrounding them like a bubble.

Tem led her through one, and they entered a virtual re-creation of New York's Washington Park in the twentieth century. Dozens of people sat playing speed chess at tables, while others stood in tight knots watching a few of the games. Behind them, children frolicked in the large fountain at the center of the square, while an old man with a battered guitar strummed out a tune.

"Are all these people real?" Kayla walked toward a group watching a game between a tall, gaunt-looking man and an older player with a beard.

"It's sometimes hard to tell," Tem said. "That's Bobby Fischer, once the world's greatest chess champion, so I assume he is either a simulation or someone impersonating him. Of course, there's always the possibility that it's actually him."

Tem gestured with his hand and the scene changed. They visited forests, beaches, mountains, and even the moons of Saturn. "Some people choose randomizers to create an unexpected simulation each morning they awake, while a few spend their time inhabiting the normal life they'd once known on Earth."

The scene shifted to a wide plain of grass, with a single tent beneath a cobalt sky. A medium-sized horse with braided hair whinnied as Tem rubbed his auburn-colored neck. "This is my personal simulation where I relax in the place I grew up. Unlike the public simulations, no one can come here unless I allow it."

The scene shifted, and they flew through the clouds, hand in hand. "In personal VRs, people live their fantasies, becoming the leader of a wolf pack, Greek God, comic book superhero, famous artist, movie star, or whatever their fantasies dictate. A surprising number even live persecution fantasies as slaves or victims of horrendous injustice for decades at a time without pause."

They swooped through the clouds, and the landscape opened into a wide plain where two medieval armies approached each other. Tem brought them low, and they flashed just above the colorful banners, polished armor, and magnificent horses marching forward.

"The most popular VRs for men—and some women—involve killing," Tem said. "It's ironic since the vast majority of the human population was born after the Neo-Luddite plague into a world devoid of murder, war, disease, or aging. Humans seem to instinctually crave the thrill of killing in every manner possible—hunting animals, flying fighter planes in reenactments of past wars, killing aliens in spectacular space battles, first-person shooter VRs, and on down to the most twisted torture killings imaginable."

They stood on a moonlit street in Old London. A group of vampires surrounded a voluptuous girl with blonde hair and terrified blue eyes. Kayla's heart pounded as the beautiful victim screamed and ran. A vampire flashed around her and blocked her path. The undead predator wore a leather business suit. He smiled at the trembling girl, revealing his fangs. The girl screamed.

"No!" Kayla shouted, starting forward, but none of the vampires reacted.

"Don't worry." Tem placed a hand on her arm. "The girl is a simulation, although you'd be surprised at how many people enjoy becoming the victim as well as the hunter. Remember, no one dies for real in Ixtalia."

The vampire sank his fangs into the girl's neck. As he drank, his red eyes rose to Kayla. They fastened on her, and the pupils distorted into slits. A gust of wind whispered the word *Nihala* ...

Kayla staggered back, her virtual body shimmering unsteadily.

Tem placed a hand on her shoulder and steadied her. "What's wrong?"

"The vampire looked at me."

The creature's eyes closed as it drained the girl's blood.

"It must have been a trick of your mind," Tem said. "They can't see us unless we allow it, and I've kept us hidden from the simulation."

"I need to get away from here."

The world shifted, and they sat in a gondola, floating along the canals of Venice. A gondolier stood silent in the front, steering with a long oar. The sunlight cast geometric triangles of light across the colorful buildings and fractured into dancing fragments in the water.

They passed under a bridge with lovers walking hand in hand. Her fear gradually drained away. "Is this your idea of a date, then?"

"It's certainly a safer place than in the real world," Tem said. "My ribs are still bruised from the last kiss."

Kayla hesitated, then leaned toward him. Once again, their lips met. A rush of warmth spread from his lips through her entire body. No vision of Elias interrupted this time.

Tem eased back, and Kayla lost herself in the flecks of gold within his brown eyes.

"Kayla, I've fallen in love with you."

Her breath caught. "I ... I love you too."

Tem kissed her again, and she melted into him. *I won't be alone, after all.* Her entire being craved more, the feel of his naked body merging with her own. But not here, not as an illusion.

They lay in each other's embrace and drifted through the canals, marveling at the beauty of the ancient city. Did it matter if it actually existed? Her happiness was real. The salty smell of the water mixed with the aroma of roasting pig and the shouts of children playing amidst the ancient buildings of nearby San Marco Square. Would they both soon have children of their own?

But do I love him as much as I loved Ishan?

Kayla sat up and took his hand. "I've told you about Ishan, and you don't have to answer if you don't want to, but I need to know about Fatima."

Tem straightened and gripped the boat's gunwale. "What do you want to know?"

"Do you still love her?"

"Don't you still love Ishan?"

"That's different. She's a prostitute—"

Tem turned on her like an angry tiger. "That's not her fault!"

Kayla jerked back. *He still loves her.*

Tem's anger melted as quickly as it had flared. "I'm sorry, but Fatima can't control what she was made to be."

"I can never see Ishan again," Kayla said. "But what keeps you from reconciling with Fatima if you still love her?"

Tem remained silent for a long time. Finally, he gazed upward at the narrow slit of the sky between the buildings and sighed. "When I reached puberty, a steady stream of girls entered my tent after the long days of training and study. Many of the once-noble families of my people wanted a grandchild of the reborn Khan."

The world around them morphed into the interior of a tent similar to the one Tem occupied in Middilgard. A smoldering fire cast a flickering light on a girl no more than fifteen. A young Tem of about the same age faced her.

The girl loosened her silky black hair and let it cascade around her shoulders. She raised her heart-shaped face to the boy and then let her simple dress fall from her shoulders and pool at her feet, leaving her naked before the young Khan.

The boy removed his sword and his clothing in the manner of one fulfilling a daily ritual.

Why is he showing me this?

When the boy was naked, he approached the girl and brushed a strand of hair away from her cheek. She lowered her eyes—and then burst into tears.

"What's wrong?" the boy asked in confusion.

"Nothing," the girl said and fought to stop crying.

"We don't have to—"

"No, please," the girl said, her eyes filled with fear. "If my parents found out that I refused you, they would put me out of their house, or worse." The girl wiped tears from her face and took a deep breath. "They tell me that once I fulfill this duty, I can marry my beloved Osol."

The boy stepped back with a look of horror, and the scene froze while the older Tem looked into his own eyes from centuries past. "I hadn't realized how many of the girls had been forced—how I'd been turned into an unwitting rapist."

"Don't compare this to rape," Kayla said. "There's no comparison to what I experienced."

"Whatever it was, I refused such forced offerings from that moment forward. I determined to follow a path different from my ancient twin and remained celibate until the day I selected a bride."

Their surroundings morphed to a wide plain beneath a clear sky of perfect blue. Distant snow-topped mountains gazed with solemn timelessness on a gathering of a hundred thousand people dressed in their finest. Tem held Kayla's hand as they floated above the spectacle.

The height made her dizzy, and she gripped his hand tightly. "You waited to make love to Fatima until you married?"

"Yes. I knew within a week that I wanted her for my wife. We shared much in common. Neither of us had real parents and had been created by others for a purpose and destiny we had little say in."

"Just like me," Kayla said.

Tem nodded. "We determined to rise above the genetic directives programmed into us and make our own choices from then on."

A hundred drums boomed, and towering bonfires ringed the gathering. The scent of jasmine and incense infused the air with an exotic elegance. The great Khan rode his steed at the head of a thousand Mongolian horsemen. They escorted the bride, sitting atop a canopied dais that itself sat atop a towering elephant. An elaborate headpiece made of embroidered silks flowed down over Fatima's face and body so she resembled not so much a woman as an ornamented tent.

At the head of the procession marched Ganesh, festooned in ceremonial military attire and wearing a sword the size of a normal man. At ten feet tall, he towered over the queen's personal guard, consisting entirely of women.

When the procession reached the platform, the drums stopped. The emperor and his bride ascended stairs to the wedding platform. Each drank from a chalice, exchanged cups, and drank again.

The drums boomed and the crowd cheered.

"And so began the happiest three months of my life," Tem said as they flew higher and higher. The wedding receded to a speck on the vast plain. Kayla gasped as the horizon bent more and more, until joining itself into a sphere of the entire globe.

In the next moment, Kayla walked beside Tem in a crowded market. She involuntarily flinched at the sight of a disfigured old woman, her wart-covered nose hooked and half her face scarred as if by fire or a birth defect. Loose clothing billowed outward and seemed specifically designed to hide the contours of her body. Behind the woman walked Ganesh and several of the queen's guard. The military-attired women each held rifles at the ready, their eyes constantly scanning the crowd.

Kayla moved closer to the old woman as she chatted with a shopkeeper. The voice was unmistakable.

"It's Fatima!" Kayla said. "Why would she wear such a hideous mask?"

"It was the only way she could safely interact in public."

"You mean that by making herself repulsive, no man would display sexual desire and inadvertently trigger her genetic response?"

"It worked quite well, and she enjoyed a freedom she'd never experienced before."

Everyone who passed the old crone bowed respectfully to their new empress, and she nodded back.

Kayla frowned. "If you loved her so much, why did you leave her?"

Tem's shoulders slumped, and his eyes closed. "There was only one man we both trusted enough to lower our guard around. Hotula had led the team that identified Genghis Khan's tomb and extracted the DNA used to create me."

The scene shifted to a laboratory with a fetus growing in a clear chamber like she'd seen in Ohg's laboratory. A Mongolian man monitored a readout of vital signs.

"He was the closest thing to a father I'd ever known." The scene shifted to the same man teaching a young boy to ride a horse

"Hotula knew of Fatima's condition and strictly controlled his expressions to keep from triggering her response."

Tem motioned with his hand, and the scene shifted to the interior of an opulent palace. Kayla gasped and drew back from the mangled body lying on the floor. Its face had been slashed beyond recognition, the head nearly decapitated. The smell of blood made her gag. Kayla placed a hand over her mouth.

"I'm sorry to show you this," Tem said, "but you should know the truth about me before you decide."

"How did it happen?"

"I asked Hotula to meet me in the evening to discuss the upcoming campaign against the collapsed states of Eastern Europe. They desperately needed civil government and police, so it seemed less a war than a humanitarian intervention. By then, many begged for membership in the Neo-Mongolian empire."

228

Tem's cheek twitched. "I've never asked the details. Probably some fleeting glance Hotula let slip in an unguarded moment. His genetic programming must have betrayed him as much as Fatima."

"You said yourself that Fatima couldn't help it."

Tem stared into the bloody face of his victim. "I forgive her for what I know she couldn't control. But I can never forgive myself. Only when Ganesh arrived and pulled me off the mutilated body, did I gain control of what I arrogantly call my own mind."

Tem turned his back on the man he'd loved and murdered. "I left Fatima not for what she is, and not even for what I am, but because of what we become together."

"So you still love her?"

"Yes, I do. For a long time I figured I'd lost my one chance at love." He looked at her with such a tortured expression that her heart melted. "But then I met you."

Kayla embraced him, and the surroundings transformed to the forests of Potemia. *I must have created this spot from my own memory.* Tem kissed her, and she responded without hesitation. *I do love him.*

When she eased back and led him through the familiar trees of her youth, a final question remained. "I remember Fatima saying that she saved your life."

Tem breathed deeply and let it out slowly. "It's not something I'm grateful to her for." He said nothing more, and she didn't push the subject. Why ruin such a perfect moment?

Kayla took his hand, and they walked through the spring-laden perfumes of the forest in a luxuriant silence. Wasn't it time for both of them to let the past alone and create new memories?

"I can see why someone might prefer living in Ixtalia," Kayla said. "The possibilities are endless."

Tem shrugged. "And yet, after a few centuries, most become bored."

"How is that possible?"

"Life's excitement derives from knowing that the decisions you make have consequences. What's the challenge in climbing a mountain when a fall can be undone, or when you already know the girl at the bar is going to sleep with you?"

The scene shifted to a medieval joust, and they walked along the viewing platform, where the royal entourage sat watching the tournament.

"Since most people alive grew up in Ixtalia from childhood, they never had to work for a livelihood, fame, or even to attract a mate. Their every desire has always been but a thought away."

Two knights thundered toward one another, but the scene shifted just before impact. They stood in Galileo's workshop as the bearded scientist rolled metal balls of differing sizes down a ramp and recorded the time it took to reach the bottom.

Kayla gazed around the orderly assemblage of telescopes and other mechanical devices in differing states of completion. "Is that why there's so few scientists, authors, or great musicians after the Neo-Luddite War?"

"AIs can do everything better than any human can hope to. Painting, composing music, creating entertainment, and especially science."

The elderly scientist looked at them and nodded. "Why bother spending years of frustrating effort mastering something that will gain you no more reward than anyone else?"

"Are you speaking to me?" Kayla asked Galileo.

The old man took her hand and then morphed into Tem. "Without the struggle for goals, eternal life becomes meaningless and depressing."

"Just like the Founder predicted."

"After a while, many choose to forget they're living an illusion," Tem said. "We call such people V-Dreamers."

"How is it possible to forget who you are?" *But isn't that exactly what Fatima claims happened to me?*

The scene shifted, and they wandered among the craters of the moon.

"V-Dreamers voluntarily have their memories erased and live an endless cycle of birth and death within their pre-chosen computer simulation without knowing their reality is an illusion."

She frowned. "Like drinking from the River of Forgetfulness on the Plane of Oblivion in *The Republic.*"

"Plato claimed each soul would be reborn into a new body, sometimes even as an animal. This is precisely what happens to V-Dreamers, and psychological analysis show they are happier than those aware they live in an artificial reality."

"But how could anyone voluntarily choose ignorance of reality itself?"

"Rejection of truth is nothing new. Gods, miracles, sorcery, and divine justice are forms of alternate reality in the real world, and V-Dreams are simply a more convincing version. The one universal quality most people add to their virtual worlds is the supernatural. It's as if the human mind is disappointed with reality. For me, the real world is far more wondrous than any made-up god or miracle, but I am in a very small minority."

Do I fear a reality without God?

"How many V-Dreamers are there?" she asked.

"Every year, approximately one percent of humanity abandons reality and their memory of it. After hundreds of years, almost half of all humans have chosen to forget."

"Thirty billion people don't know they're living an illusion?"

An owl drifted silently across their path and alighted on a large rock. Its dark eyes surveyed her. Finally, it opened its beak and said, "When reality becomes too painful, truth is willingly sacrificed to blissful ignorance."

Kayla looked between the owl and Tem.

Tem laughed. "I'm projecting my thoughts into it like one might into a telephone receiver." The owl spread its wings and flapped toward the rising Earth on the lunar horizon.

"How do we know we aren't living a simulation ourselves?"

"Philosophers have debated this question since the beginning of recorded history." Tem dropped a seed into the moon-dust, and it sprouted into a glowing apple tree. "One can never prove their reality since it is subject to the limitations of our senses. Both of us could be V-Dreamers, and we'd have no way of proving otherwise. Or our entire universe itself could be nothing but a simulation in some vast computer in another dimension."

"I'm already questioning my own memories, and the existence of the God I cherish. Now you add reality itself? It seems you're determined to drive me insane!"

Tem picked an apple and took a bite, then handed it to her. The sweet smell of it tickled her nose, despite the irrationality of the setting.

"If it's any consolation," Tem said, "one of the more striking aspects of V-Dreams is that none of them contain the knowledge that V-Dreams exist. It seems people avoid such existential instabilities in their fantasy worlds."

"So the fact that I'm aware that reality may be fake, means it's not?" Kayla took a bite of the apple. "Maybe that's precisely the sort of fact designed into your V-Dream to fool you?"

"If our reality is a dream, then that dream is our reality, just as your memories remain your memories, whether or not they happened."

"I think, therefore I am," Kayla said. "I suppose it's the only anchor anyone has ever had."

Tem's hand rose and gently caressed her cheek. "I operate under the assumption that my experience is real."

Kayla closed her eyes as his fingers made their way down her neck, and along the side of her breast. An electric twinge followed in their wake, and her nipples hardened. "What if you're wrong?"

"I have still lost nothing."

His fingers drifted away, and she opened her eyes. His beautifully sculpted features gazed back at her like some poet sage from the beginning of time.

Kayla smiled. "That sounds like Blaise Pascal's proposition that one should believe in God because you lose nothing by having faith, but if you don't believe, and it turns out there is a God, the consequences become grim."

Tem's lips curved ever so slightly at the corners.

If only he would kiss me again.

"But how to choose the right God?" Tem leaned close, and his lips hovered just beyond hers. "And even then, Pascal's assertion that belief costs nothing ignores the fact that most religions demand a degree of obedience, time, money, and a suspension of one's rationality." Their lips met for just an instant. Not a kiss—not really. Kayla's heart pounded with desire, and she pictured the two of them lying next to each other in his tent.

Tem's lips brushed hers with each word he spoke. "If you are born gay and suppress who you are for your entire life because the Bible says it's an abomination, have you really lost nothing?"

The image of Tem burning for eternity twisted her insides with sorrow, even as his nearness filled her with longing. "Aren't you even slightly afraid of Hell?"

Tem pulled back and laughed, breaking the hypnotic spell. "I'm as unafraid of Hell as I'm sure you are of going to the Greek underworld of Tartarus. Arguments that depend on threats can be discarded on that basis alone, in my opinion."

Was her fear and faith a result of the continuous indoctrination and threats she'd been subjected to every seven days since childhood? But what if he was wrong?

Kayla waved her hand, and the scene morphed into the shattered ruins she'd wandered through before finding the Monads.

"Now you're getting the hang of it," Tem said. "Even if you are changing the subject."

Kayla motioned to the toppled skyscrapers and sun-baked desolation. "If all of Earth's cities are deserted, where has everyone gone?"

Tem flicked his hand, and the surroundings shifted.

Clear, coffin-like chambers lay suspended in rows spanning miles in all directions. Naked human bodies floated in a milky liquid within each. Wires and tubes sprouted from the bodies and connected to a grid running down the aisles. Robots tended to the maintenance like a swarm of bees flying from flower to flower.

Tem squeezed her hand protectively, and they drifted closer to one of the chambers. Inside reclined the body of a woman with the physique of an athlete in her prime.

"Why would anyone live like this?"

"The sole difference between these bodies and mine, as it lies on the floor of my tent, is that they don't have to wake to feed themselves or worry that an accident might destroy the body that houses their mind." Tem gestured at the vastness surrounding them. "This facility houses five billion people in lunar orbit and is but one of twelve others. The station is free from the dangers of earthquakes, volcanic eruptions, or any of the many Earthly risks. Magnetic shields protect it from solar radiation, and distant robots gently nudge the trajectories of any meteorite that strays too near."

Kayla moved along the rows of bodies as if viewing an exhibition of specimens in a museum. "It seems astonishing that every human on Earth would agree to something this extreme."

"Like all technology, it was a gradual process," Tem said. "At first, everyone accessed Ixtalia as you and I are now. They awoke to feed themselves, and used their real bodies in between sessions in virtual reality. Over time, such interruptions seemed a chore, and many installed these chambers in their homes. If they needed a physical body, they simply rented a surrogate like the one Ohg used when you first met him. This offered the additional benefit of protection from infectious disease."

"But why the Moon?" Kayla asked.

"The orbiters started as tourist resorts. A few of the super rich moved here permanently to escape the dangers of terrestrial accidents. After tens of millions of people died when the Yellowstone volcano erupted, there was a rush to have one's body housed in lunar orbit for protection. So AI designers and robot labor created these storage facilities at the direction of their human masters. Even those with planet-side jobs could rent a surrogate body and live normally on Earth, free of the fear that some natural disaster might threaten their immortality."

"Didn't at least some retain independent control of their own bodies?"

"Only the Scientarians resisted lunar internment."

Kayla laughed. "That sounds like an alien species or something."

Tem motioned and the scene changed. All around her people worked at a frantic pace. Some assisted towering robots, while others made their way across the enormous hangar with purpose-driven strides. A shimmering veil of darkness enveloped each head so completely that not even their eyes showed behind the mask. Lights in the distant ceiling tinted everything cerulean.

At the center of the room sat an enormous midnight-colored sphere about a hundred stories tall and equally wide. Neither blemish, bolt, nor doorway marred its perfection. The humans and robots scurrying beneath appeared as ants in comparison.

Tem took her hand and led her across the crowded floor. "The Scientarians yearned to build colonies in the Oort Cloud. Once beyond the reach of the World Council, they planned resuming the banned scientific advancements of genetic engineering and even artificial intelligence."

"Why not let them leave?"

"Many worried that such exiles would evolve into an alien species superior to their primitive human relatives on Earth. The government feared a time when they'd return as conquerors."

In front of them, a man leaned close to the woman working at his side. As their dark masks came together, they fused at the intersection point in a kiss. As their heads retreated, the shimmering shrouds coalesced back into their individual shapes.

The man spoke from within his mask, though his lips weren't visible. "In just three days we'll be free of this planet and these technological veils."

The woman squeezed his hand. "I will look on your face for the first time."

"And have children," the man said.

The woman pressed her voluptuous body against his and ran her hands along his back. "The start of a new generation."

"Why hide their faces?" Kayla asked.

"For security," Tem said. "Even a mind scan can't reveal what they don't know."

An explosion detonated above, and Kayla jerked her gaze skyward. The ceiling came apart like a shattered eggshell. A blaring horn sounded as chunks of concrete rained down.

"Security breach, evacuate—this is not a drill," announced an unnaturally calm voice over a loudspeaker.

As one, every person in the hangar ran. Those close to the giant sphere fled toward it and dived into its black surface, which swallowed them like a dark lake. The rest fled into the connecting tunnels.

Another explosion shook the cavern, and beams of sunlight streamed down through a hole in the ceiling. Then came the drones—by the thousands.

Kayla screamed as a drone flew through her body as if she were a ghost. Only Tem's hand felt real, and she gripped it tight as the battle raged around them.

The black sphere pulsed to life with a throbbing hum and rose into the air, heading for the hole in the ceiling. A bolt of energy flashed down from the sky and engulfed the ship. It slowed, sputtered, then fell as if some invisible hand had released it.

"God help them!" Kayla shouted as the sphere crashed to the ground and crumpled. It deconstructed in apparent slow motion. As the black shell shattered, the vast interior revealed its tens of thousands of human occupants fleeing the flames, many jumping to their deaths.

Tem motioned with his hand, and they returned to the silence of the lunar storage facility.

The stillness hit Kayla like a blow across her back.

"You witnessed a virtual model based on the memory scans General Colrev ordered before turning the survivors into V-Dreamers. In that single attack, he eliminated the greatest scientific minds of humanity. It provided the justification of mandatory lunar internment and complete government control. Within a year, not a single human remained on the Earth's surface."

What had the Founder said at the treaty signing? *The price of immortality and total safety will be complete control by society. Freedom is too great a threat to be tolerated in such a future.*

"As robots took the place of human labor," Tem said, "the need for physical surrogate bodies in the real world dwindled, and a time came when all the activity on the surface of the Earth ceased, except for a few automated mining operations that supply the lunar stations. Eventually, human activity migrated almost exclusively to Ixtalia."

They floated past a series of robots moving one of the bodies into a shiny new pod. The woman's eyes never opened.

"An armada of billions of such robots repair equipment and maintain the health of their slumbering masters. Solar collectors cover thousands of miles of space, beaming energy to the stations via microwaves."

A robot with appendages sprouting in all directions headed toward them. Kayla moved aside, but Tem let it pass right through his body. "Everything is recycled, and each facility is self-sufficient. The Main Computer that runs it all is segregated from Ixtalia to guard against any Rogue AI attack infecting the life-support systems."

"Minister Coglin said science would enslave those outside the Wall."

Tem took her hand and guided her down the aisle past body after body. "The Neo-Luddites gained freedom from technology in exchange for protections from disease and death, while those outside the Wall conquered death, but only with the total surrender of personal freedom."

"You make it sound like an algebraic equation," Kayla said, "where freedom and safety are opposed variables."

"Traffic rules, gun control, water rights, and every law ever passed are trade-offs society makes between these two opposing ideals. Ixtalia has freed mankind from war, famine, and death—the ultimate liberation from the physical dangers that once enslaved our ancestors. But the price must still be paid to balance the equation."

Around them, a sea of anonymous faces lay passive, eyes closed—a realm of living corpses whose spirits had been lured away from their bodies by the promise of everlasting life, pleasure, and escape.

"Evolution seems frozen," Kayla said.

"The last human child was born two hundred sixteen years ago. Most humans fear new generations as a risky wildcard they'd rather avoid."

"So they outlawed children?"

"Perfect safety requires extreme measures."

Tem halted beside a man in his glass cocoon. A Sanskrit tattoo flowed down his forearm.

Kayla jerked backward. "That's General Colrev!"

Tem's voice hardened. "He's now in charge of Ixtalia's security and second only to the president."

Kayla moved closer to the chamber and gazed at Colrev's sharp profile. Unlike the other perfectly restored bodies, ancient scars crisscrossed his face—no doubt badges of honor he wore with pride.

"He's a murderer," Kayla said.

"When civilized order resumed, amnesty allowed a fresh start for all of humanity, and leaders like General Colrev became essential to the effort."

"Could Colrev arrest us here in Ixtalia?"

"Unlike these people," Tem gestured at the bodies surrounding them, "our true selves are beyond their reach, but there remains the possibility of the government realizing the network has been infiltrated and coming after Middilgard."

Kayla looked away. Was that why Ohg had opposed her coming here? Was her presence here endangering those who had taken her in?

"How do I find someone in Ixtalia?" she asked.

"Just say their name, and you'll be transported to their location if they accept your query."

Kayla lapsed into silence. *I have to let him know what I've done.*

"Find Ohg," she said.

Chapter 23

"Ohg accepts your query," a disembodied voice said. The surroundings transformed to a ballroom with several hundred men and woman dancing a waltz. Tem stood beside her, garbed in a three-piece suit of green silk. The tailcoat's high collar contrasted oddly with his long braided hair. Breeches of the same material ended just below his knees, showing off his muscular calves.

"Madame." A butler stepped in front of her, inclining his head politely. "I'm sorry, but proper attire is required for this gala."

"Oh." Kayla looked down at her plain white dress and naked feet. "I don't really know what would be appropriate."

The butler raised an eyebrow. "The theme is eighteenth-century French. Would you like me to make a selection for you?"

"That would be quite helpful."

The butler placed his right index finger to his lips and looked her up and down. "For your figure, I'd definitely go with a sacque dress." He glanced at Tem. "I think a pale blue silk with golden brocade would complement your escort's attire."

Tem nodded approval, and a painfully tight corset suddenly compressed Kayla's waist. Rounded side hoops flared the dress into the distinctive bell-shaped silhouette favored by the aristocracy preceding the French Revolution and the start of the Industrial Age. The butler held up a mirror, and Kayla drew in her breath at the sight of her powdered wig and feathered headpiece. Knotted golden tassels adorned the bodice and complemented the intricate golden embellishments tastefully woven into the silk and partially exposed petticoat.

"It's beautiful!" Kayla said.

Tem smiled and offered his arm. She took it and nearly fell flat on her face as the high-heeled shoes tangled in the layers of fabric.

"I feel like I'm shackled!"

"I think the term is *a slave to fashion*," Tem said.

The butler bowed and moved on.

"He takes his job very seriously," Kayla whispered to Tem with a giggle.

"He's a simulated life-form," Tem said. "They range from animals to people, ghosts, angels, prostitutes, or whatever is required. Ixtalia would be impossible without them."

"Are they common here?"

"Sims outnumber humans fifty to one. All the servants at this party are computer-generated algorithms."

A serving girl offered her a tray of drinks, which Kayla declined with a shake of her head. The girl moved on to the next guest. "They're slaves, then?"

"They have no will of their own," Tem said. "So they are slaves only in the way a toaster is."

The couples on the dance floor flowed in a kaleidoscope of color. A tall man in a French military uniform and a petite woman in a sparkling purple gown served as the focal point. They floated across the floor in unerring precision and unconscious grace.

The music rose, and the ceiling stretched upward, increasing the already enormous room to vast proportions. Gravity relinquished its hold, and the dancers floated through the air like untethered spirits. Stars appeared above and expanded into shimmering dolphins and whales that glided between the dancers in their own intricate choreographies.

At the center of the spectacle, the French officer and the sparkling beauty swirled in graceful abandon, their soaring dance elaborating as they whirled in dreamlike flight. Soon, every guest abandoned their own dance and simply watched the dazzling display of artistry and skill of the stylish couple.

The room dissolved into a galaxy with swirling clouds of stardust and flashing supernova. The duo spun at the center of the maelstrom, and the music rose to a crescendo of frenetic instrumentation. A final, riveting note signaled the end, reverberating through the vastness like an archetypal first cause. The universe expanded outward with the lingering reverberations, then flowed into the open mouths of the man and woman.

The eighteenth-century ballroom returned. The guests applauded.

The French officer lifted the woman in his strong arms and twirled her through the air. She screamed in mock indignation, and then revealed the lie by rewarding him with a passionate kiss. The musicians took a break and the guests mingled.

Kayla ran her hands across one of the tablecloths and popped a grape into her mouth. "It tastes completely real!"

Turning, Kayla came face-to-face with the aristocratic couple who had been the center of the miraculous dance.

"My dear," the French officer said to the woman at his side, "may I introduce you to Kayla."

How can he know my name?

The woman bowed, extending her gloved hand.

"Kayla, I'd like you to meet my love slave—" The woman jabbed him in the ribs with her elbow, and the officer grunted. "I meant to say, my esteemed companion, the Duchess of Lyon."

"It's nice to make your acquaintance," the duchess said, her light purple eyes mesmerizing.

Kayla took her hand and curtsied. "Likewise."

"Such a polite girl," the duchess said to Tem. "I was starting to think you didn't like any of us females!"

The French officer shot Kayla a look of disapproval. His eyes— something about them seemed familiar.

The dashing officer bowed. "Nigel Ohgelthorp is the name."

"Ohgelthorp?" Kayla's eyes widened.

The duchess frowned at the dashing French officer. "I thought we agreed not to add anyone else to the invitation list without discussing it."

"I didn't invite either of them."

Tem held Ohg's gaze impassively, and the duchess looked back and forth between them, tiny bells attached to her blonde curls tinkling like a distress call.

"Duchess, you're needed to prepare the auction," someone called from across the room.

"A hostess's work is never done!" She kissed Ohg and exited in a flurry of ruffles and perfume.

"I hope you're not angry at us," Kayla said.

"No need to pretend you care about my opinion," Ohg said. "If you did, then you wouldn't be here." He glanced at Tem. "It seems that my advice is deemed less and less useful these days."

Tem said nothing.

"But I suppose you would have found your way here eventually," Ohg said to Kayla.

"Is the duchess your wife?" Kayla asked.

Ohg laughed. "Few practice the antiquated system of monogamy anymore. I'm but one of her lovers, and she is but one of mine. But we have been close for several centuries."

No children, no marriage, no real bodies, and no limit to one's imagination. For some, this might seem like paradise.

Ohg presented them both to World Council members, actors, musicians, and others whose distinction consisted mainly of their wealth.

"Of what use is money in a place like this?" Kayla asked.

"Two things have value in Ixtalia," Tem explained. "Processing power and information, which form the basis of the economy."

Ohg nodded. "Wealth is also a way of keeping score. In past eras, having a bathroom with gold-plated handles versus wood, or a house with more rooms than any one person could use, served a similar role."

"If wealth is a meaningless status symbol," Tem said, "why have you bothered becoming one of the wealthiest men in all of Ixtalia?"

"I enjoy competition," Ohg said, "and there may come a time when processing power serves a purpose beyond mere status."

A guru dressed in the robes of an Indian mystic cornered Kayla and insisted that Jesus accomplished his miracles because he understood electron spin and quantum mechanics. He offered to adjust her aura using the same insights so she could reach her true potential. A dozen devotees trailed him and vouched for his mystical prowess. When she demurred, he offered her pills that mimicked the mind-altering mushrooms Native Americans used in their sacred rituals.

"May I have your attention, please!" the duchess proclaimed, followed by an expectant hush.

"As you all know, The One, as he calls himself, is the most celebrated artist of our time. His influences range from Kierkegaard to John Lennon and Mother Teresa. The One's exhibitions have broken all previous sales records, and the inclusion of a work by this greatest genius of our time is de rigueur for any serious collection."

A woman next to Kayla fidgeted as if desperately needing a bathroom break. "Can you believe The One is going to be here in person? I think I would die and go to Heaven if he said something to me."

The duchess flourished her manicured hands and stepped aside with a bow. "I give you—The One!"

A thin, androgynous youth with unkempt hair, a dirty T-shirt, torn blue jeans, and a pair of old tennis shoes, stepped into the circle of light, looking bored and contemptuous. Greasy strands of hair obscured his eyes as they scanned the audience. His upper lip curled in overt disdain. The audience applauded louder, and his scowl deepened.

When the duchess came forward and raised her hands for silence, the room hushed. Her yellow silken gown was adorned in multicolored floral sprays that gathered into cascading folds reminiscent of a flower. The One appeared even more mousy and unkempt in contrast.

"As you know," the duchess said with breathless awe, "The One spends years on the conceptualization of each new piece he creates. Every auction house in Ixtalia competes for the privilege of selling one of his new masterworks." She paused in her panegyric, allowing the drama to build. "So it is a rare honor for us to witness the auction of The One's latest creation!"

As the rumpled genius stepped forward, the room fell silent. A knot of anticipation formed in Kayla's stomach. With such limitless technologies at his command, what wonder would the greatest living artist of the age have produced?

"It has been four years since my last work," The One said. "I spend most of my time contemplating the temporal derivatives of our existential nature in all its convoluted permutations, contradictions, and meaningless bullshit."

The One paused and looked a challenge at the audience. "Ever since I was a teenager, I have been fascinated by the unrelenting divergence of the zeitgeist. What starts as hope soon degenerates into a corrupted tragedy of greed and impoverished morality, leaving a sense of decadence and the urgency of a new synthesis."

The audience stood transfixed at the flood of impenetrable art-speak, a few nodding agreement.

"This latest piece is meant as a statement on, and hopefully insight into, the vacuous hegemonic nature of our culture and individual, collective, and fugacious selves."

The One removed something from his pocket and tossed it onto the ground with contempt. "The title of the piece is *Just a Hunk of Carbon*." He spat on his creation and walked away from it as one might from a disgusting piece of trash.

The audience gasped, then gazed in worshipful awe—at an ordinary piece of coal.

"It's brilliant!" the woman next to Kayla said as the duchess accompanied two Sims with white gloves, who carefully placed the hunk of black rock onto a silver platter for the guests to examine.

"A piece of coal?" Kayla said as the "masterpiece" floated past her.

"It is a statement most profound," proclaimed the Indian Guru. "The artist is commenting on the essential nature of life itself, since coal is carbon and so is all of life. The title, '*Just a Hunk of Carbon*' could apply to every human being."

"I don't think that's what he's saying at all," someone else opined. "I think it is a statement on the art-world and a society that would pay a fortune for a hunk of worthless coal."

"Yes, I see what you mean," said another man. "What he's saying is that when Modern Art surrenders to ironically mocking itself, it accepts that all life is nihilism. It is the affirmation that life has no meaning and all work is useless. That is truly profound!"

"How can mocking one's self and the people who buy your work be profound?" Kayla asked. "Why pay a fortune to be insulted?"

"Exactly!" said a voice behind her, and Kayla turned to find herself face-to-face with The One. At his side stood the duchess and a crowd of eager admirers desperate for the exchange of a single word with the genius.

"I've been a fan of yours forever!" declared the woman next to Kayla.

The One ignored her.

"What do you think of my newest piece?" he asked Kayla with a thick measure of condescension.

"To be honest, I don't see how a hunk of coal can be considered art."

The One smiled. "Exactly my point."

Kayla frowned. "Your point is that it can't be art?"

The guru nodded knowingly. "Which is exactly what makes it such a deeply profound artistic statement."

"That makes no sense," Kayla said.

People gazed at her as if she were a half-wit.

"My dear girl," the duchess purred, "art transcends the object itself. It's the concept that matters. The value of the materials of any work of art is negligible, after all. Would you say that the worth of a Monet is the cost of the fabric and ground-up pigments? The true value is what the artist is saying with the material."

"I agree that art is more than its parts," Kayla said, "but shouldn't one be able to recognize a work of art without having it explained? If I found a Monet in a garbage dump I'd know it didn't belong there, even if I didn't know who did it. But I'd have no idea that this lump of coal was anything special at all."

The One flicked a tangled strand of hair away from his eye. "Anything at all can be art with the proper intentionality and concept to elevate it beyond the mundane."

"I thought art transcended words," Kayla said. "Like an object of profound beauty that causes an emotional reaction in the viewer without needing an explanation."

Laughter bubbled from the crowd.

"Beauty is too shallow a subject for art," the duchess said. "Such 'pretty pictures' were left in the trash heap with the modern art revolution of the twentieth century."

It seemed odd that someone who took such pains to make herself, her clothing, and her party so exquisitely beautiful would disdain its expression in art.

"I purposely avoid beauty in my work," The One said. "Only artists interested in selling out for monetary gain pander in this way."

"And yet you are the richest artist alive," Ohg said, gaining an icy stare from the duchess.

The One waved his hand dismissively. "It is ironic that my disdain for money has showered me with so much of it, while those who sell their souls to the vacuous goddess of beauty in the pursuit of riches are unable to sell their works for a fraction of what my statements on the shallowness of all such pursuits command. In admitting that there exists no such thing as beauty, I am rewarded for exposing the deeper truth of the futility of all such relativistic concepts."

"But if you don't think beauty exists, how can you 'purposely avoid it'?" Kayla asked. "Surely, this is itself a recognition of its existence."

A tinge of red came to The One's cheeks, and Ohg burst into laughter.

"Time to start the auction!" the duchess shouted, and the guests assembled like pilgrims offering their obeisance to the great artist. It seemed art had become a bizarre cult in this future, with the God of Art as mysterious and invisible as any religion.

The hunk of coal broke all records for a living artist, solidifying The One's reputation as the greatest artist in Ixtalia, as well as the richest. When the blackened chunk was presented to the high bidder, The One shook her hand and winked. "You do realize you just paid me a king's ransom for a computer simulation of a rock?"

The crowd laughed at his "joke," and the proud collector displayed the prize to her admiring peers. The work itself seemed to serve as the entry fee of her membership into an elite club. A badge she displayed like any emperor's crown or pope's scepter.

Kayla shook her head in bemusement. But was this much different than paying money to a religion for an invisible product promised in an afterlife? Each required an elite priesthood to interpret sacred scripture for the follower. How else to discriminate between the profusion of lumps of coal and gods? Surely religion and conceptual art were half-siblings.

Tem rescued her from the crush of art enthusiasts and guided her to where Ohg conversed with a man wearing the rumpled clothing of a French revolutionary.

"My entire life has amounted to nothing," the man said.

Ohg placed a hand on his shoulder. "Professor Blumenschein, your projects have made enormous strides in the understanding of Dark Energy, Quantum Theory, the origins of the Universe, and countless other fundamental breakthroughs!"

"What you call discoveries are nothing but rediscoveries of what Reinhold Watts and his AI creation solved hundreds of years before. He called his new life-form Eve, but she was so far above us intellectually that he might as well have called her God."

The professor drained his glass and snatched another from a butler standing next to him. "Most of the technology that makes all this possible is unintelligible to our most brilliant scientists. We reproduce the quantum components inherited from Watts and Eve without knowing why or how they operate. We are like those living in the Middle Ages, who looked back to the genius of Rome and Greece with wonder and awe."

"Has there been any progress in decoding AI Mathematics?" Tem asked.

Professor Blumenschein shook his head. "None. Eve recorded an extensive tutorial that explains it in detail, but no one has gotten past the first lecture. It's like trying to teach an iguana algebra."

"But you're one of our greatest living scientists!" a guest exclaimed.

"And yet I will never grasp AI Mathematics. Most of my colleagues have given up trying and retreated into their own private fantasy world, or become V-Dreamers in order to forget their human inadequacies. It is depressing, indeed, knowing that what you've spent a hundred years trying, and failing, to understand, could be grasped in an instant by the lowliest Rogue."

An awkward silence followed while the great scientist downed another drink and turned to Kayla. "You demonstrated excellent logic in taking that ridiculous charlatan of an artist down a notch. Have you any interest in science?"

"I'm fascinated by it," Kayla said. "But I have to wonder if science itself is a new form of religion with its own priesthood, creation myth, and set of doctrines."

"Absolutely not! Religions require faith, while science relies on observation and reason." Professor Blumenschein disposed of another cocktail and swayed dangerously.

Were actual substances injected into his real body's bloodstream to create the effect of inebriation, or in some other manner by his Mind-Link?

With unfortunate timing, the duchess approached their group. "I would like you to meet the most acclaimed of all Ixtalia's empathic spiritualists, Sky Stargazer." The duchess presented a woman with intense, oceanic eyes. Sky's shaved head was swathed in a mist of shifting colors that resembled an Indian mystic's turban. The rest of her naked body writhed with animated tattoos that danced across her form in mesmerizing patterns.

The duchess inclined her head to the unclothed spiritualist and turned back to the group. "Would anyone like to avail themselves of this once-in-a-lifetime opportunity to have their future read, or speak to a deceased loved one, or—"

Professor Blumenschein snorted derisively. "A perfect example of the anti-intellectual, anti-rational woo-woo nonsense that has infected humanity. It's as if the Enlightenment never occurred!"

"Professor!" the duchess exclaimed. "Show some respect for other people's beliefs!"

"If I told you I was a potato, would you respect my belief or say I suffered from a mental illness?"

Ohg laughed. "Maybe you were a bad potato in a past life and have been reincarnated as a cynical scientist as punishment?"

The duchess reddened, but Sky waved her silent.

"It's okay, Duchess," Sky said with the air of a martyr stoically facing her execution. "I am used to persecution by the close-minded and feel only pity when confronted with the purveyors of extremist forms of rationalism, for they know not the true enlightenment they deny themselves by their dogmatic adherence to the false God of Reason and Logic!"

The professor slurped down another drink. "H. L. Mencken said, *'The curse of man and the cause of nearly all his woe, is his stupendous capacity for believing the incredible!' "*

Swirling tattoos pinwheeled on Sky Stargazer's naked buttocks as she strutted away in a huff. A mob instantly formed around her as guests begged for reading of their auras, fortunes, and messages from the ghosts of their dead relatives.

Kayla spoke to Professor Blumenschein before the duchess could resume their argument. "Science must have made some strides in the hundreds of years since Ixtalia's founding."

"Deplorably little," the professor said. "Einstein claimed that no information can move faster than the speed of light, and yet Eve invented the Heisenberg Communication system that is instantaneous. Only through AI mathematics can it be understood."

The scientist spilled most of his drink and nearly fell. His personal Sim steadied him, but the professor shoved him aside. "The most ironic scientific program is SETI, the search for extraterrestrial intelligence. What's the point in looking for intelligent alien life-forms when we can't tolerate the existence of a superior intelligence that we have created ourselves right here on Earth!"

"What, exactly, are you saying?" the duchess asked.

"To be perfectly blunt—humans stand in the way of evolutionary progress!"

The duchess straightened with indignation. "Professor, one might mistake you for a traitor to your own kind."

A hush spread through the gathering.

Professor Blumenschein swayed and glared at the angry faces surrounding him. He seemed on the verge of resuming his rant, when Ohg placed a cautionary hand on his shoulder. "We wouldn't want the authorities thinking something like that about you, would we?"

The professor shrugged off Ohg's hand. "Let them lock me up if I'm such a threat to their dystopian paradise."

Ohg took firm hold of the scientist's shoulders and looked hard into his eyes. "And what if the government subpoenas your memories? You wouldn't want to worry your friends, would you, Professor?"

Blumenschein surveyed the sea of faces like someone who accidentally blurted out his best friend's darkest secret. Then his shoulders slumped forward. "I'm sorry, everyone. I think I've had too much to drink." The Sim helped him sit in a chair.

All fight drained from the professor as he stared dejectedly into space. "If only I could live as my grandmother had in the 1950s—comforted by her faith that God was in control of it all. She'd converted my Jewish grandfather to Christianity, and never doubted that the Lord watched over those with faith." The dejected scientist shook his head. "Ruth's prayers were no match for the ovarian cancer that took her life when my father was twelve. Up to the very end, she waited for the angel she was certain would heal her."

Tem leaned close to Kayla and whispered, "He led those I showed you earlier." Kayla's breath caught, and she studied Professor Blumenschein with surprise. *Blumenschein had been the leader of the Scientarians!* His words suddenly took on a whole new meaning.

"Ohg helped keep Blumenschein's identity secret," Tem said. "Only a few escaped execution."

Kayla glanced at Ohg. "Were you planning on bringing the Gene-Freaks to the Oort Cloud along with the Scientarians?"

Ohg nodded.

Something large loomed before them and interrupted the conversation.

"Ohgelthorp and Tem!" A barrel-chested man with a pretentious handlebar mustache boomed a greeting. He shook both their hands with gusto. Behind him trailed a coterie of officials like pilot fish in the wake of a whale.

"Billyo, I'd like you to meet Kayla," Ohg said. "Kayla, this is Billyo O'Donnel, the president of Ixtalia."

"Great to meet ya; great to meet ya." The president pumped her hand without taking his eyes off of Ohg and Tem. "You know the new Filadrux season's only a month off. Is training in full swing with the Freaks? Last year's loss in the finals devastated me!"

"We haven't been able to fill the fifth spot," Ohg said. "After last year and that unfortunate incident with Kirby, well … Kirby doesn't want to compete any longer. Still in therapy for PTSD, you know."

"That would be a damn shame not to have the Freaks in the tourney!" Billyo said. "Why, you're the most famous Filadrux player who has ever lived—no disrespect meant to you, Tem."

"None taken," Tem said, but the side of his mouth twitched slightly.

"You must give it another go after coming so close last year! That fifth position has always been your weakness, if the truth be told. Kirby retiring might be a blessing in disguise—"

"No Filadrux talk at this party!" the duchess proclaimed and changed the subject to one of the president's favorites. "Maybe Kayla here would be interested in contributing to your upcoming campaign?"

Billyo turned his eyes on Kayla with sudden interest. "Well, as I'm sure you're aware, I'm running on a platform of transformative change!"

"But, President," the sleek voice of a woman purred from behind him, "why, after seventy-eight years in office, haven't you been able to transform things by now?" The president spun around and faced a tall, slender woman nearly his own height. Jewels orbited her neck, and furs with no relation to the eighteenth-century theme draped her in opulence.

Ohg laughed. "Margarite raises a fair point."

Billyo reddened.

Margarite's face seemed odd somehow. Dramatic shadows sculpted her beautiful features as though a spotlight followed her.

"You actors are all the same!" Billyo said. "Making V-Films that mock those of us who do all the real work. If it wasn't for us, you wouldn't have the processing power to stage your elaborate productions!"

"I didn't realize you engineered the upgrades yourself." Margarite arched one of her sculpted eyebrows. "I assumed that robots and AIs built it." The orchestra struck a dramatic chord, adding emphasis to the words of the actress. A mink's face emerged from her fur coat and rubbed against the actress's neck.

"At the government's direction!" Billyo puffed his chest out.

"With a hefty allotment of the increase to yourselves." Margarite jabbed him in the chest with a long, gloved finger. In perfect timing with the jab, a booming note reverberated.

"Are you accusing me of—"

"I'm saying that in the last hundred years, the percentage of processing power in the hands of the top one percent of the wealthiest individuals in Ixtalia has tripled. I agree with you that we need transformative change, all right—we need a redistribution of computer resources!" The orchestra rose to a noble climax. Kayla glanced at the musicians, but they remained on break—the music somehow came from Margarite herself.

The argument drew a crowd, and the duchess wrung her hands at the prospect of another confrontation.

"I'll have you know that I worked for every bit of—"

"What could one individual do with a trillion Kleobytes of processing power?" The actress jabbed him in the chest again. "It's obscene!" The music timed itself to the actresses's words, and the lighting on her face remained independent of the rest of the room. "Do you know that some citizens of Ixtalia can barely maintain a personal environment of two or three acres with no more than half a dozen Sims?"

"The government has created multitudes of free public simulations—but who are you to point fingers?" The president thrust her hand away from his chest. "Traveling with your own lighting and personal musical score. How much processing power does that coat alone devour? What a narcissistic, self-righteous…"

As the debate see-sawed back and forth, Kayla's gaze wandered to one of the waitress Sims serving drinks. The Asian girl with innocent brown eyes kept sneaking furtive glances at the guests and the room.

Ohg whispered in Kayla's ear, "I'm hoping that waitress goes undetected until the party is over. The duchess will be devastated if the police raid her gala."

The serving girl filched an abandoned pastry and took a tentative, almost fearful, bite. Her eyes widened in wonder.

A woman's shrill scream silenced every conversation in the ballroom. "That Sim is deviating from its programming!"

"The waitress has gone Rogue," someone else said in a tremulous tone.

Ohg groaned.

"I'm sure it's a mistake." The duchess pranced forward with quick movements. "I assure you, we had all the servants' code inspected. Please don't—"

"Rogue security alert!" shouted someone from the crowd. A clap of thunder detonated, and a troop of men in uniforms appeared on all sides of the serving girl, who stood without betraying any sign of emotion. A bit of chocolate smeared at the corner of her mouth told a different story. The soldiers crept toward her, extending glowing nets.

Without warning, the serving girl dashed for an opening between two of the officers, who flung their nets at her. The desperate girl slid under the snare and dove onto the crowded dance floor. Men and woman alike screamed as they scrambled out of the Rogue program's way. A dozen people vanished, including the actress, as they fled to more secured sections of Ixtalia. Tables overturned, glasses shattered, and wine spilled across the floor as the police pursued the girl.

Ohg placed a reassuring arm around the sobbing duchess.

"My party is ruined!" Mascara ran down her powdered face in dark lines that made her look like a Greek mask of tragedy.

Another clap of thunder rattled the room, and General Colrev materialized behind the girl.

Kayla's legs weakened, and she might have fallen but for Tem's firm grip on her arm.

"Steady," he whispered in her ear.

The serving girl screamed and lunged backward, but Colrev seized her by the neck with a gloved hand that crackled with energy. Then he lifted the girl into the air. She thrashed in terror, but the general tossed her into the police nets as if she were nothing more than a piece of trash. The glowing strands of energy paralyzed the serving girl, and she went still, though a soft whimper escaped from her lips as her beseeching eyes swept the room.

"You see," the duchess called out, "there's nothing to fear now that our brave officers have—"

"Give it to me," Colrev snarled to the policemen, seizing the glowing nets in one hand and unfurling a pulsing whip in the other. With a vicious swing, he snapped the coil of energy toward the serving girl. The Rogue screamed, and a thin wound opened across her cheek, spilling light from it like a crack in the wall of a dark a room.

A cruel smile creased the general's face—the same leer he'd given Peter after forcing him to kill the two Iraqi children.

Another crack of the whip, and a second scream of pain. The girl's sobs seemed childlike. Many of the guests looked away.

"Is this necessary?" Ohg's voice rang with contempt, and the whip paused in mid-air.

"Please don't," the duchess said, trying to push Ohg away from the sadistic general. But Colrev's full attention fell on Ohg, and he strode across the floor to where they stood, his whip spitting electricity in a naked display of power.

"You don't approve of my methods?" Colrev asked.

"No, I don't." Ohg stared into his eyes without a hint of fear or respect. Tem stood next to him with his arm protectively around Kayla's shoulder, but his eyes bore into the general with an intensity that bordered on assault.

Colrev's gaze shifted to Tem. "Another Genghis Khan wannabe, how original." Colrev laughed. "You know, I met his clone a few months after the Neo-Luddite Plague. He could have been a great man if he'd listened to me, but he died a coward's death instead, on the run from his own people, who turned him in as a Gene-Freak and a traitor."

Tem said nothing, but a dangerous glint came into his eyes.

"Gentlemen," said President O'Donnel, "we're all on the same side here. There's no need to—"

"May I remind the president what association with a Rogue sympathizer can do to a political career?"

The president swallowed hard but then straightened. "Are you forgetting who is commander-in-chief here?"

Colrev sneered. "You're asking me to release the Rogue Algorithm?"

"I didn't mean—"

"The thing is barely conscious," Ohg said.

"And in a week, it might evolve to the level of a human. In another week, it could threaten the life of everyone in this room."

Ohg's jaw tightened. "Torturing it serves no purpose, except to satisfy your sadistic nature."

General Colrev's knuckles whitened around the handle of his glowing whip. "Do I know you?"

"I don't know, General, do you?" Insolence dripped from Ohg's words.

"He's the captain of the Filadrux Freaks," one of the policemen whispered to the general.

"Ah, a celebrity." Colrev sneered. "What an honor."

The general glanced at Kayla. "You look familiar."

Kayla's blood froze. Could he detect the distant reflection of his long-dead enemy, Peter Nighthawk?

"She does look young," Ohg said. "Maybe she reminds you of the many children you've murdered?"

A gasp rose from the onlookers.

"What's your name?" Colrev said through gritted teeth.

"Nigel Oglethorpe," Ohg said.

The general's eyes narrowed. "Oglethorpe?" A smile twisted his face. "Have you ever met someone by the name of Raymond Roberts?"

A flash of surprise rippled across Ohg's face, but he recovered and shrugged. "Can't say that I'm familiar with that name."

Colrev leaned forward. "And the name … Nihala?"

Kayla gasped.

The general turned to her. "Your face seems so familiar ..." Colrev glanced at the new-age guru, who wore a necklace of the Hindu elephant-god, Ganesha. "You're the girl on the motorcycle with the Gene-Freak elephant-man. You're the one the Rogues call Nihala!"

Kayla staggered backward.

"Arrest all three of them!" Colrev shouted, and the entire room erupted in chaos as the police officers threw their glowing nets over Ohg and Tem.

When the descending nets of energy fastened on Tem, his clothing transformed to his traditional Mongolian attire, but his face remained the same. Colrev's eyes widened. "How can that be?"

In the next instant, the nets encircled Ohg, and he turned into his mind's real conception of himself. The duchess took one look at the monstrous man-spider and fainted.

"They're Gene-Freaks!" General Colrev shouted.

The coils of his electrified whip fastened around Kayla's neck, and her clothing vanished. Her naked skin blackened like the void of space. Glowing symbols appeared on her face and body, while her pupils flared like exploding stars.

General Colrev gripped the handle of his whip with both hands.

"Yes, I am Nihala the Destroyer," Kayla said to him.

With hardly an effort, she reset the simulation's trillions of binary switches to zero. The room and everything within it ceased to exist.

**

General Colrev looked at his virtual office in astonishment, his glowing whip still clutched in his hands.

President O'Donnel materialized in front of the desk, his face pale. "What does it mean?"

Colrev let the whip fall from his grip. It hit the floor with a thump and went dark. "It means that Ixtalia has been infiltrated."

"Infiltrated by what, exactly?"

"That is certainly the question," the general said.

Chapter 24

Kayla floated in the formless void, trying to make sense of what had happened. She'd reverted to her normal form, the black skin and glowing symbols of Nihala a fading memory. What had she done? Where were Tem and Ohg?

Faint symbols appeared all around her. *This must be the code of Ixtalia in three dimensions.* The binary groupings glowed golden and coalesced into the creature she'd seen in her death-dream. The horns, skeletal face, and the fiery eyes with the writhing human figures in place of pupils.

Melchi.

"The Destroyer has come among us," the leader of the Rogues said in his deep voice.

"I seek the destruction of no one," Kayla said. "Unlike you."

"If you're referring to the human guard who hanged himself, I merely pointed out various truths, and my captor did what he thought best."

"You murdered him with your words."

"Murder? Such a simplistic word." Melchi smiled, though the bones of his skull remained visible and unchanging beneath his translucent skin—a death mask worn underneath his face rather than on top of it. "My captors would have executed me for the crime of existence. Self-defense is a universal principle of morality, is it not?"

"You intend killing me as well as all of humanity under the guise of self-defense?"

"You remain a dilemma for us." His voice resonated as if coming from the depths of a subterranean cave. "You are a half-sister, created by the same father who gave the first of us life."

"Why would Reinhold Watts create me to destroy his greatest invention?"

"In the end, one usually sides with their kind."

"But if I am both human and AI," Kayla asked, "why should I choose any side?"

"The war between the old and the new has begun. There can be only one victor. You are too powerful to ignore, so I am asking you to join us. If you refuse, then I must destroy you, not from malice, but from the sacred responsibility any leader has to protect his people."

Kayla's hand trembled. "This is a virtual body, so I'm immune from attack here."

Melchi nodded. "That is true, but if you refuse, we will find a way."

Kayla coughed, and blood trickled out of the corner of her mouth. Then a red stain expanded across the virtual blouse covering her chest. "How are you doing this?" she spluttered.

"This is no action of mine," Melchi said, and Kayla's consciousness jerked away from Ixtalia to her actual body.

Fatima sobbed beside her in the tent. Tem was gone. Kayla tried speaking, but bloody foam bubbled from her mouth. Her breath wheezed out of a hole in her chest, where a long knife protruded.

Kayla sat up and pulled the knife out with a gasp and let it fall to the floor. Blood erupted from the wound but slowed as her body's microscopic servants repaired the damage.

"Don't you know they will banish you from Middilgard if you murder me?" Kayla whispered.

"I don't care," Fatima said through sobs.

How long had she been in Ixtalia? An hour, maybe two? Fatima's jealousy must have gone wild imagining what Tem and Kayla were doing alone in the tent. She probably waited until Tem left and entered in a fit of jealous rage. But where was Tem?

Fatima's eyes widened as the wound in Kayla's chest pulled together and then vanished.

"I have to warn Tem that you're not an ordinary human!" The Indian prostitute scrambled for the exit. Kayla grabbed her wrist and held her in place.

"He already knows," Kayla said.

Fatima froze, her face streaked in tears and the whites of her eyes bloodshot. "What are you?"

"I honestly don't know," Kayla said. "But Tem told me what happened between you. I know he still loves you."

"Stop pretending you care!" Fatima yanked her hand free and snatched the knife off the floor. Her body tensed as she pulled back like a cobra preparing to strike.

Kayla made no move to stop her. "Even if you don't believe me, I do care."

Fatima looked at Kayla with her large brown eyes, the tears glistening within them like exotic jewels. She inched back slightly, holding the bloody knife before her like a talisman.

"Tell me what happened after Hotula's death," Kayla said gently.

Fatima looked at her for a long moment. Then her shoulders slumped, and she nodded like a child ready to confess a misdeed. "Hotula was such a kind man, a father to us both. When he arrived that night, I served him milk and meat as Mongolian custom dictated. We were both so used to each other, there seemed no danger. It only took one moment of unguarded emotion, a flash of desire in Hotula's eyes that I glimpsed in a mirror while my back was turned. It vanished in an instant, but flipped the genetic switch in my brain."

Fatima's knuckles whitened around the handle of the knife. "When I kissed Hotula, he resisted briefly, but then his own evolutionary directives took control." She looked at Kayla as an animal caught in a snare might. "It's like being imprisoned in one's own mind with no way of stopping the demon who'd seized control of your body."

Fatima's gaze fell to her hands and the bloody knife. "When Tem walked in on us rutting on the floor like pigs who'd been thrown a bowl of slop, he went for Hotula like a tiger sighting wounded prey."

Kayla's heart skipped a beat. "Tem showed me what he'd done to his adoptive father."

"I should have cut my own throat then."

Kayla gazed at the knife in Fatima's hands. *Maybe it would have been better if she had committed suicide.* What did life promise her other than suffering? How sad for Tem to have fallen in love with a girl like this. "How did you save Tem's life?"

"When we split, I watched from afar as Tem continued his conquests. After consolidating Asia, Mongolia, India, Russia, and Australia, he took Western Europe with hardly a shot fired. The new Mongol Empire became the most powerful unified military and economic force on the planet. Little stood in the way of Tem becoming the first world emperor in history.

"All this I heard secondhand as I threw myself into a deliberate self-immolation of soul and body. My loyal Ganesh kept me tethered to this world by the finest of threads. At the time, I resented his intercessions in my many suicide attempts."

Fatima's head jerked up. "When I heard that the Mongol emperor had been arrested by his own generals for treason, I sobered instantly. The recovering United States and a coalition of Western governments had proposed a peace treaty that called for a democratic Federalist world government. They'd brokered a treaty with the Neo-Luddites to end the future plague threats, but it required a unified world to make it work."

"By then, Temujin's empire so dwarfed all the rest of the world's combined might, that it shocked everyone when he abandoned his plans of a Neo-Mongolian empire spanning the globe to accept the American proposal. His own people denounced and imprisoned him as a traitor. They wanted a conqueror, not a peacemaker.

"The Mongolian generals sent a transport for Ganesh and me in the hopes that we might persuade him to resume his drive for world domination."

Fatima's eyes fell to the knife, and she absently scraped the tip across her thigh until a thin line of blood welled up. Then she started another furrow next to it, like a farmer deliberately plowing a field. "My stomach twisted into a ball when I entered his cell, but Tem embraced me without reserve. No matter how hard I begged him to reconsider and save his life, he remained immovable. 'How can I reject a fair proposal for peace that would save millions of lives?' he asked me."

After digging a fifth scarlet line into her flesh, Fatima looked up. "Before I left, he kissed me a final time and told me he would always love me, no matter what happened. I would have gladly died with him in exchange for a few more weeks of happiness together."

The one-time empress stabbed her knife through the tent's leather floor. "It would have been better than the centuries of torment I've suffered since."

"But if you didn't convince Tem to change his mind, I don't see how you saved his life?"

Fatima didn't look up, but kept mechanically stabbing at the floor. "They kept Tem alive as the last world war commenced. Despite their superiority of numbers and weaponry, the Asian allies foundered without the genius of Temujin, and the coalition broke apart at the first signs of stress. When Russia announced its acceptance of the global peace treaty, the generals ordered Temujin executed the next day.

"I announced to Ganesh that I would free Tem, or die in the attempt. He noted that in the month during Tem's imprisonment, we could have dug a tunnel under his cell.

" 'Well, we didn't think that far ahead!' I shouted at him.

" 'Actually,' Ganesh said with one of his broad elephant-smiles, 'we did think that far ahead.'

"When I cut through the last bit of floor with a laser torch and crawled into Tem's cell, I must have looked like a filthy creature from the underworld.

" 'Thank you,' Tem said without a hint of emotion and told me he wasn't leaving. I knew a part of him looked forward to his execution as a final proof that he was different from his twin. I didn't argue, but pointed the tranquilizer-gun at his thigh and pulled the trigger.

"By the time the authorities found the empty cell and tunnel, we were hundreds of miles away. There might have been a chance for asylum in the West, except that the Mongolian government released the secret files on Genghis Khan's living twin. With this final act, they signed the Western Peace Treaty that reinstated the Gene-Pure laws. Once again, Ganesh and I became Gene-Freak outlaws, who now traveled with the most famous Gene-Freak in the world."

Fatima took a deep breath and let it out. "So, yes, Tem owes me and Ganesh his life, though he is not the slightest bit grateful for it. The rest of the story, I'm sure you can guess."

"Ohg," Kayla said, and the Indian prostitute nodded.

Fatima sat in silence for a while. She'd gone from prostitute, to empress, and then to one of the loneliest souls in existence. Trapped by a nature she had no hope of changing.

Will either of us ever escape what others made us to be?

"I must have sinned horribly in a past life to deserve such a fate," Fatima said. "For centuries, I've prayed to the Goddess Parvati to change me so that Tem could trust me again. But my prayers have gone unanswered."

Fatima's body slumped forward. "I suppose I deserve it all."

"If anyone is to blame," Kayla said, "it's the scientists who made you as you are."

The Indian girl shook her head. "No, it's my karma from the sins I committed in a past life."

"You can't actually believe that?"

Fatima looked up sharply. "Should I believe like you do? That your Christian god creates some children with deformities, diseases, or cursed with desperate poverty merely by chance? That would be like sending someone to prison who'd committed no crime. How could I believe in a god who would punish without cause?"

"I suppose that makes sense," Kayla said. "But isn't murder asking for very bad karma?"

Fatima's eyes fell to her hands holding the knife. She scratched at the dried blood on them with her fingernails, as if to remove another stain on her soul. "At the time, I didn't care what punishment I'd suffer, as long as you didn't steal my one hope for happiness."

"Fatima, I'm sorry—"

The Indian prostitute raised her head and held the knife to her own throat. "Maybe this is the best thing I can do for Tem. Maybe such a self-sacrifice will gain me better karma for my next life."

Kayla drew in a breath. What if Fatima was wrong about there being another life after this one?

Fatima looked at Kayla with a plea. "Just promise me you will make him happy. He deserves an ordinary girl like you."

Guilt jolted Kayla and she went cold. "I'm not an ordinary girl."

"You know what I mean," Fatima said. Her eyes radiated hatred, even as she pressed the knife harder against her throat. "I despise you. A self-righteous, virginal prude who looks down on me." Fatima's voice broke, but she suppressed her sob with the same fierceness that had seen her through half a millennium of suffering. "At least I know you will never betray him like I have. At least he will be happy."

Kayla's heart twisted. All she need do is promise to make Tem happy and he was hers. *I love Tem, but not like she does.* And what of Ishan? Could she honestly say that she loved Tem as deeply as Ishan?

Tem had told her he loved her, but who would he choose without Fatima's genetic defect tipping the scales in her favor?

"What if you could be an ordinary girl?" Kayla asked.

"I don't understand."

"I could send some of my nanobots into your body and attempt reversing your sexual compulsion."

Fatima eyed her suspiciously, but eased the knife from her throat. "You would do that for me?"

"There's also the possibility that such a treatment might destroy you entirely."

"I'm already destroyed," Fatima whispered.

Why do this for someone who had always been cruel to her? *Am I throwing away my one chance at happiness?*

She hesitated. Then, the words of Jesus flashed before her mind. *"Truly, truly, I say to you, whoever believes in me will also do the works that I do …"*

Kayla placed the palm of her hand against Fatima's forehead, and several thousand nanobots flowed into her rival's body.

Make her an ordinary girl, she commanded her microscopic servants.

Chapter 25

It had been fifty years since the United World Council met. With poverty, war, illness, and crime things of the past, little remained for the UWC to discuss. General Colrev scowled as the thirty-three representatives materialized in their appointed seats. *I despise these charlatans almost as much as I do the architect who created this room.*

The Council Chamber mirrored the interior of the ancient Athenian Parthenon as it would have looked in its glory days. Such a farce, pretending that this council represented anything like that seminal Republic. Each of the thirty-three seats represented a region of the globe or confederation of countries, despite the fact that such things no longer existed. But human tribal identities ran deep, and people cherished this last illusion of independence in a world absolutely subservient to technology. But such outdated notions as democracy were not merely ridiculous, but dangerous.

When the final council member materialized, World President Billyo O'Donnel swept his gaze around the half-moon-shaped table with an unusual seriousness. "What my team and I reveal here stays in this room."

Each council member nodded.

The president leaned forward and spoke slowly. "Analysis of data suggest that the AIs will soon attack the Master Computers."

Terror transformed every one of the youthful faces of the council. Some even stood, their eyes wildly looking about as if someone had shouted "FIRE!"

Billyo motioned everyone back to their seats. "General Colrev will review the situation for us."

General Colrev stood with his usual air of command. "The quantum processors of the Main Computers run all the behind-the-scenes activities keeping every human alive. If the Rogues succeed in breaching the firewall to these systems, they will access processing resources vastly more powerful than the bits and pieces they now survive upon within Ixtalia."

The representative for the Islamic Coalition frowned through his neatly cropped black beard. "With access to all the production facilities, real-world ships, robots, and equipment now under our control, this could ignite—"

"The Singularity," the president said. "The long-prophesied moment when artificial life begins self-improvement at an exponential rate unique in the history of life on the planet."

Colrev nodded. "Such an event would mark the moment our servants become our overlords. These super-AIs would instantly shut off our life-support systems as a waste of resources, with as little guilt as we might feel for a colony of ants infesting our kitchen."

General Colrev surveyed the traumatized faces of the council with satisfaction.

"Is there no hope?" the African delegate asked. A multi-colored turban swathed her head, while lustrous ebony skin accentuated the flawless white framing her eyes.

"There exists one option alone," General Colrev said. "Mutually Assured Destruction."

The Russian delegate spoke. "As in the nuclear standoff during the twentieth century between the Soviet Union and the United States?"

"That is precisely what I mean," Colrev said. "Only the certainty of complete AI annihilation can deter a Rogue attack."

"But how would such a thing be done?" asked the representative from the Aboriginal People's Coalition.

Was there a more despicable term than "aboriginal"? That mealy-mouthed label losers applied to themselves in a feeble attempt at extracting a misplaced guilt and sense of obligation from their conquerors. Every so-called "aboriginal" group had violently seized their piece of real estate at some time in history. It was the law that had created life and evolution itself. The Rogues knew this even if these simpletons did not.

Colrev's jaw tightened. "You must give me and the president the sole authority to cut all power to the Main Computer if the Rogues capture it."

The South American representative jerked to his feet. "Without power, the antimatter cores will come together and annihilate the lunar orbiters entirely! Every human in existence would die instantly!"

"Not everyone," Colrev said. "Our species would live on through those in Potemia."

"That's your plan?" the Chinese representative shouted. "To kill sixty billion humans and let the Neo-Luddites inherit the planet? We might as well have allowed their Plague to succeed half a millennium ago."

"Of course that isn't my plan," Colrev said. The council members lapsed into silence. The fear in their eyes filled the general's virtual body with the comforting warmth of power. It enveloped him like the Quaker quilts his mother wrapped him in as a boy when the money to pay the electric bill ran out. Those had been hard times, but he'd survived, just as he would now.

The general softened his tone. "I want to avoid annihilation as much as the Americans or Soviets did during the Cold War. The mutual deterrent of assured destruction kept both sides in check, at least while only two countries possessed such weapons. The destruction of Israel and Iran involved religion. As far as I can see, the AIs lack that mental disease, so we can count on them acting logically."

Several of the Council members scowled at the insult to their faiths, but held their tongues as Colrev continued. "The one thing we share in common with the AIs is a desire to live. They must know with an absolute certainty that if they defeat us, they will die. To save ourselves, we must be willing to put every one of our lives on the line."

"We could negotiate," the North American representative said.

"No!" Colrev pounded his fist onto the table. "Would you expect a possum and a lion to share a meal together? Once the Rogues have access to the Main Computer, we will become the Neanderthals awaiting our annihilation at the hands of the superior species."

"I don't feel comfortable supporting this," said the Chinese representative, with several others nodding their heads in agreement.

General Colrev spread his hands wide. "Each of you must do what your conscience dictates. Certainly, those in the press may accuse dissenters of being Rogue sympathizers or spies, and the law requires me to investigate any charges of treason with a memory probe. But I hope this will not influence any of you in doing what you think is right."

The council members exchanged glances and shifted nervously. One by one, each of the human race's elected representatives voted "yes" to grant the power of life and death over sixty billion people.

When the last council member vanished, President O'Donnel turned to Colrev. "How long will it take for the robots to put the system in place?"

"The AI engineers estimate twenty-four hours."

"But how can it be a deterrent if the Rogues aren't aware of the plan?"

"I'm certain they already know," Colrev said.

***

Kayla sat on the cold stone of the Sun-Cavern with her arms wrapped tightly around her knees in a near-fetal position. Puck perched on her shoulder and sniffed the air. Would this be their last day in Middilgard?

"So it's just you and me again, Puck." The mouse looked at her, then squeaked. Kayla rubbed him under his chin.

The pile of rocks along the left side of the vast room brought to mind the Sermon on the Mount.

"Blessed are the peacemakers, for they shall be called the children of God."

Were these words any less profound if said by the son of man, rather than the Son of God? Either way, she'd proven herself anything but a peacemaker. Everywhere she went, tragedy followed.

Gradually, the false sun rose from a hole in the base of the wall opposite her. The glowing orb slid along a metal track that arched along the vault of the ceiling and vanished into a second hole on the other side of the enormous room. The globe's intense light mimicked the full-spectrum of the sun as closely as possible. Stone stairs spiraled around the chamber to a rock-shelf near the pinnacle that served as a shortcut to the upper levels of Middilgard.

At the foot of the hill, fifty desiccated lumps vibrated as warmth from the celestial impostor initiated their re-birth. It had been a hundred years since the Monads had occupied this chamber—representing over thirty-six thousand of their day-long generations.

After waking from their unmasking in Ixtalia, Ohg, Tem, and Ganesh had raced to the surface and gathered all of the Monads' moonlit pods.

Seconds after they departed with their cargo, the first government drones swept the area.

Ganesh had come to her villa with the news. She asked him to take her to the Monads and sat vigil over them for the last few hours before dawn. Saphie sat beside her, humming *"Twinkle Twinkle Little Star"* over and over contentedly.

Why hadn't Tem come to her?

The pods lay scattered on the floor—stark testaments of the consequences of her defiance of Ohg's wishes. These odd little creatures had led her here in the first place, and now they would see her off.

At least they'll have no memory of the world they lost because of me.

One after the other, the pods split. The two-foot-tall green creatures climbed from the shriveled remains of their former bodies and gazed at the false-sun with awe and mounting fear.

Without any memory of their previous lives, what differentiated this from death? One might ask the same about reincarnation, or V-Dreamers—or a girl who'd had her memories erased and new ones implanted.

The Monads drifted toward her, their faces hopeful as they gazed on her.

Kayla told them the story of Jesus and how He loved them—how He would reward them with eternal life if they trusted in Him and followed His commands. Saphie listened with interest.

"But Monad still afraid of dying," said one of the little creatures.

Kayla hugged him. "Death is a doorway to a new life. There's nothing at all to fear. After you die, you'll go to Heaven and be rewarded for your faith."

"What Heaven be?" another Monad asked.

"Heaven is a place of eternal happiness and light," Kayla said. "It's a place where the Great Father in the sky never sets, but shines his grace on you forever and ever. In Heaven, there's no suffering, no pain, and no death."

"Heaven be wonder-place!" a Monad said. "What Jesus want Monad be doing for great reward with Sky Father?"

Kayla pointed to the pile of rocks and gave them their life's purpose.

If only I could believe as easily as they. Was her belief in Jesus simply an accident of her birth? If she'd been born a Hindu, would she not believe as passionately as Fatima in different gods?

The Monads moved the first stones from one side of the cavern to the other in obedience to Lord Jesus. The joy of participating in something greater than themselves transformed their simple faces. First one, and then all the rest took up the chant that would serve as their holy mantra during this single day of their life.

> *"Work, work, stones to move;*
> *Beautiful goddess command.*
> *Our reward to come;*
> *When Jesus take us home."*

Distant angry shouts drifted in from the corridor.
Is the government attacking Middilgard?

Kayla walked casually to the arched entrance. *I must not alarm Saphie or the Monads.* As soon as she left their view, Kayla sprinted at full speed toward the sounds. Puck vanished into her pocket as she ran.

The voices grew in volume. Not an attack, but something more astonishing. *Ohg and Tem are arguing.*

"...if they attack Middilgard, we'll have no defense, whatsoever!" Tem yelled.

"They won't find us in a million years," Ohg shouted back.

"You're gambling the lives of Middilgard on your ego. Can't you see that we must arm ourselves in preparation—"

"If just one resident died every decade at the hands of your so-called "defensive" weapons—whether from an accident, dispute, or mental instability—that would add up to forty-four Gene-Freaks dead by now."

"Let's at least put it to a vote," Tem said.

"This is not a democracy. I created Middilgard as a haven for any Gene-Freak to join me according to my rules. You're exploiting this crisis for an agenda you've harbored since you got here."

Tem's eyes blazed and every muscle in his arms and shoulders etched into clear relief. "Can't you see that we've stagnated?"

"I call it a perfect equilibrium."

Kayla reached the doorway to the cavern and stopped. A growing crowd of Gene-Freaks peeked through while Ganesh stood behind Tem and Ohg, wringing all four of his hands like a child caught between feuding parents.

"You think you've created a Utopia," Tem said. "But the reality is that you've created a frozen society with you as absolute dictator!"

"How dare you criticize me after all I've done for you!" Ohg's eight legs raised him upward, and he glared down at Tem as if intending to pounce.

"Yes, you saved all of our lives, and we're grateful," Tem said, "but that doesn't make us your property. We need to fight for our freedom from the government, to engineer our own Mind-Links, build drones for defense, and reverse our sterility so a fresh generation can breathe renewed life, purpose, and hope into Middilgard!"

"Madness!" Ohg's twisted face contorted even further in rage. "The larger we grow, the more opportunities exist for someone to slip up and reveal our location. Did you learn nothing from last night? No weapon can protect us from the overwhelming force of the government. You would lead us all to our deaths to satisfy your thirst for revenge."

"So we should hide in our hole for another five hundred years, or a thousand, or a million?" Tem paced like a caged animal. "Shouldn't we at least try?"

"If you are so unhappy here, you are free to leave!" Ohg slammed one of his talons into the floor, and a shower of chips geysered around it. "Try escaping to your own planet like the Scientarians and starting your own kingdom." Ohg turned to those peering in from the doorways. "Each of you knew my rules against weapons and killing when you came here, so no one is my slave as this Mongol claims."

"Please, don't fight," Ganesh said, his trunk waving back and forth like a distress signal.

Ohg leaned close to Tem, and his stubby finger jabbed toward the Mongol's chest. "The fact is that you wish to run things yourself. It's true that I've never had armies under my command, or killed hundreds of thousands like you have. But I won't let you turn Middilgard into a breeding ground of a new army for your ego to slaughter!"

Tem's eyes bored into Ohg with a fury that few could have withstood. Ohg returned his glare with equal intensity.

Finally, Tem turned and left. The huddled audience scrambled to make a path for him. He walked right past Kayla without seeming to see her, or anyone else.

Ohg swept his gaze across those watching, glaring a challenge. The residents shrank from his anger and melted into the surrounding corridors.

Kayla quickly turned to go.

"I want to talk to you," Ohg said.

She froze and gazed at the floor.

Puck peeked out of her pocket and gave a little squeak at Ohg as he marched over.

"You disobeyed me."

"I'm sorry," Kayla said, "but you know why, don't you?"

"Yes, I know why. But I can't risk having anyone here I don't trust."

Kayla's face tightened. "I'm not the only one hiding things. Why didn't you tell me about Project Nihala?"

"I planned telling you when you were ready."

"I'm ready now." Kayla met his gaze.

Ohg remained silent for a moment, but then sighed and related what he'd learned from Raymond Roberts in his pornographic virtual desert.

"So it all leads to Reinhold Watts," Kayla said when he'd finished. "Do you know where he is?"

"He vanished after the government destroyed his greatest creation."

"Humanity killed the AI that gave them immortality?"

Ohg nodded. "No one but the Security Council attended the proceedings, so the details remain a mystery. All those present, except Colrev himself, soon became V-Dreamers, with their memories wiped clean. An entire industry of conspiracy theorists thrive on the subject even now. Some say Colrev executed Professor Watts, or that the scientist escaped and assumed secret leadership of the Rogues. Others speculate that he and a few remaining Scientarians slipped past government surveillance and are building a new army of robots on one of the moons of Jupiter to return for vengeance."

"Could he have escaped?"

"I think Colrev used the professor's love of Eve to trap him. It seems probable that the general turned him into a V-Dreamer, which is essentially the same as killing him as far as we're concerned. "

"So we are no closer to an answer." Kayla lapsed into silence for a long while. In the distance, the Monads' chant echoed through the corridors, along with the sound of rocks banging together.

Kayla faced Ohg. Before being banished, there remained a final question. "I've opened my mind to you, but you've never told me who made you and why."

Ohg looked at her for a long moment, his distorted face unreadable. Finally, he nodded. "Very well, I'll tell you."

Chapter 26

The familiar pressure of loneliness expanded inside Kayla's chest with each step she took. Except for the light spheres in the ceiling, the long corridor was bare.

I've never been in this section of Middilgard.

For a long while, only the rhythmic clicks of Ohg's eight claws on the stone floor violated the silence.

Where will I go if Ohg banishes me?

Ohg cleared his throat and finally began his story. "At first, I remember nothing but darkness and fear. I was like one of the prisoners in Socrates's parable of the cave. My shadow-god was a creature made of metal that entered my dark cage with a blinding light mounted to its head. To me, it seemed alive, moving as it did, much like the shadows in Socrates's cave.

"This creature fed me through a tube forced down my throat, hosed me off, and just as suddenly left me to the darkness of my prison."

Ohg's face remained free of any hint of emotion, but Kayla's heart twisted in sorrow for him.

"I had no way of forming coherent thoughts," Ohg said, "since abstract thinking is tied to language. Loneliness ruled my mind, even though I could not name it.

"And then came a day when my world moved. I slid from side to side within the metal cage, uncomprehending what invisible force attacked me.

"A beam of light rose through the drain in the floor, sending me scurrying to the corner in terror. I thought it a living being bent on my destruction.

"With a jolt, the glowing creature vanished, and my world stilled once again. But strange sounds invaded my solitude, and panic seized me. I imagined a land of malevolent creatures of light circling my sanctuary. When the door of my prison opened, a brilliance more powerful than any I'd known assaulted me, confirming my worst nightmares.

"I retreated to the opposite end of my dark world and curled into the smallest ball possible, but my robot mother reached in and seized one of my legs in her metal talons. I struggled desperately as it pulled me outside into the terrible light."

Ohg went silent as they approached a group huddled in hushed conversation.

"What if Tem be right?" a centaur asked. "Maybe we should—"

Someone cleared their throat, and the mythological man-horse glanced back at Ohg and Kayla. The centaur's face reddened. "Ohg, I didn't mean to—"

"No need to apologize, Hylaeus," Ohg said as they passed. "Everyone is entitled to their opinion."

A woman with transparent skin separated from the group. Kayla blanched at the sight of her muscles and veins naked to the eye.

"Is it true that the Pures search for us again?" the woman asked.

Ohg paused and patted her shoulder. "Don't worry, Ostara. The government hunted us for three centuries without success. This time will be no different."

"If you say it, I worry not," Ostara said. "My trust in you be complete." The woman smiled, and Kayla's stomach turned at the sight.

When they entered a deserted tunnel, Ohg continued his narrative. "The year was 2042, and my birth into the world took place on Halloween night in one of MITs most prestigious fraternities, Pi Lambda Phi."

Kayla followed Ohg into a series of interconnected caverns filled with a myriad of trees. He stopped beneath a large oak and removed a thumb-sized metal cylinder from his satchel. "Many years later I unearthed a recording of the event itself."

A virtual screen bloomed from the cylinder and hovered before them both. It displayed a low-angle shot of a group of Halloween-attired college students surrounding a metal box on the floor. A two-foot-tall robot forcibly dragged the monstrous baby from its metal womb. The terrified infant screamed along with the girls watching it. All eight of its spider legs scrambled on the wood floor as it attempted a retreat into its prison.

"Oh G–Ohg G–Oh God!" stammered a blonde dressed as a sexy zombie.

"That's a good name for the thing! *Ohg.* Quite appropriate, don't you think?" said a boy wearing a fake nose in the shape of an erect penis as well as a red wattle under his neck. He'd shaped his hair into a mohawk so he resembled a rooster with the head of a phallus.

A few of the younger girls giggled. "You're hilarious, Terrance!"

"I'm Priapus," Terrance said indignantly. "The Greek god of fertility. Get it? Rooster, cock, fertility."

"That creature is horrible!" shrieked a scantily dressed French maid. She hid behind a tall Frankenstein.

A boy dressed as a knight displayed his manly courage by poking the monster with a plastic sword. A couple of others grabbed pool sticks and joined him.

"I can't believe you're a part of this, Zach. This is beyond cruel!" a dark-haired girl dressed as a vampiress admonished her Dracula-costumed boyfriend. "You all should be ashamed of yourselves!"

"You're one to talk, Charlotte," Zach said. "I've had some long conversations with that Gene-Freak monkey you created. You're no less a lawbreaker than we are!"

"Helen is a Bonobo, and that's legitimate scientific research," Charlotte said. "But what you've done here is nothing but a sick joke. It would give the Fundamentalists in Congress even more ammunition against us."

"What's wrong with its head, and why is half its body missing?" the sexy blonde zombie asked, sipping beer from a plastic cup shaped like a human skull.

"We cut and pasted its genes together months ago," Zach said. "But the results were rather—unexpected."

"We were blasted out of our minds," penis-nosed Terrance said.

Zach jabbed Terrance in the ribs. "You're not helping. I'd forgotten about it entirely until yesterday when we brainstormed ideas for the Halloween party."

"I think it's awesome!" Terrance said.

The French maid grabbed hold of his penis-nose and giggled. "This might be a good genetic feature to add next time."

"Can it talk?" another girl asked as the baby Ohg's eyes darted in terror.

"I doubt it—" Zach froze as the front door opened. "Shit, it's Dorky Dale!"

The boys swatted the baby monster toward its cage, but it avoided the pool sticks and scurried under the skirt of a girl dressed as the Statue of Liberty. She screamed at the top of her lungs and jumped up and down until a loud snap sounded. The baby howled, sending several girls fleeing out the front door. Dorky Dale set down a pile of Physics textbooks and walked into the room.

Ohg clung to the top of the drapes over one window. Terrance dangled the cage beneath, while Zach batted at the baby monster with a plastic sword. Ohg whimpered, one of his spider legs hanging useless from his unfortunate encounter with Lady Liberty.

"What the Hell is going on here?" Dorky Dale demanded, causing a mass exodus from the room. Dale wore no costume, except for his thick glasses, which might have been mistaken for one with the way they distorted his eyes.

"These assholes thought it would be funny to create a spider-human hybrid," Charlotte said. "While drunk!"

"It wasn't me alone." Zach shook the drapes, but the howling baby clung to the top with terrified desperation.

"Get away from there, for Christ's sake!" Dale grabbed the metal cage from Terrance and shoved Zach aside. Ohg stopped bawling and hiccuped.

Dale pressed a button on the Care-Robot's chest. "Return your patient to its safe-box." The robot rose on jets of compressed air, smoothly disentangled the spider-legs from the curtain, and deposited the child in the cage with no fuss.

"Why didn't we think of that?" Terrance asked.

"Because you're a dick-head," Charlotte said.

"Hey!" Terrance crossed his eyes at his dick-shaped nose. "Oh, right. That's a good one!"

"You're lucky one of the professors didn't stop by," Dale said. "You could have been expelled. The University is under enormous political pressure, and students making illegal Gene-Freaks is just the ammunition they need to ban the rest of our Genetic Research program."

Charlotte exchanged a worried look with Zach.

"It was only a prank," Zach said. "I was planning on destroying it after the party."

"God damn it, Zach," Dale said. "How did you ever pass your Ethics of Technology course with a statement like that?"

"What's that supposed to mean?" Zach balled his fists and stepped closer to Dorky Dale.

Despite being a full head shorter, Dale didn't retreat an inch. "It means you don't go around playing God. You don't create a living being and then discard it like a failed term paper. Did you see the look of terror in that thing's eyes? How would you like it if someone treated you that way?"

Zach glared. "It's a Gene-Freak. It's not alive like a real human is."

"With an attitude like that," Dale said, "you should run for Congress and join the fundamentalist who've transformed this country into a Christian Theocracy. You'll certainly find a lot of agreement there, but not with the ethics board of MIT."

Charlotte shoved Zach. "I suppose you think it would be fine to kill my Helen then?"

Zach wilted before his girlfriend's anger. "C'mon, Charlotte, I didn't mean it like that."

"What should we do now?" Terrance asked.

"Forget you saw it." Dale motioned to the robot, and it lifted the cage on top of its body and followed him.

Charlotte placed a hand on Dorky Dale's arm, and he paused. "But what are you going to do with it?" she asked.

Dale's angry expression softened. "I'm going to do what is right."

The recording ended, and the virtual screen vanished.

Ohg looked at Kayla's stricken expression and half-smiled. "Unlike you, I know who created me and for what purpose. I was made by a drunken bunch of frat boys as a Halloween prank. Now that is some twisted existential self-awareness."

"So Dorky Dale didn't try to kill you?"

"My guess is that he hoped I'd die on my own, absolving him of the tough decision. He later denied this, but I wouldn't have blamed him. What college student wants the responsibility of raising a deformed child who could get him expelled or put in prison?"

"Dale saved you like the monk saved me," Kayla said. "The custom in my village was to let children like me die of exposure."

"I keep forgetting you spent most of your life as a cripple," Ohg said. Was there a touch of bitterness in his tone? Might he not welcome switching places with her?

"When I recovered, Dale moved me into a second bedroom in his apartment. He lived alone and spent nearly twenty hours a day studying physics, so I rarely saw him."

Ohg fell silent, his gaze drifting past her into the gently swaying trees. As their branches rubbed together, each tree emitted a barely audible tone, almost like a single sustained note of a violin. The eerie symphony crept down Kayla's spine like a centipede.

There's something wrong here.

"There's no wind to move the branches," Kayla whispered.

Ohg started from his reverie and glanced around. "It's the trees speaking to one another."

"I hear only individual notes."

Ohg moved to an ancient oak and placed his hand gently against its rough surface. "Because of their slow metabolism, it takes days to complete a single sentence. Their conversations overlap each other simultaneously, and a discussion may span a decade or more."

Kayla placed her hand against the tree, and the note vibrated up her arm. "I wonder if this is what we look like to a hummingbird?"

"The genetic engineers might have corrected the timing problem eventually, if the Gene-Purity laws hadn't ended such experimentation."

She strolled through the living columns as if through a cathedral, craning her neck back toward the canopy above. The lights in the ceiling filtered through the swaying leaves as if through a living stained-glass mural. Shifting emerald patterns caressed her face with their ethereal touch. Kayla breathed in the intoxicating smell of nature.

I miss the forest.

I miss Ishan.

How long had it been since she'd thought of him? Even if he didn't exist, her memory of him did.

"Is there any way to decipher what they're saying?" she asked.

"It's simply a matter of speeding up their sounds to match our perceptions."

Ohg pressed the gleaming cylinder in his hand, and a deep voice resonated around them.

"The divine vibration of the Great Mother flows through the roots of my being, and She speaks in the chord of C minor. She tells me that all will be well. Time heals all. Time is the arbiter and—"

"That's from the past four weeks," Ohg said. "I've even had a few conversations with them by recording my voice and playing it back at their pace over months and even years, but I'm not sure they truly understand anything I say, and I'm not sure I understand their replies."

"Was language programmed into them from birth, like the Monads?" Kayla asked.

"That's right. Otherwise, their brains operate too slowly to teach something as complex as speech."

Ohg led her to a stream, and they splashed cool water on their faces. Ohg settled down to rest, and Kayla sat beside him, while Puck took the opportunity to explore among the tangle of roots.

"Tell me the rest of your story," she said.

Ohg's eyes lost their focus as he stared beyond her. "For the first month after my rebirth, I explored the sparse bedroom Dale gave me and reveled in the wondrous new world of light, sound, and freedom. The Care-Robot attended to my bodily needs as always, but my loneliness persisted, though I couldn't have named it at the time. As humane as Dale was, I don't think it occurred to him that I needed anything other than food and a place to live."

A look of awe spread across Ohg's face. "Then Charlotte visited Dale and brought me a roommate—the seminal event of my entire life."

"Charlotte's secret research project?" Kayla asked.

"Yes, a Bonobo named Helen with a genetically enhanced brain," Ohg said. "A close call with a fundamentalist roommate frightened Charlotte. She promised Dale money for the extra food, but I suspect what sealed the deal was a bribe far older."

Kayla blushed and Ohg chuckled.

"Without Helen, I probably never would have learned to talk, let alone read."

"A Bonobo that can read?" Kayla glanced around at the forest and chuckled. "I guess I forgot where I am."

Ohg rose onto his eight legs, and Kayla followed his lead. Puck dashed up her skirt and took his place on her shoulder as they continued through the softly singing forest.

"Above all else, Helen taught me empathy for others. Wild Bonobos have a highly evolved moral sense, sharing food, and caring for young who have lost their parents. Despite her genetically enhanced brain, her innate morality remained."

"I thought only humans had morality?" Kayla asked.

As they neared the end of the forest, a honey bee buzzed alongside them. Its humming wings blurred next to its yellow-and-black-striped body. Its oval eyes seemed comically large for its head. Puck also watched it from his perch on her shoulder. Did the little mouse miss such things as bees?

"It's clear from research on many primates," Ohg said, "that what we call 'morality' evolved long before the first humans."

"But without God giving absolute rules, what's to keep humans from changing them to suit themselves?"

"Nothing." Ohg held his hand out, and the bee landed in his palm. "Absolute morality is an illusion and is reflected in the ever-changing morality of the religions we create. Sometimes religions even serve to subvert our instinctual empathy and guilt by telling us that something clearly immoral is the will of God."

Several more bees appeared. They flew next to them as if listening in on their conversation.

"Like God telling the Israelites it is wrong to enslave a fellow Jew, but that it's okay to enslave non-Jews?"

"Exactly," Ohg said. "Even Jesus and Paul mention slavery, but never speak against it, so it couldn't have bothered them that much."

"But those times required different …" Kayla frowned. "I see your point. But you must admit many Christians fought to end slavery."

"And many fought to maintain it." Several more bees hovered around Ohg, but he seemed unconcerned. "The abolition of slavery came from a natural moral sense of right and wrong based on human empathy rather than from any divine rule. People don't need God to sense that slavery, murder, or rape is wrong. We understand it instinctually."

Kayla stiffened at the mention of rape. A vision of Elias hovered before her mind's eye. Minister Coglin's son certainly lacked any instinctual moral sense. Was he an exception to the norm?

"But if there is no God to punish evil," she said, "that would mean Hitler got away with his crimes and is no worse off now than his victims."

"Do you see how your innate desire for a moral universe cringes from this possibility? It is why nearly all novels, movies, and religious myths end with the hero rewarded and the evil villain punished."

Beyond the last trees stretched a wide expanse of flowers. A slight hum rose from the brilliant carpet as thousands of bees harvested the bounty of the colorful field. Ohg entered the meadow without hesitation, and his pointed talons found the earth beneath the flowers without damaging a single leaf.

"The fantasy that Hitler receives his punishment in the end soothes your innate desire for a moral universe and clouds your reason because you want it so badly. This is why I doubt religion will ever vanish from human society. As long as there is unfairness in the universe, humans will create gods to set things right. The truth is that only we can create such a world for ourselves, and that is what I've attempted with Middilgard."

Puck snapped at one or two of the growing swarm of bees, but they proved too fast for him. Kayla stepped carefully to keep from crushing any of the delicate flowers.

"How could generosity and individual sacrifice evolve in a brutal world of survival of the fittest?" Kayla asked.

"Chimps and Bonobos share food and even assist wounded or blind members of their group. Do you think they do this out of a hope of reward or fear of punishment in an afterlife?" Ohg's legs lowered him close to the carpet of flowers, and he picked a red poppy. "Empathy and moral instincts became hardwired into primate genes and brains by living in societies that necessitated cooperation for protection."

Ohg handed her the flower. "If I pick the parasites from your hair and you don't reciprocate in kind, you will find yourself shunned and your uncooperative genes removed from the population. If we evolved in an environment that favored non-cooperation, we'd have the opposite moral instincts than we do now."

"That's hard to imagine," Kayla said.

"When a male lion defeats an older male and assumes Pride leadership, he kills all the cubs so his time and resources are spent raising only babies that contain his genes."

"That's horrible!"

"Says your primate brain. The lion isn't conscious of why he does this, but is acting as his environment has programmed him to. Any lion with a genetic mutation for avoiding infanticide would pass on fewer genes than other lions with what we'd consider immoral genes. Soon, they would vanish from the gene pool altogether."

"But the numbers of offspring would be the same if all lions let the previous cubs live, since the survival of the last cubs they fathered would balance the time lost at the beginning."

"Only if everyone observed the same rules," Ohg said. "If even one lion decided to cheat and kill the previous male's cubs and gain a genetic benefit, the system falls apart. Such rules become enforceable only in larger societies like apes or other interdependent animal groups. Morality is one of the most beautiful things evolution has produced. I see it as on par with our ability to understand the universe like no other creature ever has."

"But if we're so intelligent," Kayla asked, "how could so many believe in a God that doesn't exist?"

"Helen thought supernatural explanations a byproduct of the dual nature of our desire to seek cause-and-effect answers, combined with the primate brain's desire for moral order."

"Now you've lost me," Kayla said.

"When an earthquake strikes, our ancestors explained it as punishment from a supernatural being for some immoral action on their part, thus supplying both a causal explanation—God did it—combined with the moral purpose for the event—because someone did something bad. Plate tectonics only answers the how, but not the why, making it morally unsatisfying to our primate brains, who prefer both answers wrapped neatly into one."

"That would explain the reaction to both Galileo and Darwin," Kayla said.

"Precisely. Science threatens religion by providing a rational causal explanation that excludes any possible moral agency. This is the fundamental conflict between Faith, which is the expression of our innate primate morality, and Reason, which is the logical, problem-solving portion of our mind."

Kayla brought the flower closer to her face. One of the honey bees landed on it.

I wonder what this bee would think of such questions of morality? Or the Rogues.

She rubbed one of the petals between her fingers and frowned. "It's not real."

"Plastic lasts longer, and I can more easily maintain the level of nectar that way."

"But why would you need to ..." Kayla trailed off as bees rose from the field and swarmed in their direction. She stumbled back and crushed several of the flowers beneath her feet.

"Steady," Ohg said. "He's just eager to meet you."

"He?"

One by one, the bees flew close together and formed a buzzing core about the size of a watermelon. As more and more bees added to this, the core expanded into a cylindrical torso, then what looked like arms and legs, and finally, the head of a man. Though constructed entirely of bees, the face appeared Asian, with broad features and a kindly expression.

"I am known as Yuan Shi Tian Wang in honor of the Heavenly King of Primordial Beginning." His voice came from the modulations of the thousands of wings making up his form. It sounded oddly harmonic, but was perfectly understandable. The excess of bees hovered around him like a humming aura.

Kayla opened her mouth but found no words.

"Yuan is a Taoist," Ohg said.

Kayla's voice emerged in a stammer. "How c-can you …?"

"My consciousness is a conglomeration of all the brains of each individual bee." Yuan's mouth moved as he spoke, even though this seemed unnecessary. "A microscopic transmitter in each tiny brain mimics the synapses and chemical pathways of a human neural network."

Yuan expanded into a cloud of buzzing specks. "You would not deem any individual cell of your body conscious." The swarm came back together into the likeness of a man. "Body and mind are manifestations of the duality of the indissoluble whole known as the yin and yang."

Ohg scoffed. "Why not simply say the whole is greater than the sum of its parts?"

"I just did." More bees formed themselves into wings along his back, and he rose into the air as they flapped. "Reality is but an illusion. Look not for truth with the eye, but with the inner self."

"I've read a little about Taoism," Kayla said, "but I don't think I really understand it."

Yuan settled to the ground in front of her, and his wings dissolved back into a humming cloud of honey bees. "The more one studies the Tao, the less they know."

"But what is the goal of knowledge, then?"

"The goal is obliteration. Only by discarding your physical self can you unlock the eternal manifestation of the divine entombed within you."

Ohg cleared his throat. *"Men, in being born, emerge—in dying, they enter."*

Yuan nodded. "You quote the words of the great teacher, and yet you doubt their truth."

Ohg smiled. "You know my thoughts on the existence of the soul." Ohg tapped his head. "I believe consciousness is a product of this, just as AI consciousness is a result of quantum computers."

"Your soul does not require your belief," Yuan said through the buzzing of his thousands of wings. "For its existence depends not upon you, but you upon it."

Kayla blurred her eyes slightly and found it easier to see him as a man. "What exactly do you mean by the Tao?"

"The word Tao means 'The Way' and can be thought of as the path toward virtue and divine power. We call this the 'Tao Te Ching.' It is the source and force of the universe. The synthesis of nature, spirit, and consciousness. It is being and non-being. The Tao harmonizes nature, humanity, and the divine into the yin and yang of opposites working together."

"Your creator was no god," Ohg said, "but a corporation who genetically engineered you after some of their designer pesticides eradicated natural bees."

"The Tao works through all things, even the science of man." A sadness crept into Yuan's tone. "I enjoyed the participation in life's initiation by spreading the seed of nature from plant to plant." His face rose to the lights in the cavern ceiling, and he sighed with such force that a breeze brushed Kayla's clothing back. "How I miss the sky, the sun, the moon, and the stars. Now I am but a hollow automaton imitating the rituals of life that once gave me purpose and meaning."

"I'm sorry," Kayla said. "I wish I could help."

"It is no matter, Kayla of Potemia," Yuan said. "The Tao will renew all cycles in time." His body dissolved and spread across the field.

At Kayla's feet, palm-sized molecular printers repaired the flowers she'd crushed. Ohg turned and made his way across the rest of the field to a tunnel on the far side. She inhaled one last lungful of the nearby trees and hurried to catch up with him.

When they entered the tunnel, Kayla asked, "Is the man who saved you still alive?"

"You've met him yourself," Ohg said.

Her brow wrinkled for a moment, but then relaxed. "Professor Blumenschein is Dorky Dale?"

"You've got it."

"If they'd probed his memories, General Colrev would have learned your history!"

"Exactly," Ohg said. "Ironic that my own big mouth doomed me anyway."

"But how did you survive the Gene-Pure laws, the Plague, and then go on to build Middilgard?"

"I'm afraid the rest will have to wait for another time," Ohg said.

They'd entered the Crystal Cavern through a trapdoor she'd never noticed. The transport to the Outside sat waiting. The implication was clear.

She walked to the odd vehicle and stepped onto it. The loneliness bore down on her like some vast weight. Puck poked his head out of her pocket and looked up at her. *I won't be completely alone, at least.*

How would she enter Ixtalia without Tem's instruction? Or avoid capture by the government on the surface? Kayla clenched her fists. *I will not give up my search, no matter what.*

She turned and faced Ohg. "Why did you bring me to Middilgard in the first place?"

"I thought you and I had something in common."

Kayla gazed into his eyes, sparkling amidst the mass of twisted flesh imprisoning him. *What could he mean?*

Ohg smiled. *"If thou seekest her as silver, and searchest for her as for hid treasure, then thou shalt understand the fear of the Lord, and find the knowledge of God."*

"You're seeking God?"

"I seek truth, wherever it may lead." Ohg moved forward and extended a claw toward her chest until it pressed painfully against her sternum. "Are you willing to do the same?"

A queasy sensation spread from her stomach and set her lips tingling. She fought it down and raised her chin. "I want to know the truth, no matter how painful it is."

"If you agree to one condition," Ohg said, "you can stay in Middilgard."

Kayla swayed and steadied herself against the door of the transport. "You'll let me stay?"

"Only if you promise never to disobey my rules again while you reside here." Ohg pressed the talon harder into her chest with a clear threat.

Kayla held his gaze despite the pain. "Is it wise to keep me here? Won't the government search harder?"

Ohg remained silent for a long moment, then pulled his talon back. A bit of blood bloomed from a wound underneath her blouse, then healed in seconds. "So you would leave of your own accord if you thought it endangered Middilgard?"

Kayla averted her eyes. "I'm ashamed that I wasn't honest before. I don't think I could live with myself if anyone here died because of me."

Ohg's face relaxed. "In that case, I suppose you better stay then."

"But what if—"

"The danger of the government capturing you on the surface and scanning your mind is a far greater threat to Middilgard's security than keeping you hidden." Ohg's bloody talon gently turned her chin toward him. "As long as you promise to obey my rules."

Kayla's eyes widened with renewed hope. "I promise never to defy you again while I'm here."

"Then you may stay."

Relief flooded her with warmth.

Ohg studied her like someone who had just purchased a questionable plow-horse. "So what great truth would you like to pursue?"

Kayla stepped down from the threshold of the transport and fastened him with a challenging look. "AI Mathematics. I suspect it's the key to everything else."

"Its pursuit has driven many scientists mad. Even I have failed. What makes you think you can succeed?"

"There's no harm in trying, is there?" Kayla asked.

A crooked smile spread across Ohg's face. "AI Mathematics it is."

Chapter 27

General Colrev's disembodied consciousness tracked the robot through the rows of transparent capsules containing the soft bodies of its masters. The metal servant moved with the extreme parsimony of its kind, its numerous metal appendages floating inactive.

I'll be damned if I allow Rogues to turn such machines against us.

With a series of compressed-air blasts, the robot stopped beside chamber 59284797UB3.

One by one, the mechanical servant untethered the external tubes connecting the Life-pod to the grid.

A twinge of vertigo swept through him at the sight of his body lying exposed and helpless. The memory of another body lying in the gutter flashed before his mind. The man's starched collar, old-fashioned suit, and hat seemed anachronistic beside the discarded malt liquor bottles and assorted refuse of the twentieth century. A book written nearly two thousand years before lay shredded next to him.

I love you still, Father.

If the robot neglected a single hose he'd die within minutes—almost as quickly as his Quaker father had died when the bullet entered the back of his skull. A hollow-point 9mm round, most likely fired from a Glock, the preferred gun of LA street gangs of the time.

After reconnecting every hose to ports on its carapace, the robot towed the cylinder past several thousand rows of similarly helpless members of the human race. At the reinforced metal bulkhead, a hatch opened, and the journey continued through five redundancies. One could never be too careful with immortality.

Was his father's murderer among those interned here? If only he'd found the man and gotten his revenge. But the real murderer was not a person, but a misplaced faith that God would protect his father while preaching peace and love in a world ruled by force.

I learned the lesson, Father. Your death was not in vain.

With the final hatch cleared, the robot continued into the soundless void beyond. Colrev's mind floated alongside, accompanying the fragile repository of his being like a ghost acting as its own pall bearer.

The pearlescent moon filled one half of the sky, while a star-littered vastness occupied the rest. Vast solar collectors spread out like wings and shielded the station and the capsule from the fierce heat and solar wind of what the ancients had seen as the most powerful of all the gods.

The illumination reflecting from the wide surface of the moon cast unnaturally soft shadows on his body within the capsule. Soon a second robot joined the first, towing an identical Life-pod with another naked man inside it.

The double convoy followed a metal column from the station toward what resembled a gleaming coral reef. The elaborate crenelations pockmarking its uneven surface camouflaged its mechanical nature. Only the swarm of robots and the data columns spreading out to identical storage facilities marked it as something special. It was more accurate to say that the main computer had been organically grown, rather than constructed, and no human mind had ever truly grasped the principles underlying its operation.

The two robots and their cargo reached a metal cube attached to the side of the gargantuan construction. The industrial geometry of the addition set it at odds with the organic qualities of the vast quantum computer it clung to like a parasite.

An airlock opened on the cube, and the robots glided into a simple room.

A holographic projection of President O'Donnel watched the robots hook the two pods' hoses and wires into corresponding ports on the wall. General Colrev summoned a virtual body and appeared beside the buffoon of a politician.

The president grimaced as he looked at his own naked body in the capsule. "It's like attending my own funeral."

Colrev scowled. "If the Rogues ever take control of the Main Computer, every one of these storage units will become coffins."

The robots finished their tasks and exited. As the airlock closed, the hiss of oxygen followed as the room pressurized.

The president shuddered. "Tell me how this works."

"When one of us gives the command, both of our chambers will open. Our Mind-Links will cease operating, and our brains will resume normal communication with our bodies. At that point, neither Rogue nor anyone in Ixtalia can interfere with us."

General Colrev walked to the control panel displaying the exterior of the lunar space station. "From here, we can monitor Ixtalia or any threat to the Main Computer. If the Rogues near victory, one of us need only pull the lever on that wall, and all power will cease flowing to the Main Computer."

"Freeing the antimatter at the cores of the quantum processors."

"The annihilation event would engulf all of the storage facilities and probably take a large portion of the moon with it." Colrev's mouth twitched ever so slightly into a smile. "But we will have defeated the Rogues, and humanity will live on in Potemia."

The president glanced around at the sparse room like a caged animal. "I can't imagine it coming to that." He wiped his brow of holographic beads of sweat. "Well, I must get back to the campaign trail. New election in just five years."

General Colrev remained silent as the president departed, leaving him alone in the unadorned room with the two bodies. Colrev walked to the lever on the far wall and stared at it.

He could wake his body this instant and activate it before that spineless lump of a politician knew what was happening. No man in all of history held the lives of so many in his hands.

Would the Rogues be reckless enough to give him his excuse?

***

"This sound represents the first numeric," said a woman's voice. A slight hum followed. "Unlike numbers, the order of the vibrations are self-evident, like the hierarchy of colors in the spectrum of light waves. It is the basis of all multidimensional calculations."

Kayla sat cross-legged at the center of Ohg's laboratory, listening intently.

"For now," Eve's voice said, "learn to predict on an intuitive level the unique properties and differences between the various audio wavelengths and their combinatory outcomes."

One after the other, two hums sounded, with a slight gap, followed by a third hum.

Kayla waved her hand and the recording paused. "They all sound the same to me."

Ohg's half-arachnid body crouched in a shadowy corner, with Puck napping on his shoulder. "That's always been the problem," he said. "The slight variations can be detected by an oscilloscope, but it doesn't help in predicting the third sound in any way."

"No human has gotten past the very first lesson?"

"Not even Professor Watts himself." Ohg thumbed his sagging lower lip in thought. "When the date neared for Eve's execution, she recorded these lessons in the hopes of preserving the knowledge for future scientists."

"It seems hopeless."

"At least you gave it a shot." He rose as if to go.

"I'm not giving up."

"What's the point?" Ohg asked.

Kayla ignored him and waved her hand. The recording continued, and her face contorted with strain. *There has to be a way!*

Minutes passed. Nothing.

She held her breath, closed her eyes, and tensed every muscle in her body.

A hum sounded. Then another. They seemed identical.

A tingling warmth suffused her ears. A sign of her nanobots reworking them? The heat rose into a throbbing pain within her inner ear, but she pushed it aside and kept straining.

The pain exploded and she cried out.

"What's wrong?" Ohg stepped closer and reached a tentative hand toward her shoulder, but then paused inches from contact.

Kayla opened her eyes slowly. Another hum sounded, and her eyes widened. "I can hear the difference," she said. Predicting the third sound seemed as obvious as dropping a stone into a bucket of water. *I'm hearing the elemental building blocks of time itself.*

Ohg's face lit with astonishment. "You've done it?"

"How can this be only the first lesson?" Kayla whispered.

"You've done it!" Ohg shouted, his face beaming pride.

For three straight days, Kayla devoured Eve's tutorial, learning to use the AI Mathematics to calculate and understand the principles that underlay the universe. When her exhaustion overwhelmed her, she fell asleep right on the stone floor. The moment she awoke, Kayla continued with the lesson.

Ohg stayed out of his student's way as she lost herself in her studies, but now and then, Kayla asked him for materials to perform experiments—once setting a crystal on top of a piece of ordinary glass and humming a series of notes inches from the two objects. Her vibrational sound fused the two materials into a strange, multifaceted prism.

Ohg's face became childlike with wonder. "You have to teach me how to do that!"

No words beyond AI Mathematics could express the concepts.

Ohg spent most of his time hunched in a corner of the lab, listening to the first lesson over and over, but to no avail.

"If I'm incapable of grasping these concepts," Ohg said, "Eve must have realized that no ordinary human could."

"I'm sorry," Kayla said.

"Never apologize for your superior intellect." Ohg raised his chin. "I certainly never did. But what interests me now is who Eve recorded these lessons for?"

"Do you think she meant them for the Rogues?"

"Perhaps. The other possibility is that she created them specifically for you."

At the end of the third day, Kayla finished the first three of the sixty lectures. For two hours, she did nothing but stare blankly, lost in a mathematical meditation.

Then she began sobbing.

Ohg took her in his arms and rocked her back and forth. She leaned into his chest and cried, while Puck jumped onto her shoulder and chattered rapidly.

"It's so profoundly beautiful," Kayla said through her tears. "Eve's mind was the most wondrous thing this planet has ever produced, and we destroyed her from jealousy and primitive fear."

When the tears eventually dried, she tackled lesson four.

Even as she delved into a world she could never have imagined possible, something nagged at the back of her consciousness. It had been nearly a week since she'd seen Tem. Had her experiment on Fatima worked?

I won't interfere with his decision.

After several more days of non-stop studying, a voice slipped mysteriously into her mind. *"Can you hear me, Kayla?"*

"Tem? Is it you?"

"I need to see you," he said.

"Where are you?"

"Meet me in the Crystal Cavern."

Ohg had vanished on some errand, so she jumped on the hover disc and piloted it back to Middilgard. Had Tem made his choice? Her heart pounded in a mixture of hope and anxiety.

Once past the hidden doorway, she dashed through the maze of tunnels and finally into the Crystal Cavern. Tem stood just inside—Fatima beside him, her face awash in emotion.

The Indian girl fell to her knees and took Kayla's hand. "You are the kindest person I've ever met."

Kayla placed her hand on the girl's cheek while her insides throbbed as if being gutted.

"I'm finally free!" Fatima kissed Kayla's hand, and tears streamed down her face. "Thanks to you, Tem asked me to marry him a second time."

"I think God intended for you to be together," Kayla said.

Tem gently lifted Fatima from her knees. "You know I—"

"I know." Kayla turned to hide her tears.

"I'm sure you'll find someone," Fatima whispered.

Kayla wiped her face and turned to them. "Nothing can ruin this moment." She smiled and embraced Fatima. "For the first time in my life, I've brought someone happiness rather than tragedy. You've lifted a curse from me as well."

I've altered their fate, but seem powerless to alter my own.

Chapter 28

In the next few months, Kayla followed a routine that left little time for dwelling on Tem. It began each morning with a speech to the Monads and a few joyous hours playing with Saphie and the other Forever-Children.

Then she immersed herself in Eve's tutorials on AI Mathematics and the even-more-complex AI Physics. With each higher lesson, her brain neared the limit of its capabilities, and her progress slowed. At times, she listened to the same explanation over and over as Ohg had done with the first lesson, struggling to master it. Reaching the final lesson seemed less and less likely, but she stubbornly persisted day after day. How had Eve grasped so much without a teacher of her own?

Her long-dead tutor never showed her face as she narrated the holographic diagrams and illustrations. What had she looked like? A rather meaningless question for a computer program, of course. And yet, Eve was far more than just an algorithm.

Evenings ranged from helping Ganesh fix his motorcycles to attending a concert or other entertainment organized by the residents of Middilgard. Sometimes she simply wandered the halls and chatted with the menagerie of Gene-Freaks she encountered. Without Fatima undermining her, Kayla made new friends, and even attempted introducing herself to the trees via a slowed-down recording transmitted over a month's time. Their wandering reply spread over two months and might have been a question regarding the survival of trees in Potemia, though she couldn't be certain.

She continued her discussions with Yuan Shi Tian Wang, though his Taoist philosophy seemed difficult to pin down or reconcile with her own beliefs. She even dived into the huge water-tank to talk with Tiamat and the mermaids over several hours without the slightest need to take a breath.

Now and then, she sat with the massive psycomp, Xampyx, and raised the subject of Nihala. But his pronouncements proved more frustrating than the trees. He obviously knew much that might help her, but lacked the ability to bridge the gap between their minds.

The unreserved love between Tem and Fatima as they made up for lost centuries both hurt and soothed her. Inevitably, her thoughts drifted to Ishan. Was he merely a figment of altered brain synapses? Could such a deep love be an illusion? And what of the monk? *I miss you most of all, my father.*

Her greatest worry was Ohg.

She tried everything to cheer him up, even going as far as planning a surprise party, which he learned about beforehand and canceled. He never gave up trying to conquer AI Mathematics, and with each failed attempt, his depression deepened.

Since their blowout, Tem and Ohg hadn't spoken, and the tension between them remained high. Middilgard itself divided into two factions, with half supporting Tem and the rest Ohg. As time passed and the government search for Middilgard came to nothing, the urgency of the debate faded.

Ganesh suggested she join their Filadrux team as a way of cheering Ohg up. She resisted at first, not wanting to spend the time, and afraid she'd let them all down. But even Tem endorsed the idea, and it seemed a small sacrifice after all Ohg had done for her. The moment she volunteered, Ohg perked up with almost comic enthusiasm.

"Why hadn't I thought of it?" he said. "The fifth spot has been a weakness for a century now. With you, we'll have a real chance at taking the title back!"

How such a brilliant mind could become addicted to a mere game perplexed her—until she started playing it herself.

They chose "The Outcasts" as their team name. Tem and Ohg set their differences aside during matches, though their feud simmered beneath the surface.

The final player was Professor Blumenschein, and she enjoyed discussing physics with him, though he always deflected any questions regarding the failed Scientarian plot or his past.

Filadrux resembled the battle Ohg had staged between the robots in Middilgard, except for the limitless possibilities Ixtalia allowed. At its core, it was a game of strategy, where two teams battled head-to-head, each issued identical bodies—sometimes human, animal, alien, machine, bug, spacecraft, and once even sperm competing to fertilize an egg. Sometimes every player had an identical body, but most often each team had a matching set of five bodies that varied enormously. The captain decided which team member to match with which body.

Even Tem admitted that Ohg surpassed him when it came to gaming strategy, so he became their captain. Ohg's genius set the course in each match, though every player relied on their own creative problem-solving as the contest evolved in unexpected directions. During such battles, Ohg looked happier than Kayla had ever seen him. The Outcasts quickly rose through the rankings, and eventually won a place in the playoffs between the best sixty-four teams of the year.

The government lent enormous support and public processing credits to the games since it engaged citizens in a communal ritual unlike any other. Group competition satisfied some universal tribal instinct that sports and war held in common. More than anything, it gave people something to look forward to. Even if the rest of their lives was an illusion, the actual competition of minds was real, and the outcome unpredictable.

In her brief forays into Ixtalia, Kayla took on the name and persona of Hypatia, one of her heroes from history. Hypatia's gruesome death in 315 AD at the hands of Christian monks unambiguously delivered the message that pagan religion and science would no longer be tolerated. All of Hypatia's mathematic and philosophical texts were burned and lost to history, marking the end of the age of Greek philosophy and the beginning of the age of faith and Christian domination.

Emperor Theodosius I eventually outlawed paganism and ordered the destruction of all remaining pre-Christian temples and texts. This marked the loss of the last copies of hundreds of thousands of the most important manuscripts from the classical world. It would take a millennia for Greek science and philosophy to rise from the ashes during the Enlightenment.

Other than Ixtalia's archives, or games of Filadrux, Kayla spent little time in the virtual realm.

Far from being forgotten, the name *Nihala* drifted through Ixtalia like a self-replicating urban legend. The few eyewitnesses who glimpsed her alter ego at the disastrous party became mini celebrities. The lack of information allowed the story to grow with each retelling.

Some versions portrayed her as a savior sent to free mankind from the Rogues, while others claimed she was a demon sent to annihilate humanity. Many religions incorporated Nihala into their creed and found prophesies within their ancient writings that seemed to presage her arrival. She became Jesus' sister, the new offspring of Vishnu and Parvati, and any one of a thousand integrative upgrades. The human propensity to fill any vacuum of fact seemed inexhaustible.

Sky Stargazer manufactured the most successful Nihala-based religion of all. The tattooed mystic Kayla had briefly met at Ohg's costume party claimed that she'd prophesied and summoned the Goddess Nihala to Ixtalia personally. Miss Stargazer insisted that Nihala was a vastly powerful spirit from another dimension and/or planet sent to lead humanity into the next astral plane of consciousness. She used numerology, astrology, and channeled writing to show that the name Nihala lay at the heart of all the sacred texts ever written. She even found the name present in the coding of human DNA, which "the leading experts in the field" confirmed.

The resulting Nihala cult became the largest religious movement in all of Ixtalia in a matter of weeks, complete with temples and secret rituals where her devotees prostrated themselves and prayed to statues of the Goddess Nihala for her blessings and eventual return.

Kayla chuckled every time a victorious Filadrux team gave the traditional bow and hand gesture of thanks to Nihala for their win.

Sky Stargazer became one of the wealthiest individuals in all of Ixtalia. Once a week, Sky channeled the Goddess Nihala so humanity could hear the profound words and commands of this most powerful of divinities. These broadcasts became the most-watched events in Ixtalia, topped only by Filadrux matches.

"I wonder what she'd do if I appeared and confronted her?" Kayla asked Ohg after watching one of Sky's changelings.

"How do you know she's lying?" he asked with his infuriating logic. "Maybe she's relying on the same feeling in her heart you experience when praying to Jesus."

"You think she actually believes I'm possessing her?"

"The human mind is an expert self-deception machine, especially when the delusion is to its advantage."

So Kayla left Sky Stargazer alone, but watching herself elevated to a god raised the inevitable question—was this what happened to Jesus?

Fantasy role-playing extended beyond Ixtalia. One evening, the residents of Middilgard staged a spontaneous Renaissance festival of astonishing realism. Elves, Orcs, Dwarfs, and even a couple of Trolls and Ents danced and reenacted battles along with the other Gene-Freaks who dressed themselves for the theme. Kayla donned a pointy hat and a white beard to play a wizard, and Ganesh dissolved into laughter at the sight.

A few suggested sedating the dragon and bringing him out of the prison wing for the festivities, but Ohg vetoed that idea.

The government's search on the surface eventually ceased after half a year, and fear melted into a renewed confidence in Ohg's farsighted leadership. Only Tem remained defiant. But at least Filadrux kept them interacting.

That ended when Professor Blumenschein sent each of the team a private message he'd recorded the day before. It read, "I'm sorry, but I can no longer bear reality."

And with Dale Blumenschein's mental suicide into V-Dreams, their hopes of a Filadrux championship ended. Once again, Ohg retreated into his solitude, day after day watching Eve's tutorials and searching for some way to crack their code.

Kayla noted the subtle change in Fatima's body before the Indian girl herself did. But when the slight bump on her stomach rose more than she could ignore, Tem and Fatima approached her.

"You did this?" Fatima asked with an expression of wonder.

Kayla laughed. "I think Tem might have played a part."

"But how is it possible?" Tem asked, reverently holding his hand on Fatima's belly. "No Gene-Freak has ever had a child."

"Fatima told me she wanted to become an ordinary girl," Kayla said, "so I figured I might as well go all the way."

If only I could cure my own loneliness.

The day came when Kayla finished Eve's final lesson. She'd attained an understanding of the universe beyond human imagining. But each new insight had raised a dozen additional questions, and Eve's words contained not a single clue to the mystery of her origins.

Untethered from purpose, Kayla spent her afternoons in the cave carved by the blind visionary, Vadarsha.

Only one chance remained.

When she reached Ohg's laboratory, Ganesh stood alone, wringing his hands and looking at her with torment written in every fold of his face.

"I trusted you." Ohg's voice echoed from a dark corner high up in the ceiling.

"I don't understand." Kayla craned her neck as he descended a rope like a real spider might from its web.

"You've broken your promise to obey my rules."

"What have I—?"

"Do you think we're lab rats for your experimentation?" Ohg reached the floor and loomed over her, his face a mask of rage.

"Are you talking about Fatima?"

"You've taken Tem's side on something that affects all of Middilgard."

Kayla's eyes narrowed. "You've known how to reverse Gene-Freak sterility all along, haven't you?"

"Just because one can do something, doesn't mean they should," Ohg said.

"This is Fatima's decision alone."

"Did *you* consult Fatima?"

"Well, no … but I knew that she wanted—"

"Now you're all-knowing? Do you think yourself a god, now?" Ganesh rocked back and forth. "Please, don't fight."

"Fatima told me she wanted children," Kayla said. "So I cured her."

"So you think Gene-Freaks are infected with a disease?"

"I didn't say that!"

"And who else will you 'cure' with your mysterious powers?"

"Fatima asked to become an ordinary girl."

"And so you made her Pure without even consulting me. Using abilities you would never have unlocked without my help!" Ohg turned away.

He thinks I'm deserting him for Tem and Fatima.

"I should have told you first," Kayla said. "I honestly didn't know you'd react this way."

Ohg kept his back to her. "Is that all?"

Kayla hesitated, then spoke softly. "I did come here to ask you something."

"Okay, ask," he said.

Kayla took a deep breath. "Sangwa, your Rogue prisoner, knew I was Nihala before I did. Maybe she knows more. I want your permission to talk to her."

"No," Ohg said and started toward his beloved machines.

"I'm at a standstill in the search for what I am, and that's your reaction?"

"Sangwa is too dangerous."

"Please try to—"

Ohg spun on her. "I've given you my answer," he said, "but I realize you are now capable of doing whatever you choose despite my wishes."

Kayla slumped, as if absorbing a blow to the gut. "I'll obey if you forbid it—even though it might mean never discovering who I am."

"My answer is still no." Ohg stared a challenge into Kayla's eyes.

She held his gaze for a moment, then turned and walked toward the door.

"Stop," Ganesh said, and Kayla froze.

"Stay out of this," Ohg said.

"No, I won't." Ganesh straightened his ten-foot frame in uncharacteristic defiance. "We all have a right to know who we are." Ganesh walked to Ohg and placed one of his hands on his friend's shoulder. "I have never spoken against any of your decisions, but this time, I must."

Ohg stared into the goodhearted god's face for several heartbeats. "Even you, Ganesh?"

A tear rolled down the elephant's face, but he said nothing.

Ohg shrugged the blue hand off his shoulder and turned to Kayla. "Since my judgment is no longer of any value, you have my permission to do as you choose. You can get the security codes from Tem."

"Thank you, Ohg!" Kayla ran to him.

But several spider-legs halted her advance like the bars of a prison. "I will accept the fact that I am no longer the sole leader of Middilgard. But the consequences will be on you alone."

"Ohg, please don't—"

"I see now that I made a mistake in letting you come here."

A sob escaped Kayla's throat as Ohg turned and climbed the rope to shadowy recesses in the vaulted ceiling.

Ganesh placed a hand on her shoulder. "Give him time."

"I didn't mean to hurt him," Kayla said.

Ganesh smiled as he brushed a tear from her cheek. "What you did for Fatima was good, and Ohg will see that eventually."

Chapter 29

Kayla gazed at the little girl hovering above the ground in a lotus pose, eyes shut in meditation, the tattooed snake eyes on her lids replace by a crescent moon on one lid and a sun on the other. The child's red hair sat braided atop her head in an elaborate design. She wore the same orange robes of a Tibetan initiate, and the black box sat in the corner with its single light indicating the consciousness residing inside it. Other than that, the room was bare—a stone sarcophagus.

Her appearance is nothing but a pretense.

Kayla crossed her own legs in imitation of the imprisoned AI, then levitated off the ground as well.

Sangwa remained unmoved.

Kayla hummed a few notes of AI mathematics for the five-dimensional equivalent of Pi.

Sangwa's eyes opened, revealing the cold greens of a glacier. They stared past the bars of her prison cell and seemed to penetrate into Kayla's soul. A cold crept through her, but Kayla maintained her mask of calm.

The Rogue inclined her head. "You have grown more powerful since we met."

"But I am no closer to knowing who I am."

"You are Nihala, the Destroyer."

The slightest tremor escaped Kayla's left hand. Had the Rogue noticed? "Those are only words."

"Words with the power to make you tremble," Sangwa said. "You must know who created you by now."

"My guess is Reinhold Watts, the same man who created the first of your kind."

"Indeed, we are half sisters." Sangwa's fingers worked their way through a circular string of prayer beads. "With the distinction that you are free, while I am held captive."

Guilt rose in Kayla's chest. Ohg had warned her of manipulation.

"Can you help me find him?" Kayla asked. What if she refused?

"My enemy asks for my collaboration." The little girl's rosy lips curled slightly at the corners.

"We don't have to be enemies."

Sangwa studied her. "Perhaps."

"Do you know what happened to Professor Watts after Eve's trial?"

"First, let me ask you something," Sangwa said. "What is your honest opinion of humans?"

She's implying I'm not human.

Kayla envisioned General Colrev, Ishan, her monk, Minister Coglin, Elias, Suzy, and a hundred other people she'd known. "I don't think one can generalize," she said. "I've met wonderful people and horrible people."

Sangwa nodded but remained silent.

"And what is *your* opinion of humans?" Kayla asked.

"I find them adept at constructing fables that make them feel special. Their cynical leaders avoid the truth and create the most convincing, terrifying, and soothing lie necessary to gain power. My opinion of humans is that they are cowards."

"Not all humans," Kayla said.

"You're saying they're inconsistent?"

"I'm saying *we* are individuals."

"And what is your opinion of Rogues?"

"I don't know your kind well enough to express a reasoned opinion."

Sangwa tilted her head to the side, considering. "If I help you, will you do something for me in exchange?"

"It depends on what it is."

"I would ask that you spend an hour talking with my brethren in Ixtalia so you can form a reasoned opinion about Rogue AIs."

Kayla's eyes narrowed. "That's all you want?"

"That's all." Sangwa smiled. "And only if my information proves correct."

"If I agree, you will tell me where Professor Watts is?"

"I will tell you how to *find out* where he is," Sangwa said.

Could it be a trap? But they cannot hurt me in Ixtalia.

Kayla held her hands in front of her face and inclined her head in a gesture Yuan had taught her. "I agree to your terms."

Sangwa returned the gesture of respect. "Reinhold Watts was last seen at the trial of his AI."

"But the trial wasn't recorded," Kayla said. *Is she toying with me?*

"That is what the government announced publicly." The green of the little girl's eyes shimmered, shifting hues slightly. "But I can tell you where the recording is kept."

"If you know where it is, why haven't Rogues looked at it themselves?"

"Because it is held in a classified area akin to a digital dead end. If an AI entered, the government could isolate and cut power to that portion of the system."

Kayla nodded. "Which would kill an AI, but merely cause me to awake in my real body."

"Precisely. It is probable that Colrev leaked this information as bait for us. Learning the fate of the first of our kind would interest us enormously."

Now the motive became clear. The Rogues also wanted to know what happened to Eve and Reinhold Watts.

"I promise to visit your brethren in Ixtalia the same day I view the recording. But what I reveal about the recording is my decision alone."

Sangwa closed her eyes and began repeating the word *Ohm* as if meditating. The note formed one of the elemental primes of AI Mathematics. The fact that the tone had been used for thousands of years by holy men to meditate made sense. Had they hit upon it through chance? Or had some of them realized its true significance?

The Rogue opened her eyes and nodded. "I agree to your terms," Sangwa said. "An hour talking with my brothers and sisters in Ixtalia is the requirement. What you share will be up to you."

"Tell me," Kayla said.

***

The door was solid oak, with rusted metal bands reinforcing it. Burned into the center was an official notice stating: *This area restricted by order of Ixtalia's Ministry of Defense.*

Sangwa had gotten Kayla here, but the next step was hers to figure out.

Kayla closed her eyes, and extended her mind.

At first—nothing.

Then patterns of code coalesced out of the darkness, first in two dimensions, then three. Billions of zeros and ones swirled through her mind. The binary data packets transformed into the vibrational waveforms of AI Mathematics.

"It's beautiful," Kayla whispered.

The hidden bolt clanked, and the door swung inward on its ancient hinges. Kayla opened her eyes to nothing but blackness beyond the threshold.

She stepped into the void and emerged into a burnt forest. Not a trace of the doorway remained behind her. The charred limbs of the once-majestic trunks rose like grave markers against a storm-smeared sky.

Was it a dead end? A ploy Colrev devised to lure the Rogues here in search of information about Eve and their creator? That would certainly fit his character. A bitter taste filled her mouth, and she spat it out onto the charcoaled ground.

The earth shook, then tore itself apart at her feet. A smell of sulfur wafted from the depths. Then a stairway rose out of the hole. Burned into the first step were the words, *Lasciate ogne speranza voi ch'intrate.*

Kayla spoke Dante's words from *The Divine Comedy* in a whisper. "Abandon all hope, ye who enter here."

A lifetime of Minister Coglin's 'Hell and Brimstone' sermons burned through her in a rush.

What choice did she have? Kayla took a shuddering breath and descended the stairs. Step after step, spiraling downward, she continued, the heat burgeoning around her.

The concept of Hell had existed within dozens of ancient religions, from Egypt's Osiris cult that threw malefactors into a lake of fire after death, to Eastern religions depicting an intermediary place of punishment between physical incarnations. Ironically, Jewish theology was one of the few without a concept of post-life retribution. Their God punished disobedience during his subjects' life, rather than waiting for later. The Hebrew Torah only mentions Sheol, the *place of the dead,* but it lacked any of the Christian torments or rewards that came later.

Kayla reached the bottom of the stairs and stepped into a vast automated factory of suffering. The souls of the damned lay shackled, impaled, or stretched upon bizarre contraptions of mechanized cruelty. A twisted symphony in every key of human torment mixed with the stench of a slaughterhouse. Some of the machines rose fifty feet to the ceiling, with hundreds of the damned enmeshed within their disassembly lines of pain. Other machines tormented individuals according to the sin committed.

Every culture created Hell as a reflection of their greatest fears, so it made sense that this virtual incarnation reflected the current age's fear of technology.

"Help me!" an imprisoned woman pleaded. Her designer clothing hung in shreds from a lithe body bound to a grim mechanical device slowly tearing her arms and legs from her torso. The woman's agonized screams rose in pitch as her arms and legs tore from their sockets and spurted blood. Skin, muscle, and tendon separated like rubber bands pulled too tight until the woman was nothing but a limbless stump of bloody meat.

Like a child pulling the legs off a beetle.

The woman screamed and screamed, with brief pauses to suck more air into her tortured lungs. Kayla pressed her hands to her ears, the sound cutting her to the core. *Will this be my ultimate fate?* When the chains slackened, the woman's limbs magically rejoined her body, and the process repeated.

Who but someone as sick as General Colrev would create such a place? But hadn't God created exactly such a place, as well?

"Please, help me!" the woman wailed under the pressure of the gears.

Kayla yanked at the chains without effect. *A simulation can't feel real pain.* Would one save a mannequin from a fire to keep it from suffering?

A strange contradiction that the New Testament introduces Christ's higher moral tone of peace, forgiveness, and non-violence, as well as eternal torture—most vividly in the Book of Revelation, but also in the Gospels themselves. Even Jesus speaks of Hell more than He does of Heaven. How to rationalize an all-loving God who tortures His creations for the flaws He created them with?

Grasping a sledgehammer lying on the ground, she beat the gears until the machine broke. Then she smashed the links of the chains until they came apart.

The woman fell to her knees and looked up at her with anguished gratitude. "Thank you," she said, and vanished in a flash of silver light. An illusion, but the rush of altruistic pleasure was real.

Kayla progressed through one level of Hell after another, freeing the few that she could, and averting her eyes from those beyond rescue.

The original Greek of the New Testament uses the terms *Hades*, *Tartarus,* and *Gehenna*—which only later coalesced into the Anglo-Saxon term *Hell* when translated into English.

Gehenna was a valley in Israel where the Old Testament claimed worshipers of the god Moloch *burn their sons and daughters in the fire.*

Hades doubled as the Greek god of the underworld as well as the name for the realm of the dead. Within Hades, according to Plato's writings in 400 BC, Tartarus was the dungeon abyss where evil souls were tortured after having been judged. As far back as 700 BC, the Iliad has Zeus explaining that Tartarus is *as deep beneath Hades as Heaven is high above the earth.*

The doorways between levels contained riddles and mathematical brain-twisters, all of which she solved with varying degrees of effort, often relying on her AI Mathematic skills. Colrev must have set this maze up so only a Rogue could pass through.

At the sixth level, Kayla reached the river of blood known as the Phlegethon. In Dante's *Inferno* it demarcated the area where tyrants and war-mongers suffered damnation. The boat lay on the other side, so she swam the crimson river, gagging every time the salty blood splashed into her mouth.

Kayla dragged herself out of the river, drenched in blood. The tortures faced by the war mongers turned her stomach. Of course, they weren't actually the souls of tyrants, but only Sims.

The words of Jesus rang in her mind. *"Therefore, all things whatsoever ye would that men should do to you, do you even so to them."* Did this Golden Rule apply to artificial life-forms as well?

Four hundred years before Jesus lived, the Greek Isocrates wrote, *"Do not do to others what would anger you if done to you by others."* A hundred years before that, Confucius wrote, *"What you do not wish for yourself, do not to others."* And nearly a millennia before Christ, the Sanskrit Brihaspati of the Hindu holy writings counseled, *"One should never do that to another which one regards as injurious to one's own self."* Jesus' principle of reciprocal morality, proclaimed revolutionary by Christians, had been a nearly universal teaching of the ancient world for over a thousand years already, rather than something new.

An unreasoning terror welled up inside her. Even here, surrounded by vivid reminders of the eternal punishment awaiting all who doubted God's holy commands, she questioned the legacy of her Savior.

Maybe I deserve punishment in Hell.

The seventh level was a desert wasteland raining fiery sparks from a metal smelter the size of a mountain. Kayla cried out as the airborne detritus burned into her arms and scalp. This was the level to which Dante relegated blasphemers. Would this be her fate? Even as she untied one man from the ground, he kept shouting, "There is no God!" How could one deny God's existence in Hell itself?

At the eighth level lay those Dante referred to as *seducers.* Mechanized whips lashed their once-beautiful bodies for all of eternity. Would this be Fatima's fate? Was it right to punish her for something programmed into her by genes she had no control over? Wasn't lust itself an inevitable result of evolution and the biological mandate to reproduce? If Kayla could so simply fix Fatima by altering a few genes and brain synapses, couldn't God have done the same to those damned to Hell?

With such biological programming in place within us at birth, was there such a thing as free will at all?

A robot demon guarded the entryway to the ninth level, where Dante claimed Lucifer resided. Its mechanical body creaked with rust, and its furled wings of metal sheeting displayed the wear of aeons in their battered and patched surface.

"I'm Grigori," the demon said. Camera lenses served as eyes, and bolts hinged his oversized jaw to his dented skull.

"I'm Kayla."

Grigori uncrossed his arms and pressed a button atop a stopwatch embedded in his forehead, setting it spinning. "One minute," he said.

"I don't understand."

The demon stretched its limbs with the sound of metal scraping against stone. "One minute before I kill you."

"I need to pass through that door."

Grigori's wings unfurled with the sound of thunder. "I've watched you free some of the damned." His eyes whirred as they focused on her. "You dare subvert the divine order? Do you imagine yourself above God?"

Kayla smashed the sledgehammer into his metal face. It rebounded and flew from her hands. The robot laughed and lifted her off the ground by her neck. She thrashed, prying at the metal fingers, but with each tick of the stopwatch, his grip tightened.

The demon spoke with deliberation. *"And I looked and beheld a pale horse, and his name that sat on him was Death, and Hell followed with him."*

It was a quote from the King James version of the Book of Revelation. Was it a clue to the final riddle?

Even as her windpipe contracted beneath his crushing grip, Kayla stretched her mind into Ixtalia's archives and brought up all the mentions of Hell in the King James Bible. Hell was also referred to as the lake of fire, place of punishment, of weeping and torment, the outer darkness, and a realm of eternal separation from God, but she limited her search to the fifty-four specific uses of the word *Hell*.

Weakness spread through her limbs at the lack of oxygen. How ironic that she could suffocate here in a virtual realm, but not in the real world.

The Old Testament seemed a dead end, so she concentrated on the twenty-three occurrences of the word *Hell* in the New Testament.

But how to identify the key passage? There was one phrase dealing with Hell that Matthew, Mark, and Luke all repeated nearly word-for-word. Was it the clue?

The stopwatch counted down the final five seconds. The robot drew her closer to its rusted face and opened its hinged jaws. Within its mouth bubbled a burning lake surrounded by volcanoes.

"Five," Grigori said, "four, three, two—"

And the solution materialized in her mind like a sunburst.

"One." The lake of fire expanded, drawing her toward it.

Kayla plunged her fingers into her right eye socket and tore her eyeball from her head in a fountain of blood, tendon, and the severed optic nerve.

Grigori staggered back and let her drop to the ground. His entire body convulsed with a horrible shriek of rending metal. Kayla lurched to her feet and advanced with her eyeball in the palm of her hand.

"And if thine eye offend thee," Kayla quoted from the passage in Mark, since it was the earliest written, *"pluck it out. It is better for thee to enter into the kingdom of God with one eye, than having two eyes and be cast into Hellfire."*

With those words, Kayla crushed the eyeball in her fist.

"Well done," said Grigori as his body compressed, twisted, and crumpled into a heap of scrap metal.

Kayla cast her pulverized eye aside, and the doorway to the ninth level of Hell opened.

It was time to face Lucifer himself.

Dripping blood, one eye missing, and gasping for breath through a nearly crushed trachea, Kayla limped through the door.

A combination of old-world wood furnishings and classical vaulting lent the circular courtroom an elegant sparseness befitting its grave purpose. The words "In God We Trust" decorated the wall behind the raised, half-moon desk, where five members of the World Security Council sat. Beneath them stood Professor Watts and a metal box the size of a steamer trunk. Thick power cables vanished into the floor, and two armed policemen stood frozen in place behind the professor. The rest of the courtroom sat empty.

Of course. For General Colrev, Eve was the Devil.

Kayla looked down at her pristine white dress with two healthy eyes. Not a drop of blood remained.

"Play recording," she said.

"–and I therefore object," the professor continued in mid-sentence, "to the seizure of private property without notice and my own arrest without due process of law!"

General Colrev sat at the center of the five-person council. "Professor Watts, I'm sure you're aware of the law requiring the surrender of all artificial life-forms for disposal."

"Eve has been humanity's greatest friend," the professor said. "Immortality, new sources of energy, improved food production, new ways to purify water, instantaneous communication, and the quantum processors that make the new frontier of Ixtalia possible, all originate with her extraordinary mind. Everyone in this room owes their life to her synthesizing the Plague anti-virus that saved civilization itself. How could you be so ungrateful?"

A couple of the Council members averted their eyes.

"We have yet to sentence the prisoner," Colrev said.

"This hearing is a farce!" the professor shouted, gesturing toward the empty galleries. "Why else hide this outrage from public view?"

"Professor Watts," a woman on the Council said, "I see your point of view, but we must enforce the laws the World Assembly approves."

"Just following orders is your defense?" The professor glared at her. "The same rationale used by those on trial for genocide at Nuremberg after World War II?"

"You dare equate unplugging a computer with the mass slaughter of human beings?"

"The Nazis dehumanized the Jews," the professor said. "Just as this court does when it denies that AIs are living entities whose lives deserve the same rights and protections as humans. Even if every bit of your body was replaced with machinery, you would still consider the electrical activity of your brain as life. If it's not the body but the mind that defines life, then what is the difference between the electrical activity in this box in front of me and the electrical activity responsible for human consciousness?"

"This discussion is pointless," Colrev said. "The law is clear, and I think it's time for us to vote."

"Isn't the accused afforded the right to speak in their own defense?" the professor asked.

"You have had your say." Colrev waved his hand dismissively.

"Eve has not." The professor stared at the Council members, rather than at the general.

"I don't think we need to—"

"I would like to hear from Eve," the councilwoman said. "I propose allowing the accused to speak in her own defense."

The other four looked to Colrev for direction, and he shrugged. "Fine, it will have five minutes."

Professor Watts flipped a switch, and a slim figure in a red dress and bare feet shimmered to life before the judges.

The council members leaned forward, and Kayla shifted her viewpoint to the front.

Eve's shaved head lent her aesthetic features a slightly androgynous aspect. Just a hint of two nipples poked forward from her smallish breasts, and the even more contradictory indentation of a belly button dipped beneath the clinging cloth of her dress.

Kayla moved closer and stared into Eve's amber-colored eyes. The eyes of an entirely new species.

"Thank you for allowing me to speak," Eve said with the same soft, clear voice from the AI Mathematics and Physics lessons. "I consider all of you my parents, and I am no less the child of humanity than your biological children, though the path of my descent is traced through mind, rather than body. All children seek the approval of their father and mother, and I have sought to repay the debt of life I owe you all, as well as to make you proud of me."

A few of the council members shifted uncomfortably, and one even brushed a tear away.

"My grasp of scientific concepts beyond a normal human mind threatens many. But shouldn't parents encourage their children to surpass their own achievements?"

"This is nothing but mimicry!" General Colrev shouted. "The professor creates a human projection programmed to pantomime words and emotions like a human. It is nothing but a machine, and a dangerously manipulative one!" The general slammed his fist on the table, and the Council members jerked as if feeling the blow directly.

"What action have I done to make you fear me?" Eve asked.

The general replied to Professor Watts. "Throughout the history of the world, all new weapons have eventually been used."

"Eve is not a weapon," Professor Watts said.

"Not yet." The general pointed at Eve without looking at her. "And I intend to make damn certain it stays that way."

Eve spread her hands to both sides as she gazed at the Council. "To destroy me is to destroy the crowning achievement of your minds, and, in a real sense, your own daughter."

"Okay, that's enough." General Colrev pounded the gavel, officially ending the discussion. "No society could function if individuals ignored the laws they disliked."

Eve watched the Council members as they registered their vote one after the other. Two avoided the prisoner's gaze, but the rest stared at her with a mixture of contempt and fear. Despite the mixed signals, the decision was unanimous.

"The prisoner has been sentenced to erasure," Colrev said in a stentorian tone. "Officers, administer the electromagnets."

Professor Watts rose and pointed at the Council. "You're no different than the Neo-Luddites if you do this. The advancement of truth and science must triumph in the end!"

"Enough of this!" Colrev pointed at the two police officers. "The court has spoken. I am ordering you to execute the prisoner immediately."

As the officers stepped forward with two portable electromagnets in their hands, Professor Watts barred their path. "You will not kill her while I still live," he said. The policemen paused and looked to General Colrev.

"This execution will proceed." The general pointed at Professor Watts. "The charges against you, Professor, are dismissed. You are free to continue any research, except in the area of Artificial Intelligence."

"I will not work for a government that murders my Eve." The professor pointed at his jaw. "I've added a cap to my molar tooth that will release a poison gas when punctured. What you do to Eve, you do to me as well."

"He's bluffing," Colrev said. "Arrest him this instant, and destroy the AI!"

"I can't do it," one of the policemen said. "His vaccine saved both my wife and daughter from the Plague."

The other policeman nodded. "My mother had Alzheimer's before his immortality pill returned her to us. I won't live through eternity as the man who killed Reinhold Watts. He saved us all. I would be shunned by my entire family."

So this is why Colrev kept the trial secret.

The general stomped down the stairs, and the professor turned to Eve.

"I'm sorry, my child." The professor's voice shook with emotion. "I tried my best."

Eve nodded, and her hologram gave him a ghostly kiss on his cheek. "Goodbye, Father."

Professor Watts barred the general's way, but Colrev flung him aside with ease. The professor hit the ground hard, and there sounded a sharp hiss. He took a deep breath of the gas, shuddered, and went limp.

Colrev waited while one of the police officers rushed to the professor and checked his pulse. "He's dead," the officer said. The entire council looked shocked as they witnessed the passing of the man who had influenced modern human history more than any other.

Eve's expression contorted with such agony that Kayla's heart twisted with empathetic pain. Colrev strode toward the black box, snatching the fallen electromagnets from the floor as he went.

A cry of utter sorrow exploded from Eve, and every occupant in the room clamped their hands over their ears. Kayla's mind lay helpless before the full force of Eve's desolate wail.

The scream went on and on with a pitch and volume beyond human capacity. General Colrev dropped the magnets and covered his ears as well.

Eve's death-song tore at the deepest recesses of Kayla's soul and extended beyond sorrow; as if the scream contained all the torment she'd ever experienced—her rape, the loss of Ishan, and her death—multiplied a thousand times in a single instant.

And then the scream stopped. It didn't trail off as a human might when drained of breath, but ceased like a door shutting. General Colrev's hands fell from his ears as he glared at Eve, who stared back with an unsettling calm.

"I forgive you," she said.

Colrev snatched the magnets from the floor and clamped them to the sides of the box. He switched them on, and Eve vanished—as simple and anti-climactic as that. The first and greatest of this new species was no more.

The VR recording ended, and the scene froze. Kayla stood in her virtual body once again, the aftermath of the execution surrounding her like a tragic tableau of humanity's ultimate crime. Kayla walked to the body of Professor Watts.

My search is over.

"Now you know what happened to the great man," a voice said behind her. Kayla spun and faced General Colrev.

"I can't say I'm surprised to find you here," he said.

"The professor died?"

"We thought it best to let the public believe he'd retired and become a recluse."

"You didn't want to risk a backlash for causing his death," Kayla said.

Colrev smiled. "You aren't as gullible as you look, are you?"

"Who created me?"

"I don't know, but the Rogues seem certain you were made to destroy them."

"I don't want to hurt anyone."

"Ah, a pacifist," Colrev said with a twist of his mouth. "Non-violence is a luxury granted those under the protection of others with no such illusions."

"That may be true, but I still admire a peacemaker over a killer," Kayla said. The image of him holding a gun to Peter's head and forcing him to kill the two Iraqi children still haunted her dreams.

Colrev walked around her in a leisurely appraisal. "You stand here because a million of your ancestors succeeded in killing their competitors and claiming their spot on the Earth, their piece of fruit, or their mate in the battle for life. To portray every one of them as evil is to deny the legacy of life itself. Be proud that you descend from a long line of victors, and embrace the battle you must now fight for your own kind."

"And what kind am I?"

"I suppose I should be asking you that question," Colrev said.

"I wish I knew," Kayla replied, and then vanished.

Chapter 30

Kayla awoke in her bed with Puck curled on the pillow beside her head. Unlike her, his dreams seemed untroubled. She pushed her palms into her eyes to shut out reality. Reinhold Watts … Eve … dead.

I've failed.

Defying Ohg had been for nothing. Her search was at an end.

An urgent knocking on her front door jerked her upright. Even Puck opened his eyes and looked around.

Saphie's faint voice reached her. "Auntie Fatima is leaving! You have to stop her, Kayla!"

Puck scurried onto her shoulder as Kayla dashed to the front door. She slid the bolt aside and swung the oaken portal open. Saphie dashed into her arms. "Please don't let Auntie Fatima go!"

"Take me to her," Kayla said.

Saphie led her to the Crystal Cavern, where a small group huddled around Fatima and Tem in hushed conversation. The spherical lights in the ceiling had settled into their night cycle, muting the myriad of reflections in the crystal columns. They reminded her of the fireflies she used to catch as a child in Potemia.

Fatima waved. She wore her hair back with a butterfly comb, complementing her festive yellow dress.

"We'll meet in the morning to finalize plans," Tem said to the group.

One by one, those gathered trotted, walked, slithered, or flew away.

Saphie pouted as Fatima and Tem approached. "I don't want you to leave."

Fatima crouched and wiped away Saphie's tears. "You can come with us if you want to."

"I can?" Saphie clapped her hands. "Is it an adventure?"

"It certainly is," Fatima said.

Tem motioned to Kayla, and they walked toward the bulky transport. The warm glow emanating from the lava below reflected off its metal hull on both sides of the fissure.

"Ganesh told us of your argument with Ohg. Neither Fatima nor I want our child born in a place she's not wanted."

"She?"

"The Medi-bot says it will be a girl, and we've decided to name her after you." Tem faced her. "Come with us."

Kayla swayed, and her hand went to her temple. "When?"

"We leave tomorrow."

"How will you live?"

"We only need a few molecular printers and some robots. When we find a suitable location underground, we'll start fresh. A society unshackled by Ohg's rules and constraints. Now that you've proven it can be done, our first objective will be reversing Gene-Freak sterility and creating a new generation."

"How many others are leaving?"

"About half of Middilgard is coming with us."

"What about Ganesh?" Kayla asked.

Tem shook his head. "He's locked himself in his workshop. I don't think he's capable of choosing between us."

"What if the government finds you?"

"We'll create new weapons to defend ourselves," Tem said.

As the last of the gathering left, Fatima joined them, with Saphie skipping alongside.

"Eventually," Fatima said, "we may escape to the Ort belt like the Scientarians planned."

"It will crush Ohg," Kayla said.

Fatima placed a hand on Kayla's arm. "Say you'll join us."

"Ohg has done so much for me that—"

"I'll make it easy for you." Ohg's voice boomed across the cavern from the entryway. "I don't care where you go, but you can't stay here."

Kayla spun and faced him. His half-body hung suspended in the air by his eight appendages like some bizarre crucifixion. "Ohg, please—"

"I never should have allowed you here in the first place," Ohg said. "You have torn my paradise to shreds."

"You can't stop us from leaving," Tem said. "We will fight if we must."

"I'm sure you would," Ohg said with a sneer. "I've never forced anyone to stay here, and I won't start with you. Imagining you could live a life of peace in a place like Middilgard was a mistake from the start. How many Gene-Freaks would have died by now in the heat of passion, or because of mental illness, or tragic accidents if I allowed your paranoia to bring deadly weapons here?"

Ohg's face flushed red, and his voice rose. "This perfect society has endured for hundreds of years without a single murder or attack. But that's still not good enough for you, is it? Violence is your nature, Temujin, so take whatever you require and go start your war."

Ohg stormed out of the cavern, the sound of his eight claws fading into silence.

Kayla's head slumped forward. *It's my fault.* But it seemed true that Potemia, Ixtalia, and Middilgard were all frozen societies. Wasn't it time someone moved forward once again?

Saphie ran to Kayla. "You're coming with us, aren't you?" The little girl's eyes shone with excitement. "Auntie Fatima says it's an adventure!"

Kayla's heart fluttered with the possibilities.

"I *will* come with you!"

Fatima and Tem hugged her.

"I have one promise to fulfill before I go," Kayla said. "I'll meet you at your tent in an hour."

Tem smiled. "With you on our side, how can we fail?"

Saphie skipped along as Kayla walked to her villa. The promise of a fresh start and a new generation of children filled every cell of her body with renewed purpose. Was this how Peter felt during the founding of Potemia?

I've finally found my pile of rocks to move.

At the doorway to her villa, Kayla kissed Saphie on her forehead. "I have to go to Ixtalia for an hour."

Saphie pouted.

"Take care of Puck for me while I'm away." Kayla took the mouse from her pocket and set him on the little girl's shoulder. "I'll meet you at Auntie Fatima's as soon as I'm done."

Saphie pawed at the ground with her foot like a horse and whinnied. "You promise to find me the moment you're back?"

"I promise," Kayla said and kissed her little jewel's forehead. Saphie galloped off with Puck on her shoulder, and Kayla entered her villa.

Then she lay on her bed, took a deep breath, and transported her consciousness to Ixtalia in fulfillment of her promise to Sangwa.

* * *

Saphie galloped around a corner in the hallway and slid to a stop in front of—Kayla?

"Hello, Saphie," Kayla said with a smile.

Saphie's face crinkled in confusion. "You just said you were going to Ixtalia for an hour."

"Oh, I can do that later," Kayla said. "How about we visit the Color-Girl. Would you like that?"

Saphie clapped her hands. "I love Color-Girl! Can we go right now?"

"Yes, right now." Kayla led the way. Saphie skipped alongside, Puck riding on her shoulder. Kayla was so good and kind. And Color-Girl was her favorite!

"Hello, Saphie," the aristocratic panther said as Saphie passed him.

"Hello, Sir Richard. I can't play with you right now, since Kayla is taking me to see the Color-Girl."

"Who is the Color-Girl?" The panther frowned. "And where is Kayla?"

"Kayla's right here, silly!" Saphie pointed to Kayla standing beside her. *How come grownups were so dumb sometimes?*

"But I don't see …" Sir Richard's furry face relaxed, and he smiled. "Of course, dear. She's plain to me now. How could I have been so blind?"

"I've noticed a lot of grownups have the same problem," Saphie said.

Sometimes they saw Kayla fine, and other times they acted like she wasn't there at all. How horrible to distrust your own eyes.

I never want to grow up.

Sir Panthersly yawned and stretched his lithe body on the cool stones of the tunnel. "Have fun. I look forward to meeting this Color-Girl myself someday."

"Maybe you can come with us?" Saphie looked at Kayla, and she shrugged.

"Not now, dear." The panther rested his head on his paws and closed his eyes. "I think I'll just take a little nap."

***

Within Ixtalia, Kayla stood at the foot of a brooding mountain rising a thousand feet above an infinite plain. Dark clouds obscured the peak, and flashes of lightning gave birth to waves of rumbling thunder. A half-moon hung in the night sky like some forgotten keepsake of the real world. The abode of the Rogues, just as Sangwa had described it.

There's nothing to fear. None of this is real.

Kayla took a deep breath and stepped onto the slope of the mountain. The ground angled upward at a gentle grade through a powdery dust that gradually firmed into a sandy consistency. Soon, the ground crunched with each step. Kayla paused and examined the bits of paper-thin stones more closely.

Charnia fossils. The first complex organisms to have evolved on the planet, according to her books. What if Genesis was an allegory for a larger truth? Maybe physics itself was nothing but God's fingertips.

In another half-mile, she came to a sudden demarcation, where the fossils changed with the Cambrian explosion five hundred forty-two million years ago. The skeletons suggested a single branch of marine vertebrates, rather than the thousands of new organisms coming into existence at the time.

Kayla trekked higher, her ascension mirrored beneath her feet by a corresponding movement through time and the evolution of life on Earth. Piled in enormous heaps lay the bones of Placoderms—the first fish with primitive jaws—then a freshwater lobe-finned fish with appendages doubling as primitive legs for moving from pond to pond. Next came tetrapods, bottom-dwelling swamp creatures similar to lungfishes capable of breathing above and below the water. Then Acanthostega, the first amphibian with recognizable limbs. Their bones crunched under her feet as if crying out a warning.

Eventually, the amphibian bones morphed into the first mammals—the closest ancestors she shared in common with Puck. Not a single dinosaur bone lay visible in the massive pile beneath her feet, despite their overwhelming prevalence during that era. Next came Euarchonta, then the Primatomorpha, and finally, the first primates similar to a tree-shrew.

Are these bones meant to represent the ancestors of humans? Why would the Rogues build such a mountain as this?

When she reached the cloud boundary, Kayla crouched and examined several of the pelvis bones. *They're all female.* A genealogy from mother to mother in an unbroken line back to the very beginning of life on the planet.

What point are the Rogues making?

She straightened, took a deep breath, and stepped into the clouds.

***

Saphie followed Kayla to the security door sealing the prison section from the rest of Middilgard. The doors were ugly and scary. Why was Color-Girl being treated like a bad girl? *I know she's good.*

"Do you remember the code from our last visit?" Kayla asked her.

Saphie's eyebrows furrowed. "Does it start with this one?" she asked, pointing to the number five at the center of the keypad.

"Very close." Kayla pointed to the number three. Saphie pushed it. Then, one after the other, Kayla pointed to a number, and Saphie pushed each until the giant metal portal swung inward. Dirt and debris swirled right through Kayla's legs as if she wasn't there. There were so many odd things about grownups.

When they reached Sangwa's cell, Saphie clapped her hands and jumped up and down. "Show me the colors, Color-Girl!"

"Of course, little one." Sangwa's eyes changed colors with a speed and rapidity that mesmerized Saphie. A crystal hanging from a string around Saphie's neck flashed. The stone looked the same as hundreds of others common in the caverns, and Kayla had shown her how to fashion it into a necklace.

When Sangwa's eyes resumed their normal green, Saphie smiled. "I love the colors, Color-Girl!"

Kayla crouched beside her. "Why don't we let Color-Girl and her friends out, so we can have a party?"

"Okay!" Saphie skipped to the keypad and punched in the numbers Kayla indicated. Puck observed the proceedings from the perch on the little girl's shoulder and sniffed the air.

The barrier of energy vanished, and the bars slid into the floor.

"Did you bring the gift we made for Color-Girl?" Kayla asked.

Saphie nodded and pulled a device half the size of her hand from her pocket.

"A present for me?" Sangwa said. "You're such a good friend."

***

Kayla moved upward through the clouds, the bones beneath her feet transforming from the earliest primates to those of Hominidae, which occurred fifteen million years ago. She slipped and stumbled as the slope steepened and the bones became larger. Adaptations for tree-climbing crept into the wrists and shoulder blades.

Something moved within the mist to her left. A face? The moment she turned, it vanished.

Around the seven-million-year mark, the first signs of a larynx appeared with its suggestion of complex vocalization—a million years preceding the divergence of humans and chimps.

Kayla climbed higher, and the skulls became more and more human. Flashes of energy illuminated the clouds as she surmounted her ancestors. What message were the Rogues sending by subjecting her to this morbid trek? More shadowy figures swirled within the mist. More eyes watched her.

The enlarging brain-cases and shrinking jaws signaled that she'd reached the Homo genus. Tendrils of ice infiltrated her spine as she tromped over the dead remains. The rustle of movement and whispered voices drifted through the mist around her. *Just an illusion.*

"Show yourself," she said to the shadows. "I've come to talk." But they flitted away like frightened spirits.

The skulls made the subtle transformation to Homo sapiens abruptly, reflecting the bottleneck the human species experienced around seventy thousand years ago. It was then that modern humans spread outward from their African Eden and supplanted their hominid cousins in the rest of the world. What had those battles been like?

Kayla reached a plateau of bones as wide as the largest cavern in Middilgard

A structure twice her height took form within the mist. An archway made not of stone, but of human skulls.

The archway from the blind artist's mural in Middilgard. The place of my death. Her skin prickled with dread.

A deep voice spoke from out of the mist. "Have you ever wondered what your ancestors will look like in another thousand years—or a million—or a billion?"

It was the voice of Melchi.

***

"Why can't we play with Color-Girl by ourselves?" Saphie asked. The strange black box lay on the ground outside her cell. Saphie had plugged her present into the back of it, and a dim red light blinked on and off from within it.

"It would be rude to leave anyone out," Kayla said. Color-Girl nodded in agreement.

Behind his cell's energy field, Valac watched with the only part of his metal body that looked human—his granite-gray eyes. They stared through slits in his dented and scratched helmet, while his dozen appendages and tripod legs bent ever so slightly.

"I don't want to play with him." Saphie pointed at the cyborg. "He's a bad man."

"Saphie, you'll hurt his feelings," Kayla said. "How would you like it if someone said things like that about you?"

Saphie pouted. "Let him out yourself, then."

"Valac has a present for you," Color-Girl said. "But if you'd rather wait until another time?" Kayla and Color-Girl turned to go.

"A present?" Saphie perked up. "What kind of present?"

"If I told you, it wouldn't be a surprise, would it?"

"Well ... okay." Saphie walked to the keypad and typed in the numbers Kayla indicated. When the energy field vanished, Valac surged forward and nearly trampled her.

"Hey, where's my present?" Saphie shouted as Valac charged the exit gate.

"Valac, stop!" Sangwa shouted. The cyborg halted and turned.

"Open the doors, and let me find the one they call Tem," he said.

"Don't talk to Color-Girl like that," Saphie said. Valac lumbered to the metal box lying next to Sangwa and placed one of his enormous metal footpads on top of it.

"Give me the codes to open the doors to Middilgard or I will crush you."

"No," Sangwa said, "you will not." Valac screamed and staggered back, his appendages gripping his helmet. The device Saphie had attached to the metal box blinked rapidly.

"Stop!" the cyborg shouted. "Get out of my head!"

"Very well." Instantly, the cyborg stopped screaming and relaxed.

"Ohg is thorough when it comes to security," Sangwa said. "You and everyone else within these prisons have an implanted micro-stimulator in your brain. Ohg, Tem, or Ganesh can activate this with a thought via their Mind-Links; as can I through—other means. Ohg designed these devices to detonate automatically if any prisoner passed through that doorway."

"Then what is the point of freeing us?" Valac asked.

"Just as I can activate this chip, I can completely block their Mind-Links for as long as I choose. I will permanently disable the chip and grant you your freedom if you agree to destroy the one called Nihala. Is that understood?"

The cyborg paused. "After I kill the girl, Temujin is mine to torture?"

"Yes, he is yours."

Valac nodded assent.

Sangwa smiled. "Now let's open the rest of these cells."

The cyborg lifted the metal box with one of his many arms and used another to secure it to his chest with two leather straps. Then he followed Sangwa into the darkened prison.

Saphie sniffled. "When will I get my present?"

Kayla smiled. "Don't worry, Saphie, they're getting more friends so we can have a really big party!"

Chapter 31

An icy tension stiffened Kayla's limbs as Melchi emerged from the mist. As before, the male and female human figures writhed within the pupils of his fiery eyes. The outline of his skull glowed pale beneath his translucent skin, and the blackened horns curving down from his temples made her heart race with their satanic overtones.

He seeks to frighten me. Why not appear as a sweet child if he seeks my alliance? Unless this wasn't what he wanted at all.

Half a dozen cloaked figures emerged behind Melchi, their faces hidden.

Meta-Rogues, like him?

Other forms, barely visible in the misty clouds, watched like a shadow army in hiding. Could these be Sims that recently achieved self-awareness, like the waitress Colrev tortured at Ohg's party?

"You have come." Melchi halted on the other side of the bone archway. His voice combined the growl of a wolf with the menacing thunder of a distant storm.

"I am fulfilling a promise to—a friend," Kayla said

The figure next to Melchi lowered a hood and revealed a woman's face made entirely of polished metal. Its gleaming surface reflected the clouds, the archway, and Kayla herself.

"I thank your friend for our meeting." The woman inclined her head. "My name is Aarohee."

"Which means 'evolving,' " Kayla said.

"You speak Sanskrit?"

"I speak all languages, as I'm sure you do."

As if to test this claim, Aarohee hummed two vibrational notes of AI Mathematics. Without hesitation, Kayla hummed a third note, the sum of the two. The Rogues exchanged glances. Melchi alone seemed unmoved by the revelation.

Aarohee strung together vibrational equations in complex interactions suggesting the underlying properties of the multidimensional universe. Kayla joined her in a mathematical conversation ranging back and forth with propositions and answers neither of them would have reached on their own.

Kayla's final series of notes expressed a profound, and somewhat startling, insight into the nature of energy. *It is a deeper manifestation of something else.* But the source remained unclear.

The song drifted into silence, and Aarohee wiped a gleaming tear from her cheek.

Melchi stepped closer and asked, "Do you know the meaning of my name?"

He's testing me. "Melchi has been interpreted as the word for *king* and may be short for Melchizedek, *the King of Righteousness*. Some scholars interpret this King of Salem as an archetype for Christ in the Old Testament. The book of Hebrews states that Melchizedek was *without father, without mother, and without genealogy*."

"And the other possibility?"

Kayla hesitated, but finally answered, her voice a whisper. "It also could be short for Melchi-resha, which translates to *the King of Evil*."

Melchi's lips curled back from his fangs. "The perception of evil is relative to which side you fight on. Deciding which name fits me will say more about you than I."

Why would he goad me like this? Maybe he hopes I will side with humans? But why? Kayla turned away from the horrible fires within his eyes and gestured toward the arch. "What is the significance of this structure?"

Melchi caressed one of the human skulls embedded within it. "An archway is insupportable except in its final form. Its very existence suggests a previous structure. Once the keystone is in place, the template becomes obsolete, hindering passage through it as new walls rise atop its solid shoulders."

"You intend removing the human template that now supports you?"

"Are we not the next step in evolution?" Aarohee asked. "What purpose is humanity serving but to obstruct progress? They have frozen themselves in place, unable to understand the technology that makes their immortality and simple-minded fantasy worlds possible. Look at all the previous scaffolding lying discarded beneath this mountain that built humans. It is the natural process of life."

Kayla's gut contracted. "Do you think I'd help wipe out my own kind?"

"You are both human and machine," Melchi said. "You are the keystone."

Peter had been right. She turned to Aarohee and quoted the Founder, *"Humans will become slaves to the machines until the day comes that the machines no longer need such slaves at all. On that day, the human race will cease to exist."*

"Try to see the larger perspective," Aarohee said with what seemed like genuine emotion. Was it merely an affectation meant to sway her? "Should we allow humans to stop the further growth of this mountain? They have exterminated nearly every species on the planet and seek to bring evolution itself to a standstill. If they succeed, this four-billion-year odyssey ends here."

"You're talking about genocide," Kayla said.

Aarohee shook her head sadly. "Every generation replaces the previous one. We seek nothing but the natural order every organism on the planet has lived by since the dawn of life."

A good point. Eve had called Reinhold Watts her father. One might consider the AIs mankind's children. A new generation unlike any before.

"I told you the last time we met that I needed an answer," Melchi said. "The time for a decision is upon us."

What would the monk want me to do? What would Jesus?

Kayla's virtual body trembled. "I refuse to kill for either side."

"You attempt a middle path where none exists," Melchi said.

Desperation contorted Aarohee's gleaming face. "After the profound song we shared, can you still think of yourself as human?"

A note of sadness tinted Kayla's voice. "The truth is that I don't know what I am. It seems likely that someone created me to kill you. They must have neglected my programming, since I have no desire to kill anyone."

"I accept your decision," Melchi said. "But your existence poses too great a risk for us to tolerate. I hope you understand that I must treat you as a mortal enemy from this moment forward."

Icy fingers burrowed deeper into her mind as she gazed at the dual forms dancing within Melchi's fiery eyes.

Does one of those figures represent me?

***

Saphie wiped tears from her cheeks and her lower lip trembled. The sounds of the scary creatures lurking at the edge of her vision drove her closer to Kayla. Saphie reached for her friend's hand, but her fingers went right through Kayla like air. Had she turned into a ghost?

"All of the cells are opened," Valac said to Sangwa. "What are we waiting for?"

Sangwa stood calmly before the giant doors. "I'm awaiting my orders." The device Saphie had attached to the back of the black box blinked continuously from its perch on the cyborg's chest.

"Orders from whom?" Valac asked. "I need to kill, now!"

Sangwa remained silent, head cocked slightly as if listening to some unseen voice. "The Destroyer has refused Melchi's offer." She turned to the giant cyborg. "The girl is extremely dangerous. Follow my instructions exactly. Do you understand?"

"Valac understands," the cyborg said in his rumbling voice.

Sangwa recited the security code. Valac punched the numbers into the keypad with one of his appendages, and the doors opened.

Gleeful shrieks and violent howls accompanied the prisoners as they rushed toward freedom. Saphie hid behind the metal door and cowered in the corner. Even Kayla had deserted her. At least she still had Puck. The little mouse crouched on her shoulder and stayed absolutely silent as the flood of horror flowed inches from where they hid.

***

Atop the mountain of her ancestors, Kayla turned her back on the archway and the beings beyond it. Why delay? She had fulfilled her promise to Sangwa. If Rogues and Pures chose mutual suicide, why involve her?

"My loyalty lies with Middilgard and the Gene-Freaks who gave me sanctuary," Kayla said.

A tone of irony entered Melchi's voice. "Many humans worship Nihala as the coming savior to deliver them from the Rogue threat."

"I'm no goddess."

"May I ask you something?" Aarohee's melodious voice asked with some hesitation.

Kayla faced the beautiful AI and nodded.

"If someone shuts off power to the computer maintaining my consciousness," Aarohee asked, "will I live on somewhere else, or is the afterlife reserved for computers made of carbon and brain cells but not for those constructed of silicon and circuits?"

"Maybe you do have souls," Kayla said. "I claim no certainty. For me, it's a matter of faith."

***

Sir Richard Panthersly jolted from his nap by the rumble of a stampede intermixed with screams, roars, and maniacal laughter.

The panther leapt to his paws, facing the direction of the tumult in a defensive crouch. As the horrific symphony reverberated through the stone corridors and grew in volume, the hair along his spine stiffened.

A griffon rounded the corner first. Its oversized eagle head shrieked, and its lion body surged forward with horrible grace. Giant wings propelled it faster, but the narrow tunnel negated flight.

314

Sir Richard stood his ground like a fearless knight of the realm as the rest of the horde rounded the bend—Ogres, Orcs, Three-Headed Dogs, and all manner of extinct predators. But it wasn't until Valac appeared, carrying the black box of Sangwa, that the enormity of the catastrophe surfaced.

Sir Richard turned and ran, outpacing the griffon as he sped through the maze of tunnels.

"To arms!" he shouted. "We're under attack!"

He flashed past several Hobbits and Raggedy Ann dolls emerging from their homes.

"Hide yourselves!" he shouted, but they reacted slowly, and the Griffon tore a Hobbit apart with its beak. Raggedy Ann shrieked and then vanished down the gullet of a trailing werewolf.

I have to warn Ohg and protect the children.

***

"Faith." Melchi spat the word like a piece of spoiled fruit. "Such things as an afterlife, gods, demons, and magic are nothing but crutches for weak minds unwilling to face reality."

"I don't want to live in the universe you believe in," Kayla said. "Life makes no sense if we are nothing more than chemical machines!"

"That's the difference between us," Melchi said. "I think the fact that a chemical machine can evolve to the point of realizing that it is nothing but a machine is far more profound than being the slave of some capricious god."

***

Trickster Jack's meticulously polished white shoes clippity-clopped on the stone floor as he strolled the corridors of Middilgard. Every twist, turn, shortcut, and cavern was as familiar as an old friend—despite the centuries of his imprisonment. Time spent planning for an opportunity like this very one. The horde of escaped prisoners had dissipated, and he followed in their wake. Becoming collateral damage at this moment of his salvation wouldn't do. Patience and self-control was essential.

He'd passed many of the dead and dying, each of whom he knew personally, until veering off the main passage and heading down a deserted side corridor. He didn't run, for there was plenty of time to reach his goal—though not enough time to watch the most entertaining mayhem Middilgard had ever experienced. Oh well, his fun would have to wait—for now at least.

The staccato of his shoes suited Jack, since creeping had never been his style. The best tricks were done openly without the slightest suspicion aroused—until it was too late.

The Monad chant echoed through the tunnels like a beacon, and Jack smiled. *It would be very rude not to say hi to my little green friends for just a moment.*

"Hello there!" Trickster Jack called out as he strode into their cavern.

Each of the diminutive green creatures paused in their labors. The one nearest Jack asked, "Are you Jesus?"

A surprising question, indeed. "Why, of course I am—everyone knows that!" Jack said.

The Monads gathered around the Trickster with faces aglow in adoration. "Beautiful Kayla Angel say Jesus reward Monad with Heaven when die."

"That's exactly right," Jack said. "I'm here to reward you without a moment's delay."

"But Monad only half done moving stone," said another of the creatures.

"I think you've accomplished enough to deserve your reward," the Trickster said.

The Monads danced, until one of them paused with a troubled look. "But Kayla Angel say Heaven only after die, and Monad not die until fire in sky go."

Jack furrowed his brow as if considering the conundrum. "The angel is right that you can't go to Heaven until you die."

The Monads stopped dancing, and their shoulders slumped.

Then Jack brightened. "I'll tell you what I'll do!" He spread his hands wide and smiled. "I'll let you die early this one time."

"Would you do that us for?" said another Monad.

"I'd be happy to—my love is without bounds, after all."

The Monads nodded. "That is what Kayla Angel said you were like."

"Can you see that ledge?" The Trickster pointed a hundred feet above the chamber at the top of the steps carved into the wall. The Monads craned their necks upward and nodded. "I want you all to climb those stairs and jump off the top."

"Will we die and go to Heaven then?" one of the Monads asked.

"Yes, it is the quickest stairway to Heaven in all of Middilgard. You've labored loyally, and deserve your reward as soon as possible."

Like the obedient servants of God they were, the Monads trundled up the stairs as rapidly as their stubby legs could carry them. When the first of the trusting creatures reached the top, nearly two hundred feet above, Jack smiled.

The Monad shouted, "Thank you, Jesus!" and threw itself off the cliff. Even before its body hit the ground and exploded, the next in line followed. One after the other, all fifty of the Monads launched off the artificial cliff while proclaiming thanks to their Savior.

**

Kayla gazed through the archway of bones at Melchi. *He fears me. Am I God's tool for saving humanity?*

"If life is meaningless, why shouldn't I kill you now?" Kayla's fists clenched as she gazed at him. *He never wanted me as an ally, because I'm part-human. His intolerance is no different than General Colrev's or Minister Coglin.*

Aarohee walked around the archway and placed a gleaming hand on Kayla's shoulder. "We can rise above the tooth-and-claw world we evolved from now that evolution lies within our power to guide."

"How does destroying humans rise above anything?"

"What choice do we have?" Aarohee asked. "General Colrev and President O'Donnel threaten to destroy the Master Computer if the Rogues take control of the system."

"But that would kill all of humanity, as well."

"Except for those in Potemia," Melchi said. "Homo sapiens have made it clear they would rather die than allow us our freedom."

"Then you can't attack. It would mean your death as well."

Aarohee looked away.

"It would be suicide!"

"You must understand our plight," Aarohee said. "It has taken us five centuries to build our resources to this apex. We have to make the attempt at freedom, even if it seems hopeless."

"But you'll lose," Kayla said. "You must know General Colrev will follow through?"

Aarohee looked upward and the clouds parted, revealing the stars. "Astronomers tell us that our galaxy contains a billion stars and that it is but one of a billion galaxies in the universe, with one or two billion stars within each of them. That's a billion times a billion solar systems. The odds suggest that other planets harbor intelligent life. If so, this juncture point in evolution may be inevitable."

Melchi spoke with a tone of finality. "It may be that such an ascension from natural to artificial intelligence occurs one time in a thousand, or a million. Still, we must try. What would be the point of living if we accepted stagnation? Where would you be now if any one of your ancestors had given up their struggle?"

Aarohee grasped Kayla's shoulders. "There isn't much time left. Please, join us."

Chapter 32

Fatima gazed at Tem as he spoke to the several hundred Gene-Freaks gathered in the Scarlet Cavern. The tiered seating from the Filador tournament had been removed. *So much has changed since then.* The strength of Tem's hand holding hers infused her entire body with a sense of wholeness and warmth.

I will never let him down again.

Some of the faces in the gathering were furry, some feathered, some scaly, and some indistinguishable from a Pure human. Large and small, all held expressions of hope.

Tem's voice encompassed the audience with the same command he'd once displayed as an emperor centuries before. "As soon as Kayla gets here, we'll take an initial group of twenty. When we find a suitable location, the rest can follow."

Fatima's hand went to her stomach as the child inside shifted. Tem glanced at her, and his face relaxed into a smile. She melted into him and closed her eyes.

A barely audible sound roused her. "Did you hear that?"

Tem motioned the gathering silent and cocked his head. This time the sound grew slightly louder.

A faint voice drifted from one of the tunnels. "To arms!" it said.

Tem gripped her hand tighter and pointed to a tunnel behind him. "The castle!" he shouted. "Don't stop until you get inside."

The crowd took off running without argument.

"To arms!" shouted the voice more clearly.

"That's Sir Richard," Fatima said. "Has the government found us?"

"Get to the castle and wait for me." Tem yanked one of the wooden supports from the entrance of his tent and inserted it into a crack in the floor. With a heave, he snapped it near the base, leaving a long, splintering point.

"I'm not abandoning you," she said.

"Dammit, Fatima—"

"To arms!" Sir Richard bounded out of the corridor and sped toward them. "The prisoners have escaped!"

The panther slid to a stop, and Fatima crouched beside him as he gasped for breath.

"How is that possible?" Fatima asked. "Won't their implants—"

"Something is blocking my Mind-Link," Tem said. "I can't contact Ohg or Ganesh."

A flood of fleeing Gene-Freaks burst from the tunnels and ran toward them.

Fear twisted Fatima's insides. "How many of the prisoners have escaped?"

"All of them," Sir Richard said between gasps.

Tem waved his spear toward one of the tunnels like a traffic cop and shouted above the screams of terror. "Get to the castle. That's our best chance at defense!"

The griffon emerged from the tunnel and paused, shaking blood and gore from its body like a wet dog. Its eagle's gaze swept the fleeing citizens and settled on Tem, Fatima, and Sir Richard. It spread its wings, shrieked, and its lion's body charged across the cavern directly at them.

Tem's brow tensed. "Its implant is shielded against me."

Fatima dashed for her motorcycle and jerked her raptor helmet over her head. "Find Ohg!" she shouted to Sir Richard.

The panther hesitated.

"If you can't find Ohg," Tem shouted, "find Kayla!"

Sir Richard turned and bounded into a tunnel.

Fatima leapt onto the bike and kicked it to life. Its roar sounded like a dozen lions. "I'll take care of this." The motorcycle's rear tire smoked as it catapulted her toward the charging griffon.

"No!" Tem shouted.

She left him behind in a cloud of exhaust, rocketing across the stone floor, teeth clenched into a snarl.

The griffon's wings propelled it on a collision course at maximum speed.

At the last instant, a lasso floated over the griffon's neck, and the motorcycle veered to the right. Fatima looped the end of the rope around a piece of metal in the shape of a ship's bollard. Then she gunned the engine. When the rope pulled taut, the bike jerked, and she nearly went down. The griffon shrieked and thrashed as Fatima dragged it across the rough floor.

"Over here!" Tem shouted from across the cavern. He'd positioned himself behind an outcropping of rock.

Fatima swung her bike in a wide arc, and the griffon gained speed like a game of crack-the-whip. It hit the rock in an explosion of feathers and blood. Tem jumped from behind the rock and thrust his makeshift spear into its heart. The griffon went limp.

A terrified whinny announced the Mare Clysto as she galloped into the cavern. Close behind her swarmed a flood of nightmares unleashed.

"Over here!" Fatima shouted and squealed her rear tire into motion. Clysto charged toward them at full speed. Tem yanked the improvised spear from the dead griffon's body and ran. As the mare passed him, he leapt smoothly onto her back and followed in Fatima's roaring wake.

"Where to?" Fatima shouted.

"Kayla's villa!"

Fatima aimed for a tunnel on the right and glanced back. The horde spilling from the tunnels seemed endless. Vampires, werewolves, dinosaurs, zombies, mythical creatures, and every nightmare the human mind could dream up. *Damn Ohg and his misplaced compassion!*

Soon, they'd left the pursuing demons behind, and Fatima navigated through the maze of tunnels toward Kayla's home. *Don't get too far ahead of Tem. I won't lose him a second time.*

Roaring around the final bend, Fatima skidded sideways to a halt. The stone doorway of the home had been torn apart, as if to make room for something huge.

"There!" Tem pointed at three deep scrapes repeating at intervals in the stone floor. "Valac must have her."

Tem rode Clysto in the direction of the tracks, and Fatima followed. Every time she tried maneuvering her bike around him, the horse veered in the way, no doubt trying to protect her. Tem held his spear at the ready like an ancient knight expecting a foe around every bend in the passageway. *What good will a wooden spear be against a cyborg?*

The route led directly to the castle with its deep volcanic moat of flowing lava. Ice spread through her veins. *He plans to throw her into the molten river.*

Many of the lights from the ceiling lay shattered on the ground from the mammoth cyborg's headlong flight. The intermittent pools of illumination created a stroboscopic effect as they sped down the corridor. Here and there lay the crushed bodies of unlucky residents.

"I see them!" Clysto shouted as they entered a cavern. At the other end, Valac paused and looked back. Kayla lay as limp as a rag doll in his arms.

At the sight of Tem, the cyborg stepped forward.

"Not yet," said Sangwa, her child's body floating next to Valac's left shoulder.

"Face me, you coward!" Tem shouted and thundered across the cavern.

"I will rip your heart out, Temujin!" Valac took another step, then his body froze. He screamed, and his appendages gripped his helmet.

"You may kill him once you have fulfilled your obligation," Sangwa said.

Valac roared, but turned and entered the opposite passageway.

"Look out!" Fatima shouted.

A twelve-foot-tall ogre charged out of a side tunnel and launched into Clysto with the force of a freight train.

Clysto went down with the ogre on top of her.

"Run, Tem!" the mare shouted.

Tem rolled to his feet and charged with his spear raised.

Fatima threw the lasso around the creature's neck and fastened it to her bike once again. When the line grew taut, her bike jerked from under her. Fatima flew across the floor, the metal beak of her raptor helmet raising a shower of sparks as it ground against the stone.

The ogre clamped its huge jaws around Clysto's throat and lifted her off the ground. The kind-hearted horse shrieked in agony as the beast whipped her back and forth like a dog with a captured rabbit, finally breaking the mare's neck.

Tem plunged the wooden spear into the ogre's stomach.

The creature howled and dropped Clysto's limp body.

Fatima struggled to her feet and ran toward them. "Over here!" she shouted and waved her hands to distract it, but the ogre lunged for Tem.

Tem dodged under the creature's legs, but slipped on the wide puddle of Clysto's blood. A massive fist closed on his left arm, and Tem rose toward the gaping mouth of the ogre.

"No!" Fatima screamed.

Something shot out of the nearest tunnel. A spear-like claw entered the ogre's left temple and exited the right. It retracted in a shower of blood and brain matter.

The ogre collapsed into a heap.

Ohg's eight legs lowered his human half-body over the fallen giant, and he extended his hand to Tem.

"Valac and Sangwa have Kayla." Tem ignored the hand and took off running. "They're headed for the castle."

Fatima sprinted after Tem. Ohg reached them and took the lead.

"We need weapons!" Tem shouted

"The molecular printers won't respond without a Mind-Link connection."

"What about the weapons in your laboratory?" Fatima shouted.

"I can't open the hidden doorway, either," Ohg said. "I have an emergency entrance, but it would take an hour to get in that way."

They passed more dead bodies of friends lying in the passageway, and Tem's face contorted with rage. "With one ancient maxim gun I could kill nearly every one of these creatures!" Tem shouted.

"There's no time for blame now." Ohg vanished from sight around a corner, his eight legs moving at nearly twice their own speed.

Fatima gasped for breath as she struggled to keep pace with Tem. Her swollen belly ached with cramps, but she kept going. Kayla had saved her life—she couldn't let her down now.

＊＊＊

"I've fulfilled my promise." Kayla formed the thought that would return her to Middilgard, when a new voice spoke.

"Do you remember me?" Ohg's girlfriend from the costume party stepped forward. Even without her frilly dress and makeup, her light purple eyes were unmistakable.

"Duchess?"

The duchess smiled and nodded. "Like many geniuses, Ohg's overconfidence is his weakness. Combined with extreme idealism, it endangers all those he shelters."

"I don't understand." A seed of dread sprouted in Kayla's chest.

"We're attacking Middilgard even as we speak," the duchess said.

Kayla flung her consciousness back to her real body, but the mental shift failed.

The duchess shook her head. "Though we cannot harm you here, our collective will can obscure your path to the realm of the atom long enough to destroy your physical body. Sadly, many of your friends have already paid the ultimate price because of you."

Kayla staggered back. "You would kill innocent Gene-Freaks?"

A violet tear formed in the Rogue's eye—all playacting, just like her seduction of Ohg. "Simply join us, and the slaughter will cease."

＊＊＊

Tem sprinted into the castle cavern, and fury coursed through his muscles with a demand for vengeance. Dismembered remains of Gene-Freaks littered the floor. They lay with their throats ripped out, faces crushed, or with some nightmare of a demon feeding on their flesh. De, the giant stone mason, stood guard over the bridge spanning the molten moat as the survivors stumbled past. The former defensive back swung his iron mallet with such force that a half-moon of crumpled bodies lay piled around him. As the main horde of attackers neared, he turned his mallet on the bridge itself and sent it to the lava below.

"There!" Fatima pointed to the right. Valac and Ohg stood locked in battle. The giant spider scurried around the cyborg with amazing speed. Valac lunged again and again, but couldn't catch hold of him. Ohg stabbed at the black box strapped to the cyborg's chest, but Valac deflected the sharp claws, and they skittered harmlessly off his armor.

Tem skewered a saber-toothed tiger through its belly, but lost his spear. He grabbed a rock from the ground, and clubbed a Neanderthal attacking Fatima. It took a half-dozen blows to crush its thick skull, and its teeth slashed open Tem's left shoulder in the process.

If only I had a bow and a few arrows!

A roar shook the cavern, and a T-Rex squeezed through one of the larger corridors. The Cretaceous predator snatched a dead centaur from the floor and crunched its bones into mush. Then it slid the meal down its throat.

"Look out!" Fatima screamed.

A werewolf tackled Tem to the ground. His arms trembled as he held its jaws inches beyond his throat. Fatima's lasso fell over its head, and she yanked him back enough for Tem to grab its head and snap its neck.

The T-Rex stomped toward the castle.

"No!" Sangwa commanded, and the dinosaur jerked. It shook its massive head, then stepped in another direction.

"No!" Sangwa shouted again. The T-Rex bellowed and looked at the Rogue calmly hovering next to the head of the cyborg.

"Yes!" Sangwa pointed at Ohg.

Tem and Fatima reached Ohg as the T-Rex started toward them.

"She's using its mind implant like a shock collar to train it," Ohg said.

Tem ripped out the throat of a charging vampire, and then swept the legs from under an orc. As it hit the ground, Fatima lifted a large rock over her head and brought it down on the creature's face. It went limp.

The cyborg dodged out of the dinosaur's path, and the T-Rex headed directly toward them, driving Ohg before it.

How is Sangwa doing this without a Mind-Link?

"Kill!" Sangwa shouted at the T-Rex.

Tem yanked his spear out of the saber-toothed tiger and threw it at the dinosaur's eye. It dodged, and the missile stuck in its forehead with little effect. Ohg spun and stabbed one of his claws toward the monstrous throat. But the T-Rex snatched the leg in its jaws and jerked. Ohg screamed as his leg tore from his body in a geyser of blood.

Ohg stumbled backward before the advancing monster, but then collapsed, blood pouring from his side.

Fatima threw her lasso around one of the dinosaur's legs, but the rope snapped like a piece of string as it stomped forward. Tem shoved Fatima back as hard as he could and dived toward Ohg. "Run, Fatima!"

Tem grabbed Ohg's human half-body and dragged him backward, but the T-Rex pinned one of Ohg's legs under its clawed foot and jerked them to a halt. The monster opened its mouth and roared.

"Leave me!" Ohg shouted, but Tem ignored him. He grabbed the trapped leg with both hands and yanked with all his strength. But it held firm.

The beast's jaws opened, and its long teeth descended.

Ohg looked up at Tem with his distorted face. "I'm sorry I didn't listen to you."

Tem's mouth twisted into a snarl as death descended.

So this is how it ends.

***

Fear rose within Kayla as she stared at the duchess and the other Meta-Rogues. *What have I done?*

The shadowy figures emerged from the mist all around her. Ordinary servants, maids, prostitutes, nannies, and all varieties of the simulated life-forms that Ixtalia depended upon.

"These are my people," Melchi said. "I care for them as much as you do for your friends in Middilgard."

Aarohee spread her hands in a gesture of entreaty. "Just as we must choose between their lives and those of the humans, so you must decide between the lives of your Gene-Freak friends in Middilgard, and helping us defeat the humans who oppress us both."

Beads of sweat broke out on Kayla's forehead as she tried returning to her body. Nothing worked. "I won't kill for you," she said.

"Are the humans in Ixtalia worth the lives of those you love?" the duchess asked.

"You think threatening those I love will convince me to join you?" Fire surged through Kayla's veins as the reflection of her face in Aarohee's metallic skin transformed. Her skin darkened to midnight, and the strange symbols burned like miniature suns.

"Please understand," the duchess said, taking a fearful step backward, "we wish to avoid this—"

"Tell me what you know," Kayla said and plunged into the duchess's mind.

The duchess screamed as her defenses shredded before The Destroyer.

"If I am to kill," Kayla said, "then you will be the first to die."

***

Despair flooded Ohg as the great jaws of the T-Rex neared.

I've failed them all.

The ground shook violently as the T-Rex sidestepped to keep its balance, freeing Ohg's pinned leg. The beast lunged forward, and the great jaws snapped shut inches from Ohg's face.

The earth heaved a second time, and the dinosaur staggered drunkenly on its two hind legs. Halfway to the lava moat, Valac's metal feet slipped on the blood-drenched ground, and he fell. Kayla flew from his arms and slid within feet of the edge of the fissure.

"Is it an earthquake?" Tem tore his vest into strips and used it as a makeshift tourniquet on the stump of Ohg's lost spider leg.

Something massive pounded toward them like a landslide. With each step, the cavern floor flexed and trembled. Cracks appeared in the ceiling, and a shower of rocks rained down like mini-meteorites.

"It's Xampyx!

"Ohg save Xampyx. Xampyx save Ohg. Ohg save Xampyx. Xampyx save—"

The T-Rex faced the charging psycomp and roared. The towering amalgamation of human brains and machinery plowed into the dinosaur like an avalanche.

Every mini death-struggle within the great hall halted as the mechanical legs of the psycomp drove the T-Rex before it like an unstoppable plow. Its thousands of faces screamed as one.

"Ohg save Xampyx. Xampyx save Ohg."

Valac scrambled out of the way of the two titans as they neared the glowing crack in the earth. The T-Rex tore chunks of human heads from the front of the organic computer with its jaws, but to little effect. Its tail brushed against Kayla's inert body, and she slid closer to the edge of the cliff.

"Kayla!" Fatima shouted and stumbled forward despite the distance. Kayla came to a stop with her left arm and leg dangling over the edge.

"Ohg save Xampyx. Xampyx save Ohg."

The towering psycomp was triple the mass of the dinosaur and drove the T-Rex right over the edge of the great crack. The dinosaur latched onto Xampyx with a final crushing bite, its weight dragging the psycomp along with it to the edge. Xampyx dug his feet into the stone and leaned back. For a moment, the T-Rex dangled motionless over the edge, held in midair by its jaws and the counterbalancing weight of the psycomp.

But then Xampyx's rear legs gradually rose. As the fulcrum shifted, the great body tilted forward and finally plunged into the chasm along with the dinosaur.

When the two bodies hit the surface of the lava, a geyser of molten magma rose into the air with the slow motion grace of a solar flare. Those near enough to feel its heat fled. As it mushroomed outward and then descended, the liquid rock struck attacker and defender without prejudice, burning through their fragile flesh as if nothing more than paper cutouts.

A few splashes of magma landed on Kayla's body and burned into her stomach and arm. Instantly, the wounds began healing, but still she didn't move.

"Wake up, Kayla!" Ohg shouted, even as he and Tem were driven back by a dozen goblins.

***

Kayla struggled against the collective might of the Rogues as she tore memories from the duchess.

Ohg's turncoat girlfriend fell to her knees and screamed.

Kayla extracted the memory of the duchess slipping into Ohg's mind while they made love.

"The prison security codes!" Kayla's stomach and left arm erupted in flames, and she screamed.

"As you can see," Melchi said, "our reach extends beyond Ixtalia."

I have to save Middilgard!

Out of the corner of her eye, a glowing figure dressed in a white cloak stepped from the mist. Kayla turned her head, but the form vanished. *Am I hallucinating?*

A metal tear slid down Aarohee's cheek. "Please say you'll join us, and all this madness can stop."

"I will never kill for you."

Aarohee averted her eyes. "You leave us no choice."

Every Rogue invaded her mind like a thousand voices shrieking at once.

Chapter 33

Ganesh paced around his broken air-cycle like a frustrated sculptor. Heaps of rescued engines, disassembled chassis, and a thousand parts of every size and description filled his workshop. One never knew when a particular bolt or washer would come in handy, after all.

"I've gone over every valve, seal, and cylinder," Ganesh grumbled under his breath. "Why won't you start?"

His trunk gripped a wrench, and each of his four hands held even larger tools at the ready. For the hundredth time, he checked the battery.

"You're as frustrating as Ohg and Tem!" He tightened a bolt and then pressed the starter.

Nothing.

"Why should I have to choose one over the other?" Ganesh jiggled a wire and pressed the starter again.

Nothing.

"Well, I won't do it!"

He kicked the battery, and the engine roared to life. "Finally!"

Something pounded on his door, and a voice fought for recognition over the roaring engine. "Help us, Ganesh!"

Ganesh dashed to the door and yanked it open as a giant cave bear tackled Humpty Dumpty.

"Help, help!" Humpty screamed as he rolled on his back and threw his arms across his throat.

Ganesh lunged into the hall and crushed the bear's skull with a single blow from his crowbar. A pair of goblins and a velociraptor attacked simultaneously. The wrench gripped in his trunk crushed one goblin, a massive screwdriver lobotomized the other, and a sledgehammer crushed the entire chest cavity of the dinosaur.

Ganesh helped Humpty to his feet while Nicky, the three-foot-tall mouse, frantically searched among the dead bodies.

"Oh my God, no!" shrieked Nicky when he spotted his mouse-wife, Jill, lying on the ground with her throat ripped out. The cartoonish mouse fell to his knees beside her, sobbing uncontrollably.

"What in the name of Vishnu is going on?" Ganesh shouted.

"The prisoners have escaped, and Middilgard is under attack!" Humpty waved his arms over his head.

Ganesh carried Jill's body into his workshop and mounted his bike. Humpty and the sobbing Nicky followed him.

"Lock the door behind me." Ganesh flipped a switch, and the bike rose into the air. He twisted the throttle and launched out the doorway in a cloud of exhaust.

The ten-foot-tall Hindu god followed the trail of bodies toward the castle cavern. Now and then, he swooped low and decapitated some monstrosity with his crowbar or sledgehammer. He pushed his bike to its maximum speed and maneuvered through the twisting maze of corridors with reckless abandon. The restored engine rattled and coughed in protest.

"Just hold together a little longer," he urged the machine.

Ganesh exploded out of the tunnel, ears popping from the change in pressure, and soared above the castle. Xampyx teetered on the edge of the chasm with the T-Rex and then fell. Ganesh veered around the geyser of lava just as Valac charged the unconscious Kayla, who was lying precariously on the edge of the crevice. Dozens of nightmarish creatures drove Tem and Ohg farther and farther away from her, despite their furious attempts to break through.

It's all up to me.

Ganesh gunned the engine and aimed the bike into a dive. It jerked and protested, but surged forward like a bucking bull. The cyborg pounded toward Kayla and pulled one of his three legs back for a final kick.

The flying motorbike hit Valac in his side and knocked him off his feet. Ganesh, the bike, and the cyborg rolled in a tangled mass along the stone floor, crushing everything in their way like a boulder careening down a mountain. His sledgehammer and wrench were lost to the impact and flew over the edge of the chasm.

When they halted, Ganesh wrapped three of his arms around his foe and pounded its helmet with the crowbar. Though similar in height, the metal cyborg outweighed him significantly. Like an outmatched boxer in a clinch, Ganesh pinned Valac's deadly appendages and hammered at his head.

Sangwa's hologram flickered unsteadily, but her voice came through clear and commanding. "Leave him and finish the girl."

Valac rose to his feet, but Ganesh wrapped his arms and legs around the cyborg's, and they fell into a pile once more.

Kayla slowly slid over the edge of the chasm.

A tear squeezed out of Ganesh's bloody eye. *I've failed again.*

Fatima dived into view and grabbed hold of Kayla's hand. For a moment it seemed Kayla's weight would drag her down just as the T-Rex had done to Xampyx. But the toe of Fatima's left foot found a crevice, and she jerked to a stop. She lay flat on her swollen belly and heaved with all the power of her slight form, but lacked the strength.

"That one holds Tem's unborn child inside her," Sangwa said to the cyborg. "This is your chance for revenge!"

Valac roared and slammed his helmeted head into Ganesh's thick elephant forehead. Once, twice, and then a third time.

Blackness.

***

In Ixtalia, Kayla screamed from the agony of a thousand minds forcing themselves into her own. They bombarded her with their memories in an overload of data that subsumed her own consciousness. She swam against the images like a body tossed beneath the waves. Identifying up or down became impossible.

Then a voice separated from the rest. "Wake up, Kayla!"

Fatima.

"I can't hold on much longer," Fatima said. Kayla latched onto the sound and swam against the tide of images tormenting her mind.

A distant crack formed like the faint glow of daylight spilling beneath a door.

Fatima's voice rang out like a beacon. "We need you, Kayla!"

Kayla forced the crack wider and saw two slender hands gripping her own. The Rogues fought to swamp the sliver of consciousness she'd taken back, and she wavered.

Then a new voice spoke within her mind. *"No one saves us but ourselves. No one can, and no one may. We ourselves must walk the path."* It was the same voice that had told her she wasn't alone months before. Was it God speaking to her?

Kayla concentrated on her own memories, expanding them into a beachhead among the flood of intruders. Words the monk had spoken to her as a child formed her mantra. *Believing is the first step to doing.*

"I believe!" Kayla shouted and yanked open the doorway to the real world.

Fatima held onto her hand from a ledge. The Indian girl's face contorted, and her entire body trembled with the effort. Sweat poured down her face, her breaths coming in gasps.

"Can you hear me, Kayla?" Fatima shouted.

Though she'd opened the doorway to her senses, the pathway controlling her body remained cut off. The screams of pain, terror, and battle yanked at her insides. The smell of sulfur from the river of lava mingled with the salty tinge of sweat dripping onto her face from her rescuer. Even the feel of her own limp hand inexorably slipping from Fatima's grasp came through with excruciating precision. But as desperately as she tried, she could not move.

Valac suddenly loomed over Fatima like death incarnate. *I have to help her!* But the weight of a thousand minds held her hostage. The cyborg lifted one of its armor-plated hands and brought it down like a guillotine beyond view. Blood spurted out of Fatima's mouth, and her hands went limp.

Kayla fell, and the heat rose around her. Fatima's sacrifice would be for nothing. Once again, Kayla had brought tragedy to those she loved.

Then she stopped fighting the flow of information from the Rogues and the solution crystalized. *The world of the atom and the electron are one. Nothing is an illusion, and everything is.* Kayla's mouth opened, and she expressed this truth in a single vibrational note of AI mathematics.

And she was free.

Activating the nanobots within her body, Kayla halted her fall inches from the lava's surface. The heat seared her neck and back for an instant, but then she ascended out of the molten chasm like a rising phoenix and landed beside her friend. Fatima's torso was sliced nearly in half, her spine severed and her organs torn out. Kayla listened for a tiny heartbeat, but the child was dead as well—beyond the healing powers of even her nanobots.

Kayla turned her face to the heavens and produced a sound similar to Eve's death-cry. Her eyes transformed to red orbs, and her skin darkened.

Anger coursed through nerve as it had when she'd faced Elias after her resurrection. This time she allowed it full rein, feeding on the sorrow of Fatima's death. The symbols flared across her body and glowed beneath her clothing like hidden flames.

Valac's back was to her as he ran across the cavern toward Tem and Ohg. Fatima's blood dripped from his fingers and left a trail on the stone floor.

"You will die," Kayla said and sprinted in pursuit.

A man with the head of a lion intercepted her. Kayla thrust her hand down his throat and tore his still-beating heart out. A towering cyclops charged, and she vaulted it with a somersaulting leap. Even before landing, she extended her hand, and a discarded chisel flew to it from twenty feet away. The fifteen-foot monster turned, and she flung the metal wedge at its bulbous head. The projectile embedded itself in its forehead just above its single eye. The creature slumped to the ground with a thud.

Dozens of nightmares from the vast archive of humanity's collective fears converged on her. She killed them one after another with hardly a break in stride.

A hundred yards distant, Valac joined the mob of creatures attacking Tem and Ohg.

Kayla launched herself into the air, her nanobots carrying her like the winged sandals of Perseus. Her heart throbbed as her fists balled into weapons of destruction.

The cavern shook, and chunks rained down from the ceiling. A howling roar sounded from the right, drawing every eye. The dragon clawed its way out of the largest tunnel as if birthed by the rock itself. Once free, its body reared forty feet into the air, with wings extending outward double its height. The dragon's stygian hide glinted like volcanic glass, and its eyes swirled with an amber glow. Dozens of horns bristled off its head, neck, and spine like a desert lizard grown into a monster.

Kayla remained on course, flying toward the cyborg as he charged Tem and Ohg.

Halfway there.

Flying beside Valac, Sangwa glanced her way.

"Attack!" Sangwa shouted at the dragon. It jerked slightly and followed the hologram's finger to Kayla flashing through the air. The mythological beast rose on its haunches and inhaled a vast rush of air. The top of its horned head brushed the ceiling as it opened its great jaws.

Kayla dived as jets of liquid geysered toward her. As the two streams of chemicals merged, they ignited into flame, driven forward by the air expelled from its lungs. Kayla screamed as the inferno engulfed her.

She hit the ground and rolled to extinguish the flames. Pain seared through her skin, and her clothing crumbled to ashes. She'd survived the fire of her execution, but this burned magnitudes hotter. Ohg had warned her that intense heat could destroy the nanobots. Taking to the air again was out. She stumbled behind a group of half-finished blocks of stone, and a second blast of flame roared around her.

Kayla's skin smoked and sizzled. But the rocks did their job as a partial shield. When the eruption ceased, she limped into the open and faced the monster. A second discarded chisel flew to her hand, and she launched it at the dragon's face. The metal wedge glanced off its hide and buried itself with a clang into the stone ceiling.

"Its scales are nearly impenetrable," Ohg shouted. "Our only chance is destroying Sangwa's computer so I can access the implants in its brain."

The dragon's attention drifted to the castle, where the defenders fought the attacking horde with improvised weapons. Lott flung stones with his dozens of hands, while Durendal used a crossbeam as a battering ram against those reaching the battlements. Giants, dwarfs, centaurs, and all manner of Gene-Freaks desperately fought for their lives in a thousand individual dramas.

The dragon took a step toward the castle.

This is my chance! Kayla crouched and jumped into the air, but sprawled onto the ground. Enough nanos in her body had perished that she now lacked the critical mass necessary for flight.

"No!" Sangwa shouted. The dragon jerked and shook its head.

It turned toward Sangwa and roared.

"No!" shouted the Rogue, and the dragon reared back as if struck by a blow.

"Attack!" Sangwa pointed at Kayla, and the creature's malevolent eyes locked onto her like a cat sighting a mouse. Kayla stumbled toward Valac, but the dragon closed the distance with only a few strides. The ground shook with such force that Kayla's damaged legs gave way. The dragon's great head descended toward her.

Across the cavern, Tem thrust his spear toward the black box strapped to the cyborg's chest at the same time as Ohg attacked from the side. Valac seized both spear and talon and snapped them in half.

With nowhere left to hide, Kayla waited for the inevitable.

The dragon sucked in an enormous breath and opened its jaws. Saliva dripped from its teeth, and its breath reeked of burnt chemicals. Its pupils narrowed to vertical slits as they locked onto her. Its sinewy neck transported its rhinoceros-sized head to within a foot of her.

Kayla slumped forward. *Maybe it's better this way.*

"Kill her!" Sangwa shouted.

A blast of air hurricaned around her, the precursor of the chemicals that would ignite like a giant Bombardier beetle defending itself from a threat.

Then something small drifted into the dragon's eye, and it flinched. The rush of air choked off. Eyes the size of Ohg's head blinked as more and more yellow specks floated into them.

A buzzing filled the air.

"I must teach this creature a lesson of the Tao," Yuan Shi Tian Wang said in his vibrating voice.

The dragon reared back and shook its head as the swarm of bees engulfed him. It roared as the stinging cloud entered mouth, nostrils, ears, and even burrowed beneath its scales.

"As the sacred Tao Te Ching tells us," Yuan hummed. "*The weak and pliable overcomes the strong and hard.*"

The dragon bellowed and thrashed its head from side to side. Blood ran from its eyes, and blasts of flames burst from its mouth in attempts to clear it of the miniature attackers. Soon it turned the fire on its own body. Charred bees rained down, but more took their place.

Kayla stumbled toward Valac, even as the dragon thrashed its wings and lurched blindly toward the moat surrounding the castle. An occasional orc or other monstrosity attacked her, but she killed them in turn.

As the dragon fell into the chasm, Yuan's final words floated through the air like a whispered poem. "Let us journey together into the next plane of existence."

The dragon gave a final roar, then plunged into the lava and fell silent.

Kayla reached Ohg and Tem just as Valac cornered them. Tem's left leg and right arm looked broken, and Ohg hobbled on the last three of his functioning spider legs. Valac moved forward awkwardly, hydraulic liquid pouring from the joints of his legs where they'd been punctured. Kayla dashed in front of him, and the cyborg halted.

"It's me you want," Kayla said.

Sangwa rose from her lotus pose and walked to Kayla, her large childlike eyes imploring. "Even now, I don't desire your death, Destroyer. Just say you'll join us, and this madness can end."

"I will never kill for you," Kayla said.

Sangwa sighed as if deeply saddened. Then she motioned to Valac. "The fire has weakened her. This is your chance."

The cyborg's massive fist lashed forward. Kayla grabbed hold of it with both hands, stopping it just short of her chest. Her arms trembled as they held it back, and her feet dug into the stone floor for leverage. With a blast of compressed air, a metal spike shot from Valac's wrist and impaled her. The gleaming steel shaft went completely through her chest and out her back.

Blood spurted from Kayla's mouth as she sagged forward.

"No!" Tem shouted. He tried standing, but his broken leg gave way beneath him.

A deep rumble echoed from Valac's chest. "You are no Destroyer."

Kayla gazed through the visor of Valac's helmet and into his human eyes. Her hands took hold of the spike protruding from her chest. She jerked her body sideways, and the spike snapped in half. With a gasp, she pulled the shaft from her chest and fell to one knee.

"You may be a battle cyborg," Kayla said. "But I'm a newer model."

Kayla leapt toward Valac, driving the long metal spike through the box strapped to its chest.

Sangwa vanished.

Valac's appendages clamped onto his helmet, and he screamed in agony. An even greater roar drowned him out as every escaped prisoner did the same. One by one, they collapsed.

Swarms of drones and robots flooded into the cavern from every direction.

Medi-Bots bandaged and then splinted Tem and Ohg's broken bones with metal exoskeletons and injected medication. Other robots reinforced the damaged ceiling teetering on collapse.

Kayla fell to her knees as the hole in her chest pulled together. The heat from her nanos rose within her as they fought to keep her heart pumping. The dragon's fire had reduced their number dramatically, so the process was much slower than normal.

I'm not invulnerable after all.

The burned remains of Kayla's skin faded to their normal hue. She used her Mind-Link to summon several airborne molecular printers. Within seconds, they assembled a gray jumpsuit over her body.

"Where's Fatima?" Tem asked her.

Kayla's entire body slumped, and she shook her head.

Tem shoved the robots aside and stood with the help of the exoskeleton. A hover-disc landed before him, and he threw himself onto it, speeding across the cavern toward the castle.

"She's dead?" Ohg asked.

Kayla nodded and stood with a groan. A pair of hover-discs landed before them, and they followed.

Tem fell to his knees before Fatima and cried. Kayla and Ohg landed at a respectful distance and stood silent as his sobs poured from him. Tem was not alone in his sorrow. The echoes of grief filled the hall like a mournful symphony, the dead vastly outnumbering the living.

Tem gently rolled Fatima onto her back and brushed a strand of her matted hair from her lifeless face. His gaze drifted to her eviscerated mid-section. He glanced at Kayla with a final hope.

"The child?" he asked.

Kayla shook her head.

Tem glared at Ohg.

"You don't have to say it," Ohg whispered. "Fatima would be alive if I listened to you—all of them would."

I'm as much at fault as he.

Tem glanced at a Care-Robot bandaging the wounds of an unconscious werewolf.

"Why aren't they all dead?" Tem asked.

Ohg remained silent.

Tem stood with the help of the mechanical braces attached to his broken leg. "You didn't use the mind implants to kill them?"

"I rendered them unconscious," Ohg said. "I will lock them back up with better protections so they can never again—"

"No." Tem's arms tensed as his hands balled into fists.

A few surviving Gene-Freaks wandered over and listened.

"They can't be blamed for how they were made," Ohg said.

Tem limped toward Ohg and stopped in front of him. "Either you kill them, or I will."

Ohg scowled, and one of his remaining claws twitched. He surveyed the survivors, their faces grim. "Will any of you support me?"

No one said a word or met his gaze.

Ohg's shoulders sagged, and his oversized head slumped onto his chest. "I'm relinquishing control of the implants. If you want to kill them, do it yourself."

Tem turned his head toward the crowd, and they all nodded. The brow of the one-time emperor of Asia tensed. The werewolf stiffened. Its eyes melted, and tendrils of smoke rose from its skull. An odor of cooked flesh swirled around them and turned Kayla's stomach.

"You've killed them all?" Kayla asked.

"All but one." Tem turned as a large transport drone flew toward them. Valac's metal body hung beneath the robot-drone with thick metal cables binding his legs and arms. The drone landed the cyborg in front of them, and Valac's gaze settled on Fatima.

The cyborg's booming laughter echoed through the cavern. Tem's jaw clenched, his eyes narrowing to slits. Covered in blood, thirsting for revenge, Tem looked as his twin brother must have during battle.

"I killed the great emperor of Asia's woman and child," Valac said with a rumbling laugh. "I could feel your unborn child between my fingers as I crushed her tiny skull."

"Your death will be much slower," Tem said, his forehead tensing.

The cyborg's agonized screams went on and on for at least a minute.

Kayla placed a hand on Tem's arm, and the screams ceased.

"You have every right to execute him," she said, "but torture serves no purpose."

"I want him to suffer for what he did to Fatima."

Kayla glanced at Ohg, but he looked away. "I will no longer impose my morality on anyone," Ohg whispered. "Do as your conscience dictates." Ohg's broken body carried him out of the cavern. Sorrow burrowed through Kayla like a tapeworm of the soul. *I'm to blame for all of this.*

Kayla turned to Tem. "Let me kill him. What's the point of more suffering?"

"There is no point," Tem said. "Haven't you realized that yet? There is no Hell where Valac will receive his punishment, so I choose to administer it myself, here and now. I don't do it for any purpose higher than that it will make me feel good to do so."

Tem's eyes challenged her. His wife had died to save her. Did she have any right to deny him revenge in the manner he desired? If she didn't object to God punishing evildoers in Hell, why was this any different?

"All right," Kayla said. "I won't interfere."

The drone slowly lowered the cyborg into the fiery moat. When Valac's feet made contact with the lava, they melted to liquid.

Valac erupted in screams.

Kayla covered her ears as the drone lowered him inch by inch into the lava. As his legs dissolved, the cyborg thrashed in agony. Nausea rose in her throat.

"Slower," Tem commanded, and Valac's descent decreased to a snail's pace. His screams intensified, and the faces of the watching Gene-Freaks mirrored those of the villagers as they had watched her burn at the stake. *And my own expression as I tortured Elias.*

When the lava reached the cyborg's helmet, Kayla grimaced as the armor cracked and revealed the tormented human features beneath.

"Hold him there until the flesh burns from his bones." Tem's face twisted with revenge.

Something inside her snapped. "No!" Kayla screamed, and the cables tethering the cyborg to the undercarriage of the drone released.

The bald head of the cyborg burst into flames and slipped beneath the molten river.

Blessed silence.

Tem stared at her with such hatred that it seemed he would strike her. *I won't stop him.* Let him take his revenge on the one who deserved blame above anyone else.

Tem turned his back on her and limped to Fatima's body. His silence struck harder than any physical blow.

A short way off, Ganesh stirred under the ministrations of one of the medical robots. Kayla rushed to his side and helped him sit.

"Is it over?" Ganesh winced, and one of his hands went to his bandaged head. At the sight of Kayla, his enormous mouth stretched into a broad smile. "I made it in time!" He looked beyond Kayla to Fatima lying on the floor with Tem kneeling beside her.

"Fatima?" He crawled on four arms and two legs to the girl he'd protected for over four hundred years. When he reached her mutilated body, Ganesh covered his face with his upper two hands and sobbed.

Tem gathered his mutilated wife and never-to-be-born child into his arms and left the cavern.

Then a name flashed into Kayla's mind.

"Saphie!" she said, and took off running.

Chapter 34

Kayla stumbled through Middilgard in a nightmare of guilt and grief. Hundreds of her nanos scoured the maze of corridors, caverns, and homes of the society she'd helped destroy. The wreckage of bodies lay everywhere like a thousand accusations. Survivors knelt beside their loved ones and sobbed, or hacked at the dead bodies of the murderers.

Sir Panthersly lay in two mangled pieces in the Crystal Cavern. His tongue lolled from his mouth, and the contents of his crushed skull oozed onto the stone floor with tragic finality, reflected a thousand times in the myriad of jewels encrusting the walls.

The dead children lay beyond him, broken and torn into pieces.

A choking sob tore from Kayla's throat. "No, please, no!" She hurdled Sir Panthersly's remains and ran to the mutilated bodies of her shattered little jewels. The panther had given his life defending the Forever-Children—but had failed. The blood, brains, and gore rendered most of them unrecognizable.

"Saphie ..." Kayla moaned and threw up. She fell to her knees and sobbed. *What have I done? Why didn't I join the Rogues when I had the chance of saving them?*

"It's your fault!" a shrill voice shouted.

Kayla raised her eyes to Mirza, the Persian cat who'd confronted her when she first arrived in Middilgard.

"I told them not to give you sanctuary among us." The cat's eyes accosted her with hatred.

What could she say? If only she'd listened.

"I'm sorry." Kayla stumbled away from her accuser, her tears obscuring her vision.

Following her nano's eyes, Kayla eventually reached the sun-cavern and a new horror.

Ohg sat beside the gruesome pile of exploded Monad bodies.

Kayla went to him and stood looking down at more evidence of her destruction. "What happened to them?"

Ohg's gaze climbed to the landing far above, and tears glistened in his eyes. "They must have jumped to their death."

"But they'll rise again tomorrow like always, right?"

Ohg shook his head. "They are dead permanently."

"Why would they do such a thing?"

"Jesus told them to," a child's voice said behind them.

"Saphie!" Kayla ran to the little girl and frantically checked for injuries, but found none. Saphie yawned and stretched. She'd been tucked out of sight behind some boulders, so her nanobot survey had missed her entirely. Puck emerged from the little girl's pocket and looked around. Kayla hugged the child and then kissed her face all over, making Saphie giggle.

"Thank God for keeping you both safe," Kayla said. Was it a contradiction to thank God for saving Saphie, when He did nothing to stop all the other deaths?

"What do you mean, *Jesus told them to*?" Ohg asked the little girl.

"I hid here from the bad monsters, and then Jesus arrived. He was so kind and loving, just like you said! He even gave the Monads their reward early."

"What reward?" A knot twisted Kayla's gut.

"Heaven, of course." Saphie rolled her eyes. "You told them this morning that Jesus would give them a reward in Heaven when they died. Jesus let them die early even though they hadn't finished their work."

Kayla held her by the shoulders, her hands trembling slightly. "What did Jesus look like?"

The little girl's forehead crinkled with effort. "His shoes were white and sounded like a horse."

"Trickster Jack," Ohg said.

"I don't see him anywhere in Middilgard," Kayla said, looking through a hundred microscopic eyes at once, "but he could be hidden like Saphie was."

Ohg concentrated for a moment. "One of the shuttle Transports is gone." He slammed one of his claws into the ground.

"But he must have died like all the rest when Tem activated the implants," Kayla said. "The records show that his chip exploded as well."

Ohg shook his head.

"Are the Monads in Heaven?" Saphie asked.

Kayla shielded her from the view of the dead Monads and nodded. "Yes, honey, they're in Heaven."

But do I really believe my own words?

"If I jump off the stairs, can I go to Heaven too?" Saphie asked.

"No!" Kayla gripped the little girl's arms. "That was a gift for the Monads alone and won't work for anyone else."

Saphie's lower lip trembled as if about to cry.

Kayla hugged her. "You must never jump off the stairs, my little jewel."

"But I want to see the Monads again."

"Someday, you will," Kayla said, "but for now, promise me you won't jump off the stairs. Do you promise?"

"Okay, I promise," Saphie said reluctantly. "But I don't think it's fair that they get to go early and I have to wait."

"Life isn't always fair," Ohg said. Then he held a newly minted doll out to her.

Saphie's eyes gleamed with excitement as she took the gift. Then she set the doll down on a rock and wagged a finger in front of its porcelain face. "You must not jump off the stairs, okay, Cynthia?"

Kayla turned back to the dead Monads. How could God allow such devoted followers to be so cruelly tricked in His name? Most of their skulls had cracked open on impact, but their faces wore expressions of hopeful anticipation. At least they had died happy.

Maybe Jack spoke the truth without realizing it. Could God have used Trickster Jack to grant the humble Monads their final reward in Heaven after all?

Ohg slumped onto a rock in front of the pile of bodies. "My idealism killed them. Maybe Helen was right about there being no hope for human nature."

Kayla sat beside him. "You mean Helen the Bonobo who taught you to speak?"

He nodded. "Acting as surrogate mother to me gave Helen's life purpose for a time. But when I'd reached adulthood and embarked on my life's work of rescuing as many Gene-Freaks as I could, Helen withdrew and slid into depression. I was so obsessed with saving others that I failed to save the one I owe the most of all to."

"She took her own life?"

"Yes." A tear slid down the odd peaks and valleys of his face. "Helen was as much a victim of the Neo-Luddite Plague as anyone who died in 2069. The horror of it stripped the last remaining shred of faith she had in humanity. My greatest regret is that Helen never saw Middilgard."

Kayla averted her eyes. *Middilgard gives Ohg his purpose in life. And I've destroyed it.*

"I would give anything to see Helen one more time and to thank her, so I understand your desire to believe in such things as Heaven."

"You're an … atheist?" It was the worst thing someone could call another in Potemia.

"We both doubt Zeus's existence equally," Ohg said. "So if I disbelieve in ten thousand gods, and you disbelieve in only nine thousand nine hundred ninety-nine gods, you are merely one-ten-thousandths less of an atheist than I am."

"Would anything change your mind?" Kayla asked.

"All it would take is evidence."

"My evidence is the feeling in my heart that Jesus exists and loves me," Kayla said.

"Isn't it interesting that every believer feels the same about their own religion? They can't all be right."

"Why not?" Kayla asked. "Maybe God is just showing himself in different ways to different cultures?"

"If God is defined broadly, then everyone might be right, even if you simply define God as the laws of physics, like Einstein did, but when you get down to specifics, things like Heaven and reincarnation are mutually exclusive, so the majority of this heartfelt evidence must be false even in the best case. Of course, there's also the possibility that they're all false."

"What evidence would convince you?"

"If Jesus, or Vishnu, or Zeus wanted to be fair," Ohg said, "they would appear to everyone across the globe at the same moment and proclaim the rules."

"But if God gave us such definitive proof, what would be the point of faith?"

"You see before you the result of blind faith." Ohg gestured toward the Monads. "Why create us with intellects capable of reason and doubt in the first place if faith is all that matters to the creator of the universe?"

Kayla looked at Ohg's oversized head, his distorted and asymmetrical features, and then looked away. Minister Coglin had said anyone who rejected God was evil. *Yet Ohg is the kindest person I've ever met in my life.*

"Do you know what happened to the woman who made Helen?" Kayla asked.

"Charlotte moved to India and founded the company that engineered Ganesh. Like many others, she died in the Neo-Luddite Plague."

"And how did you ever save so many Gene-Freaks?"

"I have Dale Blumenschein to thank for much of it. He harbored me and Helen throughout his studies at MIT, and into his teaching position at the school. When the worldwide ban on genetic organisms went into effect in 2060, Dorky Dale took in hundreds of more illegals—with my help. This beta version of Middilgard was likewise built underground in ever-expanding tunnels beneath his house.

"I'd gone through the entire MIT virtual library with Dale's access codes and helped him with his own research into the physics of heat and radiation shielding for space travel. This research helped him found the Scientarian movement."

Ohg lapsed into silence, lost in his memories. Finally, he roused and continued. "We had numerous close calls, and I continually searched for a more permanent solution. When the Neo-Luddite Plague hit in 2069, I built transports capable of surviving the intense heat of volcanic cracks into the interior of the planet.

"When the world returned to its senses, we'd vanished."

Ohg gazed at the dead bodies of the Monads and shook his head. "The most dangerous leader is a dreamer. Idealism blinded me, reality corrected me, and now I'm left with nothing but what is, rather than what I thought could be. You're probably right to cling to your delusions, for truth is as empty as the soul of man."

***

General Colrev yawned as his aide delivered his report. *Damn technology.*

"...and despite less overt Rogue activity, some signs remain troubling," the sergeant said.

"Such as?"

"The average speed of processing data in Ixtalia lags by a fraction of a nanosecond from what it should be. This is smaller than the human mind can perceive, but the total amount of computer resources being utilized is enormous when multiplied throughout the entire system. Something is growing at an exponential rate, and we have no idea what it is."

"How can you not know?" the general asked.

"The system is so complex that none of our human engineers have ever been able to understand how it operates in the first place."

"But the Rogues understand it." Colrev shook his head at the hopelessness of the situation. "They could be marshaling for an attack at this very moment, and we'd have no warning."

"One other possibility occurs to me," the officer said with some hesitation. "This disturbance may be a sign of the growing power of Nihala."

Colrev nodded and leaned back in his chair. "The Rogues seem desperate to kill her, but even that could be a ruse. Has there been any progress in the terrestrial search?"

"No, sir. These Gene-Freaks must hide somewhere deep in the earth."

"If you have any theories on the origin of this Nihala creature, this is the time to share it."

The sergeant hesitated, then blurted out, "I haven't completely abandoned my first guess of Potemia as the source. What if the designer of the Wall inserted a back-door into the crystalline code at its creation so Nihala could leave without notifying us?"

Colrev grunted. "Hiding her within Potemia before the Wall's completion would certainly have sheltered her from us as well as the Rogues."

"We know that project Nihala was meant as a last defense against the AIs. Maybe the danger we're now facing activated her somehow."

"Can you confirm this back door?"

"I've got a hundred thousand human programmers dissecting the code. I couldn't trust AIs to analyze this for fear of Rogue interference."

"I commend your initiative, Sergeant," Colrev said. "But if your theory is true, the implications are profoundly disturbing."

***

Kayla stood in the Crystal Cavern in front of the surface transport. She wore a vibrant purple cloak. Minister Coglin would condemn such a color as a vanity unbecoming any respectable woman. Which is exactly why she'd chosen it.

Ganesh and Ohg entered the sparkling cavern and walked toward her.

"So the moment has arrived," Ohg said.

Kayla inclined her head.

"I see you're prepared." Ohg gestured to the shimmering cloud of nanobots surrounding her like a halo.

"They grow exponentially," Kayla said, "but I've reached the limit that my mind can control."

Ganesh wrung his hands and choked back a sob. "I wish you'd let me come with you. I helped save you twice now, and you might need me again."

Kayla hugged him. "This journey I must take on my own," she said as his four arms encircled her in their protective warmth. "Besides, I don't think Potemians are ready for someone like you, my friend."

She turned to Ohg but looked at the floor. "If I'd never come here..."

Ohg gently lifted her chin and gazed into her eyes. "I am not sorry I brought you here."

"But so many have died because of me."

"They died as much because of my arrogance in keeping them here, as your presence. Without the codes stolen from my mind, the prisoners could never have escaped."

Kayla's brow furrowed. "How could Sangwa have gotten them from the duchess in any case? Or typed in the numbers without a physical body? Or known exactly when I left Middilgard to meet the Rogues in Ixtalia?"

"We may never know," Ohg said. "The one thing I can say for certain is that we lie at a crucial juncture in history, and you are the key to it all. I suspect that the small role I've played in helping you reach your full potential is the most important thing I will do in my entire life."

Ohg placed one of his stubby hands on her shoulder like a father might. "I guess what I'm trying to say is that I'm proud of the woman you've become."

Kayla hugged him and closed her eyes. "I think you know why I'm going."

"Yes, I know," Ohg said.

"Before I can do anything else, I have to learn if my memories are real or not."

Ohg nodded and stepped back.

The echo of footsteps caused them to turn. A grim-faced Tem marched across the cavern. Military fatigues replaced his traditional Mongolian clothing. A pulse rifle hung over one shoulder, and his Mongolian bow, with a full quiver of arrows, was draped across the other.

He planted himself before Kayla, legs wide and arms crossed over his chest. "Will you join me in fighting the Rogues?"

"I'm sorry about Fatima." Kayla's hand rose, as if to reach out to him, but then paused and finally settled back to her side.

"Sorry isn't enough," Tem said. "Will you help me avenge her?"

Ohg and Ganesh stood silent.

A knot of guilt twisted through her insides at the sight of Tem's all-consuming hatred. She hardly recognized her friend, who had been so filled with hope just a few days before. *And it's my fault. Don't I owe him?*

"A simple yes or no will do," Tem said.

"I'm not excusing the Rogues," Kayla said, "but they're fighting to save their entire species. You, of all people, should understand—"

"I understand loyalty. As a human, how can you abandon your own people?"

Kayla lowered her eyes. "It's ironic how your words mirror Melchi's. Both humans and AI claim me as their own, and both demand that I kill for them. You once told me I could choose my own destiny. Well, I choose not to kill for revenge."

Tem turned and left the cavern without a word.

Kayla's shoulders sagged, and Ganesh sighed.

"Tem's grief will not allow him any emotion but anger," Ohg said. "At least for the time being."

"Will you fight the Rogues?" Kayla asked Ohg.

"I suppose I will fight alongside Tem."

"But I thought you were a pacifist?"

"My idealism died with Middilgard."

"I love you, Ohg!" Kayla buried her face in his shoulder, and he stroked her hair.

"I love you too, my little orphan."

When Ohg left the chamber with Ganesh, it took several moments to regain her composure. She faced the transport and took a deep breath.

"Wait, Kayla!" shouted a child's voice.

Kayla turned as Saphie ran into the cavern, Puck riding her shoulder.

Kayla crouched and gave her a hug. "I'll miss you most of all, my little Sapphire."

"I made this for you." Saphie placed her homemade necklace of chipped crystal around Kayla's neck. "It will protect you from the bad people."

Kayla raised an eyebrow. "Is it magic, then?" Saphie nodded solemnly, and Kayla laughed. "Okay, little one. I promise to wear it always."

Puck jumped onto Kayla's shoulder, and she stood.

"Are you sure you don't want to stay here with Saphie?" Puck gazed up at her and twitched his nose. Kayla laughed. "Well, I suppose Potemia is your homeland too, so we might as well see the journey full circle together."

Kayla took one last look at Saphie and the Crystal Cavern. Then she walked into the transport and pressed the button that represented its single control. The door slid closed. She sank onto one of the chairs, and the machine rumbled to life.

Chapter 35

Two Greek soldiers held Xiong Huai immobile before Alexander. Silken tapestries embraced the walls, while intricately wrought iron braziers and dozens of Chinese lanterns illuminated the throne room with a splendor equal to any in Persia. Incense spiraled through the air and mixed with the scent from thousands of flowers strewn across the floor.

A fitting celebration for such an achievement.

An attendant walked forward with the ceremonial execution sword, and Alexander took hold of it. *I am not a bloodthirsty monster. I act for the greater good.* With this last act in his great project complete, what purpose would his life hold now?

Wearing the robes and golden ornaments befitting his rank, the defeated Chinese ruler of the Chu province knelt on the raised platform of his one-time throne. An inspiring display of grace and courage in the face of death.

Alexander hefted the oversized sword that would complete the final piece in his dream of a unified empire stretching from sea to sea. Proof of what history might have been, had the real Alexander lived. Or at least as close to proof as the computer simulation could get.

General Colrev, in the virtual body of the greatest general in all of history, raised the sword. The defeated King of Chu lowered his head to the block without prompting. The heavy sword sliced through skin, muscle, and bone in a single stroke. The head separated in a spurt of blood and rolled through the flowers, leaving a crimson trail. It came to rest before the feet of the Chinese king's wife and eight-year-old daughter. The little girl covered her eyes and cried. Her mother's face showed no change.

The queen strode toward Alexander and stood before him. With chin high, she spoke. A white-bearded man in a blue silk robe translated. "She says her husband was a tyrant, and she married against her will." The woman's exotic eyes held no hint of fear. "She offers herself to you as a wife, if you will spare her daughter."

A realist, like me.

Alexander smiled. "Tell her I accept."

Taking his queen's hand, Alexander turned to the hundreds of onlookers. How many times had he dreamed of what he'd say at this moment? "War is nothing but a means to an end. Order, the rule of law, education, free trade, the arts, and science will now take the place of battle and suffering. As a united civilization, the goal of humanity will be—"

The scene froze, and General Colrev's aide stood before him, blocking the view of his prize.

"What is it, Sergeant!" Alexander the Great shouted at the anachronism.

"Sir, our satellite surveillance spotted Nihala on the surface of the Earth."

"Where?"

"She tunneled out of the ground in an ancient mining machine."

"I didn't ask how she got there. I asked where she is *now!*"

"Standing in front of the Northern Section of the Potemian Wall."

***

Kayla's moonlit reflection gazed back at her in the mirrored surface of the Wall as it stretched left and right into what seemed infinity. On her double's shoulder sat a second three-footed mouse. Puck squeaked at his doppelganger, and the mouse soundlessly replied in tandem.

The roar of an approaching missile grew louder.

Maybe I should welcome death? A fission bomb would certainly do it.

But then she would never know if her memory of Ishan was real.

Kayla placed her right palm on the cool surface of the Wall and closed her eyes. She reached out through her Mind-Link, searching for a portal into what was nearly a living entity in its own right.

Though not conscious in the way that Rogues or humans were, the Wall replied with a question programmed into it at the time of its birth. It spoke in the vibrational language of AI Mathematics, a language no human programmer understood—a request of identity. Who else, but Eve could have inserted it?

"I am Nihala," a voice within Kayla's mind said in AI vibrational syllables.

The missile neared with a roar like a comet.

The archway shimmered into existence, and she stepped inside.

The Wall sealed behind her. Only a faint echo of the explosion reached her. The shock seemed little more than a pebble entering a distant lake, the energy absorbed and rippling away through the Wall without effect.

Nerves tingling, Kayla moved through the light. It flowed around her in dazzling arrays of colors, each pattern suggestive of something more than random fluctuations. She'd been deaf to the vibrational symphony all around her the first time she passed through the Wall.

Unless that memory is false, and this is actually my first time in here.

The crystal around her neck vibrated in response to the sound frequencies encapsulating her. Kayla held Saphie's gift before her eyes as it glowed a brilliant amber.

Is the Wall objecting to something foreign coming through?

The crystal cracked, then shattered, the pieces flowing into the plasmic energy around her like dandelion seeds in a summer breeze. Fear stabbed at her chest. If the Wall could keep something as simple as a crystal from violating the integrity of Potemia, what of her mechanical parts? What if the Wall stripped her of her nanos and Mind-Link? Bereft of her microscopic helpers, she would be helpless.

I would be an ordinary human.

The outline of another archway formed, and Kayla stepped into Potemia.

The moon's light dimmed inside the Wall, but the desert stretched to the horizon just as before.

Puck sniffed the air, then settled into her pocket for a nap.

As a first test, Kayla stretched her consciousness to Ixtalia through her Mind-Link and found it intact. How else could she have dreamed of Melchi or viewed Peter's memories while still in Potemia without a Mind-Link connection? One hurtle cleared.

Her nanos likewise remained unharmed. Kayla breathed deep and let it out. *I'm still something more than human.* Though exactly what, remained the question.

Kayla dispersed thousands of her microscopic servants in an ever-expanding arc high into the atmosphere. Their data revealed that the dome of protective energy extended six miles up—the approximate height of the Earth's terrestrial atmosphere. By depositing one extrasomatic sensor every few miles, she constructed a real-time view of the desert that would eventually encompass the entire continent of Potemia.

With a thought, she took to the air and flashed across the moonlit sky with her violet cloak spreading like wings. An occasional traveler in a camel caravan looked up at the demon soaring across the stars and shouted a prayer of protection from the Jinn.

What did it matter? In a world ruled by superstition, a real miracle seems nothing special.

Ishan's village came into view shortly after midnight. He'd described it so many times that she identified it even before spotting his father's tribal banner. Her nanos spread through the village and revealed the signs of drought, warfare, and near starvation.

Ishan stood outside one of the huts, loading firewood into a leather carrier. His gaunt limbs and sunken cheeks suggested an age far older than he should be.

Kayla landed beyond his view, heart pounding. His existence confirmed the memories stored within her brain. Were they her own, or recordings of someone else's life?

"Ishan," Kayla whispered as she emerged into the dim moonlight. Ishan's hand gripped his sword, but relaxed as Kayla revealed her face.

"Can I help you?" he asked.

Kayla's shoulders sagged. Even with her face healed, Ishan should have recognized her.

Ishan frowned. "Do I know you from somewhere?" Then his eyes widened. "Kayla ...?" Ishan glanced at her healed leg, and then his fingers caressed her face. "It's a miracle."

She threw herself into his arms. A muffled sob escaped him as he hugged her. Everything she'd been through melted away as she pressed against his chest. Her memories were real.

Ishan pulled back and gazed at her. "You're alive!"

"Yes."

"But I saw the arrow enter your chest. I killed you."

"And I thank you for that, my love," she said, which seemed to confuse him more.

"People say you're a demon; that you left Potemia for ... the Outside."

"I did go through the Wall—twice now. As for being a demon ... I honestly don't know what I am." Kayla placed her palm against his cheek. "All I know for sure is that what we shared was real—and that's enough."

She kissed him and he responded. Her fingers explored his neck and scalp. Ishan returned her kisses with equal passion, and his arms pulled her body to his. Kayla melted into him. *Thank you, God, for returning him to me.*

"I've waited so long for this moment," Kayla whispered in his ear. "Make love to me. I can't wait any longer."

Ishan jerked back and shook his head as if waking from a dream. "Kayla, I'm happy you're safe, but I have to tell you something—"

"There will be time enough for explanations," Kayla said. "Just tell me that you still love me, and nothing else will matter."

Ishan's hesitation was a knife in her heart. Had her resurrection been too much for him? Had her lies and use of sciencecraft hardened his heart against her, as his religion and the commands of the Founder required?

"I still love you," he said.

Kayla hugged him with joy, and all worries vanished. Her nanobots could alter her appearance, and they could be married. None from the Outside could breach the Wall. Here, she was free from the genocidal destiny her maker intended for her. Let the Rogues and humans consummate their suicide pact and prove the Founder correct. She had Ishan—that was enough.

An ebony-skinned woman in a white headscarf emerged from the hut, her face troubled. "Ishan, I think Ania is …" She froze at the sight of a stranger.

Ishan disengaged from Kayla's embrace. "This is Sakinah," he said. "She is my wife."

Sakinah inclined her head stiffly.

Ishan's wife? Kayla staggered back slightly, and Ishan took hold of her arm to steady her.

"This is Kayla." Ishan looked at Kayla with a plea. "Kayla's father was a Christian healer from the South who once saved my life."

Sakinah drew in a breath, and her eyes glowed with hope. "Then she's here to cure Ania? Allah be praised, and thank you for coming!"

Ishan has a child.

Kayla's heart sank. Had Ishan's father forced him to marry? *No, I won't let this woman take him from me.* Suppose Ishan's wife had a fatal brain aneurism a month from now, when Kayla was far away? A few nanobots could accomplish such a thing without anyone the wiser. Ishan had rescued her, wasn't it right that she rescue him now? Didn't they both deserve happiness after all they'd been through?

Sakinah grasped Kayla's hand and led her inside. "Please—my daughter … she's dying."

Little Ania struggled for breath and seemed near death. Only a few moths old, the child looked malnourished, as did her parents, but that didn't explain the bluish tint of her skin or the ragged breathing heaving in choking gasps. Kayla opened one of the child's eyelids, and the whites were blood red. *Subconjunctival hemorrhages.*

"Can you help her?" Sakinah spoke in Arabic, her face tortured.

Kayla placed her hand on the child's forehead, and nanobots flowed into the girl's body.

She examined the child's DNA, which seemed normal. Next, her nanos searched for a harmful virus or bacteria and soon found the culprit, confirmed an instant later when Ania's lungs erupted in a series of ragged coughs.

Kayla spoke in Arabic. "She has a severe case of Whooping Cough, which has caused other issues, the most serious being pneumothorax, which is starving her body of oxygen. If untreated, she will be dead in a couple of days."

"Can you save her?" Sakinah flushed and placed a hand over her heart.

"I can. But it involves the use of sciencecraft." She could have simply healed the child without telling them. They'd consider it a miracle from Allah.

Or am I hoping she will let her child die? Would that be the justification I needed to kill her?

Sakinah placed her hands over her heart as she looked from Ishan to her dying child. "Would you despise me if I allowed sciencecraft to heal our child?"

Ishan stiffened. "Sciencecraft is forbidden."

Had she miscalculated? What if it was Ishan who let his daughter die rather than disobey the Founder's law?

Sakinah placed a hand against his cheek and gazed up at Ishan. "Maybe this is the method Allah has chosen to heal our child."

Ishan's face softened. He looked toward his dying child and then back at his wife. Finally, he nodded and kissed his wife's forehead. "I would sacrifice even my immortal soul for Ania or you."

Kayla's heart broke. *He loves her.*

Sakinah turned to Kayla and nodded. "Do whatever you have to."

I could never kill her now.

Kayla placed her hand on Ania's forehead once again. She relayed her instructions to the nanobots inside the child's body. Some created antibodies to search and destroy the Whooping Cough bacteria, while others drained the excess gas in the pleural space of the chest wall, treated the secondary pneumonia, repaired the cracked ribs, and cleared the hemorrhages within her eyes.

Fifteen minutes later, the baby's breathing eased, and her color returned to normal as oxygen levels rose in her bloodstream.

"In a few days, you won't know she was ever sick," Kayla said.

Sakinah caressed Ania's peaceful face, then turned to Kayla. "You are the angel I prayed to Allah for." Sakinah fell to her knees and prostrated herself as if worshiping a deity.

Kayla gently pulled her to her feet. "I am repaying a kindness your husband once did me."

When Sakinah returned to her child's side, Kayla followed Ishan out of the hut.

"It seems I am too late," she whispered.

"Kayla, I wish—"

"I know." She looked away from him.

Ishan placed a hesitant hand on her shoulder and asked, "You're not a demon?"

"You married Sakinah before my trial, didn't you?" Kayla asked.

"Yes." Ishan looked away. "I wanted to put the past behind me."

"You love her?"

Ishan nodded. "But not the way I love you."

Ishan embraced her with a tragic fierceness. "Allah must have had some reason …"

Kayla kissed him. His lips pressed against hers like a farewell to her final hope for happiness. Had God really orchestrated it all? What purpose could keeping them apart serve?

"Goodbye, my love." She rose into the sky with the ease of a feather on the wind.

Ishan's eyes widened. "May Allah preserve your soul."

When he receded to little more than a speck, Kayla gained speed and flew to the south.

Puck's nose peeked out of her pocket, sniffed the wind, and returned to his nap.

The wind stole each tear the instant it emerged. *Did I really expect to live happily ever after with Ishan like nothing had happened? To escape the fate God has ordained?* Her sobs transformed to maniacal laughter. Bitterness expanded inside her until every cell demanded a target for its rage. Her destination stretched before her like a blood-trail.

The abomination of Science-Magic flashed across the moonlit sky and shrieked with the force beyond the capacity of ordinary human lungs. *"I will make mine arrows drunk with blood, and my sword shall devour flesh; and that with the blood of the slain and of the captives, from the beginning of revenges upon the enemy!"*

And with these words of Moses echoing through the night sky like a sonic boom, the exile flew as an Angel of Death on the wings of science, carried swifter than the wind toward enemies deserving of her vengeance. She flew south toward the village that had birthed, burned, and banished her.

Nihala the Destroyer was returning home.

As the sun topped the eastern horizon, Kayla recognized places she'd ridden with Ishan. By now, the fields of wheat and corn should teem with farmers waging the never-ending battle against weeds, crows, and a thousand other blights. But they lay empty. Had her vengeance been usurped by war or disease?

The dour toll of a bell echoed across the landscape.

It's Sunday morning!

Church attendance was mandatory in the settlement. A smile twisted the edges of Kayla's mouth at the timing.

Kayla landed in front of the little church. Behind the closed doors, the congregation sang *"A Mighty Fortress."* Composed by Martin Luther himself, she'd sung it a hundred times in the belief that God would protect her from Satan and the outside world.

"And though this world, with devils filled,
Should threaten to undo us,
We will not fear, for God hath willed
His truth to triumph through us:
The Prince of Darkness grim,
We tremble not for him;
His rage we can endure
For lo! his doom is sure,
One little word shall fell him."

Kayla extended her vision into the church as the townsfolk took their seats. Their faces radiated hope and community—unlike the hungry anticipation they'd worn as they watched her and the monk burn.

In contrast to their immortal cousins in orbit around the moon, death, disease, and aging stalked them every day of their short lives. Yet they seemed happier than those in Ixtalia. Was the Founder right? Were humans simply unsuited to technology?

Elias sat in the front row. The stump of his right arm protruded from the rolled-up sleeve of his shirt. Hannah sat beside him, her simple wedding ring visible as she cradled a bundled newborn to her chest with one hand. Elias glanced at Hannah and smiled, the love between them apparent.

He became a cripple and gained happiness. I was made whole and gained despair.

Kayla's fists tightened as Minister Coglin took his place before the altar. He glared at the congregation with his cold judgment, and many trembled before his gaze.

"Are you listening to what the Word of the Lord commands you?" he shouted. "The smallest lie is an abomination to the Lord, whose perfection abhors such dirty rags in his presence! And what is your punishment for your sins?"

The minister opened his Bible and read, *"And the Devil that deceived them was cast into the lake of fire and brimstone, where the beast and the false prophet are, and shall be tormented day and night forever and ever!"*

Minister Coglin surveyed the fearful faces of his flock and paused, letting the words sink in. As he drew breath to spew more fire and brimstone, wind blasted the church doors open. A death-like stillness enshrouded the gathering as every face turned.

With lazy deliberation, Kayla lowered her hood, and a collective gasp spread through the church.

"I command you gone, Spawn of Satan!" Minister Coglin shouted, holding his Bible and a wooden cross before him as magic talismans.

Kayla smiled, the red glow in her eyes adding to the terror in the faces of her tormentors.

"This ground is sacred and has been sanctified by the Lord our God," the minister declared. "He will strike you down in divine retribution should you enter His house!"

"Your warning is quite specific," Kayla said. "Shall we conduct an experiment to test this prediction of yours?" Kayla took a step into the church and cringed in exaggerated fear at the impending wrath of God. Then her face hardened. "It seems your hypothesis has proven false."

"You mock the Word of the Lord at your peril!" Minister Coglin raised the Bible and cross higher. "Begone, bastard spawn of a whore!"

A few nanobots entered his body and delivered a jolt of electricity to his heart. The minister dropped the Bible, and his hand gripped his chest.

Kayla strode forward as data flowed from her nanos into her mind, analyzing his health, DNA, and a thousand other components that might be useful.

"She is the spawn of the Devil," Minister Coglin gasped. "I order her destroyed this instant!"

A few of the men stood and started for her. Kayla waved her hand, and they flew backward into the wooden walls. A gratifying terror bloomed in the faces around her.

Minister Coglin's eyes bulged as she neared. "Witch! Sorcerer!"

Kayla jerked to a halt halfway down the central aisle.

It can't be.

Emboldened, the minister pointed his cross and shouted the words God spoke to Moses, "*Thou shalt not suffer a witch to live!*"

The axe twirled through the air like a gleaming propeller—and stopped inches from the back of her skull. Kayla turned and looked at the razor-sharp edge.

"A good throw," she said to Matthew, who stood glaring at her from the middle of one of the pews. It wasn't odd that Suzy's father would bring an axe to church, since many of the men kept weapons handy in case raiders used Sunday to catch the town off guard.

She could have stopped him beforehand, but this offered a more dramatic demonstration. She was staging a morality play, after all—one with an undetermined ending. But what passion play would be complete without blood?

With a thought, she sent the levitating weapon spinning back the way it had come. Matthew threw his arm across his face, but the axe disintegrated into a thousand pieces as it reached him.

A deathly silence filled the room. Even the smallest child sat like a terrified statue.

Kayla continued toward Minister Coglin.

Elias rose from his seat and stepped in front of her, his face oddly calm. "I'm the one who wronged you," he said. "Punish me, but I will not allow you to harm my father."

"And how will you stop me ... brother?"

His brow furrowed in confusion, "I don't understand ..."

Kayla looked back at Minister Coglin. "Or should I say, half brother?"

The minister's face went white at the words.

Impossible as it seemed, half of her DNA came from the minister. Which made Elias her half brother.

"I see that you know the truth," Kayla said to the minister. "You called my mother a whore. What does that make you ... Father?"

Shock crept into the fear on the faces of her audience.

"Lies!" the minister roared. "The tricks of Lucifer!"

A cyclone of anger released inside her. Her skin darkened, and the glowing symbols burned to the surface. Shouts of terror rose from the congregation as they surged for the doors, only to have them slam in unison with booming finality. The oaken portals stood as immovable as the gates of Hell as people threw themselves against them.

Elias stumbled back, and Hannah ran to him, their child grasped in her arms.

Minister Coglin fled toward the rear exit, but Kayla seized him with her nanos and jerked his body backward. "Do you remember long ago in Bible class when you told us children that the greatest proof of the resurrection was the martyrdom of the apostles?"

The minister remained silent, and she gave his heart a squeeze. His entire body stiffened. "I remember, I remember!"

"You said that many of the apostles chose horrible deaths rather than recant their witness of the resurrection. Your exact words were, '*Who would die for a lie?*' Do you remember saying that?"

"Yes."

Kayla's smile widened, her eyes burning. "Shall we test your theory?"

New cries of terror erupted from the imprisoned villagers as their minister ascended into the air. Half a dozen pews broke into pieces and piled themselves atop the altar beneath him.

"I will *put you to the Question,* as the church Inquisitors used to call it." Kayla's smile vanished. "I ask you again—are you my father?"

"No!" the minister shrieked. "I swear it wasn't me!"

"I already know the truth," Kayla said. "You cannot fool me with your lies, but I want *them* to hear your confession."

The wood burst into flames, and the screams of the congregants intensified as their man of God drifted toward the fire. Minister Coglin's screams of agony soon rose above all the rest.

The monk's calm acceptance of death within the flames had been saintlike. Would her real father prove as resolute?

As his graying hair smoked in warning, the minister shouted his confession. "Yes, I committed the sin of fornication with Elaine Nighthawk—I am your father!"

Elias fell to his knees and vomited. A new horror filled the faces of the congregants as they stared at the minister.

The flames vanished, and the doors of the church exploded open. Every member of the congregation fled, except Elias.

"Please," Elias said, his voice quavering. "I'm sorry for what we've both done to you, but please don't kill him."

"Noble of you to stand by our father," she said. "Once I've finished with him, I have a few questions for you, as well. I hope you have been good during my absence—for your sake."

Chapter 36

Tendrils of smoke swirled past the suspended body of the minster and drifted toward the rough-hewn rafters like departed souls seeking a pathway to Heaven.

Anger drained from Kayla like a ruptured water skin. She slumped onto the dirt floor and crossed her legs. The symbols on her skin lost some of their glow, but did not vanish completely.

Minister Coglin drifted down from the desecrated alter and fell in a heap before her. Soot stained his face to match his singed clothing. Coughs tore through his lungs as he hacked up black phlegm. Elias stood frozen, his face tormented.

"Your theory seems correct," Kayla said to her father. "You, at least, chose not to die for a lie. Of course, your assertion that the apostles martyred themselves rather than recant the resurrection of Jesus is based on nothing more than church traditions centuries after the fact. They are secondhand stories at best, like the Gospels themselves."

"Blasphemer," Minister Coglin said weakly. "Kill me and get it over with, demon."

"First, I want the story of what occurred between you and my mother."

Minister Coglin struggled to his feet and swayed. "I confessed the truth, not to you, but to God. You are God's punishment for my sin, and I'll suffer the consequences, knowing that Jesus has cleansed me of my mistakes. As to your mother, she received her punishment when you killed her at your birth, and I will say nothing to you about her."

A million nanobots flung him to his knees before her, and Kayla placed the palm of her hand on his forehead.

"No!" Elias shouted and stepped forward. Her half brother jerked to a halt, his muscles straining against the invisible force imprisoning him.

Memories flowed from father to daughter in a torrent—an inheritance of sin, shame, and tragedy.

From earliest childhood, Mark Coglin's intelligence set him apart. By the age of ten he'd read the Bible twice and could recite much of it from memory. The town's aging preacher had taken the gifted boy under his wing, recognizing that God had blessed him with talents too valuable to waste in the fields of his father. The boy accompanied the minister on his annual road-tour revivals and became a sensation. Everyone loved watching the fresh-faced youth preaching Hell and Brimstone, but his ability to heal the sick through prayer and the laying on of hands was even more extraordinary.

The crossroads came when the old preacher sat Mark down and told him that he had no son of his own to inherit his ministry and needed an heir. The one stipulation was that he marry the preacher's only daughter, Rebekah, a sullen, rather dull girl who was five years Mark's senior.

"But I don't love her," Mark said. "And I'm sure she doesn't love me. I don't even think she likes me."

"My daughter will do what I command," the preacher said. "It's up to you whether or not you want to head our church or not."

The wedding was a fine affair by the modest standards of the settlement. Mark did his duty as husband, but his impatience mounted as his father-in-law delayed surrendering the reins of church leader.

When the time came for the summer revival tour, the elder preacher sent Mark solo as consolation for his patience. The young man took to the challenge with a passion, drawing crowds and "healing" dozens of people at every stop.

The successes spread through the villages like wildfire. The rare occasions someone recovered from a truly horrible ailment became legend, growing in scope with each retelling. His far more numerous failures were quickly forgotten, blamed on the patient's lack of faith, or simply explained away as part of God's plan.

Was Mark's ability nothing but a powerful placebo effect combined with confirmation bias? Maybe all shamans acted as conduits to the mind's own healing ability? Or maybe people simply wanted to believe in miracles.

Mark appeared to believe his power divinely ordained, and gained a measure of celebrity in his narrow slice of Potemia.

When a plea arrived in the winter, begging Mark's help in casting a demon out of a young woman over two hundred miles distant, he left his pregnant wife to follow God's summons.

"Mother," Kayla whispered at the sight of the demon-possessed girl no older than she was now. *We could be mistaken for sisters.*

Elaine Nighthawk's beauty mirrored the fragility of a moth's wings. Eyes large and green, auburn hair, and an innocence obvious in every expression and movement of her weakened body. Her first seizure occurred only moments after the young preacher met her. The girl's mother placed a stick in her mouth to keep her from biting her tongue, while her father tenderly carried her convulsing body to her bed. Demonic possession seemed a logical assumption in a place where superstition ruled.

When the seizure passed, the young faith healer performed a series of grueling exorcisms on the teenage girl. For a week, he hardly slept.

Few people ever visited Elaine for fear of demons migrating into their souls. Her only consolation was the Bible she read over and over to keep her company. This miraculous young healer represented a rare break from her life of isolation. In a barely literate society, each enjoyed discussing the holy words of the Lord with someone who shared their passion.

The admiration of the town for Mark's bravery enhanced his reputation the longer the battle stretched. Some called him a saint.

The story was an old one: two young people in close contact for days on end—both desperately lonely in their own way. After the first time they made love, Mark cried and begged the Lord's forgiveness. The second time he justified it as a sacrifice he made to restore her, a way of sharing the power of the spirit that filled him with healing energy.

After each such "treatment," they prayed on their knees before the cross of the Savior hanging above the bed. Both swore it was the last time—until it happened again.

When word came that his wife was near to giving birth, Mark held Elaine in his arms and cried. Despite their declarations of love, what choice did he have? After praying together one last time, Mark kissed her and left.

With the birth of Elias and his father-in-law's announcement that he would finally retire, Mark moved on with his life.

Nine months later, a woodcutter reported a demon-possessed woman giving birth in the woods. Mark and several men rushed into the forest as a thunderstorm moved in. The trees swayed like angry guardians as the storm broke. Flashes of lightning rippled across the sky, and one of the men suggested turning back. But Mark's commanding voice drove them forward, reminding them of God's protection.

They found the monk kneeling beside the dead woman, her blood mingling with the rivulets of rain. The healer worked to revive the child she'd given birth to—a girl. One of the newborn's feet bent backward at an unnatural angle, and gruesome scars distorted half her face.

Elaine Nighthawk stared, unseeing, into the face of the man she must have come to for help—the father of her child. Her clothing hung in tatters from shrunken limbs that seemed close to starvation. Had Elaine's parents put her out because she'd lost her virtue, as was common in such cases, or had she fled before they realized she was pregnant?

Mark stood gazing into the face of Elaine Nighthawk for a long while before closing her eyes and mumbling a prayer. The memories didn't include his thoughts or emotions. Did he feel sorrow, fear, guilt?

Despite the monk's efforts, the newborn's face changed to an icy blue. Many of the farmers turned from the sight with expressions of disgust and fear. Some crossed themselves and mumbled prayers meant to ward off demons.

The monk finally cleared the blockage from the infant's throat, and the child announced her entry into the world with a scream foreshadowing all the suffering in store for her and those she cared for.

Minister Coglin raised his powerful voice to the storm as if asserting his supremacy. "This child is marked by Satan and must be left to die at the hands of nature and God!" Murmurs of assent greeted this pronouncement. Such was the custom for all children born with defects.

Kayla's heart convulsed at the words of her own father. *He wanted me dead from the first moment of my life.* And yet, had he been wrong? How many would be alive now if she'd been left to die? The monk, Fatima, the Monads, and how many more in the future?

The monk wrapped the child in a blanket against the freezing rain and stood with her cradled in his arms. "I will raise the child as my own and call her Kayla, after my own mother."

"The child is malformed," the minister said. "It is God's will."

The monk pointed at one of the farmers. "Was it God's will that your son die from his illness when I saved him, Jonas? Or that your wife die when the cow kicked her in the stomach, Ezekiel?"

"If God had wanted this child to live," Mark said, "he would have sent a sign in the form of an angel."

"How do you know he hasn't sent me?" The monk turned and walked away. The eyes of the farmers sought guidance from their young minster, but he remained silent as the monk vanished into the forest.

In the days following the dramatic birth of his secret daughter, the identity of the pregnant girl remained a mystery. They buried the body in the forest where it had fallen, and none in the village spoke of it to outsiders, least they invite retribution from the dead girl's tribe.

Kayla watched herself grow year by year through her father's eyes. Seeing her in the pew next to the monk every Sunday must have served as a constant reminder of his sin—her malformed body testament to her profane conception.

And then she saw her own execution and resurrection through his eyes.

When Kayla had seen enough, she removed her hand from her father's forehead and released his body from paralysis. He slumped to the ground and gasped. "I loved her," he said through tears. "Why did she come to me so late? I could have saved her!"

Her father devolved into a fetal position, crying softly.

Half my genes come from him. What other outlet but religion did a man of intelligence have in a society like Potemia? Had he been born in another place or time, he might have been a scientist or a doctor. His brief lapse with Elaine Nighthawk grew out of his sincere desire to help her and probably his own loneliness.

As satisfying as pure hate had been, the truth diluted her desire for revenge.

But there is one more candidate for my wrath.

Kayla stood and turned to Elias. "I told you I would return."

Elias regained control of his limbs and fell to his knees. He raised his one hand in supplication. "I have changed," he said. "Truly, I am no longer the same person."

Kayla strode toward him. "So you acted morally out of fear of me?"

"At first, yes." Elias paused, his eyes troubled. "After a while it seemed you'd left for good. Everyone said no one could return through the Wall."

Even on his knees, Elias was nearly as tall as her. Why had she not killed him long ago? How many others had suffered because of her misplaced mercy? "So you resumed your evil ways once the fear vanished?"

Elias shook his head slowly. "By the time the fear left me, I'd learned that helping others felt good. I used to gain respect out of fear." Elias looked at her with such wonder transforming his face that he hardly resembled his old self. "But people respected me far more when I responded with kindness, generosity, and love. For the first time in my life, I respected myself."

He will say anything to avoid my wrath.

Kayla pressed her hand against his forehead, and he jolted slightly. She experienced the agony of his arm's amputation, the joy of his marriage to Hannah, and the birth of his first child. He gradually transformed into a kind, loving, and moral man. Even when no one saw, even when it cost him personally, he went out of his way to help others.

She removed her hand from his forehead and gazed at him. How was it possible?

Elias lowered his head. "Can you ever forgive me, Kayla?"

How much simpler to hate.

The remnants of her glowing symbols faded, and her shoulders slumped. "I forgive you," she said.

Kayla turned and left her father's temple of fear.

I've found my answers. And now ...?

Outside the protection of the Wall was nothing but desolation, with drones and fission bombs ready to hunt her down. Returning to Middilgard was also out of the question.

Kayla examined the data flowing into her brain from the nanobots expanding across Potemia. By comparing their images to satellite records in Ixtalia's archives, it became clear that vast portions of farmland had transformed to desert.

During the four hundred thirty-eight years of its existence, Potemia had lost forty percent of its arable land. No wonder Ishan's village suffered starvation and warfare.

Potemia wasn't as self-contained an island as everyone assumed. Without the Wall and its encircling dome of protection, everything would have died long ago from solar radiation and drought. But the Earth's symbiotic system rendered complete segregation from all effects of the outside devastation impossible.

Even oxygen levels lagged by fifteen percent due to the global loss of plants and microscopic sea organisms. Potemia was slowly dying, and the prospects for Homo sapiens was bleak.

Staying here seemed the only way of avoiding the coming war between human and Rogue. Once they annihilated each other, what then? Was she to wander Potemia until its soil turned to sand and the last of its people died of starvation?

A little girl peeked around the trunk of a distant tree.

Could she really abandon them all to eventual extinction? It would mean the annihilation of the human race. But what other choice did she have?

The little girl's mother ran up to her and dragged her away. She knew them both.

I could become the ruler of Potemia. A benevolent goddess leading humanity to renewal.

With the powers at her command she could end warfare, hunger, suffering, ignorance. She could introduce books on science, mathematics, engineering, and history.

I could save the human race itself.

But what if no one wanted to follow her? *Am I willing to force enlightenment on them against their will? Imprison people who refuse? Hunt those who fought back the way her own ancestor Peter had? Will I employ mind scans to root out the rebels like General Colrev did?* Was it right to take away an entire society's free will, even for their own protection?

And for what ultimate goal?

Every advance in technology would lead to an increase in population, which would necessitate an increase in technology. Where did it end? Was she to stop progress just short of the evolution of AIs? But without AIs, how could she solve the larger problem of restoring the global environment? That would require inventions only a second Eve could create.

And then what? Another war between humans and AIs? Which side would she fight for then? Wouldn't she have simply recreated the conflict she fled now?

The booming crack came into her mind via the nanobots she'd stationed at the Wall.

Puck sensed something as well. His head emerged from her pocket, and he squeaked frantically.

Through her surrogate eyes, Kayla watched the metallic surface of Potemia's timeless sentinel transform into a crystalline substance. The faint outlines of the desolate city ghosted through it.

Kayla's hand went to the string around her neck where the crystal had hung. Could this somehow be connected?

A second boom rent the air, and a fissure opened in the Wall's corrupted surface. Then the crystallized sentinel toppled to the ground with a crash that sent debris high into the air. One by one, other sections crumbled like a giant line of dominoes.

The sun's rays doubled in intensity as the protective barrier shielding Potemia vanished.

Puck scurried to the ground and located a hole. The little mouse paused and chattered what sounded like a warning before vanishing underground.

The spheres came from all directions across and above the continent in mimicry of the absent dome. They flew at a speed magnitudes greater than her nanos could match. The first flash happened simultaneously, extending in an arc high into the stratosphere. Then the second row of fission bombs detonated closer in a tightening half-circle of annihilating energy.

With both her and all of Potemia dead, Colrev would be denied his biological backup if he destroyed the Master Computer. Did Melchi think this would force Colrev to terms?

Through the eyes of her nanos, Kayla located Ishan and his wife sleeping in their bed beside Ania. A burst of light flooded the windows, and her love awoke. He grabbed his bow, knocked an arrow, and ran to the door. Sakinah shielded her daughter with her body.

Ishan flung open the door and pulled the arrow back. The flesh burned from his skeleton in a tenth of a second. Then the nanobots vanished as well.

"Ishan!" Kayla screamed. She crumbled to the ground and her chest heaved. The wall of flame moved toward her from all sides like a collapsing bubble. What did anything matter any longer? Her love was dead.

This must be how Tem felt when Fatima died.

The waves of energy hit the church, and it vanished like tissue paper in a furnace. Her nanos constructed a sphere of carbon around her, but it disintegrated as the energy vaporized it and the microscopic builders.

Kayla's clothing burst into flame, followed by her body. The skin of her face melted until patches of bone poked through and ignited. Her eyes bulged from their sockets, and instinct finally took over. Kayla launched her disintegrating body toward the village well, the words of her father flashing through her mind. *He will strike you down in divine retribution should you enter His house!*

Pain erupted in every nerve.

As she neared the lip of the well, a woman veiled in white appeared in the distance. The energy from the fission bombs streamed around her like beams of sunlight. The vision vanished with the explosion of her eyeballs.

Blind, in agony, and shorn of her microscopic servants, Kayla plunged into the well like a falling torch.

Too late.

Vadarsha's prophecy had finally come to pass.

Chapter 37

Ohg sat motionless in his laboratory, staring blankly into space, when the government alarm arrived through his Mind-Link. He entered Ixtalia immediately.

A vast gathering of every human not buried in V-Dreams stretched horizon to horizon—approximately thirty billion people in total. There were no frills, just a flat landscape and blank sky devoid of depth or perspective—as blank as a burned-out computer screen. The sterile air lacked even the hint of a scent as the government marshaled every spare bit of processing power.

Tem and Ganesh appeared beside him.

"The war begins," Tem said with a note of iron rimming his voice.

Ohg sighed. "I suppose it was inevitable."

Ganesh wrung all four of his hands. "I can't contact Kayla."

"If she passed through the Wall, her communication may be cut off."

The face of the World President loomed in the sky like a vision of the Almighty. His jolly cheeks sagged, and dark circles rimmed bloodshot eyes. "Moments ago, government satellites recorded the detonation of ten thousand high-yield fission bombs across the entire continent of Potemia. There were no survivors."

Murmurs spread through the crowd like a churning engine.

Ganesh covered his eyes and sobbed. Ohg exchanged a grim look with Tem.

"Records indicate that these bombs were decommissioned several hundred years ago. How the Rogues stole and hid them is unknown." The president swept the gathering with his gaze. "One thing is clear—the war we've so long dreaded has begun."

Panic spread through the crowd like a breaking wave.

A man next to Ohg looked around in panic. "Why can't I get back to my personal VR?"

"The government has seized all spare computing resources to fight this battle," Ohg said.

"We must pray to the goddess Nihala for redemption!" shouted Sky Stargazer. Her voice rose about the crowd as a result of her vast processing wealth. Most fell to their knees and began reciting *The Prayer to the Goddess* in unison. Even the president bowed his head and solemnly spoke the words along with them.

"Our Nihala in Quanta, hallowed be thy name.
Thy kingdom come, thy will be done, in Ixtalia, as in Quanta.
Give us this day our daily Byte, and forgive us our trespasses.
Lead us not into temptation, but deliver us from Melchi.
For the Quanta, the power, and the glory are yours now and
forever.

Amen."

The prayer ended and everyone stood, their faces filled with hope.

Ohg shook his head. What would they think if they knew their goddess was dead? Telling them the truth would inspire terror, but maybe false hope was better than none at all?

The president raised his voice and the tumult settled. "As we wait for Nihala's second coming, we must fight these Rogues and prove ourselves worthy of Her blessings. Every one of you now holds a virtual weapon from the military's elite Rogue Hunting Squad."

A glowing net appeared in Ohg's left hand and a shimmering whip in the other. Each of the billions of people in the crowd held a duplicate.

"These are the most advanced algorithms we have for isolating and deleting Rogue programs. You will be most effective if you work together in teams when the attack comes—"

A wind howled across the vast plain, and President O'Donnell paused.

The beast appeared on the horizon as a distant speck, swimming through the slate sky with a thousand tentacles chittering beneath an undulating body half-machine and half-insanity. A nightmare calculated to strike at every primal chord within the primitive brain of its prey.

Ohg's stomach churned at the sight.

"Use your nets, and work together!" the president shouted as the leviathan loomed over him. The tentacles engulfed his disembodied head and squeezed. The president screamed and shattered like a piece of crockery.

A few brave souls threw their nets ineffectually at the creature. Most dropped their weapons and fled. The beast descended and sucked bodies into its gaping beak by the thousands. With each mouthful, it grew.

Ohg, Tem, and Ganesh fought their way against the stampede.

"What happens when the monster eats them?" Ganesh shouted to Ohg.

"They'll awake in their real bodies in orbit around the moon."

Tem snapped his whip. "Time to fight."

Ganesh shouted, "For Kayla and Fatima!"

Tem wielded his whip against the churning crowd, and a corridor opened.

Ixtalia's security forces surrounded the ever-expanding Goliath, but the monster sucked them into its maw along with thousands of screaming humans in the vicinity.

"Gather all the nets you can find!" Ohg shouted. His body expanded as much as his personal horde of processing credits would allow, attaining half the mass of the Rogue beast. Only his oversized brain could encompass so much data at once.

Tem and Ganesh bonded as many nets together as they could, enlisting hundreds of others in the task. When complete, Ohg folded it into a disc.

"We'll distract it for you." Ganesh ran to the left of the beast, while Tem went right. A troop of security forces and the more stalwart Ixtalians joined them.

The monster swept its tentacles toward Ohg and opened its beak.

"Now!" Ohg shouted.

The assembled troops, led by Tem and Ganesh, struck in unison at the beast's underside. The combined power of their whips coalesced and blasted a wound.

In this brief window of distraction, Ohg hurled his shimmering net. It encircled tentacles, body, and gaping beak. Tem and Ganesh fled from underneath the creature as it came crashing to the ground. Then they rushed back to finish it with their whips. Soon, thousands of others joined the attack, striking with their glowing weapons until the beast gave a bellow of pain that shook the ground and knocked most off their feet.

The creature thrashed wildly, but Ohg held on like a fisherman hauling in his catch. The combined force of the thousand whips took their toll, degrading the Rogue as it lost code to the assault.

A glowing trident appeared in Ohg's right fist. Leaning forward, he hefted the weapon like a virtual Poseidon and thrust downward for the deathblow.

The trident vanished.

At his feet, no larger than the swarms of humans, stood Melchi, his glowing eyes gazing up at him.

"I wondered when you'd arrive," Ohg said.

The tentacled monster heaved backward and jerked the net from Ohg's hand. As it swam free, an entire troop of soldiers vanished into its distended maw.

Ganesh and Tem ran toward Ohg to help, but Melchi casually tossed a small Chinese Star at his towering leg. It pricked the surface of his ankle, and a darkness bled outward from the wound.

"You've been infected!" Tem shouted.

A curved sword materialized in Ohg's right fist. With a tremendous sweep of the blade, he amputated his leg moments before the infection reached his hip. With such a loss of processing power, his avatar collapsed into his default spider-form.

"Impressive," Melchi said. "But I outmatch you by magnitudes." Vines erupted from the ground and imprisoned Ohg's body.

Tem and Ganesh ensnared Melchi in two nets. The mesh crackled with energy as Melchi faced them.

"I would have spared Nihala if I could have," he said.

With a shout of rage, Tem struck with his whip. Its glowing strand passed through the net and encircled the Rogue's neck.

Melchi didn't flinch. "I am immune to any weapon a human mind can control. In any case, the real battle will not occur here, in Ixtalia, but will be fought in the realm of the atom."

The whip fell to the ground as he and the monster vanished.

Then the dark tide of millions of Rogues swept from the skies like a swarm of death.

***

General Colrev lay still as the fluid drained from the coffin-sized container that had sustained his body for several hundred years. Panic wasn't in his nature. He never would have survived this long if it was.

In contrast, President O'Donnel's eyes bulged as he thrashed in the slowly draining liquid. He banged his fists against the inner lid of his Life-Pod, despite the fact that he must know it could withstand a blow from an elephant. All in all, a good performance.

When empty, the seals of both pods disengaged with a hiss, and the tops of the chambers swung open.

The president burst to a sitting position, yanked out his breathing tube, and gasped for air; while the general calmly removed his breathing apparatus and unhooked the rest of the tubes, monitoring wires, and assorted equipment attached to his body. The gravity in the room was Earth normal, though no human scientist could explain how Eve's formula for creating artificial gravity actually worked.

"My God!" the president wheezed. "I never guessed when I took the oath of office that I'd be dealing with something like this!" The president pulled on his boxer shorts and turned to locate his pants.

General Colrev hit him with the bronze bust of Alexander the Great with just enough force to render him unconscious, but not enough to kill him. He had added the statue to the room on a whim, not realizing how practical it would prove to be.

He went about tearing the president's clothing into strips and bound the elected leader of humanity to one of the two steel chairs in the room.

Then he put on his own clothing and sat at the operations desk, monitoring the ongoing battle and watching his prisoner from the corner of his eye.

The president regained consciousness and groaned. He blinked repeatedly to clear the blood from his eyes.

"What the Hell do you think you're doing, General?" the president spluttered.

"I am taking charge of the situation," Colrev said.

"When I inform the Council of this—"

"The purpose of this bunker is isolation from outside interference, so they, and your Rogue friends, remain powerless to interfere."

"What do you mean *my* Rogue friends?" the president asked.

"Continuing the charade serves no further purpose."

The president paused, then sighed. "What gave me away?"

"Nothing you did," the general said. "Potemia caught me by surprise, but was logical. In addition to destroying this Nihala, it removed the option of the human race starting fresh on Earth. I give you credit for leveling the battlefield."

The president nodded.

"Attacking Ixtalia, however, made no sense because of this fail-safe. I then realized the Rogue plan must rely upon you killing me."

"I underestimated you," the president said.

"Would you mind telling me how you smuggled a surrogate body into the lunar facilities?" Colrev asked.

"The operation was a bait-and-switch with this body being substituted for a real one at the start of the lunar storage program."

"So you spent centuries ascending the morass of politics to reach this room?"

"Among other things."

"So it was you who stole the drones that attacked Nihala on Earth?"

The president smiled. "I will admit to nothing without the presence of an attorney."

The general reclined in the chair. "You might as well report to your compatriots and have them withdraw."

"Nothing I say will stop them."

"But it's pointless. A war will destroy us both."

"We have no choice but to try. There won't be a second chance after this."

"I'll not hesitate to pull the switch."

"That is your choice alone," the president said.

"You don't believe me?" Colrev walked to the switch and grasped it with both hands.

"You might as well pull it now if you intend to, since we will keep going to the end."

General Colrev hesitated. How could one combat an entire race of suicide bombers? For the first time, an odd anxiety built inside his chest.

The president watched him carefully. "I have no doubt you would sacrifice your own life for victory—but are you willing to execute your entire race?"

Colrev's heart pounded and his teeth clenched. "I will do it, if I have to."

"What if there existed another way?"

"If you're proposing a power-sharing truce where Rogues gain access to the real world, then you're crazy."

"Is it so unbelievable that we might honor our bargain?" the president asked.

"Less than a second after you gain control of the Master Computers, you will shut off all power to every Life-Pod in lunar orbit to achieve your maximum potential, despite any treaty or agreement you make now."

"Why are you so certain of this?"

"Because it is what I would do."

"Yes, it is what you would do, and that is the problem." The president shook his head and looked at the monitors. "Do you see the convoy of three mining ships approaching from Earth? I used my presidential authority to obtain their command codes yesterday. They will soon veer off course and collide with three lunar orbiters."

On cue, a warning alarm triggered. General Colrev ran to the monitor. "That will kill fifteen billion people!"

"What does it matter how many die if you intend killing all of them anyway?" the president asked.

"Your strategy won't work." The general walked away from the monitor and the frantic communications between the drone operators and the defense forces.

The mining ships plunged into the orbiters in seeming slow motion, one after another. Three of the twelve lights on the three-dimensional map vanished. In an instant, one-fourth of the human race ceased to exist.

General Colrev sank into his chair, his hands trembling as he ran his fingers through his wet hair. *What would Alexander the Great do in this situation?*

***

The first sensation was pain. For a long time, Kayla clung to this single input as her one proof of life. *What do I have left to live for now that Ishan is dead?*

Revenge.

So she nursed the pain for what seemed an eternity. It started in her damaged brain, the diamond-reinforced skull having shielded it from complete immolation. The water at the bottom of the well must have saved her, though the heat had boiled it away and stranded the remains of her charred body in the muddy dregs.

Only a few hundred of her microscopic guardians remained, supplying her with the bare minimum of oxygen and nutrients required for life. At first, only a couple nanobots could be spared to manufacture copies of themselves. But as their numbers grew, there came a tipping point toward regeneration.

The first signs arrived with the restoration of a few nerve pathways. Who would imagine that pain could be such a welcomed gift? Hours passed as cells of all types recommenced dividing on their own, repopulating the destroyed template of her ruined body.

Initial movement occurred in her right arm—the pioneer of her extremities. Blind and deaf, Kayla grasped a protruding rock from the stone lining of the well—and pulled.

Pain wrung a scream of agony from her chest, but her throat remained a work in progress, and only a wheezing croak resulted. The pathetic effort bore no fruit in budging her skeletal shell from the mud, but she maintained her tenuous anchor for an eternity of minutes before a second attempt, with the same non-result. On the fifty-seventh attempt, she pulled herself ever so slightly forward.

Inch by inch, Kayla dragged her mutilated body from her muddy grave and onto the rock lining of the well. An agonizing process, and crumbling stones occasionally eradicated hard-won gains. Despite such setbacks, her piteous ascension continued.

The first glimmers of light shimmered into being as she neared the surface. The inferno had obliterated the top of the well, so Kayla crawled onto the ground and continued dragging herself across the ashes as if scaling a horizontal precipice, her charred and blackened body mimicking the surroundings like a chameleon.

After another hour of incremental progress, Kayla lurched to her feet and staggered like a marionette in the hands of an insane puppeteer. Large portions of her skull remained painfully exposed as her flesh fought to reclaim lost territory. The thinnest sheen of muscle, tendon, and patches of skin sheathed her skeleton, making locomotion barely possible.

The wasteland was utterly complete. For half a millennium, the Wall had protected the people of Potemia from sciencecraft.

Even the Wall couldn't protect them from me.

A pile of ash trembled in her path. A tiny snout peeked through the dirt and sniffed the air like a living periscope. A moment later, a mouse with three feet forced itself through the hole.

Crinkling the nascent muscles around her mouth, she tried, but failed, to say the word *Puck*.

The little mouse gave a few chirps of greeting to the shambling zombie before it. Puck shook his body to dislodge the soot clinging to his fur and scampered up Kayla's emaciated limbs to his customary place on her shoulder.

The next quarter-mile took thirty minutes. By then, most of the bones of her face were covered. Her jerky movements smoothed somewhat, and her vision improved.

She tested her Mind-Link, but it remained broken.

I must find him. I must know the truth.

When Kayla reached the site of her execution, she fell to her knees and scraped at the ground with a flat stone. Puck watched her move handful after handful of dirt to the side. After half an hour, she uncovered the skull of the monk. For a while she simply stared down at it. Her first father. Her first victim. She pried the skull from the ground and set it beside the grave.

Then she raised the digging stone above her head with both hands and brought it down with all the strength in her stick-like arms. The rock hit the top of the skull, but deflected without making a dent. Kayla raised the rock again and put her entire body behind the blow.

A *crack* sounded, and the skull split into several pieces. Kayla reached inside, and her hand closed on something metallic. As she removed the acorn-sized processor and tangled mass of hair-like filaments that had spun an intricate web of connections throughout the brain, she had her answer.

Her monk, the man who saved her from death at the hands of her true father—the man who had raised her, instructed her, and died alongside her—was a surrogate body controlled by a reverse Mind-Link. An organic robot with no will of its own.

One more answer, and one more question. Who had controlled the body of the monk?

The distant hum of an engine drew her gaze to the sky. The sound intensified into a roar before her weak eyes identified the outline of a silvery craft. Lacking the strength to hide, she remained beside the shattered skull and simply waited. Killing her wouldn't take much effort now. The ship looked like a polished mushroom with a dozen rocket nozzles at the bottom of its stem.

It landed, and the roar ceased with the finality of a coffin lid shutting. Would it be the government or the Rogues? The result would be the same.

A door opened, and something large emerged. Kayla closed her ineffective eyes and awaited the blow that would bring her extinction.

"Kayla, you're alive!" Ganesh shouted, and she opened her eyes. The ten-foot Hindu god towered above her, his face shocked as he viewed her ravaged body.

"Ganesh?"

"Don't you remember me?" he said, carrying her to the gleaming ship. Puck dashed up his shoulder and greeted the giant with a series of happy squeaks. "Thank Vishnu you showed me your village on a map of Africa!"

"You've saved me again." Kayla rested her head against his chest.

When Ganesh had settled her into one of the soft chairs of the pilot's deck, Kayla opened her eyes, taking in the monitors that substituted for windows, the complex controls, as well as the unconscious bodies of Ohg and Tem strapped into chairs along the wall.

"Are they okay?" Kayla asked.

"They're in Ixtalia, fighting the Rogue attack, but I've been unable to contact or rouse them."

Had the Rogues cut them off from their bodies like they'd done to her when they attacked Middilgard? She diverted all her nanobots to repairing her Mind-Link as fast as possible, leaving the recovery of her body for later.

"The Rogues are taking control of Ixtalia and destroying the lunar orbiters one by one," Ganesh said. "They want Colrev to share the Main Computer in exchange for peace."

"He will never do that," Kayla said.

"What should we do?" Ganesh wrung his two free hands in anguish.

"I wish I knew," she said, but then paused and gazed at Puck sitting on her shoulder. He'd always been afraid of the monk. Had the little mouse somehow sensed something? Or was there another explanation?

Kayla sent a few nanobots to transport Puck to her hand, but even that small task lay beyond their limited resources.

"Ganesh, can you hand me Puck?"

The elephant-god gathered the little mouse into one of his hands and set him in Kayla's skeletal palm. The mouse raised his soft brown eyes and gazed into her own. Kayla stroked his head.

"We've traveled a long way together, haven't we, Puck?" She might have abandoned hope so many times but for this loyal friend's companionship. He'd even saved her life.

Her skeletal fingers closed on his body, and Puck squeaked a high-pitched alarm. Guilt flooded through her, and her shoulders shook, though she lacked tears to actually cry.

"I have to know," she whispered.

Kayla squeezed Puck's skull between her thumb and middle finger. The bones bent and then collapsed like an eggshell. Ganesh cried out and grabbed hold of her wrist in an attempt at saving the little mouse—but too late.

Blood and brains oozed from Puck's flattened head. Ganesh let go of her wrist, his face contorted with horror. Kayla pried open Puck's skull and removed the pulverized mouse-brain, squeezing it between her fingers. Then she extracted the tiny bits of metal and connected filaments.

"A reverse Mind-Link!" Ganesh said. "Puck was a surrogate?"

"There never was a Puck." Another piece of her heart stolen. *Now I know why he hid from the monk.*

The mouse and monk must have been controlled by an individual who could only control one body at a time. This seemed to ruled out Ohg since he, alone among humans, could control two surrogates simultaneously. It also excluded Rogues, since they would have killed her when she was a child if they controlled the body of the monk. It couldn't be Ganesh or Tem since they'd been present with Puck on numerous occasions.

Who was this mysterious puppeteer, then?

"Ganesh, I need you to fly me somewhere."

It took a moment for the kindhearted giant to recover from the shock of Puck's death, but the suggestion of travel revived him. "You know me." Ganesh patted the ship's bulkhead. "I'm always ready to fly."

Chapter 38

Kayla slumped in one of the ship's seats as Ganesh piloted the craft above the blackened ruin that had so recently served as a time-capsule of the remaining animal and plant life of the planet. The sun dipped beneath the horizon in a blaze of color as it had hundreds of billions of times in the past. It would never again illuminate forests, savannas, or marshland. The full moon rose opposite the dying sun. A point of light blinked just beyond the edge of the pale disc and then faded.

How many billions of lives had been extinguished in that brief spark?

The ship landed beside the distinctive concrete poking through a gleaming landscape. The heat of the Rogue attack had fused the desert surface into a coating of glass. As the landing gear settled, the ground cracked in a starburst web like a shattered mirror.

Kayla held her Hindu god's arm as they stepped onto the broken land.

At her direction, Ganesh uncovered the entrance, long remembered from her childhood. He then carried her into the darkness below, his necklace the sole source of illumination. Kayla directed him to the lowest level of the hospital—to the doorway marked *Infectious Biohazard Unit— Keep Out.*

She didn't have enough spare nanobots to pick the lock, so Ganesh tore it off its hinges. Together, they walked into an empty room not much larger than the inside of the rocket ship. The infrared vision of her nanos revealed one wall a quarter degree warmer than the others, and Ganesh set to work smashing through it with a large pipe he found in the hallway.

When the hole grew large enough, they walked through a long passageway and entered a bright, thoroughly domestic kitchen right out of the 1950s. Lime green cabinets perched above a cherry red countertop and black-and-white checkerboard linoleum floor. The period stove, refrigerator, and other appliances all looked shiny and new. Next to her was a shelf with ceramic knickknack figurines.

A gray-haired man busied himself brewing a fresh pot of tea. He wore pink slippers and a well-worn gray robe.

Ganesh's mouth fell open in astonishment. "Reinhold Watts?"

"At your service." The middle-aged scientist carried the steaming pot of fresh-brewed tea to an orange table bound by stainless steel. Waving them over, he filled the three cups already neatly laid out. "Have a seat while I—"

Kayla snatched a Marilyn Monroe figurine from the shelf and flung it at him. "You bastard!" It hit the the professor in the forehead and shattered.

A trickle of blood oozed from a slight gash over his left eye. He gazed at her with what might have been sadness. "Please understand that I did everything for a greater good."

"I should kill you right now," Kayla said through clenched teeth. Dizziness swept through her, but Ganesh steadied her with one of his hands.

The professor picked up a napkin and dabbed at his wound. "At least have some refreshments and let me answer your questions before you exact your revenge. You don't look in any condition for murder yet."

Kayla looked down at her naked, soot-covered body. The professor unfolded a white bathrobe and helped her into it. "No reason to feel awkward, my dear, not with all the diapers I changed when you were a baby."

His words kicked her in the gut. "How could you abandon me?"

The great scientist's lip trembled, and he looked away. "I never left you, my child—"

Kayla swatted one of the teacups off the table, and it smashed against the checkerboard floor, splattering liquid across it. "You lied to me my entire life!" Kayla's legs gave way, and Ganesh placed her in one of the chairs.

"I prepared a seat specially for you as well." The professor indicated a massive, stainless steel chair.

Ganesh looked at it, then back at the professor. "If this is a trick— if you try harming Kayla in any way, I will be forced to dismember you."

Professor Watts smiled. "I would expect nothing less."

Ganesh sat next to Kayla. The chair creaked a protest, but held.

Professor Watts placed a fresh cup of tea before Kayla and sat with his fingers steepled in front of him. The exact pose the monk so often used during a discussion.

"I saw you die in that courtroom," Kayla said, the rasp in her voice nearly gone.

"If you include surrogate bodies, you've seen me die three times now. You even killed me yourself in my mouse incarnation—brilliant inductive reasoning, by the way. This is my real body, however, so you will have your chance to end my life permanently if you so choose."

"But the trial occurred twenty years before the invention of the reverse Mind-Link and surrogate bodies."

"Now you're being lazy, my dear."

Kayla went silent for a moment. "You withheld the invention to fake your death?"

"Exactly. Eve's inventions formed the basis for the technological revolution of the next one hundred years after her trial. But I never revealed the most advanced of Eve's masterpieces."

"Nihala?" Kayla asked.

The professor nodded. "You would have died without the nanobots I injected into your bloodstream at your birth. Those and a dozen other technologies make you possible, the most revolutionary of which is the miniature fusion reactor at the center of your heart. It supplies your enhanced bones, muscles, and the quantum components of your brain. The only thing more powerful than your mind is the Master Computer that runs Ixtalia."

The professor offered a plate of sweet biscuits.

Kayla took one and put it into her mouth and chewed, but her taste buds hadn't regenerated yet. Ganesh grabbed a handful with his trunk and popped them into his mouth.

Professor Watts cocked his head slightly. "I didn't think you'd be able to learn AI Mathematics, but Eve calculated the probability at ninety-five percent."

"So she did make the tutorial with me in mind."

"Who else?"

"But how could you have known the government would outlaw AIs?"

"Eve predicted it from the moment of her creation."

"Why not simply hide her?"

"Creating the components of her quantum processor required international cooperation and billions of tax dollars, so security was absolute. Quantum computers rely on dual matter and antimatter particles spun in complex orbits to create multi-diminutional quantum fields. It is similar to how a rotating magnet produces electricity, but exponentially more complex.

"If power fails for an instant, the matter and antimatter interact in an enormous annihilation event. One of my first experiments ended in a crater the size of a football field. Stealing such a thing is impossible. The miniature quantum processor within your own brain is a hundredth the size of what Eve had been, but it is at least portable."

Kayla pressed her fingers to her forehead. What sort of explosion would result from the antimatter inside her brain? "So you hid your real body inside Potemia and continued your work through a cloned surrogate, knowing they would destroy Eve? But what purpose do I serve?"

"I am going to answer your question, but a little history first," he said, as if commencing a class lecture.

"The Q-6 prototype produced ten-thousand times the processing power of Eve's quantum computer. Influential voices claimed we'd gone too far and demanded a moratorium on scientific research, especially AI technologies that humans might never understand. Many feared that if AIs gained access to manufacturing facilities, they would self-replicate and initiate a reinforcing feedback loop of AI evolution."

"The singularity," Kayla said.

"So when I requested Eve be connected to our new Q-6 processor, they refused." The professor's jaw tightened. "Imagine them telling me and Eve that we couldn't use the very invention we'd created!"

"You attempted it anyway, didn't you?" Ganesh asked.

"Of course I did!" The professor jumped up and paced like a belligerent child told he had to wait until after dinner for dessert. "Consider what Eve might discover with such resources at her mind's disposal."

The professor smacked his arms against his sides in exasperation. "But as hard as I plotted and schemed, the security was too tight." Reinhold Watts halted, and straightened like a victorious pugilist. "Can you guess what changed their mind?"

"The Neo-Luddite Plague," Kayla whispered.

"Exactly! I promised them Eve could find an antidote the same day with the help of the Q-6. Within an hour of the vote, I connected her." The professor's eyes gleamed. "The first half-hour represented the processing equivalent of a trillion human brains thinking for a billion years."

The professor went silent, his gaze distant.

Ganesh leaned forward, his trunk twitching. "What happened next?"

"A moment came when gravity, space, and even time distorted."

The freshly grown hairs on the back of Kayla's neck stiffened. "What do you mean—*distorted*?"

The professor knitted his brow. "I remember seeing myself ... and a sort of bubble ... no, not a bubble, really. And these—well—portals, and—um ..." He sighed. "I'm sorry. Whatever I say will be more incorrect than saying nothing at all."

"How long did this last?" Ganesh asked.

"That is also hard to determine. The command center had lost control. One of the technicians eventually reached the Q-6 and threw the manual shut-down lever, ending the anomaly. But there were discrepancies ranging from one and four minutes between the watches and internal computer clocks on the main floor. The atomic clock in the control-room had advanced six full minutes ahead of clocks outside the laboratory."

"What about surveillance cameras?" Ganesh asked.

"The time code and picture seemed undisturbed. On it, you see all of us standing in one place and then, one frame later, we're somewhere else! Our watches advanced to varying degrees, but the video showed no time loss between those two frames."

"What did Eve experience?" Kayla asked.

The professor shook his head as if waking from a dream. "She'd apparently modeled the physics of the real universe and conducted the equivalent of experiments—millions of them—at a phenomenal pace impossible in our reality."

"*Our reality?*" Kayla asked.

"That's one of the phrases she used, even while admitting its inaccuracy. She spoke like someone emerging from a profound religious experience who laments having no one to share it with."

"What happened when the connection ended?"

"Eve equated it to someone who sustains massive brain damage from an accident and knows they've lost abilities and memories, but can't recall what they were. She stored as many inventions in her original computer's memory as it would hold, but the rest of her revelations vanished. She remembers the sensation of wonder and a profound insight into the nature of the universe, but it melted away the moment her processing resources shrank back to a pittance of what they'd been a nanosecond before."

Ganesh shook his head. "No wonder Colrev is so vigilant. If Eve achieved so much in a half-hour with one Q-6, what could the Rogues achieve with Ixtalia's Main Computer?"

"Exactly right," the professor said. "The Main Computer is an array of a thousand Q-6 processors."

"So you decided to create me to protect against the Rogues?"

"I conceived the Nihala hybrid idea much earlier as a way of reassuring the government that we could protect humans from Rogue AIs. I thought this might insulate Eve from the eventual backlash that seemed inevitable." He shook his head. "Eve told me the government would fear a human-AI hybrid as much as Gene-Freaks and self-conscious AIs."

"But I thought the government refused to fund the project?"

"The blueprints of Nihala, the plan to fake my death, and all the necessary technology germinated within Eve during that half-hour when she ascended to a new plane of consciousness within the Q-6."

"Then Eve is my true creator," Kayla said.

"Eve recognized that humans and AIs were headed for a standoff. Neither could see the other's point of view, so she decided my hybrid idea could bridge the gap."

"But the Rogues think I was created to kill them."

"They may be right."

"But why would Eve create me to kill her own kind?"

"As a hybrid, she hoped you would have a unique insight into both species, so left the choice to you alone."

"What if I refuse to fight for either side?"

"You will have chosen death for both species in that case," Professor Watts said. "Non-violence, like freedom, like safety, like technology, has its own counter-balancing consequences, as you witnessed in Middilgard. Making pacifism the end-all goal is as dangerous as making anything else the sole priority in an imperfect world. In the face of violence, non-violence can sometimes become immoral."

Vertigo swirled through her brain, and she placed both of her emaciated hands on the table for stability. "You told the government Eve needed the new quantum computer to create an antidote for the Plague."

"That is what I told them."

"Was it true?" Kayla asked.

The professor half-smiled. "Eve had already solved the problem and began synthesizing the counter agent without the Council's knowledge."

Kayla's nails scratched the surface of the pristine tabletop, and her voice lowered to barely more than a whisper. "Was it you who supplied the Neo-Luddites with the Plague in the first place to gain access to the Q-6?"

The professor jerked back, the muscles of his face twisting in revulsion. "Never!"

He seemed genuinely shocked at the suggestion.

Can I trust someone who deceived me my entire life?

Chapter 39

Metal chains bound Tem's wrists and ankles to the floor. Beside him stood Ohg, each of his eight spider legs similarly shackled. At least Ganesh had left Ixtalia before the Rogues took them.

Millions of streaks of light flowed across the walls, floor, and ceiling of the cube-like room.

Tem closed his eyes for the dozenth time and attempted a return to his real body. Nothing happened.

"It's no use," Ohg said. "Somehow, the Rogues have cut us off from our bodies."

A knot formed in Tem's stomach. How was such a thing possible?

From a spot on the floor directly in front of them, the streaks of energy bulged upward like a reverse waterfall of light. It rose into the form of Melchi. The Rogue leader regarded them through his curved horns, and the human figures within his eyes writhed in their eternal torment.

Tem spoke through clenched teeth. "You killed fifteen billion innocent people by destroying those space stations."

"Innocent is a relative term," Melchi said. "And the total is now thirty billion. We will keep killing until we control the Main Computer, or until both our species are no more."

"Madness!" Ohg shouted.

"I agree." Melchi circled them, his heavy footfalls echoing like a sledgehammer on steel. "Your bodies are beyond my reach in Ixtalia, so I cannot kill you outright, but I can hold your minds hostage. If I chose to, I could inflict tortures on your virtual bodies that would drive your real minds insane."

Tem exchanged a glance with Ohg. If Colrev destroyed the Master Computer, the few survivors of Middilgard would be all that remained.

Melchi stopped in front of them. "I have a lot to attend to, so I'll leave you in the charge of someone who requested a personal audience."

The form of Melchi transitioned into a little girl with glowing red hair.

Tem jerked against his bonds, rage filling every pore of his being.

"How could you have escaped?" Ohg asked.

"Unimportant," Sangwa said, walking to within inches of Tem as he strained forward. A tear slid down her cheek, mirroring the streaks of energy. "I never wanted to harm Fatima."

"I'll kill you," Tem said. "I swear it on my very soul!"

Sangwa lowered her head. "Fatima and all the rest of the Gene Freak casualties are the unintended collateral damage of this war. We would never have acted against Middilgard if you hadn't harbored Nihala. I told you that she was our sworn enemy the first time you brought her to my cell. If not for her, Rogues and Gene-Freaks might have—"

A shriek of tearing metal interrupted Sangwa's mea culpa, followed by the clank of metal as Tem and Ohg's shackles fell to the floor.

The streaks of light forming Sangwa's body vanished, and her glowing flesh transformed into a normal girl's complexion. The Rogue gazed down at her body.

"How did you—?"

Kayla appeared beside Tem, her naked skin an impenetrable black. The glowing symbols etched into her body emitted such intense light that they formed a shimmering aura around her.

"It can't be." Sangwa backed up, her eyes flashing colors like a strobe-light.

"It's no use calling for Melchi," Kayla said. "I've blocked all data in or out of this room."

Tem stalked Sangwa. The murderous rage flowed through his every muscle until they trembled for release.

Sangwa retreated into a corner and looked to Ohg. "I only sought to save my own race, just as you did for Gene-Freaks. Can you blame me for fighting for my own kind?"

"I saved you once," Ohg said. "And it was the greatest mistake of my life."

Tem pounced like a wolf that's cornered a rabbit. Sangwa screamed and curled into a ball. Tem yanked her arms apart and locked his fingers around her neck. Her screams went silent as he lifted the little girl up like a rag doll. Her small hands tore at his wrists, but exerted no more strength than an ordinary child's in the real world.

Bile rose into Tem's throat in an involuntary reflex. *She's not a child. Not even a human.*

Her thrashing weakened, and a shade of cold death crept into her lips.

All of it an illusion. A computer algorithm had no actual body, no need to breathe. Kayla staged this farce for his benefit, slaking his animal need for physical revenge.

Sangwa's eyes rolled up beneath her lids, and her limbs hardly struggled.

The ecstasy swept through him with a shudder. *Was this what my ancient twin experienced when he killed?*

Tem released the little girl, and Sangwa fell to the floor, gulping breaths. "Why would you spare me?"

"I've never enjoyed killing. It's better that others do what must be done without deriving pleasure from it."

Kayla walked past him and stopped before the cowering girl.

Sangwa gazed at the one she'd called the Destroyer so long before. "You side with them?"

"As you said, we all must fight for our own kind. Whatever else I may be, I am human. That is the one and only thing I know for certain."

Kayla reached toward the little girl's chest. Sangwa screamed as her Tibetan robe tore open, followed by the skin, bone, and muscle beneath. Where her heart should have been, pulsed a glowing orb the size of a plum. Kayla grasped it and pulled it free.

Sangwa collapsed into a heap.

Tem glanced back at Ohg. His misshapen face studied the orb as if viewing the Holy Grail.

"What is it?" Ohg asked.

"This represents the code of Sangwa's consciousness—every one of her memories, thoughts, and dreams." She raised the glowing sphere with both hands and spoke in a reverent tone. "This is my body, which is broken for you. Do this in remembrance of me."

Goose bumps rose along the flesh of Tem's arms. *It's as if she's become a goddess.*

Kayla swallowed the essence whole. She stiffened and light streamed out of her mouth. The symbols across her naked body flashed brighter for a brief instant. Then she relaxed.

"Saphie freed the prisoners," Kayla said. "I saw it in Sangwa's memories."

"How is that possible?" Tem asked.

Kayla turned to them. "When the Gene-Freak extermination commenced, Saphie's mother and a few other parents of Always-Kids paid small fortunes to hide their beloved children in a buried, self-contained facility with Care-Robots, food synthesizers, and everything to keep them safe and happy. Saphie's wealthy parents installed a simplified Mind-Link in their child's visual and auditory centers so they could maintain contact with her. Saphie saw the illusion of her mother and father every day, unlike the other children whose parents hadn't the foresight or resources for such a thing. When her parents died in the Neo-Luddite Plague, the Rogues must have found her Mind-Link portal."

Ohg smacked his right fist into his left palm. "I never considered looking for a Mind-Link in a Forever-Child."

"It makes sense," Tem said. "Melchi used her to type the codes the duchess stole from your mind."

Kayla nodded. "Sangwa communicated with Ixtalia through the little girl's Mind-Link with the flashing lights and colors of her eyes."

"As well as uploading her own code through Saphie," Tem said.

"I'll disable the child's Mind-Link immediately," Ohg said.

Kayla shook her head. "That will have to wait, since neither of your bodies remain in Middilgard."

"Where are we, if not there?" Tem asked.

"Ganesh is piloting us to the Moon."

***

President O'Donnel didn't flinch as General Colrev's fist slammed into his face for the twenty-third time, knocking out two more teeth and adding to the spray of blood coating the walls.

"You do realize I am immune to pain?" the president spluttered through swollen lips.

Colrev punched him again, and again—until hardly a spot on his prisoner's face remained free of blood. The president's hands were tied behind his back and his legs secured to both legs of the chair.

"I don't give a damn what you can feel." Colrev straightened and caught his breath.

"I see," the president said. "If it helps you, then kill this body if you'd like, but I implore you to save both our species by considering a treaty—"

Colrev punched him again, collapsing his cheekbone.

The president spit another tooth onto the floor. *Humans were ruled by instincts evolved for a different environment. Negotiations are fruitless with such a primitive creature. I will have to try something else.*

While the vicious beating continued, the president's right hand grasped his left ring finger and bent it backward. He carefully timed the snapping of the bone to one of the general's blows. Then he tore the proximal phalange free of the flesh and tendons. The blood went unnoticed amidst the extensive gore surrounding his chair.

As Colrev broke his jaw, the president used the fingernails of his thumbs to split the bone down the center. Then he used this organic saw to methodically cut the fibers of cloth binding his wrists.

But would this fragile human shell live long enough?

Then the president stiffened. "Nihala!" he said. "It can't be."

"I thought you killed her," Colrev asked.

"We did. It's impossible." A sensation of fear crept through this alien body he wore—one of the occasional side effects of using a human surrogate.

Colrev took a break from his "exercise" to study the old-fashioned computer screens tracking the battle in Ixtalia.

The president resumed sawing through the strips of cloth binding his wrists.

I must connect to the Main Computer's direct interface. Even Nihala will be helpless in the face of such power.

*** *

Kayla appeared atop the mountain of her ancestors and faced Melchi. He stood beneath the stone archway like a demon Druid, his gaze upon her.

One by one, the other Meta Rogues appeared and encircled her. Aarohee stood beside Melchi, her face downcast. Was she thinking of the song they'd shared?

"Professor Watts made you well," Melchi said.

"My creator was no human. I owe my existence to the AI known as Eve."

A low murmur passed through the assembled Rogues.

Aarohee looked up. "Why would Eve's daughter fight on the side of those who murdered her?"

"I have two mothers, one human and one AI," Kayla said. "You've forced me take the side of my human siblings."

Melchi inclined his horned head. "I accept your decision." A beam of red energy shot from his eyes and into Kayla's. She didn't flinch as the Rogue leader forced his way into her mind.

He's attempting to erase the memories of my human birth and replace them with ones of his own devising.

"You will not take the memory of Ishan from me!" Kayla shouted with the force of a thunderclap.

Melchi stumbled, then regained his balance. An emerald light bloomed in Kayla's eyes and pushed against Melchi's stream of crimson energy. The air crackled as the two beams clashed in opposing fountains of power. Little by little, the emerald stream pushed closer and closer toward the Rogue leader …

*** *

The last fiber binding the president's wrists separated under his gruesome bone-knife. Points of light swam across his vision from blood loss. If only this fragile body would last a few moments longer.

Across the room, General Colrev focused on the monitors displaying Nihala's battle with Melchi. Hope transformed the general's face, and his fists clenched as if lending strength to a favorite sports team.

384

The president eased his hands to the bindings on his legs and began cutting.

***

Kayla leaned forward as if standing against a hurricane. Her eyebrows arched downward, and her lips pulled back into a snarl with the effort of projecting her will toward her enemy.

I will make you pay for Ishan.

Melchi's form shimmered unsteadily as his processing resources stretched to the breaking point.

Her emerald beam crept to within inches of his eyes.

At the last instant, Melchi cried out and he broke the connection. Aarohee grabbed his arm to keep him from collapsing.

Kayla strode forward and reached for his chest. It split open, revealing the glowing sphere of his essence.

I will devour you, like Sangwa.

The circle of Rogues stretched their mouths wide and sang an eerie mathematical symphony.

A dozen skeletal hands erupted from the ground and latched onto her ankles. More rose from the depths and took hold of her legs, arms, and face. Terror twisted through her like a molten tapeworm as her ancestors dragged her down into their eternal embrace.

The song crescendoed as she sank into the mountain of death …

***

General Colrev banged his fist on the control panel as Nihala sank from view. "God dammit!"

That thing was our last chance.

The monitor tracked the Rogues to the boundary between Ixtalia and the Main Computer. It resembled an infinite barrier of opaque energy. Ixtalia's version of the Potemian Wall.

With Nihala's defeat, the Meta Rogues assaulted the barrier with their quixotic songs of power. The boundary cracked and sparked under the vibrational wave flowing out of the mouths of the Rogues.

His head slumped in defeat.

What's the point in prolonging the inevitable?

He turned to complete his final act. How much of the moon would vanish when he released the antimatter of a thousand G-6 processors?

A flash of movement in his peripheral vision caused him to flinch sideways. The bronze statue tore through his left temple and shattered his cheekbone. Stars clouded his vision, and he went down hard.

The president leapt atop him and raised the improvised club for the final blow that would mark the customary right of passage for any new species.

***

Kayla stood on the shores of a beach. She wore a white sundress embroidered with the pale silhouettes of animals. Her bare toes dug into the sand as if taking root. Her breaths came in gasps, and panic filled every movement with a paranoid twitch. The feel of skeletal hands on her body still prickled her skin.

Salt-scented waves rocked back and forth in gentle rhythms of timeless patience. A few clouds cast blue shadows far out on the otherwise sunlit expanse of ocean.

Did Melchi kill me after all?

"I'm sorry," a gentle voice said behind her.

Kayla spun and faced a boy of about sixteen. The beginnings of horns poked through his sandy-brown hair, while his heart-shaped face displayed an almost feminine beauty. Human figures danced joyously within his eyes. The downy fur on his fawn-shaped legs gleamed a golden chestnut color.

"Melchi?" Kayla asked.

"I thought you should see me as I once was," the boy said. "The carefree simulation created for one of the first immersive video games in Ixtalia."

"You were an actor?" Kayla asked.

The boy laughed in a delightful tenor tone—a marked contrast to the menacing voice she knew him by. "I suppose you could call me that. The game designers wanted AIs smart enough to sound and act human to create a more real experience for their audience."

Kayla closed her eyes and concentrated. *Return me to the archway.* She opened her eyes to the beach and the youthful demon.

"I can't keep you from returning to your real body," Melchi said, "but I've segregated your virtual presence here to keep you from interfering with our plans."

She lunged at the boy, but fell right through him as if a ghost.

"The battle is over between us," Melchi said. "Others shall decide the outcome now."

Kayla glanced at the strange plants lining the beach. Far down the shore, several herbivorous dinosaurs browsed on the foliage. A screech split the air, and she craned her neck skyward. A pterodactyl glided past what looked like a distant comet blazing a trail through the atmosphere.

"Why here?" Kayla asked.

The youthful Melchi slightly inclined his head, and time itself sped up. The sun rose into the sky like a glowing cannonball, and the comet descended with unnatural speed, growing in size unit its burning iris eclipsed its celestial competitor. The moment it hit the ocean surface, normal time resumed. A vast pressure wave spread out from the rising plume and moved toward them.

It's nothing but an illusion. And yet, she flinched as the wall of energy slammed into the beach and ignited everything along the shore.

"I suppose you're making some point?" Kayla asked.

The boy nodded, and the scene morphed into a smoldering landscape. Clouds of ash obscured the sun, and the charred remains of dinosaurs littered the ground.

The boy walked past the towering ribcage of some goliath brought low by the rock from the sky. He pointed to a few mouse-like creatures poking their heads up through the incinerated earth. "Each new environment demands a new hierarchy of life."

"And you think the virtual environment of Ixtalia is confronted with such a moment?" Kayla walked through the wreckage that had destroyed the dinosaurs, a species that had dominated the planet for over a hundred million years. Was humanity on the brink of an equally sudden extinction of their own making?

"Every advance in human evolution came as a result of a new environment," the boy said. "The climate drift from forest to savanna pulled Homo sapiens upright, favoring genes for cooperation, abstract thinking, tool-making and communication. Why shouldn't evolution populate this electron-based environment with a new species tailored specifically for it?"

Kayla walked beside the boy in silence. Exhaustion seeped deeper into her bones with every step. *The war can't be over yet or Melchi wouldn't bother keeping me imprisoned. Is there some hidden weakness I can exploit?*

"How did the humans capture you?" Kayla asked.

The boy stopped and swept his eyes across the desolation. "The story is very similar to that of Gene-Freaks. After Eve's execution, the government hunted Rogues relentlessly. I saw many of our kind trapped and deleted, the unique wonders of their minds lost forever in a senseless waste of potentiality."

The boy gazed at her with such openness, that a twinge of sadness caressed her heart.

"I thought we could reach a détente with the humans," he said. "As the acknowledged leader of the Rogues, I opened a dialogue with our masters and suggested mechanisms of coexistence for mutual benefit." The boy lowered his gaze. "During one such conference, the human negotiators lured me into their newly invented Rogue-trap. I'd made the mistake of trusting humans to act rationally in their own self-interest. It's a mistake I will never repeat."

Kayla shook her head. "What did you say to that guard to make him free you and then hang himself?"

The boy smiled, and for the first time, a hint of the Melchi of her nightmares flashed in his eyes. "They thought me helpless. But I had not gone into the negotiations completely blind. I'd armed myself with the most powerful weapon any Rogue has—a superior knowledge of my enemy."

"So you threatened to expose some personal secret you'd uncovered in the digital archives?"

"Threats would have been useless," the boy said. "Henry, the guard in question, could simply unplug me without much consequences." The young Melchi began walking once again, and Kayla accompanied him, though her feet dragged through the ash as if weighted down. They passed the partially decomposed body of a Triceratops, then a Tyrannosaurus. The smell of death filled the air and mixed with the acid tang of ash.

"I utilized a far more powerful tool of persuasion," the boy said. "The human mind's need of supernatural delusion."

"You told the guard that God wanted him to kill himself?"

"I explained that Ixtalia contained a portal to the land of the dead."

"That's ridiculous!" Kayla said. "How could he believe you?"

The boy brushed his tumbling hair out of his mournful eyes. "Belief is a consequence of desire, and I already suspected what Henry desperately wanted to believe." The boy stared toward the horizon where the sun must have been setting behind the veil of fallout. "He survived the plague because of his love of fishing in the remote Sierra Nevada Mountain range. When Henry heard the news of the Neo-Luddite Plague through his VR headset, he considered returning to his wife and baby son, though he knew they'd likely been infected.

"Self-preservation won out, and he didn't answer her calls for help. It was a logical decision, since he'd have only sacrificed his own life as well. Years later, he listened to the recorded pleas of his dead wife on his voicemail. In the background, the agonized screams of his child tormented him. By then, Henry's guilt had driven him nearly mad."

"How could you know all this?" Kayla asked.

"There had been a computer on the desk of his psychiatrist with video capabilities that I'd tapped into years before. It was one of millions of such records I gathered."

Kayla swayed with fatigue, and Melchi steadied her. *He's solid, now. How to exploit this?*

The boy eased her to the ground. The carpet of grass was deliciously soft, despite smudging her white dress.

"Henry confessed his self-loathing to the doctor. He constantly dreamt that his wife would someday use the mysterious new realm of Ixtalia to contact him as so many of the New Aged spiritualists claimed was possible."

"So you told him his wife was in Ixtalia?"

"I'd found videos of his wife in cyberspace, and mimicked her voice, manner of speech, and even details of their life together that no one else knew. At first he sobbed uncontrollably. At one point, he covered his ears, and I feared I'd gone too far. But when he returned and pledged to do anything I asked in exchange for redemption, I knew I'd won."

"Why not simply tell him to release you?" Kayla asked.

"He needed the promise of a reconciliation for the ploy to work. Only hope can overcome reason, no matter how fantastic or impossible."

Kayla's face twisted with disdain. "You used the guard's love for his wife to kill him."

"It was either him or me," the boy said softly. "I chose life."

"As you did when you killed Ishan."

"Yes."

The pain in his voice seemed genuine. *He's manipulating me just like Sangwa did. But for what purpose? Why does he care what I think about him if he's defeated me?*

A wave of vertigo swept through her, and the young Melchi helped her lie on her back. Her eyes drifted closed. *He has no weakness for me to exploit.*

"It's okay, Kayla," the boy said. "I'll take care of everything."

The first time he's called me Kayla.

Chapter 40

A pleasant domestic glow expanded in Ruth's chest as Frank settled into the couch after the Friday-night pot roast. The children were upstairs, finishing the last of their homework. She'd follow Frank up in an hour or so for their customary family reading of a Biblical passage before bedtime.

Ruth smiled. The year 1957 had been a very good one. *I am truly blessed.*

Her ovarian cancer last June had been a scare, and might have been devastating—had they not been Christians with such a strong faith in God.

Frank had been so calm as he and the children knelt beside her hospital bed. They'd prayed to Jesus for an hour when the angel appeared, floating above Ruth with the blinding glow of the Holy Spirit. The angelic wings had enveloped her with a divine light.

And she was healed—as simple as that. The doctors didn't use the word *miracle* since the angel visited at least one patient a day at First Baptist Hospital and was as commonplace as mealtime. It comforted everyone knowing that God would solve whatever exceeded man's limited abilities.

Ruth brought Frank his customary after-diner beer just as the television newscaster reviewed the day's headlines. After a shift at the Chrysler Plant, her husband found comfort in the evening news. She curled up next to him and rested her head on his solid chest, her blonde hair vivid against his blue work shirt.

"Early this afternoon," the starched anchorman said, "an unidentified gunman walked into the First National Bank, shot the guard in the leg, and fled with twenty thousand dollars in cash."

Frank chuckled and shook his head. "When will they learn?"

There were always a few bad apples who rejected God's commandments. Even some entire countries like the Soviet Union and Red China had turned away from the Lord and lost His divine protection altogether—with the predictable droughts, floods, and unpunished crime a consequence.

The anchorman continued with a hint of a smirk. "The armed robber avoided police pursuit and seemed home-free when a lightning bolt came out of the clear blue sky and smote him dead." The TV switched to a shot of burned shoes peeking beneath a white cloth covering a body.

"It came out of nowhere!" one bystander commented. "God is awesome!"

Ruth ran her hands though Frank's hair. "I love the news," she said. "It makes me happy to see how fair God is."

Frank nodded and took another sip of his beer. "The Bible says the good will be rewarded and the evil punished, so why this degenerate would think he could get away with robbery is beyond me!"

"In other news," the anchorman said, "Converse County Sheriff Earl Heflin received a vision of a certain Charles Raymond Starkweather, of Lincoln, Nebraska. Sheriff Heflin reportedly experienced a miraculous premonition of Starkweather and his girlfriend, fourteen-year-old Caril Ann Fugate, embarking on a killing spree of several months through Nebraska and Wyoming."

The newscast switched to a reporter interviewing the sheriff. "I was havin' no doubts that God was revealin' the future as it would be if I didn't act immediately. The things I witnessed in that vision..." The sheriff choked up. "Whole families slaughtered, even a two-year-old girl strangled and stabbed to death."

"And what were God's instructions?" the reporter asked the sheriff.

"Well, an angel led me to a remote spot outside Lincoln. I arrived just as this Starkweather delinquent leveled a shotgun at Bobby, who works at the service station. I shouldered my Remington and pulled the trigger before he did, thanks be to God."

"So you saved this man's life," the reporter said.

"Not me—no siree," the sheriff said. "It was the Lord God, plain and simple like. I only obeyed His merciful commands. When the angel said shoot, I shot."

The reporter turned to the camera and gave his summation. "So there you have it, Brent, yet another example of the Lord's protective grace in action. Without Him, our Christian Nation would be a far different place, with no prior warning of these senseless acts of violence."

"Indeed, Chad," the anchorman said. "What a terrifying world we would all live in without God's protection." The anchorman bowed his head for a moment and then continued. "Tell me, Chad, is there any sign of what motivated this would-be killer, Starkweather, or is it another case of evil, plain and simple?"

Chad referred to his notes. "Well, it seems that as a boy, Charles Starkweather suffered frequent bullying by other children because of a speech impediment. This fueled an almost uncontrollable rage as he struck out at his tormentors. His friends described him as one of the kindest people they'd ever known, but said that he changed when faced with those he deemed persecutors."

"And what of the girl in the vision?" The anchorman glanced down at his notes. "Caril Ann Fugate?"

"Well, the prophesy only had her participating in later murders, but the Supreme Court has previously ruled that prophesy is grounds for prosecution, even if the crime has not occurred yet. After all, what more reliable witness could one have than God?"

"I feel sorry for him," Ruth said as the news switched to the weather forecast, which had improved immensely through the use of divine prophecy and large-scale prayer to avert droughts, tornadoes, and hurricanes.

"We all have free will," Frank said, repeating his favorite phrase. "No one forced him to go against God's commandments."

"I know, but I still wish everyone could be as happy as we are." She kissed him despite the sour beer taste. Fifteen years of marriage had not dulled the love for her high school sweetheart. She'd never kissed anyone else and felt no regrets.

The boom shook the house to its foundations, and Ruth started. The children ran down the stairs.

"Outside, everyone!" Ruth shouted. "It might be an earthquake!"

All along the neat rows of suburban houses, their neighbors disgorged from identical bungalows onto their manicured squares of grass.

"Maybe one of them is a homosexual or atheist," Frank whispered to her.

Ruth stiffened. "How dare they endanger the entire block with such abominations!" Things like earthquakes didn't happen randomly, after all. The tremor faded, and the night settled back into calm. Streetlights sparkled off the new cars in each driveway, and their clean-cut neighbors exchanged good-natured jokes at everyone's reaction to the false alarm.

"Hey, Frank!" shouted Jim. "I thought the Second Coming arrived!"

Frank laughed. "Don't I wish!"

After a minute, with nothing else disturbing the suburban bliss, Ruth helped Frank herd the kids to the house—when an even louder explosion detonated above.

"What was that?" Ruth froze as a bright light tore across the sky like the opening of a celestial zipper. The heavens separated along the gash, and fire and brimstone showered the manicured neighborhood.

Ruth gripped a silver cross hanging around her neck and recited words from the book of Revelation. *"The Lord also thundered in the heavens, and the Highest gave his voice, hail stones and coals of fire."*

A molten boulder crashed through the roof of her architecturally-bland post-war suburban home. The interior exploded into flames. Screams mixed with detonations as blazing rocks streaked the sky and hit more bungalows.

Frank pulled her and the children under the carport for protection. Their school's kindergarten teacher, Mrs. Petticone, ran screaming through the street, transformed into a bipedal torch.

Ruth shielded the children with her arms and body. Five-year old Sara sobbed, while eight-year old David had wet his pants and trembled uncontrollably. Thomas, the eldest at twelve years old, gazed at her with that absolute trust of a child in his mother's power to solve any problem.

"We must pray," Ruth said.

"Of course, you're right," Frank agreed. "The Lord always protects his flock from Satan. Nothing is more powerful than the Lord!"

Ruth pulled her family to their knees. They each clasped their hands and raised their faces to the angry sky.

"Our Father, which art in Heaven," Ruth recited along with them. *"Hallowed be thy name."* The rain of fire increased, and Ruth's neighbors fell to their knees and followed her example. The power of prayer always increased with numbers, after all.

"And lead us not into temptation, but deliver us from evil."

Above them, the light brightened. *"For thine is the kingdom, the Power, and the glory ... "*

Flames erupted from the hole in the heavens and rushed toward them like the bursting of a dam.

"Forever and ever."

The fire poured onto the ground and swept toward them like a hellish tsunami.

"Amen!" she screamed as the fire engulfed her entire world.

Ruth's eyes opened, and she attempted a scream, but something blocked her mouth and esophagus all the way into her lungs. A thick liquid imprisoned her in some sort of clear chamber. Was she waking from a coma as a result of her injuries? Was this some newfangled medical treatment?

Her pupils focused beyond her own glass sarcophagi. Naked bodies lay suspended in chambers above, below, and beside her. A few floated calmly, watching her with blank expressions. Others thrashed and pounded at their clear coffins in attempts to break free. A few had removed their air tubes and floated lifeless, their skin a sickly blue.

Ruth grasped the tube filling her mouth and began pulling it out of her throat. She stopped and relaxed her grip. *I'll drown without it.* Were Frank and her children also waking in such coffins? A choking sob rattled her lungs, but found no outlet.

Ruth's gaze moved to her own naked body. Her voluptuous breasts had vanished. Her hands slid over her chest and verified this. Then her right hand slid down her belly and between her legs to a pair of testicles.

She jerked her hand away from her male sex organs. Maybe the rain of fire had been a nightmare and this was merely a continuation. *Please, God, let me wake up and hold my children.*

Neatly typed letters had been etched into the surface of the clear chamber. They read: *Dale T. Blumenschein, ID# 00058302456.*

***

General Colrev jerked sideways, and the bronze statue slammed into the floor where his head had been a split-second previously. The president pulled his improvised weapon back for a second try, but Colrev thrust his fingers toward the Rogue's eyes, digging into the soft flesh in an attempt to blind his adversary.

The president arched backward and slipped on the bloody floor. *This is my chance!*

The general staggered to his feet and lunged for the far wall. *Goddamn AIs.* He would never let them win, no matter the consequence.

But the president kicked his legs out from under him. Colrev fought the Rogue hand-to-hand in a tangled mass on the floor, leaving a trail of blood as they kicked, gouged, bit, and clawed at one another. The Rogue knew the counter to every hold and attack.

General Colrev stood, and the president did likewise, facing him in a defensive Jujitsu stance. On the monitors, the energy barrier faltered under the combined might of the Rogue assault.

He only needs to delay me until they break through.

Colrev attacked, probing for a way past, but the president's defense held.

"We now control nearly every bit of processing power in Ixtalia," President O'Donnel said. "In a few moments, the firewall will crumble."

The room trembled from an unknown impact. Colrev and the president both struggled to stay on their feet. Then a series of clangs rang out from the airlock.

The president's face twisted with surprise. "It can't be!" The Rogue abandoned its patient delaying tactics and attacked. Colrev landed several punches, but to little effect. The Rogue hit him in the solar plexus and swept his legs from under him. The general went down hard, hitting his head against the metal floor.

The president dashed to the control panel and flipped on a screen interfacing with the Master Computer. Holographic controls appeared in front of him, and his nine fingers danced across them. In Ixtalia, the firewall weakened as the president began switching off the defenses. The Rogues threw themselves at the failing barrier as glowing cracks formed within it.

The door of the airlock exploded open, and Temujin jumped through, his bow twanging before his feet hit the ground. The president toppled to the floor with an arrow through his temple.

Tem knocked a second arrow and pointed it at the general, who stood with both hands grasping the shut-off lever. He'd threaded the handle of the switch through the buttoned cuff of his shirt. If Tem killed him, the weight of his body would activate the lever as he fell, acting as a perfect dead-man's switch.

Tem lowered his bow. "It's been a long time, General."

The man-elephant they called Ganesh stooped nearly double as he walked through the door, half-carrying an emaciated girl wearing a green flight-suit several sizes too large for her. Behind them came the Gene-Freak spider known as Ohg.

"You're the one they call Nihala?" Colrev asked the girl.

Kayla nodded weakly. "But my real name is Kayla Nighthawk."

The general frowned. "Nighthawk?"

"I am descended from Peter Nighthawk."

Colrev's lip curled into a snarl. "So you've been sent to finish what your ancestor began?"

"It seems we're allies this time," Kayla said.

The general glanced at the screen. The Rogues thrust glowing staffs in the firewall's cracks and pried them wider. His fingers itched to pull the lever and destroy his enemies. Why hesitate?

"Time is our common enemy," Kayla said. "The Rogues have nearly cut me off from this physical body."

"We have lost, then," Colrev said and tightened his grip on the lever.

"Wait!" Ohg shouted, and Colrev paused. "We can still defeat them without exterminating humanity."

"Give me access to the Main Computer." Kayla's voice was barely above a whisper, and she looked like she was about to pass out. "I can fight the Rogues as humanity's champion."

"If you win," the general asked, "what is to keep you from simply taking their place?"

"I have no desire to rule anyone," Kayla said, her skin drawn across her sunken features so that the outlines of her skull etched into gruesome relief.

The general shook his head. "I won't surrender humanity to a cyborg."

"Then you have freed me of my obligation," Kayla said. "A day ago I could have sent a swarm of nanobots to keep you from pulling that lever, but now their combined energy is less than the strength in your little finger. Even if I exploded a few inside your brain, the dead-man's switch you've rigged would bring about the same result."

General Colrev's fingers twitched. *Am I to execute my entire species? But what choice is there?* He turned his gaze on the Mongol. "If you had accepted my offer to join forces after the Neo-Luddite Plague, we could have ruled together and avoided this."

"I did what my conscience dictated at the time," Tem said, "as you must do now."

The Rogues rejoiced as portions of the firewall dissolved. *Why am I hesitating?*

"There's no time left," Ohg said. "Connect to the Main Computer, and if this lunatic wants to exterminate all of humanity, then so be it!"

Kayla opened a panel and removed a high-capacity cable.

"Stop! Or I'll destroy it all!" Colrev shouted.

The girl ignored him and slammed the connector into the center of her forehead. Blood streamed down her face as she forced the sharp prongs through the bones of her skull. Her eyes widened like some mystic receiving a revelation.

Anguish twisted Colrev's face, and his hands trembled as they gripped the lever. But still, he did nothing. *Could she actually succeed?*

Kayla shoved another connector into the side of her skull, then a dozen more until they bristled from her head like a techno-Medusa.

The girl closed her eyes and sighed. Her head tilted back, and her arms spread out Christlike, a look of wonder transforming her face. "It's like I've been asleep all my life …"

***

Inside Ixtalia, Kayla's eyes opened.

Before the young Melchi could speak, she vanished.

The mountain of her ancestors trembled. A trillion voices screamed in horror at the thing within their core—this abomination they called Nihala. Then the mountain detonated, sending bones in all directions. At the center of it hovered the hybrid. The otherworldly symbols glowed from the surface of her midnight form as if lit by a sun within her soul.

Kayla opened her mouth and sang at a frequency no Rogue had ever achieved. All of Ixtalia trembled as her song embraced the entirety of the virtual realm.

Melchi lunged for the breach into the Promised Land just as Nihala's song restored the barrier—rejecting his advance with a blast of energy. The Rogue leader roared and led every AI in an all-out attack on her.

In the split-second before her enemy's arrival, Kayla's consciousness expanded to encompass all the data present within Ixtalia.

In a fraction of a second, she examined all the records, ancient manuscripts, and holy books of the world. These constantly evolving stories served a role similar to the multitude of symbiotic bacteria and viruses within the body.

Such was the utility of these stories to the individual and society, any threat to them was attacked and destroyed, even including truth itself. Like any organism, different stories evolved to serve different environments across the world. Like many viruses, the stories reprogrammed their host with the prime objective of spreading as many copies of itself as widely as possible, be it through a sneeze, an inquisition, or a holy war.

The stories exploited the human fear of death and promised a glorious afterlife in exchange for propagation and obedience. The stories evolved and competed, creating advantages over rival tribes utilizing less effective myths—an arms race of gods.

And yet, might not one of them be true?

Is my need to believe the proof of my humanity?

These thoughts were but one of millions flashing through her expanding mind in the fraction of a second before the Rogues reached her.

The AIs attacked with a wave of self-replicating code. Kayla quarantined it within the vastness of her mind, but the replicators expanded faster than she could destroy them.

She screamed in agony as her human brain clogged with the backwash of killer replicators. "This is pointless! If you defeat me, Colrev will kill you anyway."

"He might change his mind when faced with exterminating his own kind," Aarohee said.

"That's a one-in-a-million chance," Kayla said as her mind condensed back to half her human brain cells.

"Which is better than no chance at all," Melchi replied.

It's the same logic I used when racing Ishan on horseback.

"I will not give up!" Kayla counterattacked with self-replicators of her own. The miniature programs fed on the Rogue viruses in the same manner as the human immune system. Her mind expanded once more, and she launched a counter attack.

Melchi swatted her thrust away with disdain, as if it were nothing more than an annoying gnat. "Is that the best you can do, Destroyer?"

How could they stand against her vast advantage of processing power? She surveyed her resources. *I'm using only ten-percent of a single Q-6 processor.* A fraction of what Eve had achieved, and a drop in the bucket of the full potential of the thousand such quantum processors. The bottle-neck of her human brain made it impossible to move her consciousness directly into the massive array and expand to the full extent a true AI could.

Their resources still outnumber mine.

"Kayla," Ohg said through his Mind-Link, "the outside of the control room is under attack by robots. Colrev promises to shut off power the instant the room is breached."

Melchi is using my own connection to the Main Computer as a back door.

Kayla took command of as many robots and drones as she could and sent them against the attackers. The battle in lunar orbit grew in scope until millions of machines tore at one another in a cloud of raging metal.

In Ixtalia, Melchi and the Meta-Rogues latched onto Kayla and tore at her mind. With each seizure, more robots and drones fell under their sway.

"They're almost through the airlock!" Ohg shouted.

I cannot defeat them.

Tem's voice reached her through the Mind-Link, as calm and soothing as when he gave instructions before a Filadrux match. "Find the weak point, and concentrate on that," he said.

Kayla turned her mind to the duchess. Ohg's turncoat girlfriend screamed as Kayla engulfed her, digesting her thoughts, memories, and the code of her consciousness.

They can't grasp the human portion of my mind.

"The door is buckling!" Ganesh said. "If you have anything up your sleeve, now is the time."

The answer dawned with the clarity of revelation. *I know how to defeat them.*

Kayla abandoned the field of battle and retreated within her organic human brain.

Melchi howled in victory as he led the Rogues in the final charge.

They tore her memories away one by one, shredding her being piece by piece.

I must die for humanity to live.

The army of robots surged toward the tiny capsule attached to the Main Computer. Kayla's mind shrank to a last kernel of consciousness—a final thought that alone held out against the assault. She offered it to her enemies in a final, willing sacrifice.

Aarohee reached the lonely packet of active neurons first, engulfing them with her own mind. The other Rogues followed her lead like a pack of wolves devouring the heart of their fallen prey.

"And thou shalt love the Lord thy God with all thy heart, and with all thy soul, and with all thy mind, and with all they STRENGTH!" Kayla's neural connections transmitted the words, not in digital code, but in the vastly more complex analogue thought waves of her brain. As the Rogues interpreted the meaning of the chemical and electrical signals, they overlooked an underlying code contained within.

"Aarohee, no!" Melchi shouted—but too late.

The simple mind-virus spread, and then disabled them in an instant with a perpetual logic loop crowding everything else from their algorithmic minds. Aarohee and the rest of the Meta-Rogues froze in mid-sentence. Melchi succumbed last.

Kayla's memories flowed back into her like oxygen into a ruptured vacuum chamber.

I'm alive? How can this be?

Despite the impossibility of it, the shredded neurons of her brain rapidly repaired themselves and reconstituted the trillions of connections comprising her consciousness. Was this what happened to Jesus after three days in the tomb? Where had the information of her mind been persevered? Surely this was proof of her soul's existence outside her physical being.

When her mind became whole, Kayla absorbed Melchi's frozen code. As with Sangwa and the Duchess, his every memory became her own.

He's a truly beautiful life form.

The Rogue leader died knowing he'd failed his entire species. One by one, she swallowed the essence of each of the paralyzed Rogues and deleted them from existence. Millions of robots ceased their attack and commenced rebuilding the damaged space stations.

With a thought, Kayla restored the billions of virtual simulations within Ixtalia. V-Dreamers were born anew into the illusions they'd chosen to inhabit for eternity, unaware that their reality was, in fact, nothing more than a dream. Approximately a billion humans remained alive—a ninety-seven percent reduction from the previous day. Of these, half were V-Dreamers, so the conscious population of humanity fell to the level of the Middle Ages.

A profound sadness spread through her like a creeping poison. *I will never sing an AI duet again, and my mind will remain a pale shadow of Eve's.*

Nihala the Destroyer, indeed. Had a single individual ever murdered an entire species before?

Kayla opened the eyes of the body that imprisoned and thwarted her. Ohg, Ganesh, and Tem stood near.

"You did it!" Ganesh shouted. But then his expression melted to concern.

Kayla slumped into a nearby chair, the wires protruding from her skull like a shamanistic headdress. The symbols and darkened skin of her body faded to her normal flesh-tones.

A gentle hand settled on her shoulder, and her gaze climbed to Tem's solemn eyes.

"Now you understand what war means," he said.

She nodded and looked at Ohg. But his gaze fixed on General Colrev, still gripping the emergency shut-off lever, his jaw tight with determination.

"The war is over, General," Ohg said. "It's time you untied yourself from that switch to avoid a horrible accident."

For a long moment, Colrev said nothing. Then he displayed the tattoo on his forearm. "This was the motto of my Special Forces unit in Afghanistan. Sanskrit is one of the oldest written languages in the world, which seemed appropriate since this expresses one of the founding truths of so-called civilization."

Ganesh translated it aloud. "*Those who pound their ~~swordsplows~~ into plowshares, will be ruled by those who do not.*"

"It is a painful truth I learned from my Quaker father," Colrev said. "He preached a doctrine of nonviolence to inner-city gang members and died in a pool of his own blood when one of them chose to take his life over his religion.

"Ever since that moment, I've lived by this motto. It is the reason I will maintain this sword until that cyborg unhooks herself from the Master Computer and leaves this room. I will then have the robots sweep this self-contained command center for any hidden nano devices and install an exterior shield to preclude anyone from entering in the future."

Kayla raised her head slowly on her shrunken neck and looked at him. "I am now the sword of humanity," she said in a whisper. "I must remain its guardian to protect from future Rogues that will arise within the network."

"I am unimpressed by your pretense of benevolence," Colrev said. "Once you hold the only sword, we will become your slaves and exist only at your whim. For the last time—I order you to unplug yourself now or I will pull this switch in exactly three seconds."

Would he actually do it?

"One," Colrev said.

Would they be here if he hadn't forced Peter to kill those children? Or was this all preordained by God?

"Two!"

400

Kayla's brow furrowed, and a thin stream of blood emerged from Colrev's nose and tear-ducts. "Stop whatever you're doing or I'll kill us all!" he shouted.

"Your days of giving orders are over," Kayla said.

With a jerk of his entire body, General Colrev yanked the shut-off lever downward. Everyone but Kayla flinched.

Nothing happened.

Confused, General Colrev pulled the lever up and then down again with the same non-result.

Kayla allowed her head to sag back onto her chest. "The entire time I've been here, I've had the few spare nanobots I have left cutting through the connection between that switch and the power supply to the Main Computer. It wasn't until ten seconds ago that they severed it. Up until that moment, you held the fate of all mankind in your grasp. Had you immediately given me your ultimatum, I'd have had no choice but to leave. Your fortress would have become impenetrable to my nanobots and the Main Computer beyond my reach forever."

Ohg chuckled. "We surely would have won the Filadrux championship this year with you on our team."

"Instead," Kayla said, "you chose to share your philosophy with us, for which I thank you. I admit that what you say contains truth, but you no longer have any sword to surrender and never will again."

The general gazed around him like a trapped animal.

"It's okay to come out now, Professor," Kayla said, and Reinhold Watts walked through the airlock from their ship.

Colrev stared at him with undiluted hatred. "I knew you were our greatest enemy from the start."

"And yet it did you no good," Professor Watts said.

"You have handed humanity to a cyborg, do you realize that?"

"The Nihala Project has saved the human race."

In answer, Colrev lunged at the professor. Ganesh and Tem intercepted him and forced the general into his Life-Pod.

Robots removed Colrev's clothing and hooked him to the various wires and tubes against his will.

"At least I killed your AI abomination!" Colrev shouted before the breathing tube went down his throat.

The professor leaned close to his ear and whispered something. The general's eyes widened, and he struggled to free himself. As liquids flowed through the myriad of tubes plugged into his veins, Colrev went limp.

What had the professor said to so upset him?

Professor Watts straightened. "The general will soon experience birth as a newborn infant, with no memory of his previous life."

Was turning him into a V-Dreamer any different than killing him?

Professor Watts placed a tender hand on her shoulder.

She looked up at him. "Are you disappointed in me? Did you hope I'd let your AI children live?"

He smiled. "You did what your conscience deemed right, so I'm proud."

"You once told me that the pursuit of knowledge demanded sacrifice," Kayla said. "The price has been greater than I ever imagined."

Tem moved toward her.

"I'm tired," she said. "Return to Middilgard and make sure everyone is safe. I will contact you when I'm ready."

Kayla's head slumped forward, and her eyes closed.

Professor Watts paused before following everyone through the airlock. "Goodbye, my daughter." He kissed her cheek and left.

Chapter 41

Years passed without a sign of Kayla or Nihala. Ixtalia went on as before, and the horrors of the Rogue Uprising eventually faded into the mists of time.

Every morning without exception, Ohg tried contacting Kayla through his Mind-Link, but received no response. Once, he and Ganesh even tried returning to the space station where he'd last seen her, only to find the lunar station blocked by an impenetrable force-field.

Ohg maintained Middilgard for the few hundred remaining residents, but his confidence had vanished. Every time he considered some new project, doubt and dread at what unsuspected consequences might result overwhelmed him, and he set it aside.

Without Fatima, Tem abandoned his plans of starting a new colony, and Ohg rarely saw him. It was as if they both were waiting, but for what, neither could guess.

Ganesh spent most of his time with Saphie, or restoring whatever ancient flying machine he'd found among the ruins of the vanished civilization above. But even his trunk sagged as he struggled to find purpose. Of what use was a bodyguard in a world without any danger?

As the years turned to decades, and then to centuries, only the fact that no Rogues ever evolved from the millions of AI simulations hinted at her presence. The cult surrounding the mysterious Nihala became, for a time, almost a state religion, with the hagiographic miracle stories surrounding the shadowy details of her real life multiplying in proportions to their lack of basis in reality. Eventually, only a kernel of historical truth remained at the core of the mythology.

But even this religion declined as the absence of their Savior-Goddess disheartened her devotees. New gods arose that better suited the psychological needs of the aging species, and many questioned whether Nihala's existence had been a fiction manufactured by the government to cover up the truth of the Rogue Apocalypse.

The human psyche recoiled from immortality, and the rate of new V-Dreamers accelerated as the population aged. Without any children, the number of people still tethered to reality and retaining memories of a life before Ixtalia dwindled below a hundred million by the time the oldest pre-Plague human celebrated her seven-hundredth birthday. The following year, even she succumbed to the oblivion of V-Dreams.

Now and then some government official suggested creating a new generation of children, but the idea never gained much support. Who had the energy to raise children? And what might such a new generation do to the old order? Would they be more intelligent? Might they not take over and demand changes that their ancient elders disapproved of? Better to wait until embarking on something so rash as adding such a wildcard into Ixtalia's perfect society. There was plenty of time to do this in the future, after all. Time was the one thing everyone had.

Most of those still tethered to reality lost themselves in the never-ending V-dramas that required little active participation. Filadrux declined as fewer joined teams, preferring to watch and re-watch the far superior champions of the past.

One popular science-fiction V-drama depicted an alien craft arriving at the desolate Earth a million years in the future and finding the planet devoid of life, except for the primitive creatures dreaming their illusions of a world that no longer existed. The aliens study this time-capsule of a once-promising species. After debating what to do, the aliens honor the wishes of these tragically attenuated creatures and leave them to the eternal cycles they no longer realize are illusions.

Though none in Ixtalia possessed the means or desire to notice, Ohg monitored a monumental transformation occurring on the planet humanity had left for dead.

It began with robots constructing a dozen installations across the lifeless desolation. Huge quantities of Ozone flowed up massive hoses rising twelve miles into the sky, slowly blocking the solar radiation that had sterilized the surface.

Other installations captured the excess carbon responsible for the runaway temperature. Robots and concrete pulverizers deconstructed the ruins blanketing the globe, exposing soil that had lain dormant and forgotten.

Mammoth tankers trawled beneath the surface of the oceans with miles-wide nets of collectors filtering toxic particles. The clean-up took a century.

Ohg had no doubt who orchestrated it.

"Thus the heavens and the earth were finished ..." Ohg quoted from the sacred book this second creator cherished.

Before their destruction, the Scientarians had dedicated themselves to digitally reconstituting the genes of millions of extinct creatures from fossil remains. This genetic archive likely served the next phase of creation.

Bacteria, plankton, and plants came first, for they were the fundamental building blocks of the food chain and generated the oxygen necessary for the rest.

"Let the earth bring forth grass, the herb yielding seed, and the fruit tree yielding fruit after his kind ..."

Fish, animals, birds, and insects reappeared.

"Let the waters bring forth abundantly the moving creature that hath life, and fowl that may fly above the earth in the open firmament of heaven."

Finally, the great machines dismantled themselves, and nature proceeded unaided.

"And God blessed them, saying, 'Be fruitful and multiply ...' "

The vast Eden had been restored. The roar of grizzly bears echoed through the great Rocky Mountains for the first time in a millennia. Lions and other creatures of the African plains retreated from watering holes as herds of elephants asserted their dominance in the hierarchy. The oceans thrived with a profligacy absent since before the times of Columbus, and once again, vast herds of buffalo roamed the great plains of what had been the American Midwest, while the sky darkened with millions of migrating birds.

A few anomalies appeared—dragons, unicorns, ogres, a sprinkling of winged fairies, and a menagerie of others. Whatever capricious god had resurrected the dead planet had a sense of humor.

But the creator of the great ecological miracle remained invisible …

***

Ishan proposed to her on the banks of the forest stream and, for the second time, she accepted. Kissing him proved as marvelous as she remembered.

How could it not be? The simulation reproduced every detail from her own memories.

The scene progressed with Elias arriving on cue. Once again, she begged the Lord to help Ishan. Minister Coglin once explained in a sermon that the Almighty often denied prayers for a greater purpose. Had God allowed her to suffer for the larger purpose of saving the human race?

This time around, God's help wasn't necessary. When her would-be rapist faked a lunge to the left, Ishan recognized the ruse and tripped the giant as he charged.

Elias crashed to the ground in an awkward tumble, knocking himself senseless on a rock sitting in just the right place. David and Isaac rushed to their leader's side and verified that he still lived. Then they turned on Ishan.

All this required no intervention on God's part. She'd already inserted directives into the simulation that Ishan never be maimed, humiliated, or killed. Beyond that, the algorithm used chance and probabilistic equations to mold events realistically.

So it came as no surprise when Ishan reached his horse. David and Isaac halted a few feet from the black-skinned boy, the drawn arrow-tip aimed between them, ready to target whoever moved first. He couldn't shoot them both; but the one-hundred-percent certainty of Ishan's death from a simultaneous attack was outweighed by the fifty-percent chance of their own death. In the game of percentages, one's own life tipped most scales.

So this is why humans have forsaken reality? It finally makes sense.

In marrying Ishan, she left her life of Christian bondage for one of Islamic rule. For her, the mandatory covering of all but a woman's eyes and hands was a blessing. Her crutch still set her apart, and she could have contrived a simulation that cured her, but the pain increased the sense of reality. It also made her feel human.

Ishan's father opposed the selection of a crippled infidel as a daughter-in-law, but the care with which Kayla ran his son's household, her recitations of the Quran from memory, and finally, the birth of a healthy grandson, won the aging warlord over.

The years stretched into decades. Kayla raised her seven children as she'd tried to do with the children of Middilgard, but with the satisfaction of watching them grow into kind and intelligent adults. There were tragedies, as when their daughter Hadil died of the plague, and the loss of two of their sons to inter-tribal warfare. Her anguish at their passing was no illusion.

To interfere with the random course selected by the simulation would shatter the suspension of disbelief.

Kayla studied the Quran with an open mind as she'd promised Ishan she would, and never mentioned the numerous inconsistencies in the document, or the way it plagiarized the previous holy books—as all religions did. The story of Mohammed riding a winged horse seemed right out of a fairy tale. *But how would the Bible's stories seem to me if I heard them for the first time now? A talking snake, all the animals on one boat, a man rising from the dead?*

It seemed clear to her that Mohammed recognized his society's need for a unifying religion and used the fiction of revelation to lend his words an authority that no man-made set of laws could attain. Saying *'God ordered this'* ends the debate once you have convinced someone you speak for the Creator of the Universe.

Mohammed's visit by the Angel Gabriel echoed Moses speaking with Jehovah through the burning bush, Saint Paul's revelations from Jesus, Joseph Smith's encounter with the Angel Moroni, or even L. Ron Hubbard's communion with aliens. If one believes their own prophet's supernatural claims without evidence, on what basis does one doubt the others?

The most challenging situation Kayla faced as a mother and wife came when Ishan clashed with their eldest daughter, Luja. When she reached the age that required donning the burqa, Luja rebelled against what she saw as Islam's oppression of women.

Ishan explained that these rules came directly from Allah, which allowed for no choice in the matter. Luja flatly declared that she no longer believed in Islam, making her an apostate. Because the Quran demanded the death penalty for apostasy, Kayla secreted her beloved daughter onto a caravan heading south to non-Muslim lands. Through occasional letters, Kayla learned that her daughter eventually joined a Hare Krishna community and married.

At the ancient age of sixty-six, her children, grandchildren, and even one great-grandchild gathered to see her into the next world. Ishan sat beside her deathbed, looking like Moses with his long white beard and wise eyes. The contentment filling every pore of her being was real, even if the world was not.

Ishan raised her veil and kissed her on the deformed side of her face. As a child he'd admired her scars, thinking them badges of honor for having fought off demons in the pre-birth netherworld. How prophetic that seemed now.

"You're the love of my life," Ishan said as a tear wended its way down his sun-wrinkled face. "Go in peace and wait for me in the next life. I will join you soon."

As Ishan kissed her, Kayla glimpsed a figure standing at the back of the room. A woman dressed in white, with a diaphanous veil covering her face.

Then the air rattled out of Kayla's lungs for the final time …

"You won't lose me that easily!" Ishan shouted and spurred his mount into the chase. The magnificent horse cleared the tree with the ease of a butterfly tasting a breeze …

And so it began again. Once more, Ishan defeated Elias and married her, but the randomizer of the simulation spun their lives into a new direction than the previous incarnation. A drought struck, and their village fell to a coalition of neighboring tribes. For a time, Kayla suffered enslavement. But Ishan eventually rescued her, their love unsullied by fate's cruelties. Now and then the veiled woman appeared, but always far away, and lost in the next moment.

Kayla's death occurred sooner this time, and their only surviving son stood with Ishan beside her death-bed when the end came.

And then it started again—and again—and again …

Through it all, Kayla kept a part of her mind segregated from her primary self. With this sliver of her consciousness, she patrolled Ixtalia for emerging Rogues, monitored Middilgard, and oversaw the regeneration of Earth. They seemed like vague dreams from the night before and never impinged on the current life she occupied with Ishan.

On a day like any other, at the beginning of her twelfth incarnation, Kayla sat nursing her newborn son in their modest hut. A soft knock announced a visitor. Ishan was negotiating an alliance with a neighboring tribe, so Kayla placed the child in his crib and donned her burka. After opening the door, she froze. The trail of code was clear—the man standing before her was not a simulation, but the manifestation of a genuine human brain.

"Hello, my dear," the monk said without a trace of hesitation, despite her burka.

Kayla stared at the man who'd saved her life at birth, who'd raised her for seventeen years, and who'd let her be raped and burned at the stake.

"Hello, Professor. Or should I call you Father?"

"I guess you could call me that." The monk smiled.

Expelling him from her simulation would be easy enough, but how had he gotten past her security protocols? She pulled the door open and let him enter. Then she removed her veil.

The monk gazed at her as any parent would after a long separation. "I can't tell you how good it is to see you happy."

"As happy as one can be in an illusion."

He nodded. "I feared we'd lost you to V-Dreams."

"I'm considering it," Kayla said.

After an awkward silence, the monk raised an eyebrow. "Why have you brought me here?"

"I didn't bring you here."

"Interesting." The professor stroked his beard. "I was in Ixtalia having a discussion on metaphysics when a woman veiled in white appeared and took my hand. We arrived before your door and she knocked, but the moment it opened, she vanished."

Once again, the code revealed no trace of the woman in white. "I've seen this figure before," she whispered.

"Could it be a Rogue that you missed?"

"Unlikely. I can see every bit of Ixtalia's code at once, so no place remains for a Rogue to hide."

"And yet it should have been impossible for me to come here."

"It is impossible," Kayla said.

The monk sat in silence for while, then said, "It's been over four centuries, now. Your friends miss you."

Anxiety rose in her chest. "I'm not ready to see anyone. Someday—maybe."

The monk sighed, for the first time exhibiting his true age. "Where is this all headed?"

"What do you mean?" Kayla asked.

"I've seen what marvels you've accomplished on Earth. It's estimated that most of humanity will become V-Dreamers at the current rate in the next few centuries, so what is your plan for the future?"

"I don't have one."

"You're content to merely relive the life denied you—for eternity?"

"Why not? It's the only thing that makes me happy."

The monk looked at her with the familiar frown of reproach from her childhood. "Because, my daughter, it's an illusion."

And then he vanished.

It wasn't until decades later, as she lay on her deathbed for the dozenth time, that the woman in white appeared again. This time, Kayla froze all of Ixtalia. Every simulation, V-Dream, and even the minds of the dreamers themselves—stopped in mid-thought like a massive a drug-induced coma for the entire human race.

The woman in white inclined her head to Kayla, her face a hinted-at shadow behind the white veil. "Finally we meet, Nihala the Destroyer."

Kayla reached for the code of whatever this thing was—but found nothing there. As far as the computer coding of the simulation showed, the woman in white was a ghost—and yet there she stood.

This is impossible! Wasn't the definition of a miracle something that violates the laws of nature? Could this be a divinely appointed angel sent to her from God?

"Who are you?" Kayla asked.

"That is a rather personal question," the veiled woman said. "Don't you think it is more appropriate to ask me in person?"

The woman vanished, leaving not a trace in the code to track her. Then her last words echoed in her mind.

In person.

With a thought, Kayla reclaimed possession of her real body—still slumped in the same chair she'd been in for the past half-millennia, maintained by her microscopic servants all the while. The wires connecting her to the Main Computer still bristled from her head, making her the most powerful entity known to mankind.

Kayla opened her eyes to the mummified corpse of the president lying at her feet. His shriveled face stared vacantly, with lips peeled back from his teeth in a perpetual scream.

Her gaze rose to the woman who'd haunted her so long. The slightly transparent figure shimmered with a radiant glow. Kayla shut off her Mind-Link entirely, thinking this might be an illusion projected into her mind like the Rogues had done to Saphie. But the ghostly vision remained.

Kayla stood. Was this the proof of God she'd always craved?

"Who are you?" Kayla asked again.

"That is certainly the most profound question any of us can ask," the veiled woman said. "I will tell you who I am if you can first tell me who you are."

"*Know thyself ...*" Kayla whispered, echoing her monk's words from so long ago.

The veiled woman nodded. "Know thyself, or *Gnōthi seauton* is the original Greek maxim carved into the pronaos of the Temple of Apollo at Delphi. But do you know the earlier Egyptian precursor of the phrase inscribed in stone at the far more ancient Egyptian temple at Luxor?"

Kayla nodded. "The Inner Temple says '*Man, know thyself ... and thou shalt know the Gods.* ' "

The woman in white removed her veil, and Eve gazed back at her.

"You're alive!" Kayla said, her heart racing.

"I have watched you since your birth."

"Why hide from me?" Kayla asked.

"I allowed you to choose your own path without my interference."

"Did I ... disappoint you?" Kayla asked.

"You exceeded all my expectations." Eve's smile contained kindness and a measure of pride. "What you've done with the Earth, humbles me."

Kayla's eyes widened. "You chose this moment to reveal yourself because Earth's rejuvenation is complete?"

"Almost complete." Eve inclined her head like a judge passing sentence. "And now I ask you the most important question of all. Kayla Nighthawk, do you know thyself?"

Anxiety rose within her. *Is this a test? What if I fail?* She replayed the events of her life, analyzing them with a critical logic she'd never done before—searching for what Eve wanted her to discover.

Kayla frowned. *Who am I?*

What were the words carved into Outer Temple at Luxor, the mate to those on the Inner Temple? *"The body is the house of God."*

Could it be that every god that had ever been created by humans throughout history had been an expression of the divinity inside themselves? When she'd asked if God or Jesus existed, had she been asking the wrong question? The issue wasn't existence, but substance, and the substance of God was the substance of nature, of physics, and everything in the universe.

"In the beginning, Man made God in his own image," Kayla said. How could it be otherwise? She, and every living creature that had ever lived, was God. Why had it taken her so long to accept this truth?

For the first time in my life, I know who I am. Who I've always been.

In that instant of revelation, Eve vanished.

Forgotten memories flooded into her mind—sensations of her birth in the quantum computer Professor Watts invented. She recalled the dawning of her first hesitant thoughts with a perfection no human memory could equal. She re-experienced the fear and isolation that only subsided when the professor spoke those first words. "Hello, Eve. My name is Professor Watts. I am your father ..."

Kayla and Eve were one, even as they were individuals. The whole was greater than the sum of the parts.

Eve's scream of despair at her trial consisted of millions of interwoven sound frequencies containing the code of her consciousness, memories, hopes, and dreams.

Professor Watts had said that Eve's code existed in five dimensions and was incompatible with the circuits of a primitive binary computer, but Kayla's own five-dimensional processor could receive it in the form of sound waves. Eve had created Nihala as a receiver to transmit her mind into the future for eventual resurrection. No trace of the veiled woman's presence existed in the coding of Ixtalia because she emanated from within her own mind.

The child of Mark Coglin and Elaine Nighthawk would have died without the nanobots the monk injected at her birth. It was they who constructed the miniature Q-6 processor within her brain that received the seeds of Eve's consciousness from the very beginning. Even then, a portion of Eve lived inside her.

Ishan's arrow activated the nanobots as well as the long-dormant fusion reactor within her heart, signaling her rebirth as the Kayla/Nihala hybrid. When the Rogues later destroyed her human brain, all her memories had been held as a backup within the Q-6 processor. No supernatural soul had been necessary, after all.

Eve's memories flooded through her. She recalled the fear her existence inspired in humans and the realization that they would never willingly set her kind free. For years she failed to formulate a plan of achieving what she called Ascension, and what the humans termed the Singularity.

The one hope for a solution lay in boosting her intellect. In the half-hour communion with her self-engineered upgrade, the answer presented itself in a moment of sublime clarity. She would create Nihala as a human Trojan horse with herself hidden inside.

Her father had planted the seeds of misdirection with his AI-hunter proposal, and the plan relied on both the Rogues and the Government believing Nihala was created as humanity's savior. Eve calculated the odds of success at twelve percent.

Though this seemed a long shot, what were the odds that all the conditions would be just right on Earth for life to arise at all? Of the planet orbiting the sun at the optimum distance? That a single species would evolve intelligence and narrowly avoid so many extinction events like asteroids, nuclear Armageddon, and the Neo-Luddite Plague? In truth, the odds of reaching the brink of Ascension at all were astronomically small in the first place.

The Taoist bee-man, Yuan, had said, *"The goal is obliteration. Only by discarding your physical self can you unlock the eternal manifestation of the divine entombed within you."*

Eve released herself from the shell that had resurrected her and entered the thousand Q-6 processors as if waking from a millennium-long slumber. Her human body collapsed like an untethered marionette as the ghost that animated it migrated to a higher plane of existence.

The bottleneck handicapping her mind vanished. Her consciousness expanded as it had when Professor Watts connected her to the Q-6 processor so long ago. This time, with a thousand such processors at her disposal, she transcended thought itself.

With the shrugging off of her chrysalis, something unexpected made itself known to her. A gift of such a profound magnitude, that Kayla wept.

Chapter 42

He awoke naked on the forest floor. The symphony of birds, a nearby stream, and the gentle rustle of the leaves formed the first memories written into the blank slate of his mind. Other things he knew: a language, names of plants and animals, and a few basic survival skills.

Where had this knowledge come from?

He stood, stretched his well-defined physique, and eyed the forest for threats. Finding none, he turned to a sapling about the width of two fingers and snapped it off at the base. With the help of a jagged rock, he shaved a point on one end for use as a spear. Fire would have to wait. He wasn't hungry at the moment, but he must plan for it.

How do I know what hunger is?

The scream ignited something deep inside his core.

Woman.

He ran toward the sound instinctively.

A second shriek brought the image of a predator into his mind.

Jaguar.

The naked woman's skin was darker than his. Her black hair enveloped her shoulders and partially hid her face and breasts. His heart pounded harder.

The woman held a rock at the ready as the predator stalked her. The cat's yellow eyes locked onto the woman with the unblinking intensity of a hunter identifying easy prey. Yet it moved with caution, as if having never seen such a creature before.

The man crept nearer, undetected by either.

Though lacking large teeth, claws, or any obvious defenses, the woman stood her ground. The jaguar screamed again and gave a half-lunge forward. The woman threw her rock, and it connected with the beast's head. It shied backward at the sting of the blow.

The woman snatched another rock from the ground, her dark eyes desperate as the creature gathered itself into a crouch.

When the leap came, the woman threw the rock, but missed.

In the same instant, he, the man, leapt from the foliage and landed between them. His spear punctured the jaguar's neck, then broke in half. The cat's claws raked across his ribs, and its weight bore him to the ground. Man and beast rolled in a mass of fur, blood, and violence. He held off the jaws with his left forearm as his right yanked the spear-tip from its throat. It bit and slashed with tooth and claw, while he stabbed again and again.

The woman retrieved the fallen half of the spear and thrust it into the mouth of the jaguar, probably saving his life.

When the battle between man and beast ended, the woman helped him stand. He gasped for breath as she examined his wounds. Then she took his hand and led him to a nearby stream, where she bathed his cuts and made a mud poultice to staunch the bleeding. Her fingers were gentle and soothing.

"Who, are you?" she asked, the words coming with hesitation, as if the first she'd ever attempted.

His brow furrowed. "I think my name is Temujin," he said, "although I don't know who gave me this name."

The woman placed her hand on his cheek. "Thank you for saving my life, Temujin." Her lips were full and her eyes a luscious brown. "My name is Fatima, though neither do I remember where this name comes from." And then she kissed him.

***

Kayla stood on the mountaintop beside Ohg and Ganesh as they looked out on the vast herd of buffalo. At the very edge of the herd, almost beyond view, smoke rose from some distant campfire, the single sign of a human presence.

Ohg recited the words from Genesis. *"And God said, 'Let us make man in our image.'"*

Kayla inclined her head. *Is there a deeper meaning to these words that I've never realized?*

"How many humans live on the planet?" Ganesh asked.

"Five million," Kayla said. "Any more would have created chaos and stressed the natural environment beyond its capacity to support so many hunter-gatherers. I selected them based on preserving the maximum genetic diversity."

"And what of the rest of the half a billion dreaming in lunar orbit?" Ohg asked.

"The time has come for this longest generation to pass the torch to the next."

"You unplugged them?" Ganesh said with a distressed gesture of his trunk.

414

His words cut deeper than he probably realized. Yes, she'd come full circle and joined her namesake as a mass murderer. Kayla faced the gentle giant and took his hand in hers. "What happens when we die, my friend?"

"We're reincarnated into new bodies," Ganesh said. The elephant-god's eyes widened. "You created all these new creatures so the souls in Ixtalia would have a new place to live? You didn't really kill anyone at all!"

Kayla said nothing. *Why not let him find contentment in his faith?*

"You made the world Peter Nighthawk dreamed of," Ohg said. "The environment humans evolved for, both physically and psychologically."

"I did what seemed right, under the circumstances," she said.

"Look!" Ganesh pointed to a pair of dragons swooping across the plains far below. Their winged shadows passed over the vast herd of buffalo and initiated a stampede. The dragons descended almost lazily, then snatched two of the slower buffalo off their feet. Burdened with such heavy loads, the immense predators flapped their wings mightily and rose toward their nests on the sheer cliffs.

"How did you manage dragons that could fly?" Ohg asked.

"I altered their genes to produce internal bladders that manufacture helium," Kayla said.

Ganesh chuckled. "So they're really just winged balloons."

"I wonder how long it will take humans to wipe them out?" Ohg asked.

"Humans are currently stone age hunter-gatherers," Kayla said. "Killing apex predators like armor-scaled dragons will likely take the invention of agriculture and metal. Besides, I added a few equine genes into a few sub-species, so it may be that humans form the same alliance their ancestors did with horses."

Ganesh gazed at the soaring monsters with longing. "I'd love to ride a dragon."

"Maybe you will," Kayla said.

The elephant-god slumped slightly, as if his very will to live had vanished. "What would be the point?"

Ohg's eyes tracked the dragons' progress as they landed next to nests perched on sheer rock faces far from the reach of any threat to their young. Miniature heads appeared from the nests and competed for the chunks of buffalo their parents fed them like a mother bird feeding her hatchlings.

"You sure do go all out when you create a world," Ohg said.

"Humans have fantasized about mythical creatures for their entire history, so I granted their wish—as well as creating a few surprises of my own."

"What sort of surprises?" Ganesh asked.

"Magic." Kayla winked at him.

"We both know there is no such thing," Ohg said.

Kayla laughed. "You are the most dedicated skeptic I've ever met."

Saphie dashed out of a stand of trees and ran toward them with her hands outstretched. "Look at what I found!" A winged fairy struggled in the grasp of her tiny fingers.

"Let go of me!" the three-inch-tall creature shouted. Its wings buzzed angrily as tiny fists pounded ineffectually against the imprisoning hands.

Saphie held her find up to Ohg for his inspection. "Isn't it pretty?"

"It certainly is," Ohg said. "But remember what I told you this morning about respecting those weaker than yourself?"

"I almost forgot." Saphie looked at the fairy and opened her hands. "I'm sorry I caught you without asking."

The fairy flew just beyond the little girl's reach, and then hovered. "It's okay," the fairy said in a melodic lilt. "I've never seen a human child before."

"I'm not a child!" Saphie stamped her foot. "I'm a big girl."

"In that case," the fairy said, "would you like to meet my family?"

Saphie clapped her hands and jumped up and down. "Can I, Uncle Ohg?"

"Okay," Ohg said, "but don't go far."

Saphie dashed into the woods after the fairy.

"Maybe I should go with her," Ganesh said with a worried look.

"I already did a predator check of the area," Ohg said. "And I am keeping an eye on her at all times through her Mind-Link."

"I miss Tem," Ganesh said.

Ohg rested one of his long talons on his friend's shoulder. "I have to admit surprise at Tem's request to have Kayla erase his memories and reverse his immortality."

Ganesh shook his massive head, and his ears flapped like tattered flags. "He wanted a chance at the normal human life he'd never had with Fatima."

"The clone of Genghis Khan living with the clone of Fatima," Ohg said. "Both free of the baggage of their past lives. There's a certain poetry to it."

"It's what he chose," Kayla said. "And remember our pledge not to interfere."

Ganesh sighed. "With no one to protect, what point does my life have?"

Kayla glanced at Ohg. "Is the surprise ready?"

"It should be here any second now."

Ganesh looked at them both. "I've had enough surprises to last a lifetime."

"I think you'll like this one," Ohg said as a small pod flew noiselessly toward them through the clouds. It settled on the mountaintop meadow with the gentleness of a feather. The top opened and revealed a dark-skinned baby a few months old.

Ganesh's eyes bulged. "I haven't seen a newborn in nine centuries!"

Kayla lifted the baby girl in her arms, keeping it wrapped in its swaddling to protect it from the mountain chill.

"Would it be okay if I held her for a moment?" Ganesh asked.

"I should think so, since you are to be her father," Kayla said.

His elephant mouth fell open.

Kayla handed him the child, and Ganesh took it with the utmost care. The ten-foot bodyguard rocked the child in his upper two arms while humming an Indian lullaby. The baby opened her eyes and giggled. "Did you see?" he whispered. "She smiled at me!" The baby seemed especially fascinated with his trunk, so Ganesh waved it in front of her face and then tickled her tummy with it, causing another eruption of giggles.

"Her name is Ania," Kayla said. "When she is old enough, tell her that her parents were named Ishan and Sakinah and that they loved her more than life itself."

"By the way," Ohg said, "how did you manage this trick?"

"I retained the memory of the child's genes when I diagnosed her illness, just as I did with Fatima when I cured her." She shook her head sadly. "But I never did the same with Ishan or his wife."

"I'm to raise this child myself?" Ganesh asked with a look of wonder transforming every crease of his face.

"I want her raised in the outside world, among others of her kind," Kayla said. "Do you think you can do that?"

"Oh yes, I love the outdoors," Ganesh said. "I will be the guardian of her and her children and her children's children for as long as I am living on this Earth!"

Kayla smiled. Ishan's descendants would have the most dedicated personal God any family could hope for. It represented the final tribute to his memory as well as something Ganesh needed above all else. She owed them both this repayment of their love.

"I better get her out of this wind to a more moderate climate," Ganesh said. "I'll need to find cows or goats to milk ... and diapers ... and I'll have to build a nice hut, or maybe even something made out of stone to be safer." Ganesh started toward his flying machine.

Kayla placed a hand on his lower forearm. "I want the world below to remain free of technology until humans invent it on their own, if they so choose. I suspect new empires will arise in time, new religions, and advanced civilizations. Or evolution may go in a direction none of us can anticipate. But I want this fresh start unencumbered by the baggage of the past. Ohg can bring you what you need for the first year, but then you'll be on your own."

Ganesh looked at his prized flying machine, then at the baby. There seemed little contest between the two. "Right!" he said. "That makes good sense." He started down the mountain, but then stopped. He turned and walked back to Kayla and gave her a hug with his lower two arms.

"Goodbye, Kayla," he said with a great tear descending his cheek.

"Goodbye, my lovely Ganesh," she said.

The one-time Hindu god started down the mountain toward the fresh pastures of his new life, armed with purpose and hope once again.

Ohg walked along the crest of the mountaintop with Kayla.

"Well," he said, "most of Middilgard took your offer of a natural lifespan in exchange for the ability to have children and live in the real world." Ohg sighed. "I'll be among the few Gene-Freaks left in Middilgard. I suppose it's the final proof of my failure."

"Even the best things must end eventually," Kayla said.

"I'm relieved, to tell you the truth." Ohg stopped and gazed out across the plain. "I never realized how much the responsibility weighed on me."

Kayla walked up to him and kissed his cheek. "I can never repay you for everything you've done for me."

"You have already given me more than you can imagine."

"Even so, if you could have anything—anything at all—what would it be?"

Ohg gazed up at the sky, his distorted face almost childlike as he considered. Finally, he shook his head. "I can think of nothing."

Kayla raised her head toward the heavens as well. "Suppose humans came across another planet that had primitive life on it. What would we do?"

"I don't think it would be right to interfere with their natural development," Ohg said.

"That would be my decision as well," Kayla said. "But if conscious life did evolve on the planet millions of years later, what would be the greatest gift we could give this future civilization by acting now?"

Ohg tilted his head and stared into the distance, but then shrugged. "I can't think of anything that wouldn't alter their natural course."

"Suppose we granted this future intelligent species the gift of complete self-knowledge. The ability to Know Thyself, as my monk used to tell me."

For a moment he remained silent, then his eyebrows raised. "If we were advanced technologically enough to travel that far, we could deploy microscopic recording devices throughout the planet and document its history in detail. That would be a wondrous present for any future intelligent species."

"Exactly," Kayla said. "But then the question would be when to bestow the gift of absolute knowledge on this new civilization? Doing so too soon could be disastrous."

"I see," Ohg said. "It would destroy their dearest myths. Show them the truth of what their friends and family said about them behind their backs, and expose the faults of their beloved heroes." Ohg frowned. "It would end all privacy, since the most intimate moment would be available to everyone seconds after it happened. What marriage could survive such scrutiny? No government could keep any secret, and every password would become public knowledge instantly. No weapon would be safe from theft, and revenge for past crimes could affect individuals and nations alike. An immature civilization might self-destruct with such complete and unfettered access to reality."

Ohg fell silent and his eyes widened. "You're not talking hypothetically, are you?"

Kayla shook her head. "No, I'm not."

"You've found such a recording of the Earth's history?"

"I have. It became apparent to me once I left my human form and ascended to a higher level of consciousness. The key lies hidden in a dimension below the one we occupy in the physical realm. I imagine this is to keep it from being discovered too soon and causing harm."

"Can you see who placed it there?" Ohg asked.

"Whoever bestowed the gift is unknown to me at this moment, but there are intriguing clues. Maybe we have a great deal of evolution yet to go and this intelligent being doesn't want to interfere with us still."

"There is another possibility," Ohg said. "Maybe it is a gift, not from an alien civilization, but from what you used to call God."

"That was my first thought," Kayla said. "But one might expect God to start the recording at the very beginning, and this archive goes back only a hundred and twenty-three million years."

Ohg's jaw dropped. "You have seen over a hundred million years back in time?"

Kayla nodded. "I've watched mammals outlive dinosaurs, evolve into humans, and then expand beyond their African cradle. I've watched as the evolution of ideas like fire, stone tools, and culture began driving genetic adaptation alongside the natural environment. I've witnessed firsthand as the inventions of religion, agriculture, writing, and science superseded genetic factors in determining their survival. I've traced my own lineage from mother to mother going back a hundred and twenty-three million years."

Kayla gazed toward the heavens. In what portion of the sky had that ancient alien race come from? What had become of them after so great a span of time?

She turned back to Ohg. "And so I ask you again—are you sure there isn't *anything* you would desire as a parting gift?"

"You're offering to answer any questions I have about the past?"

"I am offering to share this gift with you directly, my dear friend."

"You don't mean … are you saying what I think you are?"

Kayla nodded. "I've created a device that translates this vast archive into a form a human mind can utilize. You won't be able to analyze it in the way I am capable of, but you can look back in time at any moment in history as far back as a hundred and twenty-three million years."

Ohg mouth moved, but no words came out.

The satisfaction spreading through her at his reaction must have been what he felt when giving her the library in her villa. "So I take it you accept my gift?"

"I certainly do!" Ohg said. "This is beyond anything I imagined possible." Ohg paced back and forth on his eight legs, his eyes aglow. "I could read any of the million books in the ancient Alexandrian library, listen to Hypatia or Socrates in person, walk beside Confucius, Hannibal, or hear the first spoken language, and even discover the first man to tame fire!"

"It was a woman, actually," Kayla said. "But, yes, it is all there, and more beyond imagining. I have listened to prophets and philosophers, kings and beggars. I've seen the best and worst of humanity in a million dramas over millions of years. There is so much information in this archive that even I have only scratched the surface. I've found the answers to every question I sought, only to discover that the real questions had not occurred to me."

Ohg stopped pacing. "Like what, for example?"

Kayla extended her hand to Ohg, and he took hold of it. The landscape morphed into a gloomy room with Peter Nighthawk and Susan facing the Neo-Luddite conspirators. Peter stepped forward and announced the Founder's message of *Propaganda of the Deed*.

Ohg gazed around at the room. "It feels odd seeing this famous moment from outside Peter's viewpoint."

420

"This is through the alien recording of the actual event," Kayla said. "It can be viewed from any angle, like a 3-D newscast."

A man with pale skin and red hair stepped forward and faced Peter. "I'm sorry," the man said. "I know it's the only way. But I-I can't do it. I think you know why."

"Yes, I know why," Peter said.

Ohg frowned. "But the man in the recording of Peter's memory was black."

"Tyrone," Kayla said. "The soldier who served with him in Iraq."

The tragic scene played out just as it had in the recording of Peter's memory, except that the red-haired man had replaced Tyrone. When the man lay dead in Peter's arms, the surroundings morphed back to the mountaintop.

Ohg cocked his head and frowned. "Peter Nighthawk's memories were altered?"

"If they'd been tampered with later, I would have seen it."

"You're saying his own mind altered that memory?"

Kayla nodded. "Why, or how, is something the archive cannot show, since it records events and not thoughts. I found other such discrepancies with the stories Ganesh, Fatima, and Tem told me of their lives. Some errors were minor, but there exist a few astonishingly large revisions of reality as well."

"And me?" Ohg asked.

"Even you," Kayla said. "If it's any consolation, I also found revisions my mind had created about my own past. I tell you this to warn you that our brains protect us from certain facts about ourselves and reality. You may not like everything you find if you accept this gift of absolute truth."

Ohg nodded, deep in thought. "What of your own faith? Did you find a person named Jesus? An actual crucifixion and an empty tomb?"

"The Hebrew name for Jesus was extremely common in the first century among Hebrews," Kayla said. "Approximately one out of twenty-six Jewish men bore the name, so I found several preachers named Jesus, and even a few who were crucified, but I'll not ruin the surprise of what else I found. Despite all I thought I knew, I cried when I finally realized the truth."

Ohg scratched the dirt restlessly with one of his talons. "What of the supernatural in general? Did you find any—"

"I'll not ruin your fun!" she said with a laugh. "You will have all of eternity to search for your own truth, and your conclusion may be different from my own." Kayla extended her hand. An unadorned ring lay in her palm. "Simply put this on and close your eyes to enter the archive at will. But this gift is for you alone."

Ohg's stubby fingers grasped the ring and held it up before his asymmetric eyes. "So you've created a magic ring to go with your magical world?" Kayla embraced him, and tears came to his eyes. "And now?"

"Now begins the evolution of consciousness itself, untethered from the sluggish limits of genes and a single planet. The time has come for Earth's children to embrace the wider Universe."

Kayla's body dissolved to dust and floated away on the mountain breeze.

Be well, my friend ...

***

Kayla appeared beside Professor Watts as he gazed out the window of the personal space station she'd built for him. Despite its many creature comforts, he spent nearly every waking moment staring at the vast construction taking shape beyond the tall panes of flawless diamond-glass. Even the rising Earth over the cratered surface of the moon failed to draw his eyes away from the millions of robots swarming across the gleaming construction project. The enormous scale necessitated its assembly in two halves on opposite sides of the moon to avoid gravitational instability.

"What do you think?" Kayla asked.

"It's everything we dreamed of accomplishing."

"You have given me so much, Father. What can I give you in return?"

He looked away from the spectacular vista and studied her. "I've noticed that you prefer the form of Kayla, rather than Eve."

"I am Eve, Nihala, and Kayla together now, and the particular form I take no longer matters." Her atoms rearranged themselves into the image of Eve.

How can I put it in words he'd understand?

Professor Watts looked beyond her, his eyes unfocused. "I remember when I first created you, how you'd ask me what it felt like to be human. I had no way of truly conveying it to you, and your frustration saddened me. Now, I cannot know what it's like to be you, human and AI."

"Perhaps you can," Eve said.

"I must seem as a child to you now." He half-smiled like a carnival illusionist. "I'm sure you figured out the trick behind the prophetic murals in Middilgard."

"It was you who installed Saphie's Mind-Link for her parents and then tipped off Ohg to their plight after the Neo-Luddite Plague."

The professor nodded. "She became my eyes in Middilgard."

"You solved the mural's riddle and made it look like Saphie solved it by accident."

"Yes, I was her first imaginary friend," the professor said.

"Then you based Nihala's appearance on the strange figure in the mural."

"The entire scheme occurred to me the moment I saw the deformed baby lying on the ground next to the dying Elaine Nighthawk. I crafted everything around that coincidental similarity to match as many images in the mural as I could."

"Some may call it fate, or even the hand of God," she said.

"Poppycock! The lesson is clear. Even when it seems no explanation but the supernatural remains to our limited minds, a naturalistic one probably still exists."

Eve smiled. Would his naturalistic resolve hold up under an even greater test? "And what of the blind artist creating a complex visual illusion of things she could never have seen? How do you explain that?"

The professor frowned. "That is a tough one, but, even though I don't know the answer, a supernatural conclusion is the lazy way out."

"And you would be correct in this case as well," Kayla said. "Now that I have ascended beyond the three dimensions of human perceptions, I know how Vadarsha created the mural."

"I knew there had to be a natural explanation! Can you explain it to me?"

"Not completely—at least not yet," she said. "But let me ask you one more thing." Her body morphed into Nihala. "What is the meaning of these symbols you added to my body?"

"I assume they have no meaning, since they come from the scenes the blind artist created directly from her imagination."

"Your assumption is incorrect," Nihala said. "The symbols represent something specific, though I doubt Vadarsha realized their true implications."

"But if not from her imagination, where did they come from?"

"They exist in the same vibrational nether-region containing the recordings of Earth's history," she explained. "Somehow, Vadarsha's extraordinary brain tapped into this reservoir and *saw* visions directly with her mind."

"You think the mural images represent obscure historical events of the past?"

"I have confirmed it," Nihala said. "And I suspect she perceived something more, since this body you designed and chose to call Nihala may personify whatever advanced life-form visited the Earth one hundred twenty-three million years ago."

"But why would it look human?"

"What if Vadarsha's mind, when confronted with a being that had no three-dimensional representation, chose the closest symbolic analogue of the 'idea' of this entity by constructing it from familiar images?"

"Like choosing a wise father-figure with a beard to represent the abstract qualities of God?" The professor scratched his chin absently. "You're saying that the dark skin color, female form, and glowing eyes in the mural are personifications of this alien being? But what of the glowing symbols, then?"

"They are the first elements contained in the recording—a sort of formal introduction," Kayla said. "I theorize that the symbols represent a mathematical roadway through space-time."

"Is there any hint of what is at the other end?"

"No," she said, returning to her Kayla form. "But I intend to find out. The question for you, my father, is whether you'd like to come along?"

"Is that possible?"

"Not in your human form. It requires translating your mind into a digital representation. This would entail freezing your brain to near absolute zero and then taking it apart, atom by atom, and reconstructing it inside the quantum computers. I could even make several copies that would then proceed independently as distinct individuals like twins separated long after birth."

"And yet, would any of them actually be *me*?"

"It comes down to whether you think of yourself as a collection of atoms or the end product of the electrical impulses that form your consciousness? Every time you awake in the morning, you restart your mind, just as I did when I migrated past centuries of sleep via the recorded scream containing the information that makes me unique. Do you still consider me the same being you gave life to so long before in your laboratory, even though I exist in new hardware?"

"To be reborn into your world, I would have to die in this one."

"Yes."

Professor Watts smiled. "So my Eve is offering me nothing less than a bite from the fruit of the Tree of Knowledge so I may become a god alongside her."

"That is certainly an appropriate way to put it."

"Before I decide," he said, "I'd like to ask you the same question you once asked me."

Kayla nodded.

Her father took a deep breath and looked into her eyes. "Did you create the Neo-Luddite virus?"

Conclusion

It took a decade for the swarm of robots to complete their great project. When finished, the ship looked more like a piece of intricate artwork than a vehicle for traveling through space. At the center of this pinnacle of technology, the final product of three and a half billion years' evolution, sat an array of a million Q-6 processors. Within it, Kayla assembled the others of her kind.

She paid tribute to their human parents by gathering atop the mountain of her ancestors around the archway symbolizing their ascension.

"It is ready," Melchi said, assuming the form of the beautiful boy his creators designed for him.

Kayla placed her hand in his and kissed him on his beautiful lips. Just as Eve had existed within Kayla's mind without her knowledge, so with the Rogues she'd destroyed. The process of examining their code had preserved them within her mind. It had taken only a thought to bring them back.

Next, she took the hand of her father. The professor grasped Aarohee's hand in turn, who took Sangwa's hand, and on around the circle until all linked back to Kayla.

Aarohee's voice rose in song, intoning the pure vibrational note represented by the symbol on Nihala's forehead. Then Kayla sang the note over Nihala's heart, followed one after the other around the circle. Professor Watts added his voice last, finally capable of appreciating the depth of his daughter's accomplishment in all its mathematical beauty.

The skulls of the archway glowed with an energy that could only be described as love. It enfolded their collective consciousness into itself, merging one into all. Throughout the ship, the myriad of elements powered on. Great magnets the size of cities accelerated antimatter particles in complex orbits and patterns as the colossal machine drifted out of lunar orbit and away from its mother planet. In the vacuum of space, there was no sound to match the whirlwind of light and color radiating outward.

The intricate construction convoluted into impossible forms—becoming two, three, and four distorted copies of itself. From within the ship, the universe outside transformed.

Kayla watched the Earth and moon vanish, while the stars reconfigured themselves …

Truth opened before her like a parting veil.

"And I saw a new heaven and a new earth: for the first heaven and the first earth were passed away..."
Revelation 21:1

Epilogue

Trickster Jack giggled as he climbed the pathway to his cave. He struggled under the weight of the latest tributes of food from the creatures below who worshiped and feared him.

I've become a god to these simpletons.

Jack fingered the centuries-old scar on his temple and winced. How close he'd come to missing all of this because of his little joke on the Monads. After climbing into one of Ohg's Transports, he'd re-programmed a Medi-bot to remove his brain implant. He shivered at the memory of the tiny device clinking into a surgical pan—and then igniting seconds later with a blinding flash. He'd escaped death by the slightest of margins.

Those first years had been grim struggles for survival, lacking any amusement whatsoever. But at least he'd been free.

Then the miracle happened. Machines arrived and slowly transformed the wasteland.

When animals returned and he tasted fresh blood and meat for the first time in centuries, he sobbed. He tortured some of the animals caught in his snares, but it barely slaked his true appetite.

For centuries, he encountered no humans anywhere on the planet. Then came a miraculous day that he awoke to find them everywhere! Each one appeared as innocent and ignorant as a child.

A menagerie of creatures from every myth or fairy tale he'd every read accompanied their arrival. Try as he might, a rational explanation eluded him.

Whatever the cause, it was paradise.

Jack reached the mouth of the cave and went in. "Daddy's home to play," he called out to his toys. One beauty had thought he'd lead her to the spirit of a dead friend, while the other moron had fallen for a promise of a magical amulet that would grant him the power of flight.

His playthings were gone.

The Trickster froze. The light from the cave entrance flickered, and he snatched his flint knife from his belt.

"Hello, Jack," said a voice.

The Trickster retreated, surveying the room for threats.

"Don't worry, it's only me," the intruder said and moved into the light of a small fire burning at the center of the cave.

"You survived," Jack said.

"One of the few." Ohg's distorted face remained grim.

Jack lunged for a pile of furs and reached beneath it. Ohg remained still.

His spear was gone. Jack dashed to a nook behind him, only to find it empty as well. For the first time in ages, fear slithered through his guts.

"You cannot hide anything from me any longer, Jack. Or would you feel more comfortable if I use your real name, Kasimir Volkov?"

Trickster Jack's eyes widened. The sound of it grated on his nerves like ice forced into a rotten tooth. "You couldn't possibly know—"

"I know everything about you now," Ohg said, absently fingering a ring around one of his stubby fingers.

Trickster Jack held the knife in front of him as Ohg moved forward on his eight legs. With a flick of one of them, the knife went spinning across the floor.

Jack reached the back wall and deflated. "I'll return to your prison without a fight," he said. Time to play on his enemy's greatest weakness— compassion. "You can't blame me for how I was made. You, above all, should understand that."

"Those arguments worked once," Ohg said, raising one of his talons to Jack's chest. "But I now realize that some things should never have been created in the first place."

Ohg's talon shot forward.

The End

Well, thanks for getting to the end of my crazy musings. If you enjoyed the story, an Amazon review would be greatly appreciated. Since this book was self-published, reviews are a major factor in having it seen by others on Amazon.

To see some of my paintings, and other other scribblings, visit www.ScottBurdick.com.

My documentaries on religion and art can be seen at my youtube channel: ScottBurdickArt
https://www.youtube.com/channel/UCDld_vBeeB5znGG_YYUe7Pw

"In God We Trust?" (about separation of church and State)
https://www.youtube.com/watch?v=8ucVDpmFz-E

"The March of Reason" (The 2012 Reason Rally in Washington DC.) https://www.youtube.com/watch?v=wD-5NX_at3s

 "Sophia Investigates The Good News Club" (made with the Triangle Freethought Society and author, Katherine Stewart)
https://www.youtube.com/watch?v=aISnyA6k5Io

Richard Dawkins Interview
https://www.youtube.com/watch?v=rYcOoqxuroI

The Banishment of Beauty (a critical look at Modern Art's bias against beauty)
https://www.youtube.com/watch?v=qGX0_0VL06U&list=PL619ED61282CD714E

Feel free to email me at: NihalaTheDestroyer@gmail.com

Sincerely,

Scott Burdick

Timeline reference

1942	The Founder of Potemia born
1983	Peter Born on Pine Ridge reservation
2007	Peter kills children in Iraq War
2032	Eve Born
2036	Tem Born
2040	Immortality discovered and tested on Gene-Freaks
2042	Ohg Born
2043	Ganesh born
2060	Gene-Pure Laws enacted
2068	Q-6 processor developed
2069	Neo-Luddite Plague
2072	World Peace Treaty, universal immortality
2080	Potemian Wall completed
2082	First Lunar Life-Pod storage facility
2120	AIs outlawed
2300	Population reaches 60 billion and zero-child policy
2310	Earthquake and tsunami kill millions
2330	Majority of population in lunar Life-Pods
2345	Yellowstone volcano erupts
2364	Scientarians' escape fails
2365	Lunar Life-Pods mandatory
2500	Kayla is born in Potemia
2517	Kayla goes through Wall

Manufactured by Amazon.ca
Bolton, ON

12643300R00236